The Gift
of Asher Lev

The Gift
of Asher Lev

✤ ✤ ✤

CHAIM
POTOK

✤ ✤ ✤

ALFRED A. KNOPF

New York   1990

THIS IS A BORZOI BOOK
PUBLISHED BY ALFRED A. KNOPF, INC.

Copyright © 1990 by Chaim Potok
All rights reserved under International and Pan-American Copyright Conventions.
Published in the United States by Alfred A. Knopf, Inc., New York,
and simultaneously in Canada by Random House of Canada Limited, Toronto.
Distributed by Random House, Inc., New York.

Library of Congress Cataloging-in-Publication Data
Potok, Chaim.
The gift of Asher Lev: a novel / by Chaim Potok.—1st ed.
p.   cm.
Continuation of: My name is Asher Lev.
ISBN 0-394-57212-2
I. Potok, Chaim. My name is Asher Lev.   II. Title.
PS3566.069G54   1990
813'.54—dc20   89-43401   CIP

Manufactured in the United States of America
First Trade Edition

A signed first edition of this book has been privately printed
by The Franklin Library.

Surely all art is the result of having been in danger, of having gone through an experience all the way to the end, to where no one can go any further.

RAINER MARIA RILKE

BOOK ONE

✦ ✦ ✦

1

✤ ✤ ✤ Afterward I lived in Paris, in the same apartment where I had painted the *Brooklyn Crucifixion*. I married Devorah, and we moved to the Rue des Rosiers. Some years later, Devorah gave birth to a girl, and we named her Rochel, after Devorah's mother, of blessed memory, who was taken away in the July 1942 roundup of French Jews. We called her Rocheleh, beloved little Rochel.

I made many drawings and paintings of Devorah and Rocheleh, but I kept most of them for my own collection and would not show or sell them. I made many drawings and paintings of Paris and of the old ones in our neighborhood and people eating on the terrace of the café diagonally across the street from our apartment house on the Rue des Rosiers, and Lucien Lacamp, one of the righteous of the Gentiles, and Max Lobe, Devorah's cousin, who came often to visit us.

Then Max went to live in the south, and Jacob Kahn, who was in his late eighties, came to live in France, and I made many drawings of Jacob Kahn. "You are even better now than when I first taught you," Jacob Kahn said to me one day. "But you do it too easily, Asher Lev. You are too comfortable. There is no sweat in your armpits."

One afternoon I was tending to Rocheleh, who was ill, coughing and wheezing in the chill air of the Rue des Rosiers apartment, when Lucien entered, his square features oddly tight, his usual soldierly carriage gone slack. It was a Sunday afternoon in early April. "The master is dead," he said, his eyes wide and moist. He had been a paratrooper with the French Foreign Legion in Vietnam, and now there were tears in his eyes. For days afterward I saw clearly within myself, as if thrown upon some inner screen, the ghostly face of the Spaniard. There it lingered in myriad ways: young and with the black hair combed diagonally across his forehead; broken and rearranged in Cubist forms; grotesque as in his crucifixion painting; middle-aged and furious as when he worked on the *Guernica;* old and lecherous as in his erotic drawings; skeletal with stark terror-filled eyes as in his final self-portrait. Jacob Kahn, himself old and weary, wrote me: "The king is dead. Endless memories. The past is a parade before my eyes. The secret language we invented during those years in Montmartre and Montparnasse. It was a glorious birth. We brought into the world a new child. Dirty, cluttered studios in rotting buildings in decaying neighborhoods. Our best years. He was our center. Who replaces the king, Asher Lev? No one. In art, chaos is now king. Your old teacher and friend who asks you to take care of yourself and to sweat. Jacob."

Then Devorah and I and Rocheleh moved to the south, to Saint-Paul-de-Vence. A son was born to us, and we named him Avrohom, after Devorah's father, of blessed memory, who was also caught in the July roundup, and we called him Avrumel.

We lived in the warmth and golden air of Saint-Paul. I traveled a great deal, alone: exhibitions, commissions, the needs and politics of art. In Paris I drew the face of a student who had been clubbed by riot police. In Italy I drew the face of a terrorist on trial for assassinating the minister of justice. In Japan I drew the face of a survivor of Hiroshima. Some of the drawings I later turned into paintings.

Two or three times a year the Rebbe would write me and send his blessing. He wrote when Rocheleh became ill, and Devorah framed the letter and hung it on the wall near the bed in Rocheleh's room. He wrote when Avrumel was born. "I give your son my blessing, Asher Lev. May he grow up to be a leader of his people."

Once, only once, two years after the Rebbe sent me away, I returned home to stay overnight with my parents in Brooklyn. There was the phone call, and I never went back. Every time I thought to return I remembered the phone call. I told Devorah about the phone call, but not my parents. The whispery voice, a ghostly sibilance from the Other Side, the sitra achra, the realm of the demonic created by the Master of the Universe for reasons known only to Him. I traveled everywhere, but not home. That voice.

In the Galilee I drew the face of an Arab man working for Israelis on a kibbutz. In the Old City of Jerusalem I drew the face of a young soldier standing guard on the Temple Mount not far from the Mosque of Omar. In Meah Shearim, the very religious neighborhood of Jerusalem, I drew the face of a retarded Hasidic girl. In Hebron I drew the face of an Arab boy talking about the Jews. In America I drew the face of a sick, aged Indian woman on a reservation in South Dakota and the face of a homeless black man on a glacial street in New York. In South Africa I drew a legless man on a bunk in a vile hovel in a black township outside Cape Town. The customs people were angered by my drawings. I told them I didn't make the drawings to cause trouble; I was an artist, and an artist draws what he sees and feels and thinks. But they tried to confiscate the drawings anyway and that made the newspapers and later they said I could never go back to South Africa.

In Paris in the winter of last year I had a show, and the critics were disappointed and angry. I was repeating myself, they said; it was all getting too easy for me: the superlative technique, the resplendent avant-garde flourishes, the virtuoso renderings of color and line. *Le Monde* called it "Rococo Expressionism" and "a false continuity." The *International Herald Tribune* talked about Asher Lev mired in technique and treading dangerously the paths of a potentially mawkish sensibility. The critic for *Le Figaro* wrote, "Miserabilism might be acceptable if you are 16 years of age and your name is Pablo Picasso. It is not acceptable if you are 45 and your name is Asher Lev." Even a noted music critic joined in: "In the case of Anton Bruckner, it is sometimes difficult to make a distinction between 'establishing an individual style' and 'repeating oneself'—unlike the Asher Lev exhibition currently on view at the Maeght, where the latter judgment is clearly the more judicious one." John Dorman, the American writer who lives in the house next to mine, suggested I go away for a rest. Max Lobe agreed. Douglas Schaeffer called and urged that I put Paris behind me and prepare for a show in his New York gallery. The Paris newspapers kept writing about the show. Then the magazines began to appear.

Afterward I went to Switzerland alone for a while, and then I returned home to Saint-Paul. But I couldn't work. I was very tired, and the primed canvas seemed large and unconquerable, and even after I covered it with a wash of umber it was still too large, and it would be there looking at me when I came into the closed studio every morning to begin my work. That was the winter.

Then my uncle died.

He had often been a father to me during the years when my own father was away on long journeys for the Rebbe, and for a period of time I had lived in his home. My mother phoned us around midnight. "Your Uncle Yitzchok is dead. . . . Yes, very sudden. . . . A heart attack." She was weeping.

Instantly, I saw his face: round and smiling; the parallel ridge-lines across his forehead; the little mole on the cheekbone beneath his right eye; the moist thick lips around the cigars he favored; the long flow of untrimmed white beard. I heard his loud and cheerful voice. My Uncle Yitzchok.

Devorah called a friend of ours who worked at the airport in Nice and got us four seats on a morning flight to New York. We began to pack.

I called Max Lobe and listened to his soft voice. "This is the uncle who visited a few years ago, who bought a drawing from you when you were six? I am very sorry, my friend. Do you need me to come over? Devorah is all right? Do not worry about anything. You will be away ten days? What of Rocheleh? Will she not be affected by such a long trip? I will ask Claudine to take in the mail and see to the gardener and all the rest. Is the studio locked? Travel well. My condolences to your family."

I called John Dorman and heard his slurred words. "Real sorry to hear that, Lev. Heartfelt condolences. Ten days? It's okay to take your daughter? Listen, do me a favor, get me some decent

American writing pads while you're there. Can't stand these French pads. Safe trip."

Devorah woke the children at their usual time and told them we were going to New York. They looked bewildered and a little frightened. Rocheleh put on a brave face and helped Avrumel get dressed. Neither of them remembered Uncle Yitzchok from the one time he had visited us in Saint-Paul.

The taxi arrived. It was a lovely spring morning, the sun glistening on the red-pantiled houses of the villages, the air cool and clear and honey-colored all through the cypress-studded valley to the green hills and the sea. The driver helped me load the bags. I locked the house and the gate, and we drove to Nice to the airport.

We were on line waiting to board the flight when Avrumel, five years old and still confused by the abrupt wrenching from his comfortable world, suddenly realized he had forgotten to bring Shimshon, the Samson rag doll that had been his companion since birth and with which he held long, intimate conversations. He began to cry. Devorah said she was sure we would be able to buy him a new Shimshon doll in New York, but he was inconsolable. She held him as he cried. Eleven-year-old Rocheleh, pale of face and large of eyes, said, in her tone of grownup disdain, "He's such a child."

Avrumel had on his high red sneakers and green jogging suit. He sat next to me in the Airbus, weeping. I took my drawing pad and a soft-leaded pencil from my attaché case and quickly drew from memory an exact and realistic picture of Shimshon, shading it into three-dimensionality with the side of my small finger. Avrumel watched through his tears as his rag doll came to life under the point of my 4B pencil: frayed right ear, gouged right eye, thick-chested, broad-shouldered, wearing a tunic and sandals, its chiseled face topped by an enormous shock of hair. I gave him the drawing, and his freckled face broke into a smile of delight. He hugged it to himself.

"Ça va, Avrumel?"

"Ça va, Papa."

I sat in my seat looking at my son and seeing the face of my uncle and listening to his voice.

. . .

We were seated in the four-seat center row: Rocheleh on the aisle, Devorah, Avrumel, and I. The Airbus bumped through dense clouds and turbulent Mediterranean air. I felt it banking and saw through the window to my left a hazy pale-blue world of sea and sky. Avrumel fell asleep. Rocheleh was reading *Alice au pays des merveilles,* in which she had been living for the past three days. Her light-brown hair was combed back into a high ponytail. She wore blue sneakers and white knee socks and a lilac-colored dress-length jersey with a picture of Madame Curie on it. Madame Curie was Rocheleh's love ever since she had read a *cadet biographie* of her by Eve Curie a year ago. I had drawn the picture of Madame Curie, and a T-shirt shop in Nice had baked it onto her jersey.

Devorah sat holding tightly to the armrests of her seat as the Airbus bucked on its climb through the clouds. She wore a light-gray cotton suit and a gray print blouse and had on her brown pageboy wig, which normally gave her a young, almost schoolgirl appearance. But now her face was locked with anxiety. Her eyes kept darting about. She had never flown before. Was the sealed interior of the aircraft bringing back poisoned memories?

"Are you all right, Dev?"

"I am so-so. How long is it to New York?"

"I think about nine hours. Can I do something for you?"

"Did you say the prayer for a safe journey?"

"I said it."

She sat very stiff and straight, staring into space. The Airbus went on racing through the clouds on its climb to cruising altitude.

I closed my eyes for what I thought would be a brief sleep and when I opened them we were out over the Atlantic, hours into the flight. Some minutes later, a young couple came down the aisle and stopped at our row. Devorah and Rocheleh had gone to the lavatory. Avrumel was asleep, my drawing of his Shimshon doll still clasped to his chest. The man had on a pink shirt and plaid trousers, and the woman wore a short-sleeved yellow cotton dress. Was I by any chance Asher Lev, the artist? the man asked. I said yes, I was. He said they were on their honeymoon and had been to Rome, Florence, and Venice. They lived in Chicago. His father was a collector and owned two of my paintings and some prints. The man talked with the hearty self-assurance one sometimes sees in wealthy Americans. His bride seemed nervous. He asked for my autograph. Then they wanted to shake my hand. I shook the man's hand but politely declined the woman's because it is not permissible in my tradition to shake a woman's hand, and she looked surprised and hurt.

A few minutes later, a middle-aged man came over and asked if he could take my photograph. He took the picture and thanked me and went away. I closed my eyes, feigning sleep, not wanting to be disturbed again. But I was quickly in a real sleep, and as in a fever dream saw myself as a child in my uncle's jewelry store, asking if I could live with him because my parents were going to Vienna on a mission for the Rebbe and I did not want to go with them. I was frightened of Vienna; it was a city that hated Jews. My uncle took the cigar from his mouth and said something to me, but I could not hear him.

Devorah and Rocheleh returned to their seats. I woke, dazed.

The intercom crackled. The pilot announced that we would be late coming into New York because of strong headwinds. Devorah, busy with our food—she had made sandwiches and hard-boiled eggs and cut up some raw vegetables before we left Saint-Paul; the airline had not had enough advance notice to prepare kosher food for us—Devorah gave me an apprehensive look. Her eyes blinked nervously.

Rocheleh ate with her customary daintiness. Avrumel, as always, was reducing his food to its rudimentary state of powder and paste.

The movie came on—something about the game of baseball; it did not interest me. I closed my eyes. As if I were the screen for some mad projectionist's bizarre amusement, I began to see inside my head brief, clear, disconnected pictures of my past world, like a series of superrealist slides of my swaddling-clothes years: the Brooklyn apartment in which I grew up, its small rooms and white walls; my closetlike room and its paint-it-yourself furniture; my father praying in his tallis and tefillin near the living-room window, tall, dark-eyed, heavy-shouldered, thick red hair and beard;

my mother at her desk, small and slight, clear brown eyes, high-boned cheeks, long, thin, delicately boned fingers; my image of my great-great-grandfather, garnered from stories told me by my parents, coming to me in dreams like some mythic ancestor and thundering that I was wasting time drawing pictures; my father in his dark coat and hat, carrying his bag and attaché case and *New York Times,* ready for yet another journey for the Rebbe; my mother standing at the window of our living room, gazing out at the parkway, waiting for him to return; Jacob Kahn and I stripped to the waist, painting; Jacob and Tanya Kahn and I in their summer home in Provincetown: the shimmering heat, the sun on the baking sand, the hot wind blowing in from the ocean; Paris and my two crucifixion paintings; the rage of my Brooklyn community; the Rebbe saying to me, "Go to the yeshiva in Paris. You did not grow up there. People will not be so angry in Paris. There are no memories in Paris of Asher Lev." Pictures flashing kaleidoscopically into and out of view, a chilling slide show of memory.

To get the pictures to stop, I recited silently and by heart some chapters from the Book of Psalms. That calmed me. I took from my attaché case one of the books I had brought along, a gift from John Dorman, the English translation by Joel Agee of Rainer Maria Rilke's *Letters on Cézanne.* The exquisite still life on the pale-blue cover: bottles, apples, a glass, a cloth. What was it the Spaniard had once said about Cézanne? "If there were not anxiety behind those apples, Cézanne would not interest me any more than Bouguereau."

In the Rilke book I read:

> It seems to me that the "ultimate intuitions and insights" will only approach one who lives in his work and remains there, and whoever considers them from afar gains no power over them. But all that already belongs in the area of personal solutions. Basically it's none of our business how somebody manages to grow, if only he does grow, if only we're on the trail of the law of our own growth.

I read that again and closed my eyes and saw a brief slide show of the words "if only we're on the trail of the law of our own growth" and then went on reading until I read these words about Cézanne:

> I know a few things from his last years when he was old and shabby and children followed him every day on his way to his studio, throwing stones at him as if at a stray dog. But inside, way inside, he was marvelously beautiful, and every once in a while he would shout something absolutely glorious at one of his rare visitors.

I closed the book. Cézanne an old man and children throwing stones at him as he trudges to his studio. The image persisted.

The flight dragged on. The plane was about half full, its interior dim, most of the shades lowered. Passengers sat watching the movie. I listened to the rhythmic revolutions of the two huge engines and the rushing streams of wind and saw ourselves miles above the earth in this sealed tubular craft sailing swiftly through the blue sky; the vision chilled the backs of my legs. Avrumel grew restive. I told him a story about the Rebbe in Paris during the war. Rocheleh coughed, but it was nothing; she had merely swallowed some water too fast. Devorah, working now by the overhead light on the manuscript of her children's book, looked pale, apprehensive. From time to time she would raise her eyes from her work and gaze about anxiously. She would look at the children and at me, and return to her manuscript.

We crossed the coastline and banked toward Boston and New York. The captain came on the intercom and said a storm was moving into the New York area and we would circle over Connecticut for a while and if the storm did not run its course before we ran low on fuel we would set down in Philadelphia, refuel, and return to New York. I saw Devorah look up from her manuscript and stare into space and murmur words I could not hear.

We sat belted into our seats, the passengers still, the giant aircraft circling. Below us was a world of dark clouds menacingly shot through with silvery tints; above us, the pale-blue sky of the spring day. The engines suddenly changed pitch, and the captain came on the intercom and said we had been cleared for landing in New York. We entered the clouds and bucked and bounced and rode the air currents like a carnival roller coaster. I was certain Rocheleh would be ill, but she sat calmly through it all, reading about Alice and her Wonderland. Avrumel wanted to know if it was like riding a horse, and I told him I didn't know, I had never been on a horse. Devorah sat very straight, her small chin rigid, her eyes closed. Then we were through the clouds and I could see water below, slate gray in the rain, and brown sodden earth and rows of private homes and cars on the wet roads. The ground tilted and rose swiftly toward us and the wheels bumped heavily on the runway and we lurched and slowed and then rolled on for a while and came to a stop.

After a moment, the captain told us that all the gates were in use, there would be a gate for us in ten minutes. Thirty-five minutes later, we rolled into a gate and disembarked.

I carried Avrumel. He clung to me. I felt his warmth and his slight weight and his cheek against my bearded face. Rocheleh walked alongside Devorah, her eyes behind her glasses taking in the long herdlike trek through corridors and the waiting lines at passport control and customs and the dense milling crowd outside. We started through the crowd.

"Papa," Rocheleh called, and pointed.

A bearded young man stood along the edge of the crowd, carrying a large white sign on which was written in thick red letters: "Asher Lev." People kept passing him and looking at the sign.

We steered toward him.

He was in his early twenties, deep-voiced, heavily built. He wore a dark suit, a tieless white shirt, and ritual fringes that dangled beneath his jacket.

"Asher Lev?"

I said yes, I was Asher Lev.

"The artist?" he said.

I nodded.

He said my father had asked him to meet us; we were two hours late. He told us his name was Binyomin. He shook my hand and said it was an honor to meet me, he had known my uncle, what a terrible loss, a tragedy for the entire Ladover world. He led us through the glass exit doors and across a wide busy road to a traffic island. He told us to wait, and hurried off.

Avrumel said he was hungry. Devorah took him from me and held him. "Soon," she murmured in his ear. "Soon." He held tightly to the drawing of the Shimshon doll. Rocheleh stared at the traffic in the rain and the churning crowds and people on the island rushing and cars loading up and pulling away and buses and vans stopping to let off and take on passengers.

A long blue station wagon drew up alongside the island and stopped, and the bearded young man jumped out. He held on to the brim of his dark hat with both hands as a gust of wind threatened to lift it from his head. We loaded our bags and climbed inside and moved into the traffic.

I sat in the front seat next to the young man and watched the terminal slide slowly away. An odd coldness settled upon me, a fearful and darkly textured sensation that was like a gust of fetid wind from the Other Side, and a curiously colored slide dropped into view, smoky reds and blacks beneath a dusky glaze, and I had a precise, stark, lucid presentiment that I would not be returning to this airport for a long time.

He took us along the Belt Parkway. It was raining hard. The highway was glutted with slow-moving afternoon traffic. The rain fell drearily from low clouds and washed across the road. Wipers arced rhythmically, and I saw the blurred faces of drivers through streaked windshields. Here and there the road was under repair. The traffic crawled and stopped and crawled on again. The car was old, its interior shabby. A used Styrofoam cup lay on the seat between me and the driver, on top of a folded Yiddish newspaper and a crumpled copy of the *New York Times*. He kept talking about my uncle. A true Jewish soul. A gift to us from the Master of the Universe. One of those who held the world together. A good heart. Always happy. A rare soul. One who binds up the wounds of the world.

We drove a long time in stop-and-start traffic. Avrumel, on Devorah's lap, began to whimper. Rocheleh sat glassy-eyed, staring out her window at the traffic and the rain. Devorah looked haggard. Her wig was slightly awry. It was night for us. In Saint-Paul the children would have been long asleep, and Devorah and I might be sitting on our terrace with Max Lobe and John Dorman over drinks, talking. Suddenly the driver said the road was impossible; we would be better off going a different way. He took the next exit. "Longer, but faster," he said.

We rode along a wide boulevard, crossed an intersection, and entered a narrow one-way street. Scraped and broken asphalt lay open to its dirt and crushed-stone layers. The station wagon creaked and groaned, its tires encountering with jarring shocks the rain-filled holes that pocked the street as in the aftermath of a cataclysm. Lining the broken, caved-in sidewalks were five-story red-brick houses, some with windows boarded, others open to the rain like eyeless sockets. One of the houses had suffered a fire; it stood scorched, its roof partially collapsed into its top floor, the center section of the floor deeply fissured, the cleft like an ax wound to the head, bricks littering the cement walk in front of the house. All through the street and around the houses and over the occasional empty lot lay the detritus of the neighborhood: beer cans, whiskey bottles, newspapers, dog droppings, a decaying mattress, an abandoned chair, an infant's crib, a gutted television set—an infernal rubbish heap that was like the graveyard of all hope. The street was empty of people. An occasional car lay near a curb, doors open, wheels gone, stripped to its core: a metallic corpse abandoned to aboveground putrefaction. I turned in my seat and saw Avrumel asleep on Devorah's lap and Devorah and Rocheleh staring at the blighted urban world through which we were passing. The driver, short in height and sitting low in the seat, kept craning his neck to spot the ruts and potholes. "Only a little more," he muttered. "Patience, patience." He hummed a light Ladover melody.

After two more blocks of bucking and lurching, he turned left into a wide two-way street, paved and glistening in the rain, and heaved a sigh. He glanced into his rearview mirror.

"Everybody okay back there?"

"We are well," Devorah said in English.

He drove swiftly and skillfully through Brooklyn streets still unfamiliar to me and then into the fringes of my old world. Then we were deep into that world, and I saw Ladover Hasidim on the streets and newly renovated homes and new shops and the parkway torn up, huge machines scraping at its entrails and heaving up the raw reddish earth.

"They're repaving this whole section of the parkway," the driver said. "Months they're working on it. New trees also they'll put in."

The rain had eased. He turned into a tree-bordered street and came to a stop in front of a red-brick ranch-style house. He switched off the engine.

"Here we are," he said in a somber tone. "I wish I was bringing you home on a happier occasion. I'll help you with your bags."

He had parked beneath a leafless sycamore. Rain dripped from the branches onto the car. The late-afternoon air was gray and cool. Gusts of wind blew through the street and rippled the puddles and shook the rain from the trees. I helped Devorah out of the car. Avrumel, in deep sleep, clung to her. The driver was busy with the bags. Rocheleh gave me her hand and stepped from the car to the sidewalk, just as a gust of wind splattered rain onto her startled face. The door to the house flew open, and two tall dark-bearded men came hurriedly down the walk that divided the front lawn. They wore dark suits and dark hats and tieless white shirts. They came over to us and, without a word, took our bags and hurried back up the walk and into the house.

I thanked the driver.

"An honor," he murmured.

Holding Rocheleh's bony, fragile-feeling hand, I followed Devorah into the house.

My mother stood just beyond the doorway, inside the entrance hall. She embraced Devorah lightly so as not to waken Avrumel and pointed to the men who were carrying our bags through the hallway to the interior of the house. Devorah followed quickly behind them. My mother murmured, "Rocheleh, Rocheleh," and bent down and held my daughter to her for a long time, her face against the face of the child, and I noted fleetingly how alike they looked—straight nose, wide eyes, small lips, high-boned cheeks. "Grandmother, it was a long trip, and I am very tired," Rocheleh said in French. My mother responded in French: "But yes, dear child, of course. Everything is ready for you." She looked at me and asked in Yiddish, "How are you, my son?"

"I am well, thank God, considering the circumstances. How are you?"

"How should I be, Asher? Your uncle's death is a terrible tragedy."

"Where is Papa?"

"Next door. They are making the final arrangements for tomorrow. The Rebbe himself will speak at the funeral. You look pale, my son."

"It's been a very long day, Mama."

"Papa, I am very very tired and I would like to go to bed now," Rocheleh said.

"I am so sorry," my mother said. "You have just flown thousands of miles, and here I stand talking. Come along with me, dear child. Asher, your room is on the left, over there. Come, Rocheleh."

"Good night, Papa."

"Good night, Rocheleh. Remember to say the Krias Shema."

"I always remember, Papa. Will Mama bring me my medicine?"

"I'll remind her."

They went off down the hallway and turned a corner.

I entered the room my mother had pointed to: twin beds in honey-colored wood, a desk, chairs, a dresser, beige carpeting, off-white walls bare save for a picture of the Rebbe over the desk, a large sliding glass door that led to a flagstone terrace and a length of wet lawn bordered by a tall juniper hedge and a towering mottled sycamore. I had not been in this house before. The apartment had been old and cramped: small rooms, a narrow hallway, two bedrooms, mine closetlike, its single window looking out on the cement paving of a back yard encumbered with garbage cans and hungry cats. This house, new, spacious, seemed filled with light even on this murky day of rain.

There was a noise behind me, a familiar tread: my father's slightly limping stride, the lingering residue of the infantile paralysis he had sustained as a child in Soviet Russia. He entered the room and I moved toward him and he shook my hand: a powerful grip even in grief. He had not yet removed his coat and hat; they were stained with rain. Sorrow and shock clouded the dark and mesmerizing eyes. He ran a hand through the dense white length of his untrimmed beard and then across his forehead: long-familiar gestures of distress and fatigue. He spoke in Yiddish.

"The children are all right? I have not had a chance to see them. Your mother says they are asleep. Devorah looks very tired. How are you, Asher?"

"I'm all right. I'm so sorry about Uncle Yitzchok. Was he ill?"

"No. It was very, very sudden. He was in the living room of his house, he gave a little cough, and he was—he was gone. Your Aunt Leah Golda was with him, and some friends. One minute here, the next minute gone. God gives, and God takes. That is the way of the world, Asher. What a blow this is, what a tragedy. I cannot reconcile myself to it. My brother. . . ." He closed his eyes and shook his head, and a tremor coursed through him. "The Rebbe will speak at the funeral in the synagogue. That is a great honor. . . . I cannot believe this is happening. . . . I should take off this coat. . . . An awful day outside; a terrible rainstorm we had earlier today. Your mother worried about all of you flying in such a storm. . . . I must take this off. . . . It is really good to see you and your family, Asher. Too many years. And they go by so quickly now. It is the only good thing that has come of this, that you and your family are here. This is not a time for conversation. We will talk when things settle down a little. You and Devorah should go to sleep. I know about jet lag."

He stepped out of the room and into the hallway and was gone. The space he had occupied vibrated softly. A residue of his presence remained in the room, a palpable afterimage that faded only after some moments passed.

The bags had been set down at the foot of one of the twin beds. My attaché case was on the desk. I began to unpack.

Devorah entered the room.

"The children are asleep."

"Did you remember to give Rocheleh her medicine?"

"Of course." She took off her wig and stepped out of her shoes. She put the wig on the dresser. Without her shoes and wig, she looked diminutive. "Avrumel woke up and asked for Shimshon."

"What did you tell him?"

"He fell back asleep before I could get a word out. How do you feel, my husband?"

"Very tired and very sad."

"Do you think any good will come of this, Asher? Can God have a plan? That's what I used to think when I was in that sealed apartment in Paris. That God had a plan, a big plan. Sometimes I would lie awake at night and try to guess what the plan was."

"My plan is to shower and go to sleep, Dev."

"Go ahead, my husband. I will unpack. But wouldn't it be interesting if there was a plan to this? Wouldn't it?"

"Absolutely. My uncle dies suddenly as part of some big plan. You're more of a Hasid than I am, my wife."

I headed for the bathroom and the shower.

Standing naked before the full-length mirror in the bathroom, I can barely see myself for the vapor that clouds the glass. Droplets cling to the wallpaper: lacy dogwood as in a rain. Pallid features, dark eyes, red hair and beard beginning to gray, narrow shoulders, white skin sheathing a scrawny frame down to the reddish triangle above the genitals, and then the legs, white, bony, all seen mistily, distorted, misshapen, through the fog of vapor thrown off by the hot, jetting water of the shower.

I lift my right arm and with my index finger trace slowly and with care the outline of my head and beard and then put in the locations of the eyes and nose and mouth. With my right index finger I draw the outline of my left shoulder and arm, and with my left index finger I draw the outline of my right shoulder and arm. I step back.

The drawing of me in the foggy mirror is awkward, doll-like, diminished, an ungainly semblance of myself.

Eighteen years before, I spent a night with my parents in the apartment where I grew up. I came out of the bathroom after a shower and went into my room. The phone rang. My mother tapped on my door. The call was for me. I went out into the hallway. The air was cool. I felt it cool on my face and the back of my neck, where the hair was still damp.

"Hello," I said into the phone.

"You are Asher Lev?" a whispery, muffled voice said.

"Yes."

"Asher Lev, the artist?" There was an eerie quality to the voice, a hollowness, as if it were coming to me over a long tube from a great distance away. "You made the crucifixion paintings?"

"Who is this?"

"I will tell you who this is. Listen to me, Asher Lev." A pause followed, strangely sinister. "I am the Angel of Death."

Cold air brushed across the backs of my legs. Beneath the damp hair of my head my scalp tingled.

"By morning you will no longer be among the living," the voice said. "You hear me, Asher Lev? By morning I will have taken back your corrupted soul. So perish the enemies of the Lord."

The line went dead.

The phone in my hand was suddenly alive, pulpy, reptilian. I slammed it down, trembling, and returned to my room. Sitting on my bed, I felt soiled and thought I must take another shower, but I lay down instead and tried to sleep. I woke in the darkness of the early morning and thought I heard the phone ringing and an arctic presence in the room and the reeking stench of goatish breath. I climbed out of bed and walked in the chill night silence of the hallway to the bathroom and urinated and looked at myself in the mirror. That voice. Cold, menacing, faintly accented, sinister, like a messenger from the Other Side.

Now, on the night before my uncle's funeral, I stand gazing at the drawing of myself in the bathroom mirror in my parents' home, watching it slowly dissolve, dripping mist.

I had always thought of my uncle as a simple, cheerful, good-hearted man, successful in his business, devoted to his family, and loyal to the Ladover movement. But his funeral astonished me. It was the funeral of a man of power.

I was told afterward that more than three thousand people attended, many from out of town: Boston, Philadelphia, Chicago, Miami, Los Angeles, Montreal, Toronto. I spotted two men in the crowd I knew from the Ladover community in Paris. The crowd, hushed, respectful, jammed the synagogue and spilled out onto the sidewalk and the parkway. Police on horses and in cars patrolled the parkway and diverted traffic from the lane adjoining the synagogue. In their identical dark coats and suits and hats, the men turned the street into a vast silent black lake. Loudspeakers had been set up outside so all could hear the service and the eulogy, which was to be delivered by the Rebbe.

I sat in the front row of the synagogue next to my father, who wore a dark suit and a dark tie and a dark hat and sat tall, self-controlled, an imposing presence, his eyes fixed upon the sealed simple pine coffin that lay on trestles between him and the lectern. On the other side of my father sat my uncle's two grown sons, and next to them were representatives from the office of the mayor and the governor, and some members of the city council. My father told me there were prominent lawyers and judges in the crowd. I thought I caught a glimpse of a well-known West Fifty-seventh Street art gallery owner. Why would the owner of a distinguished art gallery be at my uncle's funeral?

Close to two thousand people crowded the synagogue, sat jammed in its seats, stood along its walls, craned their necks from the back rows, blocked the entrance hallway. Somewhere in the women's gallery overhead, peering through the openings in the decorative arabesques of the concealing wooden screen, were my Aunt Leah, my uncle's two grown daughters, my mother, Devorah, Rocheleh, and Avrumel. The air in the synagogue was stale, warm, faintly malodorous. I hoped Rocheleh would be all right.

All faces, raptly attentive, were turned toward the Rebbe, who sat in his tall-backed, thronelike, upholstered chair to the right of the Ark, facing the congregation. Accompanied by two tall, brawny, dark-bearded men, he had entered through the door near the Ark, and I had felt the cold touch of shock at how old he had become: wizened, slightly bowed, walking with hesitant steps, hair and beard astonishingly white. He sat down in his chair, and the two men stood on either side of him, waiting.

One of the elders of the congregation approached the lectern near the Ark and recited a Psalm in a low, quivering voice. He returned to his chair. The Rebbe slowly rose and walked the few steps to the lectern. He wore a darkly glistening brocaded silken caftan, dark trousers, a white shirt with a dark tie, and a dark hat. All the gathered dismay of the grieving crowd focused itself upon him. He seemed haloed in unearthly light.

He spoke in Yiddish into the temporary microphone set up on the lectern for the service, and the speakers magnified his softly quivering, whispery voice and sent it in faintly echoing waves throughout the synagogue and out into the corridors of the building and the street and the parkway.

"Our dear Reb Yitzchok Lev, of blessed memory, has been called to the True World by the Master of the Universe. The mind is numb, the heart is heavy, the tongue cleaves to the palate. Sorrow weighs upon us all, and the years have placed upon me their added weight, so it is difficult for me to speak. I will therefore say only a few words. Let everyone listen with great care, so that my words will enter the heart. I will say a little that will contain much.

"Out of primordial chaos came order. Without order there can be no world. The first sign of order is light. 'And God said: Let there be light.' And Light, as we know, is the essence of the Messiah. The Messiah was created at the beginning of time.

"Now we live in another period of chaos. Everywhere, chaos. Hatred, terrorism, drugs, hooligans, murder in the streets, the abuse and death of little children, families falling to pieces, greed everywhere, homeless people in every corner of the land. We wait for a new light. We wait for the Messiah.

"Reb Yitzchok Lev labored hard to bring the Messiah. All knew his outward appearance, his cheerfulness. Few knew his soul, his inwardness, where the fire of Torah burned, where the teachings of Hasidus were for him a light, where he clung to Godliness."

He paused for a moment and seemed to need to gather strength before he was able to continue. Then he went on. "Listen to me, for it is important that you know this truth. Every Jew has it within his grasp to become a vessel for Godliness. Our dear Reb Yitzchok was just such a vessel, as was our Patriarch Yitzchok, who stood ready to be sacrificed on the fires of the altar, fires of Godliness and light. Why was our Patriarch Yitzchok prepared to let himself be sacrificed? Because he understood that the future of our people depended upon his act, his acceptance, his yielding, his faith, his willingness to be the sacrifice. He saw with perfect clarity what had to be done—as did our dear Reb Yitzchok, who gave of himself, his heart, his wealth, his entire being, to our community and to the

Ladover cause so as to hasten the coming of the Messiah and bring order to the chaos that surrounds us.

"Now listen with care, all of you here today, listen to my words. My father, of blessed memory, taught us the power of the riddle. Yes, the riddle: the seed that yields the flower; the acorn that yields the oak; the word that yields the book; the truth that must be uncovered slowly and with great care lest its fires burn and its power destroy. On this day that we have come together to mourn the departure from our midst of Reb Yitzchok Lev, of blessed memory, I say this to you as a message from the departed and from your Rebbe. I say to you: Three will save us. The third is our future. Do you hear me, my people? Three will save us. The third is our future."

He paused. I glanced at my father and saw his eyes had narrowed and his mouth had opened slightly. I was aware of the entire synagogue behind me, of the hush that lay upon it, as if even the possibility of sound had been drained from its walls. We seemed encapsulated in a dimension of silence I had never experienced before: light as air; dense as water; faintly vibrating; the emptiness carried by soundless echoes to the farthest reaches of the synagogue and out through the corridors and doorways to the parkway and the distant blue sky overhead.

The Rebbe leaned heavily upon the lectern and continued. "This our dear Reb Yitzchok, of blessed memory, understood. We thank the Master of the Universe for his life. We pray that his soul will forever find itself before the light of the Presence. May he labor for us in heaven to speed the coming of the Messiah. May his memory be a blessing forever and ever."

He stood motionless. The synagogue was still, as if all the current of its pulsing life had suddenly ceased. A moment later, he turned and walked slowly back to his chair.

An old man with a long white beard approached the lectern and recited two Psalms. Another old man chanted the El Moleh Rachamim prayer. "O Lord, full of compassion," he sang, in a soft, sweet, melancholy voice.

The Rebbe stood and, accompanied by the two tall men, left the synagogue through the door near the Ark.

Together with my two cousins and three others, I stepped over to the coffin. We lifted it off the trestles and slowly carried it—how astonishingly light it was!—up the center aisle of the synagogue as another elder, who walked before us, recited a Psalm. The air seemed suddenly stifling; I could not breathe. I worried about Rocheleh. We were outside. I inhaled deeply the cool air. The crowd silently parted as we came through, and there was the hearse, black and gleaming in the sunlight, and then the coffin was inside behind the curtained windows and someone was guiding me toward a glistening black limousine.

I sat next to my father in the back seat. There were two other men in the car, colleagues of my father whom I had known since childhood. We rode in silence. The cortege of funeral cars was two blocks long. My father sat gazing out the window. We drove through ruined streets and graveyard neighborhoods. A moment after we swung onto the Interboro Parkway, my father sat back and put his hand over his eyes. He remained in that position until we reached the cemetery.

The cars came to a halt in the section of the cemetery that contained the graves of Ladover Hasidim. I walked on the gravel road to the hearse and helped remove the casket. The crowd stood in silence. An elderly man, reciting from the Book of Psalms, led the procession to the edge of the open grave. I looked into the earth, saw the deep wounds made by the wielded shovels of the gravediggers, who stood idly by, watching. Abruptly, I felt my legs go weak and a sudden careening of the world. All around me were the muted sounds of weeping. My uncle's white-pine casket was lowered into the earth, the gravediggers swiftly and adroitly maneuvering the straps and then standing aside. My aunt sobbed and sagged into the arms of one of her daughters. My father stood beside me, biting his lips, all of him rigid. The starched white collar of his shirt, visible above his dark coat, glinted in the sunlight. I saw my mother in the crowd, her face ashen. Devorah, I knew, was not there: she had taken the children back to my parents' home.

My uncle's two sons began to fill in the grave. I took a shovel from one of the gravediggers, dug with it into the reddish-brown earth heaped along the rim of the grave, and lifted and let earth and pebbles and stones fall into the grave; heard the hollow sounds of the stones and earth striking the wood. My father took the shovel from me, and a moment later someone took it from him. My aunt stood nearby, loudly sobbing. The open grave filled rapidly. My uncle's two sons stood before the mound of raw turned earth and recited through tears the special Kaddish that is said at the grave of one newly buried. The crowd stirred, moved, divided itself into two lines between which the members of the immediate family moved through murmured words of consolation: "May God comfort you together with all the mourners of Zion and Jerusalem." My aunt walked supported by her two daughters. The cars began to fill up for the return journey.

I walked among the Ladover graves, all carefully tended, the grass cut, the paths raked, the gravestones clean. I saw the gravestone of Yudel Krinsky, the Russian Jew who had once owned a stationery store in our neighborhood and had sold me my first oil paints. The Hebrew letters carved into the polished stone gave the dates of his life and said of him that he was a righteous man, true to the ways of his fathers and a loyal Ladover Hasid. I saw him clearly: short and thin, with nervous bulging eyes, a beakish nose, pinched features, and the Russian cap he always wore. I had heard that he had died. I placed a small stone on his grave, a symbol of eternity, and recited by heart in his memory a chapter from the Book of Psalms.

Someone was standing alongside me.

"Sholom aleichem."

I recognized him: a high-school classmate. He had sat behind me in the yeshiva, often taunting me mercilessly for my drawing. "Aleichem sholom."

"I am very sorry about your loss."

"Thank you."

"You remember me?"

"Dov Brenner."

"Yes." He seemed pleased. He was short and heavyset, with small dark beady eyes and a long dark beard, long wisps of which ran down across his mouth. "What is Asher Lev doing these days?"

"The same."

"We read about you everywhere."

"You should not believe everything you read. What does Dov Brenner do these days?"

"I head the Ladover house here on the campus of New York University. Where your mother teaches. I'm the director."

"That's very nice."

"Your uncle was doing great things. This is a terrible blow. Between you and me, his sons are not of his caliber. How long are you staying?"

"Just through the week of mourning."

"It's nice in the south of France, yes?"

"Yes."

My father came over to where we were standing. I saw Dov Brenner stiffen and take on a respectful air.

"Dov Brenner, how is your father feeling?"

"He is better, thank God."

"Tell him I wish him a complete healing."

"I thank you, Rav Lev."

"We are waiting for you, Asher."

On the way back to the limousine, walking with my father along the graveled path between the rows of tombstones, I said, "Does the Rebbe usually speak in riddles at a funeral?"

"I cannot recall him doing it before."

"What does the riddle mean?"

"I have no idea. The Rebbe's riddles are not always easy to decipher."

"Is the Rebbe all right?"

"The Rebbe is eighty-nine years old," my father said. "May he live a long and healthy life."

The seating arrangements inside some of the limousines had been changed for the journey back to accommodate those traveling to similar destinations. The two men who had accompanied us to the cemetery were gone. I sat in the rear of the limousine with my parents.

The driver was negotiating the same blighted streets we had driven through earlier. I sat sideways in one of the jump seats, so

I could see my parents. My mother looked pale but dignified and poised. She had on a short-haired brown wig and a dark coat, and wore on her pale face the wrinkles of her age with a serene elegance. My father sat very straight in his dark coat and hat, gazing out the window, early-afternoon sunlight on his troubled features.

"The children are beautiful," my mother said.

"Thank you."

"Devorah is very good with them. Very patient."

"She needs patience with those two."

"Rocheleh behaved very well."

"Rocheleh is eleven years old. She sees childhood as a waste of time and considers herself an adult. How did Avrumel behave?"

"Avrumel is five. What do you want from the child? When you were five all you did was draw pictures and cry."

"I don't remember crying."

"I remember. Your father remembers."

"I remember drawing."

"How long are you staying, Asher?" my father asked, gazing out the window.

"Just for the week of mourning and the day after."

"That's all?" my mother said. "Such a trip, and you will only stay for eight days?"

"Rocheleh has school. I have my work."

"Rocheleh can go to school here for a while."

"How can she do that?"

"The Hebrew classes in her yeshiva in Nice are the same as they are here. Isn't that right, Aryeh?"

"Yes, that is right," my father said.

"Your father built that yeshiva. Rocheleh's English is very good. She will have little difficulty with her classes here."

"Devorah is in the middle of a new book."

"Devorah can use the room I showed her yesterday. There is even a computer in the house, if she needs one." The yearning in her voice. All the years that had to be made up for; all the opportunities torn away by my exile; all the shattered hopes and normalcies because of her inexplicably aberrant son. "And if you want to paint, can't your dealer find you a studio in the city?"

"I have to be in Paris next week."

She fell silent. Outside the windows of the car: broken side-walks, pitted streets, splintered brick façades: the ruins of an abandoned world. We rode quietly awhile.

"Asher," my mother murmured. "Eight days."

"There are things I have to do," I said.

"We cannot persuade you?"

"I can't stay."

"Asher."

"Rivkeh, leave it alone," my father said. "Let it be as he wishes." He sat staring out the window.

We rode on in silence.

My uncle had built a neighborhood jewelry and watch-repair shop into a citywide chain of stores called Lev's. He was to jewelry and watches what another Hasidic enterprise, located in the Forties in Manhattan, was to cameras and computers.

The chain of stores built by my uncle throughout New York City helped support the chain of Ladover yeshivas built by my father throughout the world. The acquisition of new sites, the renovation of old buildings and the construction of new ones, the purchase of Torah scrolls and Ladover texts; scholarships, emergency funds, travel expenses, deficits; the maintenance of dining rooms, dormitories, medical facilities, gymnasiums—all nourished from the endlessly flowing fountain of funds whose source was my late uncle's expanding watch and jewelry business. One of my cousins told me that my uncle had been considering further expansion into New Jersey, Connecticut, and Pennsylvania before he died.

His family lived in the house next door to my parents' house: a three-story, Tudor-style sprawl, with a large front lawn, a deep expanse of grass in the rear, bordering hedges, flower beds, and a towering ailanthus along the rim of the back terrace. I had lived in that house for a time; had painted in it when my parents had been away together in Europe, traveling for the Rebbe. Most of the paintings I had made in that house were now in museums or private collections.

The limousine turned the corner and moved slowly along the

orderly residential street. A hushed crowd stood in front of my uncle's house, spilling down from the porch and out onto the wide front lawn. The limousine came to a stop at the curb.

The driver stepped out quickly, opened the rear door, and helped my parents out onto the sidewalk. I climbed out on the street side. The afternoon sun shone through the bare trees and into my eyes, and I thought fleetingly of clear bright sunlight and terraced hills and the Cubist houses of the valley and the distant silvery radiance of the sea.

I stood with my parents on the sidewalk near my late Uncle Yitzchok's house. Behind us, the limousine pulled slowly away from the curb and drove off.

"Asher, come," my father said.

His strong fingers were on my elbow.

We moved toward the dense silent crowd: mostly young men, dark-garbed, freshly bearded, standing about: the new generation that had grown up while I was in Europe. My uncle's death had touched them deeply; they stood there with somber eyes, mournful faces, sagging shoulders: the body language of sorrow. They parted silently before my father, as if a hidden signal had been given. I walked in the wake of the looks of awe and reverence directed at my father. From somewhere in the silent crowd I heard a voice say, "That's Asher Lev." I saw my mother's brief embarrassed response—she shut her eyes and shook her head—and felt the immediate momentary tightening of my father's grip on my arm. We walked up the cement path and the stone steps to the porch. A young man suddenly appeared before us with a basin, a pitcher of water, and a towel. We washed and dried our hands and went on through the front door into the house.

The silent crowd in the entrance hall parted for my father. "Coats on the second floor, first room to the left of the stairs," someone said in a near-whisper. I took my parents' coats, and they continued on through the crowd into the living room. I climbed the stairs.

The house gleamed with the opulence of its owners: thickly carpeted floors and stairs; richly textured wallpaper with floral designs; expensively framed prints by contemporary Jewish artists on the walls of the second-floor hallway: Agam, Nachshon, Bezem,

Bergner, Ardon, Bak, Rubin, Ticho, Moreh. How curious, all that art. The only art on the walls of this house during all the years of my growing up in this neighborhood had been calendar reproductions of medieval Hebrew manuscripts, pictures of the Rebbe, and my own work.

The room to the left of the stairs was small but tastefully furnished. Coats lay everywhere: on the bed, chairs, desk. This room had once been mine, but when I lived in it the furniture was plainer, more in keeping with my uncle's then modest earnings. How I had worked! The cascades of color and form; the images that had possessed me: I would gaze at them inside myself, watching them grow from the empty point of their beginnings, from the void of nonbeing, to amorphous, shapeless lumps, and then simmer slowly into a molded nucleus of life, fragile, tender, frightened, incomplete. That constant wide-eyed looking at the shapes inside myself. That strange sense of being possessed by the Other. What a fearful and exquisite and frenzied time that had been—here in this room and in the attic overhead!

I put my parents' coats on a chair and started out of the room, then noticed the mezuzah at about eye level on the doorpost: the small filigreed silver container with the Hebrew letter *shin* boldly on top like a silver crown, and the parchment within visible through the tiny glass window set in the opening cut out of the decorous front. Standing in the hallway, I saw mezuzahs on the other doorposts as well: at the rooms once occupied by my cousins, and at my aunt's and uncle's bedroom, and at my uncle's study near the—

I looked carefully. The door next to the master bedroom led to my uncle's study. It was closed, and there was no mezuzah on the doorpost. The door to the narrow stairway that led up to the attic was also closed and had no mezuzah. I remembered clearly the mezuzah on its doorpost when I had lived in this house: a plain, unadorned metal container. I looked again at the door to my uncle's study and at the naked doorpost. I started back downstairs.

The silent crowd now extended halfway up the stairwell. I moved slowly through the press of bodies down the stairs and into the hallway and the living room.

Wooden folding chairs had been set up in rows in the center of the room and were now filled mostly with bearded, dark-garbed elders. I stood against a narrow section of wall near the wide picture window that looked out on the front lawn and the street. Most of the wall to my right was taken up by a fireplace and a mirror. The wall to my left was the entrance to the room. The only entirely unobstructed wall in the room was the one across from me. In front of it, on low stools, sat my Aunt Leah and my four cousins. Corpulent and normally as cheerful as my Uncle Yitzchok, Aunt Leah now wore on her fleshy features a look of stunned bewilderment. The two daughters sat to her left; the sons, to her right. They were all eating the ritual meal that traditionally follows a funeral.

The wall contained two large reproductions of micrographic drawings—lines formed of minute Hebrew letters. Both were from a Pentateuch printed in Germany in the thirteenth century. One drawing showed Aaron tending the lamps of the Tabernacle during the period of the Israelites' desert wandering. The second depicted the binding of Isaac: Abraham, his arm raised high, was about to slaughter his son.

Between the two drawings was a large, ornately framed oil painting of the Rebbe.

The painting was based on a photograph; the Rebbe did not sit for oil paintings. It showed the Rebbe seated at a table, his right hand raised in greeting, his left hand resting on a white cloth. His beard was white. He wore a dark suit and a dark hat. His eyes were sharp, clear: eyes that looked. The Rebbe in the painting was twenty years younger than the Rebbe in the synagogue. I glanced away and saw my parents seated together, deep in conversation with a white-bearded man; my mother was doing most of the talking. Looking again at the picture of the Rebbe, I see it shimmering faintly in the too-warm air. A trick of lights and shadows brings a rush of life to the face: the eyes flame; the hand moves slowly, beckoning. I look quickly away.

My aunt and cousins complete their meal. The dishes and low tables are removed. Someone announces that the Afternoon Service is about to begin. My mother and aunt and the half-dozen or so other women in the room rise and leave, for the service cannot begin if there are women in the room with the men. One of my cousins leads the service. He stands in front of the picture of the Rebbe, praying softly. The Rebbe gazes out from the picture, scrutinizing me, looking.

The service was over. People began to leave. New people entered. The air buzzed with movement and subdued conversation. I took a chair next to an old man and watched people going over to my aunt and cousins and murmuring the words of consolation. Yesterday at this time Devorah and I and the children had just come off the Airbus. Two days before, the air blue and warm and fragrant with spring, she and I were sitting on our terrace with Max Lobe and John Dorman, drinking good cognac and talking about the differences between writing and painting, and the future of painting, and the aimlessness of postmodernism. I sat now in the hot and crowded living room of my Aunt Leah's house, thinking of my Uncle Yitzchok.

"Reconcile yourself to your son," he had once told my father. "He cannot help what he does."

"Only an animal cannot help what he does," was my father's response.

My mother had returned and was seated again next to my father. They were deep in conversation with two white-bearded men, who were listening intently to my mother. The old man who had been sitting silently beside me stirred and turned to me with an abrupt motion. I had the impression he had suddenly made up his mind about something.

"You are Asher Lev?" he asked. His voice was low, quavery. Beneath the brim of his worn dark hat a network of furrows lay weblike across his forehead. Lines of tiny wrinkles crisscrossed the pouches below the deeply socketed watery eyes. The pale flesh of his face above the line of long untrimmed beard was like brittle old paper.

I told him yes, I was Asher Lev.

"The son of Rav Aryeh Lev?"

"Yes."

"I have heard about you."

I wondered what he had heard, but did not ask him.

"Where does Asher Lev live these days?"

"In the south of France."

"There are Jews in the south of France?"

"We have a fine community in Nice."

"Ah, yes. Of course. The yeshiva was built by your father." He paused briefly, glancing over at my parents. "He is a great man, your father. So was your uncle, may his memory be for a blessing. Great men. Good men. God gives, God takes away. That is the way the world is." He nodded and closed his eyes and was still. I thought he had fallen asleep. But after a moment he stirred and gazed at me, his eyes moist and lustrous with the high sheen of age. "Tell me, Asher Lev, you knew Jacob Kahn?"

"He was my teacher in art."

"I knew his father. A learned man. He was my teacher in Torah. We were among those who came to America with the Rebbe during the war against Hitler, may his name and memory be erased. Jacob Kahn also lived for a time in the south of France. You knew him there?"

"Yes. We lived near the same village."

"Tell me. Before he died, Jacob Kahn became a Torah Jew? He returned to Yiddishkeit?"

I shook my head.

His aged face took on a look of profound grief. "It hurts the heart," he murmured. "What children sometimes do. How old are you, Asher Lev?"

"Forty-five."

"Forty-five. How young. Do you know how old I am?"

"No."

"Take a guess."

"Eighty."

"Ninety-two. Yes. You look surprised. Ninety-two. What these eyes have seen. When you live in this world for ninety-two years, you see a lot." He shook his head sadly. "It hurts me to hear that Jacob Kahn did not return to Torah." He looked away and closed his eyes.

The room was becoming crowded. I gave my chair to an elderly woman and made my way into the thronged hallway and then into the dining room, where a few women stood about, talking quietly.

There on the wall above the heavy mahogany buffet was the oil painting I had made of my uncle and his family when I lived with them—a gift for renovating the attic and turning it into my first studio. It hung in a baroque frame that was much too opulent for its facile realist genre; I had painted it in straightforward fashion, thinking my uncle and his family would have little appreciation for the ambiguous and mystifying flourishes of a modernist style. How they had loved it! My uncle proudly called it his first "authentic Lev" and boasted about the money it would one day be worth. There he was, in the picture, rotund, dark-bearded, smiling, a small dark skullcap on his head, the cigar in his hand, his wife beside him, the children to their right and left. Uncle Yitzchok. Dead and in the earth. Together with Yudel Krinsky. And Jacob Kahn. And Anna Schaeffer. May their memories be for a blessing.

I came back out into the hallway and glanced into the living room. A small crowd had assembled around my father and was listening absorbedly to something he was saying. I saw through the open door the quiet, milling crowd on the porch and the lawn. The stairway was clear, and I climbed it to the second floor.

I walked quickly along the empty, carpeted hallway. The doors to my old room and my cousins' rooms were open. I stopped at the door to my uncle's study and tried the knob. The door was locked. There had been a mezuzah on its doorpost once, but even the marks of its nails were now gone. I went back along the length of the hallway to the door beyond the stairway that led up to the attic. It, too, was locked, with no sign on its doorpost of the mezuzah that had once been there.

A riddle. What can be put into a room that will so profane it that the mezuzah should be removed from its doorpost?

I went back downstairs to the living room. My mother was ready to leave to prepare supper; my father would remain awhile longer. It was late afternoon. I would return for the Evening Service.

The crowd in and around the house had thinned. I stood with my mother before Aunt Leah and my cousins and spoke the words of consolation.

My two female cousins averted their eyes and shied away from me, as though fearful of contamination. One of the male cousins assumed an air of bravado. "How you doing, Asher? Long time no see." The other gave me a look of contempt.

"He loved you," Aunt Leah said to me through her tears. "He thought the world of you."

My cousins avoided looking at her.

"When are you going back?" my aunt asked. "Will I get a chance to see the children?"

"Asher is returning after the week of mourning," my mother said.

"I'll ask Devorah to bring the children over," I said.

"Only one week?" my aunt said.

The girl cousins looked relieved. The male cousins were not paying attention to the conversation.

"It's a shame Asher cannot stay longer," my mother said.

"How he loved you, Asher," my aunt said. "He would never say it, but I know he loved you."

I went back upstairs and got our coats. The second-floor hallway was silent, deserted. Downstairs, I helped my mother with her coat and looked into the living room and saw my father talking quietly to a group of elderly men, one of them the ninety-two-year-old man who had sat beside me earlier. I came out of the house with my mother and breathed deeply the cool early-spring air.

My father stayed in the house of mourning after the Evening Service, and I waited for him. The living room was never without a crowd. Many non-Ladover people came: city politicians; the district representative to the statehouse; the local Republican committeeman; men and women who worked for my uncle in his many stores. Two Japanese men showed up, stayed awhile, offered their condolences, and left. The art dealer I had seen in the synagogue earlier that day suddenly appeared, a trim, dapper man in his late sixties, nattily garbed, silver hair combed smoothly back, a pale-blue handkerchief in the breast pocket of his expensive dark-blue suit. We had met briefly here and there in the past at parties and openings, and shortly after Anna Schaeffer died, he had made an attempt to prize me away from her gallery. How was the Blue Coast, and what was I doing these days? he asked, with both the

accent and the studied politeness of a Central European. I asked
him how he had known my uncle. Oh, he had sold him a print
now and then, this piece, that piece. He seemed disinclined to let
the conversation go beyond the conventional banalities. To my
aunt and cousins he expressed his condolences in low, courtly
tones. A moment later, he was gone.

I gave up my chair to an elderly woman and went out to the
crowded hallway and then up the stairs to the second floor. The
Bak print beckoned, and I looked at it with care: two huge keys set
in a hilly boulder-strewn green landscape through which meanders
a stream that reflects the clear blue light of a cloudless sky. One of
the keys, huge, antique, of the sort one sees on a castle ring, stands
on its head; the other reclines upon a rock. The distant blue sky is
penetrated by shimmering white light shaped like a huge keyhole.

Near the door to my uncle's study was a Moreh print. Over a
landscape devastated by torrential waters in which helplessly bob
humans, animals, rodents, boats, birds, and trees, a robed figure
hangs suspended in the air, attached to a stake that is connected at
its foot to a wheel. The Hebrew words above the center are from
the Book of Psalms. "Out of the depths I call you, O Lord. O Lord,
listen to my cry. . . ."

The figure, a bearded old man, hangs from the stake, arms
extended, feet crossed: the position of one crucified.

My uncle's study was to the left of the Moreh print. I tried the
knob again. The door was locked. I started back down the stairs.
Behind me, vague sounds moved through the hallway: air fluttering; feet sliding softly upon the carpeting; a distant whistling.
Cold winds touched the back of my neck. I turned.

The hallway was empty.

I stood there a moment, listening.

Then I went back downstairs to the living room. My father was
ready to leave. We walked home together.

Later, we sat in the kitchen over cups of coffee. My mother was
in her study, grading examination papers, and Devorah was with
Rocheleh. Avrumel, suffering jet lag and a low-grade fever, was
asleep.

My father sat in his shirtsleeves, collar open, gazing somberly
into space. His velvet skullcap lay like a dark crown on his thick

white hair. Even in grief there was an aura of stateliness to him: his demeanor controlled, faintly majestic and imperial. He ran his fingers slowly through the vigorous white hair of his beard and drank from his cup.

The cup was from a set of six—all fired in earthen colors strewn with drawings of parakeets—he had brought back with him once from a trip to Australia. The house contained other, less frivolous tokens of his travels: an eighteenth-century Haggadah published in Warsaw and discovered by my father in a secondhand bookstore on some back street in Munich; a battered seventeenth-century Havdalah spice box rescued by my father from an attic in Vienna; a nineteenth-century white silk Shabbos chalah cover found amid a pile of rags in the basement of a home in Prague, the Hebrew word *shabbos* exquisitely sewn into the silk with multicolored threads; a filigreed seventeenth-century silver pointer used by Torah readers, which my father had acquired from a high government official on one of his trips to South Africa. He didn't know how the pointer had fallen into the official's hands, but, as he had put it to me earlier that day while showing me around the house, "Such an object does not belong in the hands of such a person."

Here and there on the walls of the house were reproductions of medieval illuminated Hebrew manuscripts, gifts from my uncle over the years. There was also an unusual micrographic drawing of the Rebbe's great-grandfather. The most prominent picture hung in the living room: a large, ornately framed color photograph of the Rebbe taken about twenty years ago—around the time he had sent me away from the Ladover community in Brooklyn because of my crucifixion paintings.

My father put down his cup. "Do you want some more coffee, Asher?"

I told him if I had any more coffee, I wouldn't be able to sleep.

"You have trouble sleeping? Your mother cannot sleep. Four hours, and she is up. Does Devorah still need a light?"

"She can fall asleep with a night light now."

"A night light. We have one in the house somewhere. Remind me later, and I'll get it for you. Rocheleh looks frail. While you are here, you should let a doctor examine her. I can arrange it so the Rebbe's own doctor will do it. He is at Mount Sinai."

"Rocheleh has been seen by specialists in Paris, Lyons, and Nice. Everything is under control."

"It can't hurt for her to be seen by an American doctor."

"What difference will it make? There's no cure for asthma."

"Every day something new is discovered."

"If anything is discovered, her French doctor will know about it. I don't want her upset by new examinations."

"As you wish, Asher. You are her father. Devorah asked me today if I knew where she could purchase a Shimshon doll for Avrumel. I told her to ask your mother. There are stores all over the neighborhood that sell toys and dolls. This is, thank God, a neighborhood filled with children. Where did you get a Shimshon doll?"

"John Dorman got it for Avrumel in a store in Nice. Avrumel thinks he was born with it."

"John Dorman is the writer who lives next to you?"

"You met him. We were over at his house the last time you were in Saint-Paul. A man in his seventies, reddish face, white hair."

"The man who drinks."

"He has a drinking problem, yes. The novel he published in the late thirties is a classic."

"You told me he no longer writes."

"He writes, but he doesn't publish."

"What happened to him?"

"I don't know. He says he lost his beginnings. His first world, he calls it. He lost his first world. Also, he was with the Communist Party for a while, and left when Stalin signed the pact with Hitler."

"I remember we talked about communism. He seemed to me a lonely man, a person without a community." He paused a moment, looking at me. "And you, Asher? Are you all right?"

I was quiet.

He leaned toward me. "Asher?"

"There are problems."

"What happened in Paris? Your mother and I heard about the exhibition."

"The show sold out. But the critics hated what I did. They were ... nasty."

"Sold out? You mean everything was sold?"

"Yes."

"How many paintings were in the exhibition?"

"Eighteen."

There was a pause. "The critics are important, Asher?"

"The important critics are important. They tell you what you already know and are afraid to admit. I'm repeating myself, and that's not good."

"I know less than nothing about art, Asher, but it seems to me that Max Lobe repeats himself."

"Max Lobe is a fine artist, but he's not an important one. Everyone loves Max, but the critics don't pay much attention to him. They pay a lot of attention to me because they know who my teacher was and what I've been doing all these years, and they're warning me to consider where I'm going. Who knows? Maybe they're right. Maybe I'm another John Dorman."

"John Dorman is a good friend?"

"He's a very dear friend. To me and to Devorah."

"A drunkard is your dear friend?"

"He's an alcoholic. He can't help what he does."

"Asher, an animal cannot help what it does. A human being is able to control himself if he wills it."

"I think we've been through this conversation before."

"That is God's gift to us. It is what separates us from the animals. Our minds and our will."

"John Dorman's mind is pickled in alcohol, and his will isn't strong enough for him to stop. He's not an immoral person. He's sick."

"That is very sad, Asher."

"It certainly is. It's the great American success story."

"Success? Where is the success? It is a tragedy."

He shook his head and drank from his cup. The irony was lost on him. Someone once told me the Japanese have no sense of the ironic. Tell a Japanese on a rainy day that the weather is just great, and he will look at you in bewilderment. Perhaps one should not affect the ironic mode in the presence of one who has just buried a beloved brother. Was there anything in the Talmud or in Hasidic teachings on that? Do not be ironic in the presence of death. When else, if not then? I was feeling tired and light-headed. The too-long day. Jet lag. The prints in my uncle's home. The locked doors. The doorposts without mezuzahs. The doorways in my parents' home had mezuzahs on them. That was the way you did it in a traditional Jewish home: you obeyed the biblical commandment "And you shall write them on the doorposts of your house and upon your gates." Every door, except the door to the bathroom, had its own mezuzah, its own little case with the small rolled-up scroll of parchment bearing on one side the first two paragraphs of the "Hear O Israel" from the Book of Deuteronomy, carefully rendered by a scribe, and on the other side the Hebrew word *Shadai,* one of the sacred names of God. Devorah had bought mezuzahs for the front doors of Max Lobe's house and John Dorman's house, and we had all made a ceremony of putting them up. Mezuzahs are sacred; they are believed to possess power. Some years ago, after a bus disaster in Israel, one of the Hasidic Rebbes in Brooklyn announced that children had been killed because the mezuzahs in their town had not been checked in a long time and some were probably spoiled, the writing worn after too many years. The acrimony, the verbal attacks against that Rebbe by so many other Jews, that had followed that announcement! But the Rebbe had stood by his statement. And now, two doors without mezuzahs in my uncle's home. Did my father know?

"I like the art Uncle Yitzchok has in his house."

"Art?"

"Bak, Agam, Ardon, Moreh. All the others. Very nice. I had no idea Uncle Yitzchok was interested in art."

"He was interested," my father said, looking down at his cup and indicating by his tone that he himself was not at all interested in talking about it. He had not the vaguest notion about art. He was a graduate of Brooklyn College, where he had majored in political science, had a master's degree in political science from New York University, read widely, subscribed to magazines and journals—the house was strewn with current and back issues of the *New York Review of Books, Commentary, National Review, Time,* the *New Republic, Foreign Affairs, France Today, Soviet Life,* and other, more technical publications in his field. A sophisticated man—yet blind to the world of art: Greek, Roman, African, Asian,

Christian, secular, Jewish; it made little difference to him. The boundary of his artistic appreciation was the kitsch of a calendar scene: Abraham at the Covenant; Isaac on the altar about to be slaughtered; Moses at the parting of the sea; Miriam and the women dancing; Moses on Mount Sinai. The vast, rich, nuanced, exhilarating, disturbing, iconoclastic world of modern and contemporary art was locked to him.

"I read an article on Picasso a little while ago," he said now, looking up from his cup of coffee. "He was not a nice man."

"That's right, he certainly wasn't a nice man."

"You admire Picasso?"

"Do we admire Maimonides? It'll take the world of art three hundred years to absorb the work of Picasso."

He was shocked. "You compare Picasso to Maimonides?"

"Niceness and greatness are two very different qualities."

"Not in Yiddishkeit, Asher. Not among Hasidim. What a person does is what he is."

"Not in art."

"A man can be a murderer and still be regarded as a great artist?"

"A man can be a good doctor and not be nice."

"Would you put Rocheleh into the hands of a physician who is a cruel person? You live in a world where a man like Picasso is your king. What a strange world you are in, Asher."

"Picasso has been dead for fifteen years. No one is king in art today."

"It is not a world I thought my son would belong to."

He lapsed into silence. We sat quietly. He stared a long time into his cup. Then he looked at me and shook his head. "I am sorry, Asher. I spoke out of anger. This is a difficult time for me. My brother's death. I cannot reconcile myself to it."

I was quiet.

"So much depended upon him. He was my—my support. His sons are not as generous as he was. Especially Yonkel. Very angry and very greedy."

"If the Rebbe tells him—"

"The Rebbe is old, Asher. The Rebbe is tired. Not everyone listens all the time to the Rebbe."

I stared at him.

"There are times," he murmured, "when I think that—" He stopped and took a deep breath and shook himself. He looked wearily around the room, blinking. The kitchen gleamed. Hidden sources of energy fed its appliances: the refrigerator, the two ovens, the microwave, the two dishwashers. "Enough," he said. "That is the work of the sitra achra. It enters you and wants you to wallow in sadness and self-pity so your work cannot be done. Enough. All will be well, with the help of God. Yes, Asher? All will be well."

He fell silent. The refrigerator hummed into life, its soft pulsing filling the kitchen.

"Asher, you are certain you cannot remain for a while after the week of mourning?" It seemed an effort on his part to ask that: entreaty was for him an utterly uncharacteristic act.

"I have to be in Paris next week. I promised Max I would work with him on a print."

"You cannot change the appointment?"

"Printers are involved. We've reserved time and a press. Max says he needs my help. It has to do with a new process he wants me to teach him."

"You will teach Max Lobe? He is fifteen years older than you."

"I learned the technique from Jacob Kahn. It's a complicated process."

"You have been with us only once in twenty years, Asher."

The phone call returned frighteningly to mind. That cold hollow satanic voice. "I have my own life now," I said.

"All right, Asher. As you wish."

The refrigerator hummed in the brittle silence.

There were footsteps in the hallway. My mother entered the kitchen, wearing a pale-blue housecoat. From beneath the edges of her yellow kerchief protruded an occasional curl of her short-cropped silver hair.

"Forgive me for interrupting. I came in for a cup of coffee."

"Rivkeh, Avrumel forgot his Shimshon doll in Saint-Paul. Asher wants to know if there is anyplace nearby where we can get him a new one," my father said.

"I already told Devorah about a store on Kingston Avenue. We will go there tomorrow."

"I told you your mother would know," my father said to me.

"He prefers the old, but he will settle for the new," my mother said. "You have lovely children, Asher."

"Devorah is the one to tell that to. She's with them day and night."

"I have told her. I must get back to the examination papers. The way young people write English these days. It is absolutely a scandal. It is as if English is a foreign language. Do you want to hear some examples of American writing? 'Intents and purposes' someone writes as 'intensive purposes.' 'Fallen by the wayside' is 'fallen by the waste side.' 'Next-door neighbor' is 'next-store neighbor.' 'Dog-eat-dog world' is 'doggy-dog world.' Can you believe that? It is a mystery to me where they learn to write like that."

"Your mother wants to retire so she can travel with me and spend time visiting with you," my father said.

"And finishing my book. I must finish that book." She was writing on the Politburo and the changes in the processes of succession in the Soviet Union. Some years ago, the University of Nice had asked me to do a mural for its library building, and one day, while passing through the catalogue room, I had looked for my mother's name: "Lev, Rebekah." Three of her books and one volume of her published papers were in the library, in French. She taught Russian history and political theory in the Russian Studies Department of New York University.

I watched as she poured herself a cup of coffee. Short, slight, delicately boned, a fragile look that belied her tenacity and strength. The soft lights and pastel colors of the kitchen. The hypnotic hum of the refrigerator renewing its energy. My mother sipping from her cup and nodding with satisfaction. "I teach only one class tomorrow. We will get the Shimshon doll for Avrumel tomorrow. Now I'm going back to those papers, so I won't wake up at four in the morning, worrying about them."

She took the coffee cup with her out of the kitchen. I heard her receding footsteps.

"Mama looks good," I said.

"She is well, thank God. She looks forward to retiring."

"Will you retire, too?"

"I? Of course not. The work of the Master of the Universe is never over."

"Artists don't retire, either. They just fade away."

My father smiled sadly and sipped from his cup. "Paris was that bad?"

"Paris was a disaster."

"I am truly sorry, Asher."

"The thing is, I'm not sure I know what to do now. That's the thing. I don't know where I'm going."

He did not respond.

"It's nice to be able to retire. Comforting."

"You think so?" he said.

"Isn't it?"

"No," he said. "Endings are never nice."

I wandered alone through the hallways of the house. Mezuzahs on the doorposts. Rocheleh was asleep, breathing tranquilly, covered to her chin with a light blanket. I hoped her pillow was all right. Avrumel lay snoring slightly and looking forlorn even in sleep, his blanket a shambles. Where was the drawing I had made on the Airbus? No doubt crumpled somewhere amid the chaos of his blanket. Devorah and my mother were talking together quietly in my mother's study. I went to our room and got out of my clothes.

In the bathroom I brushed my teeth and washed and saw on the full-length mirror the faint outline of the awkward drawing I had made of myself the day before. The vanishing vapor had left a residue on the glass: the mark of my finger in the fog.

Devorah was in the room when I came back. Her head was uncovered.

"Your mother and I had a lovely talk."

"That's nice."

"It's a pity all these years have gone by and we never got to know each other."

"It wasn't my doing."

"No one is blaming you, Asher."

"Of course everyone blames me, Dev. Haven't you heard? I'm

not in control of my mind or my will. Listen, I'm tired. It's four o'clock in the morning Saint-Paul time."

"They say you should adjust your body clock immediately to your new time zone and not pay attention to where you came from."

"I intend to pay careful attention to where we came from."

"You are in one of your moods, my husband."

"My father wanted to know what happened in Paris. My mother is talking about retiring. I'm ready to go home tomorrow."

"Do you really want to?"

"I want to, yes, but we won't."

"Your mother suggested we put Rocheleh into the Ladover yeshiva for the time that we're here."

I looked at her. "How can we do that?"

"She'll be in the same grade she attends in the yeshiva in Nice."

"What does Rocheleh say?"

"She is willing to try."

"Are you sure it's all right?"

"What can be wrong with it, Asher?"

"And Avrumel? What will you do with Avrumel?"

"He can go into the kindergarten. Your mother says the yeshiva has a very fine kindergarten."

"I guess it's okay. You'll have time to work on the book."

"There are also other things I can do. I want to get to know your parents."

She went to the bathroom. I lay on my bed in the silence of the room. Off-white stippled walls, a French-style bureau, a beige carpet, two soft chairs, twin beds. The Rebbe gazed at me from the wall above the rolltop desk. That picture, too, was about twenty years old.

Devorah returned and climbed into her bed. The mattress barely moved beneath her weight.

"Will you want the lamp on, Dev? My father gave me a night light we can use."

"Leave the lamp on for tonight, Asher."

She lay with her hands behind her head, slender, small-boned, her elbows pointing outward, her thin white wrists jutting from the frilly sleeves of her pink cotton nightgown. Her short brown hair, streaked with wisps of gray and always concealed beneath a wig or a kerchief when she left our room, grew in tiny curls upon her head. She looked over at me. Her gray eyes were blurred and moist.

"I am wondering what John is doing."

"Drinking, no doubt. Maybe writing. Missing you, that's for sure."

"Poor John. Let's not forget that we promised to get him some American writing pads."

"It's on my list. American writing pads for the ex-Communist John Dorman."

"You *are* in a mood, my husband."

"Devorah."

"Yes."

"Do you want to stay on longer than the week of mourning?"

"We should think about it, Asher. Can it hurt to stay on a week or two longer? Grandparents have a right to enjoy their grand-children. Now I am very tired. How is it I am not yet asleep? Good night, my husband."

"I have to be in Paris next week with Max."

"That's one of the reasons God gave us the telephone, Asher. Appointments can be postponed. Max will understand. I am al-ready asleep, Asher. I am talking to you in my sleep."

She recited softly to herself the Krias Shema, then turned on her side, her face to me. Almost immediately, she was asleep.

I lay wide awake in the bright light cast by the lamp on the night table between our beds. From the hallway outside the closed door came the sounds of shuffling feet and a low, soft whistle. I shivered and closed my eyes and lay still in the light. The Bak print entered my eyes: the keys in the rock-strewn landscape, the luminous keyhole in the sky; and the Moreh print: the bearded old man on the wheeled crucifix-shaped stake hovering over a grim and water-scourged vista. The look of loathing on my Cousin Yonkel's face, as if I were decaying vermin forbidden to the touch. Aunt Leah weeps. Will I get a chance to see the children? The Rebbe beckons to me from the oil painting on the wall between the drawings of

Aaron in the wilderness and Isaac bound to the altar. I fall asleep with the Rebbe still beckoning to me, the light of the lamp full in my eyes.

A cement walk divided the front lawn of my parents' home. Rows of rhododendrons separated the lawn from the sidewalk and the two adjoining properties.

The house had been purchased for them by my uncle about ten years after I had left the neighborhood to live in Europe. When my mother wrote me about the purchase, I imagined hearing my Uncle Yitzchok saying, "You can't live in this tiny apartment any more! How does it look? The right arm of the Rebbe, and you live this way? People come in to see you, and they see *this*? The Master of the Universe has been good to me. Why shouldn't I be good to my brother and sister-in-law?"

To the right of my parents' home stood the three-story home of my aunt and uncle. Three houses down from my uncle's home, on a rise beyond a gently sloping lawn and a juniper hedge, stood the large red-brick home of the Rebbe.

Every morning that week my father and I rose early and walked together to my uncle's house. About fifty feet of sidewalk separated the cement walks that led to the porches of the two homes.

On the first morning after the funeral we came out the front door into a gray and chilly dawn. Mist clung to the bare branches of the trees. I felt the cold air sting my face, and I shivered. Once I had played with my mother in snow, running with her through drifts, our galoshes kicking soft sprays into the frigid air. She would toss snowballs at the trees, her arms making the awkward motions of a little girl. I had loved the snow and made many drawings of my mother in it. Now the mild cold of an April morning seemed unendurable to me.

About thirty men were in the living room of my late uncle's house, some sitting quietly in their prayer shawls and tefillin, others still winding the straps around their arms and foreheads. Everyone wore the early-morning look of recent sleep and fresh beginnings. I took a chair in the back row, wrapped myself in my tallis, and quickly put on my tefillin. Someone slid into the chair next to mine: the same ninety-two-year-old man who had sat there the day before. His large tallis was yellow with age; the uncommonly wide straps and oversize boxes of his tefillin were shiny black. He gave me a faint nod and turned his attention to the Book of Psalms in his hands.

The younger of my uncle's two sons, Cousin Nahum, a short, round, balding man in his forties, led the service in a thin, unmelodious voice. I was quickly caught up in the words, lost awareness of where I was. The images in the morning blessings moved before me. Opens the eyes of the blind; clothes the naked; sets the earth firmly in the waters. The binding of Isaac. The Psalms. The Song at the Sea. The Unity of God. And entering now the breadth and length and depth of the river, stepping into the first flow aboveground, the trickle of water, exploring it to its expansion at its underground source. And the head filled with images but the hand mysteriously inert. I stare at my right hand: the skin coarsened by pigments and chemicals; the fingers thin, bony; the nails broken, chewed; the hand of a longshoreman. Once the fingers would twitch of themselves, initiate the motions of art as if they were creatures of their own, separately attached to the images within my eyes. But not any longer. The hand lies dormant.

The service came to an end. I began to remove my tefillin. My aunt and her two daughters entered from the hallway, where they had sat throughout the service, and now returned to their stools in front of the oil painting of the Rebbe. Cousin Nahum and Cousin Yonkel finished removing their tefillin and prayer shawls. People came over to them, spoke the words of consolation, and hurriedly left. It was a weekday, and most of the men had work to go to and a living to make.

Next to me, the old man finished folding his prayer shawl and said, "Good morning, Asher Lev."

"Good morning."

"You pray like a true Ladover."

"Why not? I am a Ladover."

"I must say to you I never imagined that a man who paints the kind of pictures you do would pray in such a way. It is a perplexity to me."

"Why?"

"The Torah forbids such pictures."

"Where is it written?"

"In the Ten Commandments."

"The Ten Commandments forbid the worshipping of pictures, not the making of them."

"Asher Lev, they forbid the worshipping *and* the making. How can pictures such as yours *not* be forbidden?"

"Not all understand the Second Commandment in that way."

"It is the way the Ladover understand it. Tell me, are you truly a Ladover Hasid? What a father is, is one thing. A son does not always follow a father."

"I consider myself a Ladover Hasid."

"Then how does a Ladover Hasid paint such pictures? I do not understand."

"In this matter, I disagree with the Ladover."

"It is not a small matter. The whole world knows of Asher Lev and what he paints."

"With all respect, it is not a clear issue. The Code of Law forbids full-face pictures." I cited the passage. "And yet look there at the painting of the Rebbe."

His aged eyes flew open. He seemed horrified. "You compare a picture of the Rebbe to the pictures you make? God forbid!"

"I did not mean to upset you."

"Such a thing to say! A shame, a scandal!"

He clutched his tallis and tefillin bags to himself as if he feared a touch from me would pollute them. He shook his head and muttered as he went past me. I watched him go over to the mourners, speak to them briefly, and hurry out of the room. He walked fairly briskly for a ninety-two-year-old man, urged on no doubt by his need to distance himself from the demons in Asher Lev.

The wooden folding chairs stood in disarray, and I went quickly through the room, setting them in their orderly rows. The room was now empty of visitors. My father and my uncle's family went into the kitchen. I was alone in the living room with the oil painting of the Rebbe, and I went over to it. Smooth and slick. But he had caught the eyes and the mouth. The eyes followed you, the mouth smiled its benevolence upon the viewer, speaking a silent blessing. Three will save us, I heard the mouth say distinctly in the silence of the living room. The third is our future. I looked quickly around. I was alone in the room.

My aunt was calling me. I joined my father and my uncle's family in the sunlit breakfast room. The picture window looked out on the terrace and the back lawn. Two large-leaved potted plants sat on the sill amid an array of charity boxes. Set in a wall was a bookcase filled with cookbooks and paperbacks. One of the paperbacks was a collection of essays by a contemporary New York art critic. I knew it contained a chapter on me and my work. I wondered who in this house was reading art criticism.

I sat between my father and Cousin Nahum. My two women cousins looked uncomfortable with me in the room. The table, large and round, was arrayed with smoked fishes, bagels, cream cheese, fruit juice, coffee.

"How are you, Asher?" Cousin Nahum asked. "We haven't had a chance to talk."

"Asher, have something to eat," my aunt said gently.

"How's the paint business?" Cousin Yonkel asked. He was younger, taller, and thinner than his brother, had an untrimmed dark beard, an angry mouth, and glittering dark eyes that had long ago found the answers to the world's difficult questions.

"Yonkel, it's too early in the morning for your jokes," Cousin Nahum said.

"Did you hear the Jackie Mason line?" Cousin Yonkel said. "It took Michelangelo twenty years to paint the Sistine ceiling. Did you know that? Twenty years. Jackie Mason says his brother-in-law could do it in two days."

"Yonkel," one of the sisters said. "This is not a good time for jokes."

"It's a funny line," Yonkel said.

"Yonkel," my father said quietly.

That stopped him. He gazed down at the table and ate in silence.

"We read about the exhibition in Paris," Cousin Nahum said.

I looked at him and did not respond.

"We may not like what you paint, Asher, but we also don't like it when you're hurt."

"Speak for yourself," Cousin Yonkel said.

"Yonkel," Aunt Leah said. "For your father's sake, let there be peace."

Yonkel lapsed back into dour silence.

"Asher," Cousin Nahum said. "Can you stick around awhile?"

"Sure."

"I want to show you something."

I saw Cousin Yonkel raise his eyes and stare at his brother. "What do you think you're doing?"

"It's not your affair," Nahum said.

"What do you mean, it's not my affair. Are you the only son in this family?"

Cousin Nahum looked at my aunt. "Mama?"

"In this matter, Nahum decides," Aunt Leah said. "That was the wish of your father."

I looked around the table. It was clear to me that I was the only one there who did not understand what was happening.

"What's going on?" I asked.

"Finish your breakfast," my father said quietly. "Nahum will explain it to you later."

"All I want to do is show you something," Cousin Nahum said.

"Asher, how are the children?" Aunt Leah asked.

"They're fine. Avrumel is running a little fever."

"Rocheleh starts in our yeshiva today," my father said.

"Really?" my aunt said. "What a good idea!"

"It was Rivkeh's idea," said my father.

"Bring them over later, Asher," said my aunt.

"She is a very smart girl, our Rocheleh," my father said. "Her English is excellent."

"How can a child of Asher Lev's not be smart?" Cousin Yonkel said.

"For God's sake, Yonkel," Cousin Nahum said. "Asher is a guest in our house. How often do we see him? Ease up a little on the sunny disposition."

Cousin Yonkel returned to his gloomy silence and his food.

We finished breakfast and quietly said the Grace After Meals. My aunt and her daughters began to clear the table. My father and Cousin Yonkel returned to the living room.

"Asher, come upstairs with me," Cousin Nahum said.

I followed him through the dining room and the hallway and up the stairs. He walked slowly and seemed to have difficulty breathing, and I wondered if he might have something wrong with his heart. One flight of carpeted stairs, and he was wheezing and sweating. It occurred to me that I didn't know where he lived. A private house? An apartment? I didn't know where any of my four cousins lived. I had never even met their wives, husbands, or children.

I followed him along the second-floor hallway to the door of my uncle's study. He fished in his pocket, brought out a key ring, selected a key, and opened the door.

"My father said you'd appreciate this."

We stepped inside. The door closed smoothly and soundlessly behind us.

I had been in my uncle's study many times when I lived in this house. Now I could barely make out the furniture and the walls for the dimness. Heavy drapes lay across the windows. The air in the room was fresh. I heard a faint humming sound as from some muffled machine.

"I'll get the drapes," Cousin Nahum said, and crossed the room to the windows.

Morning sunlight entered the room as the drapes were slid aside. The room was entirely different now from when I was last inside it, more than twenty years before. I saw an ornately carved desk, a tall-backed dark leather chair, a dark leather recliner, a lavish Oriental carpet with a floral and bestiary design, a large dark wood door near the door to the room, and, on the dark-paneled walls—*paintings*. Three large paintings. The easily recognizable styles leaped out at me. I felt myself stunned by the shock of their utterly unaccountable presence in this house.

"My God!" I heard myself say.

On the walls were a Matisse landscape of the south of France done nearly in the full spectrum of Matisse's palette: cadmium red, purple red, emerald green, Prussian blue, cobalt blue, ultramarine, cadmium yellow, ochre, burnt sienna, black, zinc white; a Cézanne oil on canvas of Mont Sainte Victoire seen through and over a line of tall leaning cypresses; and a shimmering Renoir of a garden made when he lived in Cagnes, a few kilometers from my home.

I was finding it difficult to breathe.

"Neat, eh?" Cousin Nahum said. "You like them?"

"I can't believe what I'm seeing here."

"Yonkel hates them."

"Yonkel is a barbarian."

"He thinks in this matter Papa was the barbarian."

"These are magnificent paintings."

"I'll tell you the truth: I don't know anything about art. To me it's all the same, this painting, that painting. Someone told Papa that art was a good investment, so he invested in it like he invested in stocks."

"Who advised him?"

"A dealer from Chicago. A Ladover sympathizer. He knew my grandfather, Mama's father, may he rest in peace."

"Smart man."

"Who? The dealer? Papa?"

"Both."

"They're worth a lot of money?"

"Money! There are great human souls in those paintings."

He gazed at the walls. "I see souls in Torah and in the commandments, not in paintings. Are they worth money, Asher?"

"Are you serious? There's a fortune on those walls."

"There is? Well, that may make Yonkel a little happier. I don't know the first thing about it. It reminds me of a friend of mine, not a Ladover but an observer of the commandments, who collects rare wine, even though we're forbidden to drink goyishe wine. I asked him once why he collects wine that he can't drink, and he told me it was for an investment. Wine for an investment! Can you believe it? I don't understand it. Wait a minute. I'll show you something else. Come on."

He drew the drapes and led me back into the hallway and locked the door. "You'll remember this. It's where you worked when you lived with us."

I followed him to the doorway that led to the attic. He opened it with a different key from the one he had used on the door to the study. The narrow stairway led up into deep shadows. He flicked a switch on a panel just inside the door, and a burst of light flooded the stairs and the area overhead. The wooden stairs, raw and scarred when I had worked there, were now thickly carpeted. I followed him up into the attic.

The air was cool and fresh. When I had worked there, the attic, redolent of my oil paints, was often sweltering in the summer and freezing in the winter. The room, nearly as large as the entire expanse of the house, had been bare, its wooden floor naked, its ceiling beams exposed, its single tall window facing the trees on the street outside and always open to the light. Now the floor was covered with rich carpeting; heavy drapes concealed the window; and along the walls were deep floor-to-ceiling metal racks filled with canvases, drawings, and prints.

Cousin Nahum pulled out drawings and held them to the light. He showed me a harlequin drawing by Picasso, dated 1919; a drawing of Virginia Haggard by Chagall, with his signature— "Marc"—under the words *Pour Virginia mon amour,* and dated Vence, 1952; a painting by Magritte of a man gazing at an image of himself in the forehead of another man, whose features were identical to those of the first man; drawings and canvases by Chirico, Bonnard, Modigliani, Soutine. I watched him return a Soutine canvas to the rack, and then I asked him if he would let me look through the racks by myself, and he said sure, but we would have to go down soon, people would be coming into the house. In one of the racks I found oil paintings and prints by Reuven Rubin, Raphael Soyer, Bergner, Bak, Ardon, Bezem, Theo Tobiasse, Ben Shahn. In another were drawings and lithographs by modern masters; there was one by Picasso of a *Guernica* study that I had not known existed. A third rack was entirely filled with my own work—oils, drawings, pastels, prints. I went through that collection very quickly—Cousin Nahum was becoming impatient—and noticed that my uncle had acquired a copy of my first carborundum print, the one I had made in Paris with the help of Jacob Kahn during one of the early years of my exile. His copy was numbered 7/20. All the copies of that print were in museums and private collections; none had entered the market in over ten years.

I saw no nudes anywhere in Uncle Yitzchok's collection.

Cousin Nahum was telling me there would be other times for me to look at the art; we had to go back downstairs. I followed him down the narrow staircase. He turned off the lights and locked the door. We went down to a living room crowded with dark-garbed men and kerchiefed women.

That was a long and wearying day, that first full day of mourning. I sat in the living room listening to Torah discussions and praise of my uncle and chatter about this one's illness and that one's children and sober talk about security problems in the neighborhood and the rash of recent street violence. A small crowd had gathered around my father, who listened and responded, and I noticed how silent people became when he spoke, how they leaned forward to catch his words. There was a soft electric intensity to his rhythmed speech, to the slight nasalities that accompanied some of his words, to the way his nostrils flared on occasion and his lips worked. Even seated he looked taller than anyone else in that room.

People seemed to be coming from everywhere. My mother's sister, Aunt Leah Chayah, who had been unable to attend the funeral because her husband had undergone bypass surgery the day before, flew in from Boston. She was a short, robust woman in her late sixties or early seventies. Yes, the surgery was successful. The miracles they can do today. We have to thank the Master of the Universe. She sat quivering and talking to my father and to my uncle's family. My mother was teaching a class at the university and would come in the late afternoon. There were people from Philadelphia, Cleveland, Detroit, Chicago, Miami, Albany, Tucson, Houston, San Francisco, Seattle. I met the art dealer who had helped my uncle put together his collection, a cheerful, round-faced man named Abraham Vorman, who wore a pale-blue suit, pink shirt, light-green tie, earth-brown shoes, and a dark-red Alpine hat with a yellow feather in its band. I wondered who advised him on his clothes: he looked like a Fauvist painting. "Honored, Mr. Lev. Truly honored. Too bad for me you have a dealer, or we could talk serious business. Douglas Schaeffer treats you well? Ah, too bad. Anytime you are looking for greener fields, anytime."

The head of the Ladover movement on the West Coast showed up and was introduced to me by Cousin Nahum. "Rav Yosef Kroner. Asher Lev." He was a short, intense, dark-visaged, dark-bearded man about my age, with darkly gleaming eyes and a frosty smile. "You are Asher Lev? The trouble you make for us!" Later, I saw him talking in the hallway to a group of younger Ladover men and heard him utter the words *meridoh bemalchus*—a term meaning "rebellion against the kingdom"—spitting them out with a venomous anger that left me chilled even though I had no idea what he was talking about.

The front door opened, and in came Shaul Lasker, who was head of the Ladover yeshiva in Paris. Short, chunky, jovial, his brown beard going gray. He greeted me somberly. "A tragic loss, for you, for all of us. Without your uncle there would be no yeshiva in Paris, nothing in Milan or Nice." Wasn't I supposed to be in Paris next week? Yes, working on a print with Max Lobe. He remembered Max Lobe. The artist, Devorah's cousin, the one who had introduced me to Devorah. He and Devorah had spent the last two years of the war in a sealed apartment in Paris, hiding from the police. Yes, he remembered Max Lobe. "Call me when you get to Paris, Asher." He went over to my father, and my father saw him, and I saw Shaul Lasker bow slightly to my father and sit down next to him.

During the Afternoon Service, the ninety-two-year-old man sat far away from me; in his place sat a scraggly-bearded young man, who murmured a brief word of consolation and was otherwise silent.

My mother arrived and began to prepare supper. The house emptied of visitors. My father sat reading the Book of Job. For a while I studied some passages in one of the works written by the Rebbe's grandfather, which were in my uncle's collection of sacred books in the bookcase near the entrance to the living room. I put the book back on the shelf, scanned the titles, and took down another book by the Rebbe's grandfather, a volume on riddles. It was written in Hebrew, as was the previous book I had looked at, and the opening words caught my eye:

Even the most unlearned of men knows that the truly important matters of life are those for which we have no words. Yet we must speak of them. We speak, as it were, around them, under them, through them, but not directly of them. Perhaps the Master of the Universe thought it best not to give us those words, for to possess them is to comprehend the awesome mysteries of creation and death, and such comprehension might well make life impossible for us. Hence in His infinite wisdom and compassion the Master of the Universe gave us the obscure riddle rather than the revealing word. Thus we should give thanks to Him and bless His name.

I leafed through the book. It was a thin volume, printed on rag paper in small print around the turn of the century in the Russian town of Ladov, the original seat of the Ladover Hasidim. I read some of the riddles. "One I don't know, the second I don't see, the third I don't remember: death, age, and birth. You are in me, and I am in you: the soul. Faceless in a face mask: riddle." I read on for a while, but the ideas began to become very complex, and I lost the chain of thought and put the book away. Then Devorah came over with the children. Avrumel showed me his new Shimshon doll, and I gave it a big hug. He seemed a bit wary of it, treating it more as a new acquaintance than as an old friend. We all sat around the dining-room table, eating supper. I kept looking at the painting I had made of my uncle's family and thinking of the paintings in the study and the attic. Aunt Leah, delighted by the children, asked Rocheleh to describe her first day in the yeshiva. Rocheleh studied her for a moment and then delivered, in her French-accented English, a detailed and lengthy account of her school day—her reactions to her teachers, her classmates, her subjects. Aunt Leah was charmed. My parents beamed.

"Never ask Rocheleh a question unless you really want the whole answer," I said. "Avrumel, on the other hand, is a very different proposition. How are you feeling, my son?"

"Ça va, Papa," Avrumel said, his lisp somewhat aggravated by this company of strangers. "Walk with Papa?"

"Get well and we'll go for a walk."

"Avrumel is cured," Devorah said.

"What did he have?"

"The most common malady known to man. Fever."

Later that night, I walked with my father along the stretch of cement that separated the two homes. The air was cold. I asked him if he knew about Uncle Yitzchok's art collection.

"Of course I knew." There was an edge to his voice. "The yeshivas my brother helped me build are more important than the art he collected. The money should have gone to us rather than to his fancy Chicago art dealer. It is a mystery to me, the money and energy he put into that collection."

Rocheleh was asleep when we came into the house, but Avrumel was bouncing on his bed. "He's waiting for Godot," Devorah said wearily.

I kissed him and covered him with his blanket and listened to him lisp his way through the Krias Shema. The new Shimshon doll lay on the pillow next to his head.

"Walk with Papa?" he said, half asleep.

"Tomorrow when you come back from school."

"Thchool," he said, his tongue working.

"School," I said. "School."

In our room, lying in her bed, the lights on, Devorah said, sleepily, "I will ask you if anything interesting happened today, but only if you promise not to become angry when I fall asleep in the middle of your answer."

"Let's both fall asleep." I was getting out of my clothes. "What did you do today?"

"Today was Avrumel day. In the morning we went on an expedition for a Shimshon doll, and after lunch he slept and I read a book of poetry I found in your mother's library. Good poetry. Browning. 'The Melon-Seller' and things like that."

"That must have been nice."

"It was very nice. Until I remembered a story Max once told me about a place called the Island of Poetry. One of the many stories he told me during the two years in the apartment. The Island of Poetry. All these years I forgot it, and I remembered it today."

"What's the Island of Poetry?"

"Its people dream a lot and don't talk very much. They conceive their infants in their heads and give birth to their children through their fingers. Yes, their fingers. Many of the children are monsters, but the people don't cast them away; they feed them with a special nourishing meat called 'esteem.' When one of the islanders dies, he is embalmed. Trumpets are blown at his funeral. There is no politics on the island. The people spend all their time wandering like lonely clouds along the shore, watching the waves, or sitting near streams, writing poetry. That is the Island of Poetry. I am very sleepy—but, see, I am still awake. Was it terribly boring? You shouldn't ask me a question, Asher, unless you are prepared for the whole answer."

"Max Lobe told you that story?"

"Yes."

"Where did he get it from?"

"I don't know. A book, I suppose. Wasn't it strange that I remembered it today? Oh, I am falling asleep."

"Good night, Dev. When we get back, we ought to do something about Avrumel's lisp."

"Your mother told me you used to lisp."

"Really? I don't remember that."

"Nobody remembers lisping. Do you remember wetting your bed?"

"Remember to remind me to tell you about my uncle's art collection."

"God is merciful in what He sometimes lets us forget."

The apartment has been dark forever in the past, and I know it will remain dark for all the future. The people in it are asleep: some snore; one moans. An icy wind strikes the closed shutters. Outside, the cobblestone street is empty of pedestrians and traffic; only the occasional sounds of steel-jacketed boots echo through the darkness. From the cold plaster wall, as I put my ear to it, comes the cry of an infant, muffled, rising and falling and rising again, a distant stridency—suddenly gone. The wooden floor is cold and hard, and when I put my ear to it, it makes strange sounds, an eerie sighing, a groaning, as if it can no longer bear our weight. Water rushes through pipes; a bedspring creaks; a woman softly laughs. Barely the dimmest of light comes through the shutters when the sun rises; by it, Max sits against the wall of the living room, drawing, and I lie on the floor, dreaming of skies and clouds and the soaring of birds and the orange-red trumpet vines on the side wall of the country house I once saw in a picture. On cloudy days no light at all comes through the shutters, and we barely know when to eat and when to sleep. Sometimes my body is so heavy I am turned to stone; sometimes I am so thin and light I am able to slip through the slits of the shutters and float about outside on the wind high above the stolen streets. But I know that I will be in this room for all my life and beyond, forever and ever and ever, and beyond even that. I know that with absolute certainty. Knowing it, knowing it fully, and feeling and tasting that cold knowing of it, absolutely and fully, I climb steeply from the dream and lie staring into the light of the room I share with Devorah in my parents' home.

The house is silent.

Devorah is asleep in her bed, her face tranquil in the light of the lamp on the night table. I listen to the soft snifflings and gurglings of the air that passes in and out of her nostrils. She lies on her right side, facing me, her hands under her cheek, her short hair curling out from the pillow beneath her head. All the tender suffering softness of her beneath the blanket and sheet on the bed.

I have dreamed that dream before, the dream of Devorah's life in Paris during the war. I have never painted it; it is not my life or my dream. It happens on occasion when you are married a long time: you dream the nightmares of the person you love.

The morning was cold. A steady rain fell through the trees. Cars moved cautiously along the dark street, headlights on and wipers working. On the way to my uncle's house I asked my father if the Rebbe would visit during the week of mourning.

"The Rebbe rarely goes out."

"He came out for the funeral."

"A tribute to my brother. The Rebbe goes out on a Shabbos sometimes. The holidays."

"Does anyone ever talk about the future?"

"That is all we *ever* talk about, Asher."

"I mean the future after the Rebbe."

His face emptied of expression, locked. I felt the sudden icy silence that surrounded him. After a brief moment, he said, "We do not talk about such matters, Asher. The Rebbe expects that any day the final redemption will come."

"The Rebbe has no children."

Again, the locking out of expression, the iciness, as if I were treading on forbidden ground. "That is what I mean, Asher. Would God leave the Rebbe without children unless the final redemption was certain? The final redemption will come in the Rebbe's time. An end to the exile. An end to suffering for all our people and for all the world. Any day now, Asher. The Rebbe is certain of it. That is the reason we work the way we do. Everything we do, every Jew we bring close to Torah, brings the redemption closer to us. We do not talk about after. There is no after."

His voice was low, tense; the voice of certainty, finality, faith. We walked through the rain to my uncle's house.

Inside, two dozen men had already assembled for the Morning Service. Shaul Lasker of Paris and Yosef Kroner of the West Coast were there, in tallis and tefillin. Many more regional directors and heads of Ladover yeshivas would be arriving today and tomorrow, my father had told me. The regard all had for my uncle; the honor they now paid him. It had been decided that all would remain through the weekend, for meetings with my father and the Rebbe after the week of mourning came to an end. They had plenty to talk about: budgets; fund-raising; where to open new yeshivas; which universities should be targeted for future Ladover campus houses; what regions in the world needed circumcisers and ritual slaughterers; the implications of *glasnost* for the Ladover Hasidim in the Soviet Union.

Cousin Yonkel led the service in a manner so dull and dry the words seemed to be coming from him after a lengthy journey through a barren wilderness. How had my cheerful Uncle Yitzchok raised so arid a soul as my Cousin Yonkel? Another riddle.

Yosef Kroner sauntered over to me after the service. Close up, his beaked and surly features gave him the appearance of what I have always imagined to be the look of those birds of prey the Torah forbids us to eat.

"Good morning, Lev."

"Good morning."

"You are well known on the West Coast. People write about you and talk about you. A producer told me recently he is considering making a movie of your life."

"I'm not dead yet. Why would he want to make a movie of my life?"

"I don't know. Maybe he thinks it's interesting and people will pay money to see it."

I put my folded tallis into its velvet bag. The tallis had been my father's gift to me when I married Devorah. Its silver edging became caught in the zipper, and I had to move the zipper back and forth a few times to work it loose.

"On the West Coast people wonder if you are still a Ladover Hasid."

I looked at him and did not respond.

"People keep asking me, 'Is Asher Lev really a Ladover?' "

"And what do you tell them?"

"I tell them that as far as I know he still is. That confuses them, because they know what you paint."

"I regret the confusion."

"It's nice to be an artist and not have to worry about what people think."

"That's right. That's why I became an artist. So I wouldn't have to worry about what people think. You hit the nail right on the head, Kroner."

"It isn't funny, Lev. You don't have to live with it day after day. It's an embarrassment."

"I regret the embarrassment. And I am not being funny. I genuinely regret it."

He stared at me for a moment out of wary, distrustful eyes, then turned abruptly and walked away.

I went into the kitchen. My aunt had not come down for the service; she was not feeling well. We sat around the table, eating in silence, my father gazing through the window at the rain falling on the ailanthus and azaleas on the rear lawn. Wisps of mist curled across the low bushes and young spring grass. I thought of the garden in the Renoir painting on the wall in my uncle's study, the lavish and sensuous play of luxuriant colors, soft, so soft, as if brushed on by feathers, like the creamy pinks and whites on the breasts and thighs and buttocks of his nudes; brushing them and brushing them, feeling them upon his fingertips through the bristles and the wood, the copious and sumptuous softness of them, the—

Someone was talking to me. "Hello, Asher. Hello! Where are you?"

"Asher goes off like that sometimes," I heard my father say, as if from a distance. "You have to get used to it."

"With all due respect, I'm only his cousin." It was Yonkel talking. "I don't have to get used to it. Asher, are you there?"

I drew painfully back from the Renoir.

"What do you think of Papa's art collection?" His sour look and crabby tone made what he thought of it exceedingly clear.

"It's a magnificent collection, Yonkel. Actually, it's three collections. The Jewish work, the modern masters, and my own work. Very cleverly done."

"You want to know what I think? I think it's a desecration of the name of God."

"Oh, stop it, Yonkel," Cousin Nahum said. "What do you know about it?"

"And you? You know a lot about art?"

"I know at least to ask questions."

"I don't need to ask questions about art. I say that it's an outright desecration of the name of God. It's idol worship, that's what it is!"

"Oh, for God's sake, Yonkel! Enough!"

"Wait a minute, wait a minute! Let me talk my mind! This is family. If a man can't talk among his own family, where then? Tell me. Where?"

"Let Yonkel talk, Nahum," my father said.

"For years I couldn't sleep in this house because of that collection. Images and idols in my house. I can't sleep now. I lie awake thinking of those pictures."

"It's art," I said. "It's not Satan or the Angel of Death."

"That goyishe art in this house!"

"A lot of it is by Jews."

"Goyishe Jews! Including your own stuff, Asher, if I may say it. That's how I feel! I'm sorry. It comes from my heart." His lips trembled inside the blackness of his beard. "A spirit must have entered my father when he decided to buy such things."

My father's face darkened. But he remained silent.

"I promise you this," Cousin Yonkel said. "The first chance we get, we will sell it."

No one around the table—neither his brother, nor his sisters, nor my father—said anything.

"My father was a kind man," Cousin Yonkel said. "A good man. I loved him. But in this matter, he was wrong."

He rose from the table and shuffled in his slippered feet out through the dining room and into the hallway, angry, bowed, carrying on his narrow shoulders all the melancholy my cheerful uncle had tried all his life to stave off.

I asked Cousin Nahum if he would mind my going upstairs to have another look at the collection.

"Why should I mind? If you can't look at it, who can? Take the keys."

I went up the stairs and along the second-floor hallway. The door to Cousin Yonkel's room was partly open, and I saw him lying on his bed in his stockinged feet, his hand over his eyes, his long dark beard spread upon his thin chest. I thought I heard him reciting quietly verses from the Book of Psalms—no doubt to ward off the evil spirits he felt were emanating from his father's art collection.

Quietly, I opened the door to my uncle's study, stepped inside, and closed the door behind me. I had noticed, the day before, the panel with two mercury switches near the door. They glowed softly in the darkness. I flipped one of the switches and nothing happened. I flipped the other. Ceiling spotlights fell upon the three large paintings on the walls. The colors glowed, luminous, breathing. I stood there and stared at the paintings. Then I noticed thin ribbons of light leaking through the edges of the large door near the door to the study. I tried the knob; it was locked. One of the keys on the ring Cousin Nahum had given me opened it.

I stepped into a large storeroom lined with shelves. The air was cool, faintly musty; the air of library stacks. One of the shelves contained orderly piles of magazines, art journals in English and French, and art newsletters. There was a ragged pile of announcements and invitations to openings of exhibitions I had had over the years, in New York, Paris, London, Tokyo, Buenos Aires, Cape

Town, Geneva, Brussels, Venice, Nice, Rome, Tel Aviv, Berlin. Along the other shelves were dozens of cardboard boxes, neatly arranged and labeled. I opened two of them and hastily went through their contents: articles in English and French on some of the works I had seen yesterday in my uncle's collection; a study of Cézanne's evolving style; an account of some of the major works by Matisse and where they belonged in the body of his oeuvre. There was a lengthy article in French on facture and passage. Another was a study of Picasso's early contributions to texturing. Articles in English and French dealt with Chagall, Renoir, Bonnard. A monograph in English compared the crucifixion paintings of Asher Lev, *Brooklyn Crucifixion I* and *Brooklyn Crucifixion II*, with the *White Crucifixion* of Chagall. In the box with the article on Picasso's use of texturing was a lengthy description, taken from a French art magazine, of the carborundum printmaking technique used by Jacob Kahn and his protégé, Asher Lev. Under that was a description of a drawing made by Picasso when he was twenty-five: a crucifixion.

I closed the boxes, put them back on the shelf, and went out of the storeroom. For a long moment I stood in the study, gazing at the Matisse and Cézanne and Renoir on the walls. I looked at my uncle's recliner, saw the declivity shaped by his body, and imagined him sitting there, overweight and grinning, smoking his cigar and looking at his paintings. I locked the door to the storeroom, turned off the lights, closed and locked the door to the study, and went back downstairs.

There was a small crowd in the living room, mostly women, seated in the front row of chairs and talking with my aunt, who was apparently well enough now to have returned to her low stool of mourning. Devorah was among the crowd, leaning forward into the penumbra of grief surrounding my aunt, and talking to her. I went through the living room and into the den to use the phone. The den was large, paneled, carpeted, lavishly furnished with leather sofas and chairs. A dark wood desk with a tall-backed leather chair stood near a wall. Tall, wide sliding glass doors opened onto the flagstone terrace and the rear lawn. Rain was falling heavily on the sodden earth and the black trees. I sat down in the leather chair and gazed outside. Then I picked up the phone on the desk and tapped in a number. A woman answered. I asked for Douglas Schaeffer and told her my name.

He came on the line immediately. "Ash? How are you, dear boy? How's the weather?"

"It's the same weather you've got in Manhattan."

"What do you mean? Where are you?"

I told him.

"What are you doing in Brooklyn, dear boy? Did someone die?"

I told him.

"The uncle who bought your drawing when you were six? I'm so sorry to hear that."

"Thank you. Listen, Doug, can I see you Monday morning?"

"The gallery is closed on Mondays, dear boy. Remember? Catherine and I are going out to Connecticut to her sister's. Can you come on Tuesday? Very good. Tuesday, then. Terribly sorry about your uncle. Catherine says hello. She's right here. What? No, his uncle. Condolences from Catherine, Ash. Goodbye."

I hung up the phone and sat back in the leather chair and looked out the glass doors at the rain. It fell bleakly through the dismal mist-laden air onto the drenched earth and into the grave of my Uncle Yitzchok. Cold and gray, it struck the wet stones of graves everywhere and seeped into the graves of Yudel Krinsky and Anna Schaeffer. It washed across graves old and new, oozing silently through the waterlogged earth and around the pebbles and stones and through the wood onto the lifeless flesh. Uncaring, merciless rain, lashing the living and the dead.

There was a writing pad near the phone and a tall pen fixed point downward in a greenish block of veined marble. With the pen, I drew on the pad, in a single continuous line, a profile of my uncle. Then I drew my uncle full face, as he had been when I was a child: round, dark-bearded, full moist smiling lips, merry eyes. My uncle appeared beside the chair and looked at the drawing of his face. He picked up the drawing and put a coin on the desk. Now I own an early Lev. You will one day be another Picasso. Who is Picasso? He is the greatest artist in the world. What does he look like? He is short and bald and has dark burning eyes. How do I know such things? I read. Someone who is a watchmaker is not necessarily also an ignoramus. I was drawing a profile of Anna

Schaeffer: oval features rich with the wrinkles of age, short silver hair, her eyes mirrors of grace and accomplishment. You have Chagall's pale face, Asher Lev. Do you suffer fainting spells? Are you really very religious? You believe your Rebbe is a gift given to your people by God to help you make your lives holy? Is that what you truly believe? Art is not for people who want to make the world holy. If you want to make the world holy, stay in Brooklyn. Very well, very well. You will study with Jacob Kahn. He will teach you, and I will sell your paintings. He will make you into another Picasso. "No," I heard myself say loudly. "My name is Asher Lev."

Someone was calling me.

"My name is Asher Lev," I said again.

"Hello, Asher Lev," someone said. "How do you do? My name is Devorah Lev."

I opened my eyes, startled.

Devorah was standing in front of the desk. "You fell asleep in the chair. Did you have a dream?"

I looked at the pad and the pen. They lay untouched on the desk.

"You kept saying, 'My name is Asher Lev.' "

I opened the pad. Bare paper stared back at me like the expanse of huge blank canvas in my studio in Saint-Paul.

She came over to the chair and leaned over me and put her arms around the back of my head. I felt the warmth and softness of her, felt her lips upon the hair on the side of my face. "Do you want me to stay with you, my husband?"

Where were the faces I had drawn? Surely I had drawn them. I had felt the pressure of the pen upon my fingertips, had seen the lines come to life. Where were the drawings of the faces?

"Are you all right?"

"No. But there isn't anything we can do about it."

"They're serving lunch, Asher."

I followed her out of the den and into the kitchen. Where were those drawings? I kept asking myself. Could I have dreamed those drawings?

I sat at the table eating lunch and hearing nothing of what was being said around me.

All that afternoon people came and went. The rain slackened, then stopped, but the mist remained in the azaleas and in the branches of the trees. Devorah said she was leaving to bring the children back from school.

"Rocheleh wants to walk home by herself with her brother, starting tomorrow."

Independent Rocheleh. One afternoon she had disappeared from our home in Saint-Paul and walked by herself up the long road and through the entire village to the cemetery at the far end of the wall, and then all the way back—at the age of six.

"Is it safe, Asher?"

"How do I know? Ask my mother."

"She said children walk back and forth all the time during the day."

"Then I guess it's safe."

The end to the rain increased the traffic into the house. My mother came through the crowd and was immediately given a seat next to my father. Cousin Yonkel sat on his stool, looking dry and crabby. Cousin Nahum was listening and making efforts at talk. My aunt and her two daughters looked weary and desolate. Dark-garbed men and kerchiefed women crowded the porch, the hallway, the dining room, the living room, the staircase. A low buzzing sound hung in the air, the hum of a hundred subdued conversations occurring simultaneously. I heard someone mention a recent talk given by the Rebbe on the radio and cable TV. Others were discussing the diamond business, the jewelry exchange in Manhattan, the market for Japanese cameras and computers, the night security patrols along the streets of the neighborhood, a fund-raising drive for the local Ladover yeshiva, a fire in the Ladover yeshiva in Jerusalem, local city politics, politics in Israel. I sat on my wooden chair with my eyes closed, lost in the murmurous flow of the talk all around me and wondering where my drawings were; I was certain I had made them. It had all been so real: the faces, the conversation; it had all felt so good, so exhilarating, as though at the morning of the world.

I heard a distant shout. All around me startled faces looked about, debate faltered. I heard the shout repeated, the words indistinct. It was outside somewhere, on the street, then on the walk, then on the porch. A strange and tangible whispering began to move through the air, like the trembling breaths of a hundred simultaneous astonishments. There was a sudden stirring and a concurrent movement of chairs. Everyone around me rose, and I rose, too, and stood looking at the crowd that jammed the hallway and blocked the door to the house. Silence invaded the house, and stillness, as though sound and motion had suddenly abandoned the world. In the hallway the crowd began abruptly to part, in silence, with a barely audible shuffling of feet, and through the divided crowd walked two tall dark-bearded men in dark coats and hats. Behind them, walking slowly with majestic stateliness and supported on his left arm by a third tall dark-bearded man, came the Rebbe. Behind the Rebbe walked a fourth man, very tall, his eyes glancing left and right. The Rebbe wore a dark coat and suit and an ordinary dark hat. His beard was stark white, his face pale. His eyes, gray and piercing, gazed out from the shadow cast by the brim of his hat. The tall men walked slowly through the crowd and passed close to where I stood, and I could smell the moisture of the still-damp air on their coats, see the wariness and determination on their faces and the fingers grasping gently but firmly the Rebbe's left arm, see the Rebbe scanning faces as if searching for a face he knew. Then I felt his eyes upon my face. He stopped for the briefest of moments, his eyes upon my face, and he nodded, once, and moved on—and everyone in the room saw that nod. A quiver of subdued motion passed through those around me. I sensed the nod as a palpable movement across my face: a hand had brushed my cheek. Over the heads of those near the front of the room I saw my father, his face showing clearly his surprise at the appearance of the Rebbe. My Cousin Yonkel stood dry and rigid, his mouth open. Cousin Nahum looked ecstatic. Instantly an easy chair was placed beside my father. The Rebbe carefully sat down. All took their seats. The Afternoon Service began, led by Cousin Nahum.

The Rebbe sat very still in his chair, praying. The sounds of the brief service filled the living room and seemed to echo on the porch outside. Those on the porch were praying, too. The Rebbe stood for the Silent Devotion and the Kedushoh and the final prayer. The Mourner's Kaddish was recited. A Psalm was said, and the Kaddish was repeated. Cousin Nahum returned to his stool.

Everyone sat in silence, waiting, eyes upon the Rebbe.

The Rebbe turned to my father and nodded briefly. Someone brought my father a tractate of the Talmud. He opened the huge volume and began to teach a passage of Mishnah from the tractate *Sanhedrin*.

" 'All Israel have a portion in the world to come,' " my father intoned. " 'For it is written, "Thy people are all righteous; they shall inherit the land forever, the branch of My planting, the work of My hands, that I may be glorified." But the following have no portion therein. . . .' "

All eyes were turned upon my father. He spoke in a softly melodious tone, the traditional resonances for the teaching of a Talmudic text. I sensed the focused attention of the crowd and, at the same time, became gradually aware of a subtle dwindling in the light of the room, as though a vaguely discernible blurring shadow had settled across the chandelier in the center of the ceiling. The shadow slid slowly along the ceiling to the corner behind my father's stool. There it settled, gathering its edges into itself, becoming the thinnest of clouds. I saw the cloud gather depth and color and take on form, and it was my Uncle Yitzchok, and he stepped from the cloud and came toward me.

" '. . . He who maintains that resurrection is not a biblical doctrine,' " my father went on. " 'And he who maintains that the Torah was not divinely revealed; and an epikoros.' "

My uncle moved slowly and effortlessly through the crowd and into the hallway and up the stairs. I heard my father continue reading from the Mishnah.

My uncle moved soundlessly through the second-floor hallway and through the door into his study. He turned on the lights and sat in the recliner.

" 'Three kings and four commoners have no portion in the world to come,' " my father said.

My uncle sat in the recliner, gazing at the paintings on the walls. On his white-bearded features was a look of awe; he seemed in the presence of mysteries of creation he knew he could never fathom. Surely the Master of the Universe was at the heart of this mystery! But what if not? What if at its core was the befouling sediment of the pagan, the menacing allure of centaurs and satyrs, garlanded and gamboling naiads and dryads, or, worse yet, the stark demoniacal world of the sitra achra, the Other Side, the Destroyer? Clearly such works did not emanate from the world of Torah. All the more fascinating, then, their allure! All the more blissful the gazing upon them, the slaking of one's thirst with their colors and forms! One could think of them at one moment as creations of the Master of the Universe, and at another moment as monstrous birthings from the realm of darkness. Two sides of the same coin? Yes. Dancing and flickering lights and shadows. Is that why there are no mezuzahs on those doorposts, Uncle Yitzchok? Because you're in rooms that are weighty with the possibilities of reverence and corruption *simultaneously?* How calmly he sits in his recliner, my Uncle Yitzchok. How he drinks in the paintings. God is everywhere, even in a Renoir. Or is He?

My uncle rises from the recliner and turns off the lights. The paintings vanish. I am in the living room. The Evening Service is at an end. I hear the final Mourner's Kaddish being recited by Cousin Nahum and Cousin Yonkel.

Inside the living room everyone was seated. Those in the hallway strained forward, watching. My aunt and her two daughters slipped silently into the room and sat down on their stools.

The Rebbe rose. Immediately, everyone in the living room, except the mourners, stood.

The Rebbe walked the few steps to my aunt and cousins.

"May God comfort you together with all the mourners of Zion and Jerusalem." His voice was soft, tremulous. "He was a good soul, a good man. I loved him as one loves a brother. I give you my blessing for strength in this time of darkness. Soon, soon the redemption will come, and there will be an end to our exile and suffering. Soon. . . ."

He turned away and, together with his tall dark-bearded retinue, went slowly through the living room and the hallway and then through the front door and out of the house.

A silence followed. People stood about or moved slowly, as though fearful a sudden flurry of sound or action would tear apart the fabric of sanctity brought to my uncle's home by the Rebbe.

The house slowly emptied.

Later, we sat around the dining-room table. Devorah came in with the children. "Did anything special happen in school?" I asked Rocheleh. I always asked her that when I saw her after a school day.

Nothing special had happened to her, Rocheleh reported.

I turned to Avrumel.

"Ça va, Papa," said Avrumel. It came out "Tha va."

"Nothing special to report?"

"My teacher asked me if my papa is Asher Lev."

"Oh? And you said?"

"I said of course my papa is Asher Lev."

"And your teacher said?"

"My teacher said nothing."

I looked at Devorah. She shrugged. My father glanced at my mother. I thought I heard him sigh.

"What does the child say?" Aunt Leah asked.

I translated.

"Even in kindergarten they talk about Asher Lev," said Cousin Yonkel in his best sour manner.

"What an honor to Yitzchok, of blessed memory, that the Rebbe came," my mother said, in an effort to change the direction of the conversation.

"Better my husband should be alive," my aunt said, "than the Rebbe coming to console me because he is dead."

"The Rebbe almost never goes out," my father said. "I am astonished that he was here."

"Better my husband here than a thousand such astonishments," said my aunt.

In the kitchen in my parents' home later that night, I said to my mother, over a cup of coffee, "Have you and Papa seen Uncle Yitzchok's art collection?"

"Of course."

"Yonkel said they'd sell it the first chance they get."

"I'm not surprised."

"Yonkel would probably burn it if it wasn't worth all that

money. Someone put a lot of thought into that collection. What a shame it will be to break it up."

"It's theirs to do with as they wish."

"Renoir, Matisse, Cézanne, and Uncle Yitzchok. What a pretty picture!"

"You should get some sleep, Asher. You look very tired."

My father had returned home from Uncle Yitzchok's house exhausted and had gone to bed. Devorah was putting Avrumel to sleep. Rocheleh was in her room, reading her French *Alice in Wonderland*.

"Devorah tells me she is trying to persuade you to stay on for another week or two," my mother said.

I said nothing.

"You don't want to?"

"I'm in the middle of a lot of things."

"We should have come more often to see you in Paris and Saint-Paul. We were both always so busy, your father and I. And the travel is so expensive. It was very difficult, especially for your father."

"Difficult when he wasn't there, or difficult when he was?"

She smiled sadly. "Both were difficult, Asher."

Difficult. They had visited us twice in Paris, and once my father had come alone. And they had been with us once in Saint-Paul, and each had also come alone. They had sat in our apartment in Paris on the Rue des Rosiers and looked at our walls. The walls were crowded with paintings and posters and prints. They sat there looking around the apartment and seeing a strange world of color and form: oddly shaped sculptures in corners and on bookshelves; modernist and occasionally grotesque figures and designs on the walls. Outlandish mobiles hung from the ceiling and turned slowly in invisible currents of air. My father sat and fidgeted and stared and combed his beard with his fingers. What nightmarish congruence of fateful events could have made possible the issuance of such a son from such a father? Had he thought evil thoughts while lying with his wife? Had the moment of conception somehow been invaded by a corrupting spirit from the Other Side? Another riddle! He sat and stared at the walls and shook his head, and fled as soon as he could.

Difficult. So why does he want us to stay? Maybe it's easier for him with us here because this is his world. Maybe it's easier now because we're all older, tireder, closer to the gray time before the final darkness.

Devorah put her head into the kitchen. "Godzilla wants his father," she said. "And I want a cup of coffee."

I went into Avrumel's room. "Go to sleep," I said, "or I will never let you pose again for a painting."

"Yes pose," he said, undaunted by the tired threat. He had posed once, had recognized himself in the result, thought it magical that he could somehow be present inside and outside himself simultaneously, and had posed three times more. Twice I had painted him with his Shimshon doll. On occasion he would slip silently into my studio and sit holding the Shimshon doll on his lap, watching me work, waiting to be painted.

I kissed him. He smelled of warmth and fresh nightclothes and a bath and soap. He clung to me a moment, his red curls against my face. Then he let me cover him. A little more than halfway through his Krias Shema, he fell asleep.

I went back into the kitchen. Devorah and my mother were at the table. I refilled my cup and joined them.

My mother said, "I was telling Devorah about your Uncle Yitzchok's art collection."

"When did he start it?"

"Exactly when? I'm not sure. Perhaps your father knows. I think it may have been after your New York show, the show with the—with those paintings. He said to me once that he bought one of the paintings from that show."

"No, he didn't. A museum bought both crucifixions."

"No, not one of those. He would not buy one of those. He bought another of the paintings in the show."

"I don't remember that. I'm always told who buys my paintings."

"Someone bought it for him. He didn't want you to know."
"Why?"

"Because the show caused all the . . . trouble."

"Then why did he buy a painting?"

"He was very proud of you and also ashamed of you, both at the same time."

I glanced at Devorah. She was looking down at the table, circling the rim of her cup with a long, slender finger.

"A year after he bought it, someone—I think it was his lawyer or his accountant—offered him more than twice what he had paid for it. He said he began to realize that there was more to art than meets the eye. Those were his words, Asher. He got in touch with your Aunt Leah's family friend, the dealer in Chicago, and started to collect art."

We sat in silence awhile, drinking our coffee and listening to the soft rhythmic noises of the kitchen. It had begun to rain again, and we could hear it on the windows.

"Asher, what can I do to persuade you to stay on a little longer?" my mother asked.

I looked at Devorah. She kept circling the rim of her cup with her finger.

"Asher," my mother said. "For the sake of peace in the family."

"Let me think about it," I said. "You really believe it will bring peace? I'll think about it. But it won't bring peace."

In the bathroom I showered and toweled myself dry and gazed at the streaky outline of my face and shoulders that I had drawn in the mirror my first night here. The steam of the shower had brought it back: ghostly lines sliced into the vapor on the surface of the glass. I put my face and shoulders into the outline and stood there with the towel around my loins and my head and beard still wet. How the Spaniard hated mirrors! He saw his dying each time he looked in one. I brushed the towel brusquely across the steamed glass surface. The outline blurred and smeared and vanished.

When Devorah entered our room a few minutes later I told her I did not want us to change our plans; we would be returning home on the Tuesday-night flight.

"You will hurt your parents," she said. Suddenly she looked her full fifty years, weary, leaden.

"We're going home," I said. "I've had my turn here."

Her eyes blinked nervously. "I do not understand."

"They're trying to suck me back in, and then they'll kill whatever I've got left."

She looked stunned.

"We're going home, Dev. We came for my uncle's funeral, not for mine."

The day dawned wet and disheartening. During the Morning Service the clouds broke and a pale sun emerged. After breakfast with my uncle's family—Cousin Yonkel going on about being unable to sleep because he kept feeling the waves of contamination from his father's art collection—I went out of the house and walked to the end of the street and turned up the avenue toward the parkway. I passed a fruit-and-vegetable store, the produce in open crates on the sidewalk and arranged colorfully inside; a large Hebrew bookstore, its windows crowded with books and toys and pictures of the Rebbe, its interior deep and tiered with floor-to-ceiling shelves of books in English and Hebrew for adults and children, stationery items, games, toys, T-shirts with Ladover mottoes—BRING MOSHIACH NOW; SAVE A JEW AND HEAL THE WORLD; KOSHER IS IN—and nearly an entire wall filled with framed color pictures of the Rebbe in a variety of poses. Farther down I passed a real-estate storefront, a cosmetics store, an art-supplies and picture-framing shop, an all-night cafeteria. The street, bare of trees, lined mostly with two-story brick houses, and thick with pedestrians and Friday-morning traffic, wore a tired look; its better days were long behind it. Beyond the small neighborhood of the Ladover, the side streets were home for urban poor and drifted off into griminess and decay.

I turned into Brooklyn Parkway. It lay raw and exposed in the resurfacing project, manhole covers projecting above the brown-red earth, noisy construction machines impeding traffic. Boys in skullcaps and ritual fringes, girls in coats and long stockings, rushed to school. Sunlight slanted between the tall red-brick and whitestone apartment buildings and shone like a limpid orange-red wash upon the cracked cement squares of the sidewalks, the leafless trees, the dark asphalt. A boy went past me, ten or eleven years old, red hair, dangling earlocks, thin pale features, a dark velvet skullcap on his head, hurrying along, bent slightly forward—and the years all seemed to turn to glass, all their blurring opacity miraculously gone, and I could see through them with shocking clarity, and I had to restrain myself from asking him if he had been born with a gift for drawing pictures.

On a corner stood the apartment house where I had been raised: five stories, red brick, wide cement walk leading to the double entrance doors. The living room facing the parkway and the trees; the window where we waited for each other to return home, where our eyes smarted with the watching and waiting and our hearts beat with dread at the dark memory of my uncle's—my mother's older brother's—early death while on a mission for the Rebbe; my mother waiting for my father to return from *his* missions for the Rebbe; and my father and I waiting for my mother to return from her graduate-school classes; and my mother waiting for me to return from my long painting sessions with Jacob Kahn. The Window of Waiting. Like the wait for the end of the exile, for the redemption, for the Messiah. Endless waiting. Who lived in that apartment now? Who slept in my room? Were they Ladover Hasidim? I hadn't asked my parents. I didn't want to know.

A block and a half from where we had lived stood the Ladover headquarters building: three stories, tawny stone façade, leaded stained-glass windows bordered with whitestone in a Gothic style, flagstone front porch with a whitestone railing. A wide cement walk led from the street through a low red-brick wall to the wooden entrance door. Always parked in front of the building was a police patrol car with two cops inside. No one here worried about terrorist bombs the way we did in Paris. No one here was blown up in a synagogue or a Jewish restaurant. Paris and Lucien La-camp, and the restaurant across from where we had once lived on the Rue des Rosiers. The bomb must have shattered all the front windows of the apartment, spraying glass into the rooms. If not for Rocheleh, we would still have been in that apartment. But we were in Saint-Paul by then. Who was living in that apartment when the bomb went off? I had never asked. I didn't want to know.

I turned off the street and went up the cement walk and entered the headquarters building.

Off the entrance hall, a wide flight of wooden stairs climbed to a well-lit second floor. To the right and left of the hall ran corridors that led to warrenlike offices, many behind half walls topped with glass partitions. The doors to the offices kept opening and closing. Men in dark suits and dark skullcaps and beards kept going in and out of the doors. They spoke to one another in Yiddish or English. I heard phones ringing and saw computers on desks everywhere. I walked slowly through the building. My father had worked here for years until he had become the Rebbe's personal secretary. The Rebbe himself had lived in an apartment on the second floor and then had moved into the more comfortable home where he lived now. On the second floor I wandered past a television studio; and a room lined with telephones under which were the names, it seemed to me, of most of the big cities of the world; and a large tinted plate-glass window behind which was a room crowded with the boards, panels, tapes, and switches of a radio station. None of this had been here when I was growing up.

A man in his late twenties emerged from the door to the radio station. He was stocky and red-bearded and wore a dark skullcap and a white shirt, the sleeves pushed up to just below the elbows. He started hurriedly along the corridor, spotted me, and stopped.

"Can I help you?"

"Thanks, no. I'm just looking."

He was looking, too—at me, his eyes narrowing. Baggy trousers, rumpled shirt and windbreaker, fisherman's cap. Weary, bearded, and somewhat bedraggled. A street person looking for a handout, a bathroom, a place to sleep?

"I'd be happy to help you. Are you looking for someone in particular?"

"No. If I'm not supposed to be here, I'll leave."

"Do I know you from somewhere? May I ask your name?"

"Asher Lev."

He stood very still, looking at me. "Ah," he said. "Well. Asher Lev. No problem. Please look around. I'll be happy to show you the building myself."

"I know the building."

"Ah. Sure. Right. Well, good to meet you."

He went hurriedly into an office.

By the time I was halfway down the staircase, office doors had opened along the corridors on the first floor and bearded men stood in doorways, staring at me. I went out of the building.

Computers. Radio. Television. Books. Newspapers. Magazines. More than two hundred yeshivas all over the world. Synagogues everywhere. Campus houses. Liaisons with governments. Emissaries crisscrossing the planet, journeying, journeying—for Torah, for Ladover Hasidus, for the Rebbe, for the Master of the Universe. How had it happened? From one man fleeing Eastern Europe and France, the Nazis at his heels; from a few hundred followers in a neighborhood in Brooklyn—an empire! In Paris he had lived awhile with Devorah and her family; her father, of blessed memory, had been a follower of the Rebbe's father and then of the Rebbe. She remembered the Rebbe, even though she was only four at the time. She told stories about him to Rocheleh; bedtime stories about the struggles of the Rebbe to save Jews, clandestine meetings, comings and goings in the night. She told them to Avrumel, heroic stories, tales of selflessness. A family saved here, a Jew saved there, false passports, exit visas, deceiving the French police, escaping from the Gestapo; fleeing, fleeing. To Brooklyn—where he rode the waves of the renaissance of American fundamentalism and built the Ladover movement into a worldwide evangelical Jewish movement, sending out its good word only to Jews: love one another; be proud of your Jewishness; light Shabbos candles; observe the commandment of family purity; put mezuzahs on your doorposts; recite the blessings over the palm frond and the citron; worship the Master of the Universe with wisdom and joy; support the Rebbe in his efforts to hasten the redemption. The Rebbe is the Rebbe not only of the Ladover but of all the Jews. The Rebbe prays not only for the Jews but also for the righteous among the Gentiles. The Rebbe is king. The Rebbe is the Messiah. The Rebbe is a gift from God to the world.

John Dorman told me one evening as we sat over drinks on the terrace of Max's home, "You're in the middle of it, Lev. That's why you can't see it." Max refilled his glass, and he went on talking. The Ladover success as a fundamentalist movement on America's essentially secular soil was what kept it in the news, John said, put it on front pages of the *New York Times*, gave it full-page spreads in the religion section of *Time*, splashed it on the cover of *New York* magazine, made of it sufficient high-culture interest to warrant multipart treatment in *The New Yorker*. The movement was an American success story. That was why it could not easily detach itself from its most notorious son: Asher Lev. He was their perpetual dilemma, their Great Embarrassment. The movement prided itself, announced to all, that it was both profoundly traditional *and* part of the contemporary world. Any story about the Ladover invariably mentioned Asher Lev, the contemporary artist; any story about the iconoclastic Asher Lev unfailingly took note of his fundamentalist Ladover origins. They were inextricably linked. Ladover and Lev. Lev and Ladover. "It's as plain as the yarmulka on your head, Lev," John Dorman said, sipping his drink and looking out across the green valley at the walled village and the Cubist dwellings and the far range of hills. "You're a pain in the ass to your own people. At the same time, you're one of their most valuable *ass*ets. Ha, ha. Very sorry. I'm an old drunk, Lev, and Elizabethan wit is not my bag."

Walking through the neighborhood now, past the yeshiva, which Rocheleh and Avrumel were attending, past the Ladover synagogue, where my uncle's funeral had taken place earlier that week, gazing at the people and the traffic, at this unkempt Crown Heights world, this miracle of a birth, I longed to be back home amid the flowered silences, the exquisite gardens, the scented air, the hills and valleys and sea of southern France. They had sent me into exile; exile had given me a new home. I was now in exile in Brooklyn.

I walked slowly back to my Uncle Yitzchok's house.

Mourning is suspended on Shabbos. Sadness is forbidden on the Seventh Day.

That evening, after my mother and Devorah and Rocheleh lit Shabbos candles, I walked with my father to the synagogue. During the service, Cousin Nahum and Cousin Yonkel stood and quietly recited the Mourner's Kaddish. The Rebbe did not appear. Afterward we all walked back together in shadows cast by the streetlamps and the trees. Cousin Yonkel seemed restive, unusually irritable even for him. I was growing weary of Cousin Yonkel.

Later, in my parents' home, we sat around a resplendent dining-room table and ate the first of the three Shabbos meals and talked and sang zemiros. My father enchanted Rocheleh with some intriguing riddles.

"What is 'riddle'?" Avrumel asked at one point, looking up from the chaos that was his meat plate.

"C'est une énigme," Devorah explained.

"Énigme," Avrumel repeated, tasting the new word; it did not clarify matters but offered some comfort by virtue of its being in his native tongue. He shoveled vegetables onto the table and into his mouth.

"Look at you," Devorah said. "You even eat like Godzilla."

"Never mind," my mother said happily. "We have a new washer and dryer in the basement."

We ate and talked and sang, and there was an abundance of food and wine and brandies and liqueurs, and the light softened and filled with haloes. My mother began to talk about the book she was writing on the power structure of the Politburo: a sequel to her earlier volume on postrevolutionary Russian-American relations, which had been published about ten years before and had earned her scholarly applause and a full professorship at New York University. She had been in her mid-fifties then. She had come late to scholarship, worked long and grindingly at it while being a wife to a roving ambassador and a mother to a gifted and troublesome child. She had published a great deal over the years; lonely hours at home while my father was on journeys for the Rebbe had finally turned her away from the living-room window to a pen, a typewriter, a computer. Her study, a small room adjoining the master bedroom, was crowded with file cabinets, boxes of cards, papers, the computer and printer, her desk, and two chairs. Most of her personal library was in her office at the university.

How many hours a week did she spend on matters having to do with the Ladover? I asked her.

"Many," she said. "Two or three meetings, position papers for your father and the Rebbe. Many."

"Is the Rebbe at the meetings?"

"Sometimes."

"We should not talk about such matters on Shabbos," my father interrupted. "Shabbos is for the Master of the Universe and for

Torah. Let's sing more zemiros. Do you have a favorite, Rocheleh? Yes? Sing it for us."

She sang, in her high, tremulous voice, a song taught her by Devorah—a song Devorah's father used to sing at the Shabbos table. "Mosai yovo hamoshiach," she sang. "When will the Messiah come . . ." The candles flickered upon her pale, thin face, her head slightly upturned so the words and the melody could flow more easily from bronchial tubes that turned treacherous at times and sealed off her breathing. Devorah sat looking down at the table, containing herself, chewing her lower lip. Then my father joined Rocheleh in the song, and a moment later we were all singing it together. "Mosai yovo hamoshiach . . ." Then my father sang his father's melody to Yoh Ribbon Olom, a melody I had heard only rarely from him—when his mother died; when my mother became ill—yet whose haunting tune remained fixed in remembrance, a poignant testimony of pain and faith and hope. Avrumel watched him for a long moment, awed, his mouth open; and then suddenly he was down off his chair and on my father's lap, and my father held him gently as he sang. His voice had deepened with the years and had lost some of its quaver. His eyes closed, his upper body swaying back and forth on the chair, he sang softly, slowly. ". . . Ant hu malka, melech melech malchayoh . . ." He took in a tremulous breath. "Ovad gevurtaich vetimhayoh . . ." From the corners of his closed eyes, like glistening beads, tears fell slowly across the ridges of his cheeks, breaking into minute rivulets along the creased skin and vanishing inside the thicket of white beard. Avrumel stared at the tears and then reached up and brushed at them with his little fingers. I turned my head away and remembered how, in childhood, I had heard him sing that melody for the first time when his mother died, and I had later drawn him singing it; again and again, drawing my father singing his father's melody.

Later, as we were clearing the table, I found myself alone in the kitchen for a moment with my mother, and I asked her where my father had picked up the idea of playing riddle games with children; he had never done that with me.

"He saw your Uncle Yitzchok, of blessed memory, doing it with Nahum's children. Isn't it a fine idea?"

I agreed that it was a fine idea.

The food, the wine, the singing, and the late hour had a wondrous narcotizing effect upon Rocheleh and Avrumel, who were yawning halfway through the Grace After Meals and asleep soon afterward. I sat with Devorah and my parents in the living room, and we talked about Uncle Yitzchok. My father told stories about his cheerfulness, his goodheartedness, his devotion to the Rebbe and the movement, his optimism about the future. Uncle Yitzchok was certain the redemption would come soon. Wonders and miracles awaited us. The Messiah was coming, speedily, at any moment. For Uncle Yitzchok, the future of the Ladover movement was joyous and golden. For me right now, it looked like a good idea to use the immediate future for sleep. And, indeed, my father was soon asleep in his armchair, his skullcap slightly askew. My mother woke him, and they went off to their room.

Devorah and I sat alone in the living room. "It feels good here," she said, after a moment.

I was quiet.

"The children love it here. There is community here."

I said nothing.

"Hello. Are you there? Is anybody there?"

"A crazy artist is here," I said.

"And here sits his wife, trying to talk to him."

"I went for a walk today and saw where I grew up."

"Ah, yes? And how did you feel about it?"

"I felt so-so. Somewhere between nothing and forlorn. I felt ready to go home."

"Poor Asher. You don't like Crown Heights?"

"No. And Crown Heights doesn't especially like me."

"I don't like Paris."

"I love Paris. But I didn't grow up there. I didn't lose my parents there. I didn't spend age four to six in a sealed apartment there. So what do I know? Right?"

"Yes. Correct. What do you know about Paris?"

"Exactly what you know about Crown Heights. So let's go back to Saint-Paul. We both agree about Saint-Paul. Yes?"

"How did we survive our childhoods, my husband?"

"We were helped by a merciful God."

"Yes? I wish He had been a little more merciful. I wish He had been a little more merciful toward my father and my mother, toward my aunts and uncles, toward my—"

"Dev."

"Just a little more merciful."

"We should go to bed."

"She sang beautifully, our Rocheleh. Didn't she sing beautifully?"

"Yes."

"My father sang beautifully. He was a tenor. I never told you? Yes. Once he taught me a Christian song. In case I would ever have to hide in the countryside with the peasants, I would be able to fool the Nazi soldiers. 'Je me croyais au Paradis,' she sang softly, 'entre les bras de Jésus Christ.' Would you ever believe that my father taught me that? A Ladover Hasid. He learned it from a farmer he did business with. I heard him tell my mother he would go to his death proudly as a Jew, but he wanted his children to survive the war and build a future. Well, he died. Isn't it a lovely Christian song? How old was I when he taught it to me? Three or four. More than forty-five years ago. I still remember it. A kind of goyishe Krias Shema. My father told me to memorize it because my life might depend on it. But I never had to use it. Oh, yes, God is merciful."

I went over to where she was sitting and helped her to her feet. I walked with her to our room and helped her out of her clothes and into her nightgown. She seemed dazed, half asleep, and kept singing the French song about the arms of Jesus. Then she came suddenly fully awake and stared about her, startled, and remained awake long enough to wash up and brush her teeth. She climbed into my bed and dropped off into sleep as if drugged.

The desk light was on. An automatic timer would soon turn it off, for we do not tamper with electricity on Shabbos. I got into my pajamas and washed up and sat at the desk reviewing the Torah portion of the week, as I did always on Friday night. After a while the desk light went off. By the dim glow of the night light I climbed into Devorah's bed and was quickly asleep.

She woke me in the middle of the night. Through sleep I felt my blanket and sheet being pulled back and, half awake, I felt her slip into the bed beside me and, fully awake, I felt all her warmth and nakedness and the ferocity with which she clung to me. I loved her so much, my Devorah; her arms tight around my neck and her legs against my thighs. "Hold me, Asher. Tight, tight. Yes! Tell me God has a plan. Tell me. Come into me, my husband. Oh, my Asher. Oh, my husband. Oh!"

The Rebbe entered the synagogue the next morning during the Shacharis Service. He entered through the door near the Ark, helped by two tall dark-bearded men. They all wore their prayer shawls. Near the Ark was the Rebbe's tall-backed chair with the stand before it, both inside a small area bounded by a low wooden wall decorated with arabesques of wood. The wall was about the height of a tall man's knees and had a wooden gate set in it that swung in and out. The Rebbe wore his tallis over his head and the tall men left him sitting in his chair and took seats in the front row of the synagogue.

The synagogue was crowded. I sat between my father and my cousins in the front row. The sounds of more than a thousand men and women praying set up a rhythmic, murmurous humming. The Rebbe sat with his head covered by his tallis; even his beard lay concealed beneath the white-and-black-striped fringed cloth. The elderly man leading the service took the congregation through the Shema and the Silent Devotion and the Kedushoh.

As the leader of the service continued chanting aloud the public repetition of the Silent Devotion after the Kedushoh, a gray-bearded man came over and handed me a small card on which was printed in Hebrew the word *maftir*. He did not even glance at me as he gave me the card, but walked quickly away, affording me no opportunity to refuse. I slipped the card into a pocket of my suit jacket.

A few minutes later, the Ark was opened, a Torah scroll was removed, and the Ark was closed. The Torah scroll was brought to the podium in the center of the synagogue, beneath the huge brass chandelier. The Torah reading began.

Years ago, on a trip to the United States, I had prayed one Monday morning in a synagogue outside the town of Spring Valley, New York. They gave me the honor of being the third man called to the Torah during the reading. I approached the podium and stood before the sacred scroll and was about to make the blessing when I felt someone tap me on the shoulder. I turned, and a tall, thin bearded presence slipped between me and the podium. He had on his tallis and tefillin, and he stood between me and the scroll and shook his head at me and pointed to the scroll and shook his head once again. He was in his early thirties, his eyes dark, his face set in rigid lines, determined. I reached forward to touch my tallis to the scroll and make the blessing, and he brushed my hand away and pushed hard between me and the podium and would not let me move around him to make the blessing. The men standing at the podium stared at him in astonishment but did nothing. With my face flaming and my heart pounding, I backed away from the podium and returned to my seat. I could feel my knees weaken and the anger rise inside myself. "Our rabbi is a fool," one of the congregants, an elderly man, said to me afterward. "For us it is an honor to have you here. For him it is a desecration. We apologize to you. What do they teach them in yeshivas nowadays? Where do they learn to behave that way?"

I was being called to the Torah in the Ladover synagogue. I heard my name. "Rise, Asher son of Rav Aryeh, maftir."

I walked to the podium and made the blessing. A white-bearded man chanted the Torah portion. I made the second blessing. The Torah scroll was raised and removed from the podium. I stood alone at the podium, aware of the silence in the synagogue as I read the portion from one of the prophetic books. I could see out of the sides of my eyes the white stillness that was the Rebbe inside his tallis. I came to the closing verse of the reading, and a chorus of voices joined me in the final words. I chanted the concluding blessings and, with the echoing "Amen" of the congregation in my ears, turned to leave the podium, when a flash of light, a movement, caught my eye. I looked across the distance between the podium and the Ark and saw the Rebbe's hand, only the hand, the wrist and the fingers protruding from the fringe of the tallis, beckoning to me. Then it withdrew into the mound of white.

Everyone in the synagogue saw that beckoning hand.

A silence settled upon the synagogue, an absence of sound that had about it a physical density. I walked quickly through that silence, feeling myself pushing through strangely thickened air, and climbed the short steps to the area of the Ark and went through the low wooden gate. The hand moved out again from under the tallis and I grasped it, felt its cool dry papery smoothness, its age—and found myself looking into the eyes of the Rebbe, dark-socketed gray eyes that were like soft clear pools and that would certainly go on and on beyond the lives of all of us there. He clasped my hand and put his other hand over mine and, holding my hand in both of his, leaned toward me and spoke in Yiddish, in a barely audible voice. "May your strength be straight, Asher Lev. I wish to speak with you about some matter after the week of mourning. Someone will call you." Then he released my hand and withdrew into his tallis.

I returned to my seat in a silence that was the holding of a thousand breaths.

My father sat looking at the prayer book on his stand, his face without expression. Cousin Nahum and Cousin Yonkel gaped at me in astonishment and disbelief.

The service continued. Immediately after the Musaf Kedushoh, the Rebbe left the synagogue, together with the two dark-bearded men. The final Mourner's Kaddish was said, and the service came to an end.

My father embraced me and wished me a good Shabbos. Cousin Nahum pumped my hand. Cousin Yonkel managed a parched smile that barely concealed the incredulity still on his pinched face: his painter cousin invited into the sacred space near the Rebbe, and the Rebbe taking that painter's contaminated hand and clasping it! The whole world was upside down!

I was caught up in the crowd leaving the synagogue. People I did not know murmured Shabbos greetings and shook my hand. On the street in front of the synagogue people kept coming over to me and shaking my hand. Devorah and the children were near the police car that was parked at the curb. I moved toward them through the crowd. Rocheleh looked lovely in the red coat my mother had bought her during the week; Avrumel stood in stiff discomfort in his new dark suit and dark cap. My parents stood near Devorah. Children stared at me as I went past.

I felt as I did at one of my openings: unveiled, paraded, displayed; the whispers, the glances, the stares. I shouldered my way through the crowd and greeted my mother and Devorah and the children.

"My papa talked with the Rebbe!" Avrumel promptly informed the policeman who sat behind the open window on the curb side of the patrol car.

The policeman gave him an indulgent smile.

We started home.

"What did the Rebbe say to you?" Rocheleh asked.

"The Rebbe said he wanted to talk to me."

The glance that passed between my mother and my father was not lost upon me.

"About what?" Rocheleh asked.

"The Rebbe didn't say."

The children walked on ahead with my parents.

"What do you think it means, Asher?" Devorah asked.

"I have no idea."

We walked on awhile. "Was I terrible last night?" she asked.

"You were wonderful last night."

"I mean about the song."

"What song was that?"

"You know what song. The goyishe song."

"I only remember the together-time song. It was beautiful."

She smiled joyfully.

"It was my Island of Poetry," I said.

"What was?"

"Last night. Birth through the fingertips."

She turned crimson. "You are awful."

"And you are beautiful."

"There's a demon in you, Asher Lev."

"That's hardly news."

"I love that demon."

"That's news."

"We should not be talking this way on Shabbos."

"If not Shabbos, then when?"

She laughed delightedly. We walked on together behind my parents and the children.

. . .

After the long Shabbos meal we all slept for a while, and then Devorah and I and the children went on a walk through the neighborhood. Avrumel brought along his new Shimshon doll. I showed them the apartment house where I grew up and the streets where I used to play and the parkway benches I would sit on, drawing the old people who sat with their faces toward the sunlight and the children skipping past me and the young Ladover couples with their many babies.

"Did you ever draw the black people, Papa?" Rocheleh asked, and I said yes, sometimes, but I drew the Ladover more often here and the black people more often when I was in South Africa or wandering through the streets of Manhattan.

"Why are there so many black people in America?" Avrumel wanted to know.

"They were brought here to be slaves," I said.

He looked confused.

"Like we were in Egypt," Rocheleh explained.

He gazed up and down at the many blacks on the street. "They are still slaves?"

"No," Devorah said. "They were freed a long time ago."

"Did Hashem give them the Torah?"

"No," Rocheleh said. "Hashem gave the Torah only to us."

It was a warm and sunny afternoon. The streets were filled with strollers. A black youth sauntered past, a huge radio on his shoulder, blaring. Rocheleh and Avrumel watched him go by. "Why is the music so loud?" Avrumel asked.

"They like it loud," I said. "Like we do at weddings and on Simchas Torah. Come on, let's walk to the museum."

I showed them the façades of the museum and the library, and they stared in awe at the vast traffic circle with its statuary and arches.

"Now I know why you like Paris," Devorah said to me. "You grew up with a boulevard in your neighborhood."

Then we walked along Prospect Park to the lake where my mother and I used to go rowing; to the zoo, with the lions and tigers and elephants and monkeys; then back to the botanical gardens, which would soon be nearly as explosive with color as the Renoir garden hanging in my Uncle Yitzchok's study.

Avrumel held my hand with one of his hands and the Shimshon doll with the other. From time to time, he turned to the rag doll and engaged it in intimate conversation. "This is the lake where my papa used to row with his mama. This is the library where my papa used to take out books." Rocheleh kept on with a barrage of questions. Where had her papa bought his first oil colors? When had her papa gone to the museum for the first time? What kinds of pictures were in the museum? Had her papa been permitted to see the nudes? She was a Ladover, our Rocheleh, but she was also French and the daughter of Asher Lev. She knew about nudes. Max Lobe had a large collection of nudes. There were paintings of nudes on the walls of our home in Saint-Paul and reproductions in books written about me.

Unusual for Avrumel, he was actually listening this time to his sister's conversation. "Nudes?" he said. "That means the paintings of women without clothes?"

"That is correct," Devorah said, glancing around the street, which was crowded with passersby.

"Papa paints nudes," Avrumel announced to no one in particular.

"Yes," Devorah said. "But it is not necessary to go around shouting it to everyone."

"He's such a child," Rocheleh said. Were the Ladover upset when her papa painted nudes? she wanted to know. Somehow she had never thought to ask me that before.

Yes, they were upset.

Why did her papa paint them?

Because her papa was an artist.

"This is Shabbos talk?" Devorah asked. "Nudes?"

"Nudes," Avrumel chanted. "Nudes."

An elderly Ladover couple, approaching us, glanced curiously at Avrumel, and went on.

"Avrumel," I said. "If you don't stop that, there will be no more posing for me."

"Yes posing."

"When are you going to grow up?" Rocheleh asked him.

"When the Messiah comes," he said. He had turned irascible, a sure sign of fatigue. The walk had wearied him. He mumbled something to the Shimshon doll. Then he said, loudly, "When I grow up I am going to be an artist like my papa."

"God forbid," said Devorah.

I looked at her. The words had come out impulsively. We laughed.

"I am going to be an artist and paint nudes," Avrumel said.

"Whatever God wishes you to be, you will be," I said.

"An artist," Avrumel insisted loudly.

"All right, let it be an artist."

That mollified him. He let us walk tranquilly the rest of the way home.

Later that afternoon, some friends of my parents' came over to the house—most of them couples their age and a little younger, a few my age, with little children. The men wore dark suits and dark hats; the women were handsomely wigged and garbed, many of them looking as if they had studied current high-fashion magazines displaying the most elegant long-sleeved, high-necked dresses. The air was warm, and they sat in chairs on the terrace, talking about the morning's Torah portion and midrashic comments on it, and one thing led to another and somehow they began telling stories about the Rebbe and the Rebbe's father and grandfather. The adults sat alone; the children were inside the house somewhere, playing together. Someone told a story about the leader of another Hasidic group, and that led to talk about the Ba'al Shem Tov, the eighteenth-century founder of Hasidism, who had lived and taught in Eastern Europe. Someone mentioned the quarrels among the first generation of disciples of the Ba'al Shem Tov, and that started them talking about the rivalries among the different Hasidic sects. One of the older men talked about the strange silence of the Rebbe of Kotzk, decades of silence, during which he said nothing to his people or his family; the fight among his followers; the split in the sect. Another of the older men told about the breakup of the Rhyziner, one of the greatest of the Hasidic dynasties of the last century. Then he talked about the quarrels among the Belzer Hasidim, the Karliner, the Satmarer. There was some murmuring when he mentioned the Satmarer, for they were the sworn enemies of the Ladover, had been so in Europe and continued so on the streets of Brooklyn: verbal and physical assaults between the two sects were not uncommon. It was strange, intimate, brooding conversation, unusual for a Shabbos afternoon among Ladover Hasidim—and I began to sense in the group an undercurrent of concealment; discussion circling a subject all conceded was crucial but about which no one truly wished to talk. I had grown up in this community; my nerve ends were still connected to it; I could read its unwritten texts, hear its unspoken dialogue. There was something going on here, something inarticulate hovered in the air, an unspoken dread. Sunlight colored the sycamore and fell upon the redwood flooring of the terrace and the bare patches of earth gouged out of the lawn by the winter snows. Here and there tufts of young grass speckled the lawn, and there was the barest beginning of buds on the hyacinths. A fly buzzed lazily in a slanting sunbeam and then flew off into the shadows of the sycamore. The talk went on—tales of rivalries and quarrels and breakups—and I noticed my parents were not participating. My father sat in silence, gazing down at the wooden floor of the terrace. At a certain point in the conversation, he suddenly looked up and made a quiet remark. Someone immediately reacted to it, and a second person countered the reaction, and a moment later I realized how gently and expertly my father had steered the talk away from the subject of dissension to something as innocuous and joyful as the projected new summer-camp program for Ladover children. My mother realized it, too; I saw her knowing smile.

The afternoon slowly waned. I went with the men to the synagogue for the Afternoon and Evening Services. The Rebbe did not appear. After the final Mourner's Kaddish, my father and I returned with my cousins to my Uncle Yitzchok's home. The period of mourning resumed.

I did not think a private home could contain as many people as my uncle's home held the next day. Many who had been there the previous week returned; others came for the first time. It was the final full day of mourning. Ladover arrived from Rome and London; two arrived from the Ladover village in Israel; one from

Bucharest; one from Buenos Aires. There were muted conversations with my parents; condolences were repeatedly offered my aunt and cousins. The shuffle of tight bodies and chairs; the subdued voices; the body-heated air. It was very late when my parents and I returned home.

The children were asleep. Devorah was in bed, reading. I fell asleep with the lights on and dreamed I was in Jacob Kahn's studio in Manhattan, painting a nude, and my father sat nearby, watching, his face the shape of a sphere, smooth and without expression.

The next morning, after the service and the final Mourner's Kaddish, my uncle's family and my father sat for a while on their low stools. About two dozen men occupied the wooden folding chairs. They sat there talking quietly about my Uncle Yitzchok. Then the men filed past the mourners and spoke the traditional words of consolation—and the mourners rose from their stools and left the house and walked slowly around the block and returned to the house. The week of mourning was at an end.

The house was silent, empty of visitors. I helped Cousin Nahum and Cousin Yonkel fold and stack the chairs. I asked Cousin Nahum for the key to his father's study. Cousin Yonkel glowered, but Cousin Nahum gave me the key ring without a word. We went into the kitchen for breakfast.

My aunt sat at the table, crying. No consoling crowd now; no distracting bustle. She fled into the den, and her two daughters and my mother went after her. Cousin Yonkel and Cousin Nahum said they had business to take care of; they excused themselves and left. My father said he wanted to look at the mail that had accumulated in his office during the past week. I found myself alone in the kitchen with the dishes and the food and the sudden crushing silence of the house. I sat and stared out the window at the terrace and the lawn and thought of Max Lobe and John Dorman and the valley and the walled village on the hill, and was eager to return home. Tomorrow morning the meeting with Douglas Schaeffer. Tomorrow night the flight home. I sat there thinking of home.

Afterward I climbed the stairs and went along the carpeted second-floor hallway and opened the door to my uncle's study. How velvety the silence, how feather-soft the stillness of calmly anticipated astonishments! I turned on the lights and sat down in the recliner and gazed at the paintings on the walls.

Each painting was encased in the sort of gilded decorative frame accorded vaunted classics. Each glowed beneath the lights; each appeared to be sending forth waves of light from the pigments on the surface of the canvas. The tiny color planes in the Cézanne, like the pieces of a riddle, exquisitely explored, investigated, probed, resolved, each daub of color another piece of his answer to the greatest riddle of all: how we see and think the world. Trees and valley and mountain and sky; put together piece by piece, with infinite peasant perseverance. Prussian blue here; pale violet there; ultramarine here; cadmium red there. Trees and valley and mountain and sky suddenly a world on a two-dimensional surface. What an act of creativity by a painter's fragile fingers! And the flowers and leaves of the Renoir; the climbing red and white roses, the flood of geraniums, the trumpet vines, the peonies and impatiens; the blurred and heady gushing of color from the potted and earth-sown plants. And the cadmium yellow of the curtains and the burnt-sienna arabesques of the balcony and the cobalt blue of the sea and the cadmium-red goldfish in the emerald-green bowl and the purple and red and ultramarine of the walls in the Matisse. What joy to be able to sit and gaze at leisure upon these paintings after such a week of sadness! I wished there were a blessing that could be uttered over such a display of pagan beauty!

I sat alone with the paintings. After a while I turned off the lights and went out of the study and down the stairs and out of the house.

The late-morning air was warm and burnished with sunlight. Soon there would be leaves on the trees and grass on the lawns. An elderly couple walked along the street, leaning on canes. Three doors away was the Rebbe's home. White-bearded elders stood on the sidewalk, talking quietly, and dark-garbed men kept going in and out. A stray dog loped by in front of my uncle's house, urinated against the maple, and ambled off. I went up the walk to my parents' home and let myself in.

I was very tired. I lay down on my bed in my clothes and fell asleep. Devorah woke me for lunch. She had gone to the nearby

Hebrew bookstore and returned with books for the children: *In the Streets of Moscow*, *The New York Express*, *The Mezuzah Maker*, *A Children's Treasury of Chassidic Tales*, *Tales from Reb Nachman*, *Emunah*. We ate together in my parents' kitchen. Was there anything I wanted her to buy for me before she began to pack for the return trip? There was nothing. Oh, yes, let's not forget John Dorman's writing pads.

That afternoon I sat on the terrace of my parents' home and with a soft pencil made a drawing of my uncle. I drew him as I remembered him from twenty years before, dark-bearded, round-faced, smiling. I drew him gently—the small radiating lines in the outside corners of his eyes; the rounded fullness of his nose; the high forehead with the ridge below the hairline and the slope to the lined valley below and then the twin rise of bone above the eyebrows. I made the lines soft and wispy, brushing passages from plane to plane with my middle and small fingers, drawing it the way Renoir would have painted it. Rocheleh and Avrumel returned from school and must have seen me through the glass doors of the living room, because suddenly I was aware of them on the other side of the doors, watching me. They stood silently until I put down the pencil and looked up at the sunlight on the high branches of the sycamore.

"Who is it, Papa?" Avrumel asked. He held the Shimshon doll by one of its hands, its feet dragging on the floor.

"My Uncle Yitzchok."

"That's not the way you draw," Rocheleh said.

"That's right. It's a special drawing."

At supper that night we sat around the kitchen table. My father talked about the mountain of mail that had greeted him when he returned to his office, the meetings he had attended all day, the people who wanted to see him, decisions that needed to be made, travel plans that had to be finalized, budgets that had to be reviewed. He looked weary.

I had something for him, I said. A gift. And I opened the large drawing pad I had been holding on my lap and pulled out the drawing of Uncle Yitzchok and showed it to him.

He sat looking at it, his mouth slightly open.

"Asher," my mother said in an awed tone. "It is exquisite."

"You made him . . . alive," my father murmured. He blinked, and brushed a hand over his eyes. Suddenly he was weeping, silently. He sat there, silently and unashamedly weeping, the drawing in his hands. Devorah looked down at her plate. The children were very quiet.

"This kind of art I appreciate," my father said through his tears. "Please excuse me for a moment."

He went from the kitchen, taking the drawing with him. A few minutes later he returned, without the drawing. We finished the meal. He had to go back to his office. Meetings, he said.

Some minutes later, the phone rang. Devorah poked her head into our room and said it was for me. I turned away from the drawing pad on the desk and looked at her.

"Who is it?"

"I didn't ask. Do you want me to ask?"

Sudden memories of that sibilant voice and that threat of death. "No."

I took the call in the hallway.

"Is this Asher Lev?" said the voice at the other end, clearly, nasally.

I said it was.

"I am calling you from the Rebbe's office. My name is Rav Hershel Specter. I am one of the Rebbe's aides. The Rebbe would like to speak to you."

"All right."

"Alone. Tonight."

"Tonight?"

"Eleven o'clock. In his house."

"Yes."

"Come a few minutes early."

"All right."

"Did you go to the mikvah today?"

"No."

"You should go to the mikvah before you see the Rebbe. When you come, one of the men at the door will tell you what to do and where to wait."

"Thank you."

"Be well, Asher Lev." He hung up.

I put the phone down and could not stop the trembling of my hands. I returned to the room and the desk. The pencil danced and quivered upon the page. Wavy curves. Jagged lines. I kept remembering the phone call of eighteen years ago. Devorah asked what the call was about, and I told her. I sat staring at the photograph of the Rebbe on the wall over the desk and could not continue drawing.

A few minutes before eleven, I left the house and walked along the street toward the home of the Rebbe, treading carefully in the shadow-laced lamppost lights shining dimly on a cracked and broken sidewalk that was yielding to the relentless upward thrusting of tree roots. The air was cool, the street still. Yellow rectangles of light shone from the windows of houses. I shivered in the cool air; the hair on the back of my neck was still damp from my immersion in the mikvah. My uncle's house was dark and silent, Aunt Leah no doubt asleep, my cousins gone. Cousin Nahum had wished me a safe trip back to Saint-Paul. Cousin Yonkel had said he hoped he would not see me again for a long time, because we would only be seeing each other again in a time of sorrow, since there was no reason on earth for us to see each other otherwise. Cousin Nahum shook his head and rolled his eyes. "It's the truth," Cousin Yonkel had said. "I am telling the truth. If it hurts, so be it."

I turned off the sidewalk and started up the narrow walk to the stone porch. Two tall dark-bearded men stood on either side of the wide wooden front door. One of them told me to wait in the large room to my right just off the entrance hall. I stepped into the house, and the door closed silently behind me.

I was in a large hall with a parquet floor and bare white walls and two arched doorways on either side open to rooms beyond. At the far end of the hall, a wide carpeted flight of stairs led to the dimness overhead. Voices sounded somewhere in the house, distant, indistinct. The room to the right was large, carpeted, furnished with chairs and low tables on which were numerous Ladover publications: newsletters, children's magazines, catalogues of books published by the Ladover press, the most recent radio and television talks given by the Rebbe, magazines for teenagers, application forms for Ladover summer camps for children. The publications were in English, Hebrew, Yiddish, French, Russian, Italian, and Spanish. The walls were bare save for a large oil painting of the Rebbe, ornately framed in a style reminiscent of the frames that contained the Cézanne, Matisse, and Renoir in my Uncle Yitzchok's study. I sat down in one of the chairs near the window that faced the street. Across the room from me was a white wall with a walnut-stained door, curls of dark metal embedded along its wooden surface, long triangular wedges of black metal clinging to its frame. Faraway voices kept drifting into the room from somewhere in the house.

A clock struck eleven times, the sound reaching me as if muffled by thick curtains and wall hangings. I sat quietly, waiting.

The door opened silently. A man stepped into the room, closed the door behind him, crossed the room, and sat down in the chair next to mine. He wore an old windbreaker and baggy brown trousers. His craggy features were windblown and deeply lined, and his hands were huge, the fingers callused and stained with paint. He had a thick shock of flowing white hair, on which he wore a dark beret. I stared at him and felt the sudden jolt of astonishment and the swift dizzying whirling of the world.

The man gazed at me and smiled through his walrus mustache. "It is a surprise to me how young you look. Are you really thirteen?"

I nodded.

"You are so skinny and pale. Like Chagall."

"My name is Asher Lev," I said.

"Yes," he said. "I know your name. My name is Jacob Kahn."

We shook hands. He had a powerful grip. I felt myself drawn into his pale-blue eyes.

"Do you have any idea what you are doing? Better to become a carpenter, Asher Lev. Become a shoemaker."

I did not respond.

"I know your father. He will become my enemy."

I said nothing.

He sighed. "Our Rebbe is very clever. If it isn't Jacob Kahn who teaches you, it will be someone else. He prefers to take a chance with me. My father was all his life a follower of his father. I myself am not an observant Jew. But I will watch you. Yes, we have a clever Rebbe." He looked at me sharply. "Do you know what you are getting into, Asher Lev? It is a world without peace. Do not expect redemption if you enter the world of art. Redemption is death to art. Tranquillity is the poison the artist takes when he is ready to give up his art. Do you hear me, Asher Lev?"

"Yes."

"Are you listening?"

"Yes."

"Asher."

I opened my eyes.

"Asher." My father stood before me. I stared up at him and felt myself trembling. "Are you all right?"

"I dozed off for a moment."

"Do not expect redemption, Asher Lev," Jacob Kahn said from the chair where he was sitting.

"Come with me," my father said.

I got to my feet and followed my father to the wooden door. Glancing over my shoulder, I saw that the chair on which Jacob Kahn had been sitting was empty.

My father stopped in front of the door. He was a tall and distinguished presence in his dark suit and dark tie and white beard and small dark skullcap—and for the first time in my life I felt a rise of pride in what he had achieved for himself, this position as chief of staff to the Rebbe. All the years of travel; all the anguish over my mother's illness and his son's slide into the alien world of art; all the energy he had given to the founding of Ladover schools in America and Europe; all the focused tenacity of his selfless determination to succeed in behalf of the Master of the Universe and the Rebbe—all the sum of his life had brought him to this exalted position as the right arm of the Rebbe. Now he touched me lightly on my arm, and in that touch I sensed his reverence for the person who sat in the room beyond the door, and I recalled his words to me the first time I had gone to see the Rebbe, the week I had become a bar mitzvah: "Remember with whom you will be speaking."

My father opened the door and stepped aside and beckoned me

across the threshold. I entered the room. The door closed sound-lessly behind me.

I stood at the door. The floor was carpeted. Near the opposite wall, in front of a tall leaded stained-glass window, was a large dark wood desk with ornate carvings along its edges and legs. Floor-to-ceiling bookcases laden with books covered the walls. Three armchairs stood in front of the desk. Lights burned dimly in a burnished Oriental chandelier suspended from the stippled ceiling and fell softly upon the bookcases and the desk and the figure who sat behind the desk in a tall-backed dark leather chair.

He looked so small, his dark clothes so indistinct against the leather of the chair, that at first I could barely make out his face, the stark white beard and pale features and dark eyes. He seemed all face, luminous, suspended, unsubstantial, flesh so rarefied after all the decades of consecrated leadership that only the soul now showed. I stood gazing at him from across the room, and I saw him raise his hand and beckon to me, and I went up to the desk.

He wore a dark suit and an ordinary dark hat. His eyes seemed to gather the dim light in the room; they glowed through the vague shadows cast by the brim of the hat. He pointed to a chair. "Sit down, Asher Lev." His voice was faint, gentle. "It is a long time since I have seen you alone."

I took one of the chairs.

"How is your wife?"

"Thank God, my wife is well."

"How is your daughter? Her illness is controlled?"

"Thank God, yes."

"And Avrumel? How is Avrumel?"

"Thank God."

"And how are you, Asher Lev? The years have been good to you, yes?"

"I thank the Almighty."

"The world hears from our Asher Lev. The world knows of our Asher Lev. Who has not heard of Asher Lev?"

I was quiet.

"I remember the first time you came to me, at the time of your bar mitzvah, when you met Jacob Kahn, of blessed memory. I remember you came to me later, when I asked you to study Russian. I remember when I sent you away because of your paintings. All those times I remember."

I said nothing.

He leaned forward in his chair; the vaguest of movements, a shifting of shadows. "To send you away was a severe decree, a terrible thing. But it was better for everyone that you went from us."

The tremor that passed through me, like a shattering of myself, was so tumultuous I felt certain he had seen it. He gazed at me in silence. Then he closed his eyes and his head slowly fell forward upon his chest and I thought he had fallen asleep. I sat there, not knowing what to do. Interminable minutes passed. I had decided to go quietly to the door and leave, when I heard him say, his head still upon his chest, "Asher, I want to tell you something. It is important that you listen carefully to my words." He raised his head and gazed at me unblinking from beneath the rim of the dark hat. "My father, of blessed memory, once said to me, on the verse in Genesis: 'And He saw all that He did and behold it was good'— my father once said that the seeing of God is not like the seeing of man. Man sees only *between* the blinks of his eyes. He does not know what the world is like *during* the blinks. He sees the world in pieces, in fragments. But the Master of the Universe sees the world whole, unbroken. *That* world is good. Our seeing is broken, Asher Lev. Can we make it like the seeing of God? Is that possible?"

He paused a moment, then went on. "Once I told this to Jacob Kahn, of blessed memory. Yes, these same words. And he said to me that an artist, too, must see the world whole, he must somehow learn to see during the blinks, he must see where no one else can see, he must see the connections, the *betweennesses* in the world. Even if the connections are ugly and evil, the artist must learn to see and record them. I said to Jacob Kahn that a Rebbe, too, must see the connections, and if a Rebbe truly sees, if he is able, through the goodness and mercy of the Master of the Universe, to see as the Master of the Universe Himself sees, then he will see that all is good. Jacob Kahn said to me, 'It is the task of the artist to see. If what he sees is good, then fine. If not, then not.' But all agree, Asher Lev, that it is the task of a Rebbe and of an artist to see, to look. That is understood?"

I nodded, slowly.

"It is understood?" the Rebbe asked again.

"Yes," I heard myself say, as if from a distance.

"It is understood. Good. Very good. Then listen to me, Asher. There are things I am able to see that I cannot reveal to you. You must understand that what I will now ask of you comes from that seeing. Listen. I ask you not to return to France tomorrow. I ask you to remain here with us for another week or two. Stay with us. I am told you must go to Paris. I ask you not to go."

There was a long silence. I sat very still.

He leaned forward slightly in his chair. "Asher Lev, I give you and your wife and your children my blessing."

With his right hand he made a slight gesture. Then he sat back in the chair and seemed to disappear into its shadows.

I went silently from the room.

The house was still. I poked my head into my father's office, near the stairs. He was seated behind his desk. He looked up. I told him I was ready to leave. He said to go ahead, he still had work to do and the Rebbe would be seeing more people later tonight. I went past the two dark-bearded men on the porch and down the path to the sidewalk. I walked quickly in the light-speckled shadows beneath the trees.

Devorah was at the desk in her nightgown, a writing pad open before her. She had removed her wig; the low-cut brown hair, with its wisps of gray, gave her white slender neck an oddly elongated appearance, like the necks of women in medieval French tapestries and manuscript illustrations. She turned and gazed at me over the top of her glasses.

"I was becoming worried. You were with the Rebbe all this time? What did you talk about?"

"The Rebbe asked us not to go home tomorrow but to stay on here awhile longer."

She removed her glasses and looked at me.

"What do you think?"

"It will make your parents happy."

"One week, Dev. At most, two."

"The children will be very happy. Did you notice how Avrumel has taken to your father? You will have to cable or phone Max."

"We'll need to change the flight. I think we'd better ask for open reservations." I looked over at the desk. "Are you working on your new book? It's marvelous that you can write here. I haven't drawn a thing except that picture of my uncle."

"Husband mine, what do you want from yourself? You have just been through a week of mourning."

"I am really tired. How does the Rebbe stay up the way he does? He was seeing someone else after me. What's the story about, Dev?"

"You look half asleep, Asher."

"Isn't it a bedtime story?"

She laughed softly. "Do you really want to hear about it now? All right. I had the idea that it might be wonderful if we could find a world where we could hold on forever to the good feelings we get from a story or a song, keep those feelings inside ourselves forever instead of having them only for fleeting moments. We hear a song or read a story, and the good feelings we get don't remain inside us. We are either anticipating them, or we've had them and they're gone. We never experience them as *now*. Do you know what I mean? I'm writing a story about a little girl who discovers a cave where there is a lasting now."

"What are you calling it?"

"The Cave of Now."

"That's clever. *The Cave of Now.* Boy, I am really tired, Dev."

"Then get undressed and come to bed."

"The Cave of Now. Very clever. Now or never. Now and forever. If not now, when?"

She smiled patiently.

"We'll stay another week, Dev. Then we'll go home. I don't want this place to become my permanent now. I don't live here any more. One week. At the most, two. That's it. For the sake of peace in the family. Now I'm going to get washed."

I left her with her writing pad and her dreams of now and went into the bathroom.

I wake and lie with my eyes open, staring into the dim halo cast by the night light. Devorah is asleep in her bed. I hear her quiet, liquid breathing. The room pulses softly, alive.

Slowly, the door to the room opens, but no one enters. It opens wider. I raise myself on the bed and look below the level of the doorknob and see Avrumel, his hair disheveled. He leans against the doorpost, holding his Shimshon doll and staring into the room.

"Nightmare, Papa," I hear him say, and he begins to cry.

Devorah does not waken. I go to him and hold him to me, all the trembling warmth of him, his freckled face against my beard, and bring him back to his bed.

"What did you dream?"

"Don't remember. Very frightened, Papa." He holds the rag doll tightly against his chest.

"Sha. Go back to sleep. Papa is here."

I stay with him until he sleeps. Then I return through the silent hallway to my room. Walking to my bed, I sense a stirring in the curtains before the wide glass door to the terrace and the back lawn. I open the curtains slightly and peer out.

A full moon bathes the terrace in a bluish-white light. I see shadows near the mottled trunk and beneath the tall-branched tangle of the sycamore: flitting fields of darkness moving back and forth through the eerie pale wash of night light. I close the curtains and climb back into my bed. It is a long time before I am able to fall asleep.

In the morning, during breakfast, Devorah and I told my parents and the children that we would be staying on awhile longer. My mother was overjoyed to the point of tears. Rocheleh said it was a good idea; it would give her a chance to finish something that had begun in her class. Avrumel, a look of triumph on his face, turned to Shimshon and said, "You see, I told you we would stay," got down off his chair, climbed onto my father's lap, and hugged him. My father gazed at me over the top of Avrumel's head. His eyes were shiny and there was, deep inside them, a strange dark knowing look.

2

❀ ❀ ❀ I descend the stone stairway into the Kingston Avenue subway station. Cool stale earth-smelling air blows stiffly along the stairwell. I have the odd, chilling sensation that I am joining Uncle Yitzchok, Jacob Kahn, Anna Schaeffer, and the Spaniard in their cold graves.

I wait on the dimly lit crowded platform for the train to Manhattan. Then the thunderous passage through dark tunnels. The last time I was on a New York subway train, years ago, the walls seemed to twitch and shudder beneath the weight of the frenzied graffiti they bore; now the stark clean walls of the car glisten in the overhead lights.

In Manhattan I climb up the crowded dirty stairs and out of the subway into thronged streets and towering angles of shadow and light. I wander along looking into galleries, at the art in windows and on walls. I see Pop Art, Minimalism, Conceptualism, figurative painting. Consummate technical skill. The Bouguereau Effect, someone called it. Art without risk. The art of the eighties. A leading critic recently labeled it Importance Art: big, incoherent, a studied flouting of taste, tacky application of paint, indifferent drawing, a repellent choice of colors, everyone aping a big brother. Galleries glittered like department stores. A carnival of sorts. Art as Mardi Gras. The ordinary was king. And the courtiers were: popularization, shallowness, doubt, cynicism. The century was exhausted.

I wished I were back in Saint-Paul. I would stay here a week, at most two. Something odd was happening in Brooklyn. I could feel it even in Manhattan, amid the towers and tumult and crowds and street people: a shadowy stirring by the Ladover; a drawing forward; a vague sense of myself being reeled in. I could not give it a coherent word or feeling. Something.

I turned off the street and entered a tall building and rode the elevator to the fourth floor. I had last been here three years before, for the opening of a show. The critics had been kind, though I detected notes of hesitation. "Lev's style borders on stylishness," one had written. "On occasion it loses the deeper tones that satisfy our profoundest needs, and flirts dangerously with sentiment and melodrama." I disregarded it at the time, and remembered it after the Paris show. A good critic. Sympathetic and understanding in the past. A warning sign. Unheeded.

I stepped out of the elevator, onto a thickly carpeted floor, and found myself in front of a large sculpture of a female figure by Matisse. The languid flow of line from shoulder and torso to the rise of rounded thigh. A show of Matisse sculptures was in progress. About a dozen people wandered among the pieces. The soft flow of unhurried sensuality glowing in the light from overhead.

Across from the elevator, at the far end of the gallery to my left, was the same large dark intricately carved desk once used by Anna Schaeffer. Behind it sat a blond-haired, beautiful woman, Douglas Schaeffer's receptionist, talking into the telephone. She saw me and quickly concluded the conversation. Mr. Schaeffer was expecting me, she said. I went into the back office.

Douglas Schaeffer sat behind a small, pale lacquered wood desk that had belonged to a French nobleman who had lost his head to the guillotine. Douglas was peering at papers on the desk through Benjamin Franklin glasses. On a long table behind him stood a computer, a fax machine, and a telephone in a transparent box through which intricate wiring, like a network of veins and arteries, was intriguingly visible. The walls were covered with the works of his artists. One of my smaller paintings was there: *The Artist's Son and His Samson*. Dapper, of medium height, trim, dressed in a dark-blue blazer, gray trousers, a pale-blue shirt and red bow tie, with a light-green handkerchief in the breast pocket of the blazer, Douglas had about him the grace and old-world elegance of his mother. He was in his mid-forties and had Anna's cool searching eyes. His smooth face was tanned; his straight light-brown hair was combed back and parted; his nails were manicured. The air in the room was faintly scented with his cologne.

He looked up as I entered, came quickly around the desk, and took my proffered right hand in both his hands. "It is so good to see you, Asher. How are you? How are the children? Rocheleh is well?" It had taken him a while to learn how to pronounce the guttural in her name. "And Devorah? Sit down, dear boy, please. Sorry about your loss. Your only uncle. Sad. Very sad. Did you see the Matisses outside? They are splendid, aren't they? What a noise the show is making, especially among the critics and scholars. When do you return to France?"

He loved the atmospherics of high art: exhibitions, critics, scholars, the media, private collectors, museum and corporation curators. He was a Harvard graduate, with a bachelor's degree in fine arts. He had gone on to Oxford for a master's degree in art history, and had naturally and successfully taken over his mother's gallery during her last illness, about ten years before. Three years back, he had opened branches of the gallery in Los Angeles and Tokyo, both now highly successful ventures. He had been the executor of Jacob Kahn's estate. Three of the largest paintings in my last show had gone to museums; the fourth he had acquired for his own collection. It hung on a wall in his Upper East Side home. He possessed his mother's genteel haughtiness and elegance of manner, and every time I saw him he reminded me of her and, by immediate association, of Jacob Kahn, my teacher and his mother's closest friend.

I told him I would be in Brooklyn with my family for another week or two. I told him it would be good for the children to get to know their grandparents; it would be especially good for Avrumel, who had taken a liking to his grandfather. Devorah and my mother were getting along fine. It made sense to stay on awhile longer. But as I said it, there seemed attached to the words an aura of darkness. Had my father known that the Rebbe would ask me to stay? Had he urged the Rebbe to ask me? That knowing look in my father's eyes at breakfast this morning.

"What about you, dear boy? What will you be doing?"

I told him I would be taking long walks and from time to time resting amid the creations in my uncle's collection.

"What collection is that?"

I proceeded to describe my Uncle Yitzchok's art collection: the paintings that made up its cornerstone; the drawings; the prints; the Jewish artists; my own works; the magazine articles and monographs and vernissage announcements. As I went on, I saw him remove his glasses and place them in the pocket of his jacket behind the green handkerchief. He stared at me. When I was done, there was a pause. He touched his bow tie with a manicured finger and coughed lightly.

"It seems an estimable collection."

"I would say so, yes."

"Isn't it rather an odd thing for a man like your uncle to have done?"

"He started it as an investment. Then I think it became something he admired. He may even have come to love it."

"What will your uncle's heirs do with it?"

"Oh, they'll sell it off. They can't wait to get their hands on it. Especially one of my cousins, whose middle name is greed. They'll open a dozen stores with the money they make from it."

"A shame, dear boy. If you are at all interested, I would be happy to handle part or all of the sales for your family."

"I'll certainly suggest it to them. Doug, to change the subject, I wanted to ask you if any copies of my first Paris print have surfaced?"

"The one you made with Jacob Kahn? Dear boy, no collector in his right mind would divest himself of that print. Not with your market the way it is now."

"I need a copy of it."

"Where are your artist's proofs, Ash? Didn't you receive artist's proofs?"

"They were in that truck that was robbed when we moved south."

"Ah, yes, I remember. Bad luck, that."

"I saw one in my uncle's collection, and I suddenly remembered

I had promised someone a copy years ago and forgotten completely about it. What do I do?"

"Who was the printer? I forget."

I told him.

"Well, write to him or call him and ask if he still has the bon à tirer. They usually save them, because sometimes they become valuable." He was talking about the final test print, on which the artist writes "bon à tirer"—ready for the press—and signs his name. "I must say, dear boy, I cannot get over the news of your Hasidic uncle's art collection. It is quite astonishing."

"My uncle's family can't get over it, either."

"I can imagine." He regarded me closely. "You don't look well, Ash. Are you recovered from Paris? How do you feel, really?"

"So-so."

"You must not let them affect you this way. You must get on with your work."

"That's what I came here to talk to you about. I'm going to stop painting for a while, Doug. There's been too much light these last years, and I need to rest awhile in the shade."

He looked shocked. "No painting at all? You are not thinking of ending your career simply because the Paris critics showed you a bad time."

"Not ending. Resting. Just resting."

"For how long, dear boy?"

"I don't know. Whenever it starts up again."

"This is most disconcerting. I had hoped we would have something from you for the fall season."

"Not this fall, Doug. Give my place to Max. Max always has something ready."

"Well, this is distressing. I do hope you are not quitting. Not doing the Duchamp thing, are you?"

"No, I don't think so."

"*Think?* You are upsetting me, dear boy."

We talked for a few more minutes about business matters and then shook hands. Normally he accompanied me to the elevator, but I told him I wanted to see the sculptures, and he went with me as far as the door to his office, a look of consternation on his face.

"You must take care of yourself. The art world cannot afford to lose an Asher Lev. There is too much ersatz work being done now, calculated gestures everywhere, cultural entertainment. Bear that in mind as you bask in your shade. Please give my very best wishes to Devorah and the children."

I went past the receptionist and walked slowly through the gallery. It was a little before noon, and there were about twenty people inside. Plush light-gray carpeting, inviting creamy white walls, soft lights, sensuous sculptures. A handsome woman moving among the sculptures looked at me for a moment and then said quietly to the man who was with her, "I think that's Asher Lev." I moved away from them. The two crucifixion paintings had first been shown in this gallery. This was where my parents had seen them, on the huge wall before the turn to the elevator. The look of horror on my mother's face; the frozen grimace of disbelief and shock on the face of my father. The murmuring of the crowd: "It's their faces on the paintings." Then my parents' raging departure from the gallery. The paintings were in a New York museum now, where they hung side by side in a vast gallery. On occasion people would come over to me: "We saw your crucifixions, Mr. Lev. Stunning." Or: "We saw your crucifixion paintings. What, exactly, were you trying to say? How does someone raised as a Ladover Hasid come to paint crucifixions?" In the early years I tried to answer their questions: I wanted to paint suffering, and there are no motifs in Jewish art that I could use as an instantly recognizable aesthetic vessel for the depiction of my mother's anguish during all the years my father traveled for the Rebbe and I journeyed for my art. I wanted to put her pain into my painting. I needed an aesthetic mold that immediately said: *Body and soul in protracted solitary torment.* I wanted ... I needed ... I required ...

Some nodded as if they understood. Most looked at me glassy-eyed. After a while I stopped answering their questions. It seemed to harden people's anger, those attempts of mine to explain, justify, rectify, elucidate, make amends. Who really understood the mysterious clockwork of the artist? I wished I had never needed to paint those crucifixions. I wished I hadn't caused all that pain. I wished they weren't in that museum for everyone to see. I wished ... I wished ...

I went out of the gallery and rode the elevator down to the street and walked quickly to the subway.

I got out at Ninety-sixth Street and Broadway. A haze of brownish dust and gasoline fumes hung over the dense traffic and crowded sidewalks. I walked along Broadway for a while, then turned down a side street that sloped toward a parklike spread of hillside studded with trees and bordered by a low stone wall. Beyond the wall lay a highway and the wide slate-gray expanse of the Hudson River.

I stood in front of a tall old building and was barely able to recognize it. The once grimy façade had been sand-blasted clean and the graystone exterior glistened in the sunlight. It had been a building of high deep lofts, with a front door of rusting metal and dirty glass, and a dim and cavernous interior hall. Now a green awning led from polished glass entrance doors to the curb. The interior was of light-gray marble veined with branching bluish lines. A thin man in a dark suit sat at a desk near the elevator, and on the wall behind him was a bank of television monitors. Where the lumbering and clanking elevator had once been, with its ancient folding iron gate and sliding door, there was now a glistening brass door with a small window in its upper section.

A uniformed doorman stood at the entrance under the canopy, heavy-shouldered, olive-skinned, dark-eyed, muscular. I saw him looking at me.

"Help you?"

"Someone I knew had a studio in this building once, on the fifth floor."

"Yeah? When was that?"

"Back in the fifties and sixties. I used to work with him."

"Yeah? Well, it's all condos now. The ones that owned the building, they made apartments out of the lofts."

"When did they do that?"

"About ten years ago. Who'd you say had a studio here?"

"An artist named Jacob Kahn."

"He didn't buy in?"

"No. He moved to France."

"Jacob Kahn. Don't know as I heard of him. What does he paint?"

"He's dead. He was a great sculptor. And also an Abstract Expressionist painter."

"I don't know anything about—what you call it. Is that the stuff with the paint all over the place? Yeah, I know about that. Lots of people couldn't buy in when they went condo. All the artists left. The owners fixed it up real good and sold it and made a pile. You should see it inside. Nice. But I can't let you in unless you got an appointment or know someone."

"Well, thanks."

"Sure. Don't mention it."

I walked down to the end of the street. It sloped steeply toward the river. Like the street I had lived on in Paris, where I had worked that first year and painted the crucifixions and met Max and Devorah: the narrow cobblestone street that ran into the boulevard. Max climbing to the top floor of the five-floor walk-up with Devorah that first time, bringing her to me because I had just completed the crucifixion paintings and would not answer the telephone and was oblivious to the world; telling her she could do a story on me for the magazine she wrote for; me answering the door naked to the waist and in my underpants and scurrying to put on jeans and a shirt, the two of them standing in the doorway, Devorah astonished and red-faced and Max laughing.

The urban highway beyond the wall was thick with speeding cars. A Circle Line tourist boat glided past on the water, going north, its passengers crowding the rails. River birds wheeled over a passing barge, white in the sunlight, calling. In a nearby playground children played in sandboxes and on monkey bars and swings, closely watched by mothers and maids. A young woman in a yellow sweater and jeans walked past me, wheeling a baby carriage. What did she see when she glanced at me? A middle-aged man, red hair and red beard going gray, a pale face, a windbreaker, baggy pants, a fisherman's cap. How startled Anna Schaeffer had been the first time she met me in Jacob Kahn's studio in that loft building now turned condominium! She had stared at my skullcap, my dangling sidecurls, which I no longer wear, my thin pale face. "You did not tell me," she said to Jacob Kahn. And Jacob Kahn replied, "He is a prodigy, Anna. A prodigy in payos." The glorious enormity of that studio. Its magnificent clutter. A tall wall of windows facing a cloudy sky that seemed to press down upon the sheets of glass; a skylight set in a slanted roof; bronze, stone, and wood sculptures scattered about everywhere; easels and canvases and worktables on trestles; and the heady smells of pigments and linseed oil and turpentine and raw stone and wood—the luscious perfumes of art. For five years I worked in that studio, traveling from our apartment in Brooklyn, once, sometimes twice a week, some weeks every day. Starting at the age of thirteen. Thirteen from forty-five. Thirty-two years. Do people see in my eyes the sense of rushing time that sometimes leaves me hollow with dread?

There was a wooden bench under a tree near the stone wall, and I sat down and raised my face to the sun that filtered through the bare branches. A warm and comforting caress, that sun on my face. A wind blew across my eyes; the branches softly stirred. Were those buds on that lacy canopy? In Saint-Paul the spring was in full riot, our terrace an Eden of flowers. Max Lobe would be going to terrace parties in Nice; John Dorman would be wandering among the flowers in his garden. He liked peering into a flower's heart. "The heart of brightness," he called it. "A peek into the mystery of being." Once I heard him refer to it as "the only opening worth thinking about anymore," and immediately apologize. "I'm a drunken old man," he said. "And a writer. What the hell can you expect from a writer?"

After a while, I left the bench and started back up the hilly street toward Broadway. Afternoon sunlight shone on the gleaming façade of Jacob Kahn's old building. The uniformed doorman looked at me as I went past him. The street seemed oddly disquieting, its shaded areas queerly angled, its noises muted: a Chirico street of uncanny shadows and dreams.

I took the subway back to Brooklyn. The sun was pale when I came out of the ground onto the parkway. I walked up Kingston Avenue and turned the corner into the street where my parents lived and saw immediately the flashing lights of the police car.

. . .

The car stood in front of my parents' home. A small crowd of neighbors had collected on the sidewalk. The lurid red and blue revolving lights of the police car reflected off their anxious faces. I heard the crackle of the police radio as I went quickly through the crowd.

The front door was open. Two uniformed policemen stood in the entrance hall with Devorah and my parents. Avrumel was near my father, clutching his Shimshon doll.

"Rocheleh hasn't come back from school," Devorah said when she saw me. Her eyes blinked nervously, and she looked ashen.

Rocheleh had sent Avrumel home with one of her classmates and had gone off somewhere alone. Devorah had called classmates, teachers, friends, acquaintances. Rocheleh was more than two hours late.

The policemen stood by, listening to Devorah talking to me in French. One of the policemen politely interrupted and asked Devorah for a description of Rocheleh. Hair. Eyes. Clothes. Distinguishing marks. Had there been a quarrel at home before she went off to school? Had she ever done anything like this before? Had she been in a fight with anyone in school?

"What did she tell Avrumel?" I asked Devorah in English.

"To go home with one of her classmates, who lives on this block."

"She didn't say anything about where she was going?"

"No. We've been through this, Asher."

My parents stood very quietly near the wall mirror. I saw my mother close her eyes and her lips move. My father did not put a supporting arm around her; they never held one another in someone else's presence.

"Does she have her medication with her?" I asked.

"Of course," Devorah responded.

"What medication is that?" one of the policemen asked.

"For asthma," I said.

He made a note in his pad. "Could that be disorienting?"

"No."

"We ought to call this in and get it to the hospitals," the second policeman said to his partner.

I felt the back of my neck go cold and a sudden chilling weakness in my legs.

"I have already telephoned the hospitals," my father said. "No child of her description was brought into emergency today."

"We'll do it anyway," the first policeman said. He went out. Through the open door I saw the crowd on the sidewalk and the police car and the flashing lights on the faces and on the trunks and branches of the trees.

"There are many cars with our people going through the entire neighborhood," my father said to me in Yiddish. "With God's help, she will be found." His face pale, his eyes dark with dread, his white hair in some disarray beneath his velvet skullcap, my father wore his fear visibly but with reserve.

"Exactly like her father," my mother said. She was trying to lighten the fear, and failing: her voice too high, her eyes wide and darting. "He went off on his own. Long walks, came home late, worried me sick. I would stand at the window, waiting. Exactly like her father."

"The gendarmes will find Rocheleh," Avrumel said in French to his Shimshon doll. "Wait and see."

A girl about Rocheleh's age came through the crowd and walked up to the house. She stood in the doorway: wide, dark, frightened eyes; long pale face; dark braided hair; high gray stockings.

"Rocheleh isn't home yet?" she asked in Yiddish.

"No," Devorah said. "We are very worried."

I recognized the girl, had seen her playing with Rocheleh on the terrace. "Sarah, what did Rocheleh say to you?"

"She said to walk Avrumel home and bring him to the front door."

"That's all?"

"She said to tell her mother that she would be home soon."

"In which direction did she go?"

"I don't know. She told me this in the schoolyard."

"Did anything happen in school today? Was there a fight?"

Her lower lip trembled. She was nearly in tears. "I don't know about any fight." She said she had to go home for supper and went out the door.

"Master of the Universe," I heard my mother say in Hebrew.

Her eyes were mirrors of the memories of all her own waiting—
for my father, for me. The past had suddenly been returned to her
by her grandchild.

The policeman was standing on the sidewalk and talking into
the radio transmitter. The red and blue car lights rotated and
flashed across his face and uniform. He seemed a character in a
grisly crime movie, the sort that Ladover Hasidim would never
permit themselves to see. A car came slowly along the street, its
emergency signals blinking. The policeman looked at the car. It
stopped behind the police car, but I could not see who was in it
because of the crowd. Avrumel loudly asked my father if the
Master of the Universe would soon find his sister. I saw my father
lift him and hold him and Shimshon in his arms. The policeman
who had made the radio call was walking back through the crowd.
There was a man with him I thought I recognized. It was a
moment before I remembered he had met us at the airport in his
car and brought us to my parents' home. He walked with his hat
tilted back jauntily, a smile on his face. The two men came out of
the crowd, and between them walked Rocheleh, carrying her brief-
case. She seemed calm and poised, unperturbed by the crowd
around her.

"Hello, Asher Lev," the man said. "I bring you your daughter."

"Rocheleh is home!" Avrumel shouted happily in French to
Shimshon from his perch in my father's arms.

"Where was she?" I asked.

"On the parkway, walking home. She is a very bright girl."

"Thank you."

"You are welcome. A mitzvah on my patrol night."

"Thank God," my mother said.

"You did well, Binyomin," said my father. "I thank you."

The man bowed slightly toward my father. Devorah was with
Rocheleh.

"Where were you?" Devorah asked. "Do you know what time
it is?"

"In the library," Rocheleh said, gazing at the crowd and the
police.

"The library at the beginning of the parkway?" I asked.

"Where you took us, Papa."

"Rocheleh, this is New York, not Saint-Paul. You do not go for long walks here by yourself. Couldn't you call us when you saw it was late?"

"I used up all my money on the copying machine. I had to borrow twenty cents from the librarian."

We were talking in French. The two policemen stood listening patiently. I told them where Rocheleh had been.

"The library," one of them echoed.

"The Grand Army Plaza library?" the other asked. They looked at each other. "Are you all right?" the first policeman asked her. "No one hurt you or bothered you in any way?"

"I am very well, thank you," Rocheleh said.

"Sorry about this," I said.

"Glad it ended this way," the second policeman said. "Got a kid of my own this age."

"We are very grateful to you," my father said.

"Doing our job," the first policeman said.

They went out of the house. My mother closed the front door on the street and the crowd.

We stood there in the entrance hall, looking at Rocheleh.

"I am very sorry for causing you all to worry about me," Rocheleh said.

"Why didn't you tell Sarah you were going to the library?" Devorah asked her.

"I was afraid she would say it was too far away and wouldn't take Avrumel home. You didn't have to call the police. I am not a child." She then announced that she was very hungry and was going to her room to put away her books and wash up for supper.

"Call your friend Sarah and tell her you're alive," I said. "And next time you're out late somewhere, use the telephone first and then the copier or whatever. That's why God let us invent the telephone. So we could save each other heartache."

Avrumel followed his sister out of the entrance hall.

A few minutes later, I passed by Rocheleh's room and asked her what she had been looking for in the library.

"I put it on my bulletin board, Papa."

My mother was calling us in to supper, and I did not stop to see where Rocheleh was pointing. After supper, I looked into her room and saw tacked to the cork bulletin board over her desk half a dozen clear photocopies of my two crucifixion paintings.

She had made one copy of each of the paintings, one enlargement of my face, one of my father's, and two enlargements of the face of my mother. The photocopies, each eight and a half by eleven in size, were arranged in three vertical rows and took up the entire surface of the bulletin board.

She was bent over her desk, writing.

"Rocheleh, can I disturb you?"

She looked up, squinting at me slightly through her glasses.

"Why did you bring these home?" I pointed to the photocopies on the bulletin board.

"Because I needed to."

"Do you know what they are?"

"They are copies of my papa's paintings about the way the god of the goyim died."

"You know about the crucifixion?"

"Of course. I am not a child, Papa."

"Who are they for?"

"They are for my English teacher."

"Your English teacher asked you to write something about my crucifixion paintings?"

"She asked us to write two hundred words about what our fathers do. I am writing about my father, who is an artist."

"Where did you find the reproductions you copied?"

"In a book about my papa in the library."

"They let you into the adult section?"

"I didn't ask to take the book out, Papa. I found it by myself and made copies of the pictures."

"What are you going to say about them?"

"That's what I'm writing now. I'm writing that my papa made those pictures because he is an artist. The book says you made them because there is no Jewish image that expresses suffering. I don't understand what that means. Why did you put Grandmother's face in the painting?"

"It's very complicated. One day, when you're older, I'll explain it to you."

"I am going to write what you just said. Is that what Grandfather looked like before his beard became white?"

"Yes."

"And that's you when you were a boy?"

"I'm a little older there than a boy. Rocheleh, listen, I don't think you ought to keep them up there on your wall like that. If your grandparents see them, they will be very upset."

"I'll take them down as soon as I finish writing. It helps me when I can see all of them together like that. I don't like the paintings, Papa. They give me a bad feeling."

"I'm sorry. Maybe you'll feel differently about them one day. Will you remember to take them down when you're done?"

"Yes."

I went along the hallway and looked into Avrumel's room. He was asleep, curled up in a corner of his bed, the new Shimshon doll on the pillow beside him. Tacked to his bulletin board was the pencil drawing I had made of the old Shimshon doll we had left behind in Saint-Paul.

I said to Devorah later in our room, "Wait till she finds the ones I painted of you after the wedding. She missed those in the book."

Devorah's face turned crimson. "You will please tell her I did not pose for those paintings. They are entirely from your memory and imagination."

"She won't believe me."

"Sometimes, my husband, I think you enjoy being wicked."

"Only when I'm with my wife at certain hours of the night."

"Did you ever think such a thing might happen when you made those paintings?"

"No. But even if I had, I would have painted them anyway. When I paint, I think of the truth of the painting. I try never to think of the consequences."

"Some truths are best left buried, Asher."

"Then God should not have given me this talent. I'm going to bed."

My father said to me as we walked to the synagogue early the next morning, "Your mother could not sleep last night. She kept remembering how you would come back late from school."

"Rocheleh won't do that again."

"She went to the library to do research?"

"Yes."

"On what?"

"On her father, the artist."

"I did not know there is a book about you."

"More than one."

"What is she writing about?"

"The crucifixions."

He stared at me a moment and shook his head. "There is no end to how your work pursues us."

I said nothing.

" 'A mistake once implanted cannot be eradicated,' " he quoted in Aramaic from the Talmud. "All these years, and I still do not understand why you do what you do. Does it satisfy you to do those things? Does it make you happy?"

"I've never known of a serious artist who was happy. Except maybe Rubens."

"Then why do you do it, Asher?"

"I don't know. I do it. Why do you work for the Rebbe?"

"For the sake of heaven."

"Maybe I do it for the sake of earth."

"What do you mean?"

"Maybe it's another way to get to the truth."

"Your crucifixions and those other paintings you have made are a way to the truth?"

"If there wasn't something true about my work, do you think people would bother with it? Someone told me there are sixty thousand working artists in Paris alone. Sixty thousand. Critics, artists, curators—why do they bother with my work? Why do they bother with *me*?"

"Who are those people, Asher? They are goyim. What do they have to do with *us*?"

"Do you think goyim are fools? Is that what you're saying?"

"They are not fools, Asher. But their way is not our way. They have nothing to do with us."

During breakfast, I said to Rocheleh, "Did you finish your composition?"

She nodded.

"You look very pretty. I like the bow in your hair."

"Grandmother bought it for me."

My mother smiled. "A small gift."

"It's school time," Devorah said to Rocheleh and Avrumel. "Breakfast is over."

"I must go to Boston today," my father said. "I will be back for supper."

"Have a safe journey," said my mother.

In the doorway to the house I asked Rocheleh, "Do you have the composition with you?"

"Of course."

"Who will bring me home today?" Avrumel wanted to know.

"Rocheleh will bring you home," Devorah said. "Today, tomorrow, every day. Understood?"

"Yes, Mama."

"Rocheleh, do you understand?"

"Mama, I am not a child."

We watched them go up the street together. "What are you doing today?" I asked Devorah.

"Writing. And you?"

"I'll think of something."

My parents left. Devorah was at the desk in our room. I went over to my uncle's house. Aunt Leah was home. She gave me the keys to the study and the attic. I spent the morning with my uncle's art collection.

I returned to my parents' house for lunch and found Devorah in one of her writing trances. I put together something from the refrigerator for the two of us and brought her plate into our room and put it on the desk. She sat bareheaded, her wig off, her neck long and slender. By the light of the desk lamp I saw the tiny grooves in the corners of her mouth and the beginnings of the lines in her smooth pale cream-colored cheeks. She looked all her fifty years during those moments of writing; wore all the weight of her age and memory.

Later, I went back to my Aunt Leah's house and was inside my uncle's study, lost in the paintings, when someone knocked on the door. It was Aunt Leah. There was a telephone call for me. They had called me at my parents' house, and Devorah had told them I was here. There was a phone in the bedroom; I could take the call there.

The phone was on the mahogany night table between the two meticulously made twin beds. I sat down on one of the beds—my uncle's? my aunt's?—and picked up the receiver. There was an odd trembling in my hand.

"Hello," I said.

"Reb Asher Lev?" It was a man's voice.

"Yes."

"Reb Asher, this is Rav Shlomo Greenspan. I am the principal of the yeshiva your children are now attending."

"Sholom aleichem."

"Aleichem sholom. Reb Asher, your daughter's English teacher and I were wondering about something. We were wondering if you could come into the school tomorrow and perhaps give a little talk about art to your daughter's class, and maybe answer some questions put to you by the children."

I looked at the walls of my aunt's and late uncle's bedroom. An exquisite garden by Bonnard. A vase of flowers by Chagall. A street scene by Utrillo. An explosive Expressionist landscape by Soutine.

"Tomorrow?" I heard myself ask.

"In the morning. Ten o'clock."

"Are you sure you want to do this?"

"Oh, yes. Very sure." He had a cheerful, boisterous voice and spoke without an accent. "By the way, your daughter's composition about your work—you know about the composition, yes?—it created a stir in the class. I was called in by the teacher. Maybe you should come a little before ten, so we can talk a few minutes."

"All right. Is there anything in particular you want me to say or do?"

"We leave that up to you, Reb Asher. You are the artist."

I hung up the phone and sat on the bed, looking at the paintings on the walls of my uncle's bedroom. The Soutine was magnificent: there it was, one of the birthplaces of Abstract Expressionism. How the Spaniard had disliked Bonnard! Once, entering a room with a Bonnard, he turned the painting to the wall. The Chagall flowers were lush; one could imagine their living scents. How still the Utrillo street was: heavy with melancholy and brooding. The silver mezuzah on the doorpost gleamed in the hall light. Why a mezuzah here and none on the doorposts to the study and the attic? Because he shared this room with his wife? Because there was no collection of monographs and drawings here and the paintings could be regarded as mere decorations? Another riddle. After a while, I went out of the bedroom and returned the keys to Aunt Leah and went home.

Rocheleh returned from school with Avrumel in tow and announced that she had read her composition to the class and some of the students were horrified. Many had not known about the paintings. They all knew about that man, the god of the goyim, the one that the goyim accused the Jews of having killed. How could Rocheleh's father make paintings having to do with that man? Wasn't Rocheleh's father a Ladover Hasid, a loyal follower of the Rebbe? Didn't the Rebbe speak to him in the synagogue just this past Shabbos in front of the entire congregation? Why would Rocheleh's father do such a thing? And how could Rocheleh write about those paintings and talk about them in the same room where there was a picture of the Rebbe? The principal had to be called in to quiet the class.

She told us her grade. A for content, B for spelling.

Devorah said she would like to read the composition.

"The teacher kept it to show some of the other teachers," Rocheleh said, and went off to her room.

Avrumel, clutching his Shimshon doll, let it be known that he, too, had had a busy day. He had listened to stories about one of the great rabbis of the Talmud, Rabbi Akiva, during the war against the Romans; about the Rebbe's grandfather and his fight against the Russian Communists; about the Rebbe during the big war against the Germans. Then he had played and made pictures. He was tired, he said, and wanted to lie down for a while.

My mother returned home a few minutes later and announced

that she had had a long, wearying, and worthwhile day. Teaching; a meeting of the university senate; a tenure committee meeting; a graduate colloquium on *glasnost* with an academician from the University of Moscow who had confided to her that the immediate effects of the new policy upon the Jews would be significant but he did not think the policy would succeed in the long run because of the power of the Communist Party and the byzantine maneuvering of the entrenched Soviet bureaucracy. But he could be wrong, he said. There might be surprises. It was like Peter the Great dragging Russia into Western civilization.

My father came home from his office, where he had stopped on his return from Boston. Over a cup of coffee, he informed us that some people had called the Rebbe's office during the day about a problem in the yeshiva that had to do with Asher Lev's daughter. Because my father had been out of the city, the problem had been handled by one of the younger men in the office.

" 'A mistake once implanted cannot be eradicated,' " my father quoted again, looking at me over the rim of his cup.

My mother, busy together with Devorah at the kitchen counter, asked me how my day had been. I said I had not done anything all day. Nothing.

"An artist," my mother said.

In our room that night Devorah said to me from her bed, "Do you want to know what I did all day, Asher?"

"What did you do all day, my wife?"

"I was writing, and all of a sudden I remembered something I had forgotten for more than forty-five years."

"What was that?"

"The time the Rebbe lived with my family in Paris before the Germans came. I was about four years old. One Shabbos at the table the Rebbe was singing zemiros, and suddenly he stopped and looked at me. For a long time, he just sat and looked at me. My mother thought he had become ill, but my father signaled her not to disturb him. I remember the Rebbe had black hair and a black beard and burning gray eyes. He looked at me as if he was seeing my beginning and my end. I thought his eyes would reach out and pull me into them. I began to be a little frightened, when suddenly he blinked a few times and continued to sing. I just remembered it today while I was working on the book. How strange time and memory are. That's what I did today."

I told her about the telephone call from the school.

"What will you talk to them about?"

"I'll think of something."

"Please do not do anything to embarrass Rocheleh."

"I cannot understand why they want me there. A talk about art to eleven-year-old children in a Ladover yeshiva. This must be divine punishment for painting those crucifixions."

"Go to sleep, Asher. You've had a difficult day."

"A difficult day? I didn't do a thing all day!"

"For you, my husband, that is the most difficult kind of day you can have."

Mist clung to the trees, and the early-morning air was gray and cold. I walked with my father to the synagogue. The machines used for resurfacing the parkway lay like dormant mammoths in the mist. After the service I mentioned to my Cousin Yonkel that I liked the paintings in his parents' bedroom, and he looked startled. I explained why I had been in that room.

"Did your father have paintings anywhere else?"

"My father's paintings are no concern of yours."

Sweet Cousin Yonkel.

I walked back with my father in a heavy rain. He had a cup of coffee and left immediately for his office. Devorah decided to walk with the children to school because of the rain. I sat alone at the kitchen table. My mother was at the sink, an apron over her dress.

"Have you thought what you will tell the children in the classroom?"

"I've thought, but I don't know."

"Do they ever ask you in Saint-Paul or Nice to talk to schoolchildren?"

"Not to go to the schools. Sometimes children come to my studio and ask me about my work."

"The schools organize that?"

"Yes."

"You look disturbed, Asher. Are you sorry you stayed?"

"No."

"It is giving your father and me much pleasure, your staying. The children are beautiful. It is so good to have time together. Do you notice how well your father gets on with Avrumel?"

"That part is nice."

"Are you bothered that you cannot paint? Do you need something built for you here? I can have a carpenter come in."

"I don't think I can paint now."

"You used to paint all the time in the apartment. It didn't matter that there was no space. There is so much space in this house."

I heard the front door open and close. Devorah came into the kitchen.

"It's pouring. Your son discovered that he enjoys parting the Red Sea. He didn't miss a single puddle between here and the yeshiva."

We sat around the table, drinking coffee and talking. After a while, my mother left for the university. Devorah's face took on a tired, drawn look.

"Are you all right, Dev?"

"Bad dreams. Sealed apartments."

"Can I get you something?"

"A new childhood, perhaps."

"Not even the Rebbe can make such a miracle."

"What are you going to tell the children in Rocheleh's class?"

"I have no idea."

"Poor Asher. Self-doubt even in the face of eleven-year-old children."

"What I don't understand is why they're even letting me in the front door."

I left the house shortly after nine-thirty. The trees were wet and dark, and there were rain puddles on the sidewalks and along the curbs. Rain dripped from the branches and drummed on the umbrella. The stores along Kingston Avenue were deserted. In the all-night dairy cafeteria I saw young men in dark suits and dark hats sitting at tables, drinking coffee, smoking cigarettes, and talking. I stepped into a stationery store and from its bearded, skullcapped proprietor bought a box of soft chalks of various colors. I looked around the store as the owner counted out the change.

Yudel Krinsky had once owned a store like this, a few blocks from here. A Russian Jew somehow saved by my father and brought to Brooklyn. My first drawing pencils, charcoal sticks, drawing pads, fixative, oil colors, canvases—bought from him. How I had loved that man! Dead now. In the ground not far from my Uncle Yitzchok, and the rain seeping slowly into his bones. Magnified and sanctified is the name of God. Along the parkway people walked leaning forward into the rain. Cars maneuvered tortuously through the roadway construction. The wet spring morning wore the dismal look of a dying winter afternoon.

The wide four-story Ladover yeshiva stood to the right of the Ladover headquarters building, facing the parkway. Rain fell heavily upon its windows and red-brick façade. I went quickly along the cement walk to the front double doors.

The entrance hall was large, its floor tiles a dark-brown brick design, its walls pale green and bare, save for the large framed color picture of the Rebbe on the wall opposite the doors. To the right of the hall was a door with a plaque on it that read MAIN OFFICE. I went inside.

The walls were covered with announcements, schedules, calendars in Hebrew and English, and a picture of the Rebbe. A stout woman with gray hair and half-moon glasses sat behind the reception desk. She looked up from her typewriter and her eyes drifted over my raincoat—one of my father's old coats, two sizes too large for me—and my bearded face and fisherman's cap.

"Can I help you?"

"My name is Asher Lev."

She stood up. "Rav Greenspan is expecting you." Standing, she picked up her phone and pushed a button. "Mr. Lev is here." She put down the phone and came around the desk. "Please," she said. I followed her to a door marked OFFICE OF THE PRINCIPAL. At the door, she said in a low voice, "I love your work, Mr. Lev. I saw your last show in the Schaeffer gallery. Was it three years ago? The painting of the women dancing, the one that was so—uh—controversial. I loved it. I bought one of your prints. The waiter in the café in Paris. I love it."

"Are you and your husband collectors?"

"I collect a little. My husband, of blessed memory, has gone to the True World. He was a great follower of the Rebbe. But all he knew was diamonds. I do this"—she indicated the office—"to keep busy. Are you staying long? You must go back and make more pictures." She opened the door for me, and I stepped into Rav Greenspan's office. She closed the door quietly behind me.

A tall, barrel-chested, dark-bearded man stood behind a desk, listening to the telephone in his large hand. He kept moving back and forth behind his desk. He saw me and, reaching across the desk, took my hand in a powerful grip, put the mouthpiece against his chest, and said, "Sholom aleichem," in a resonating voice.

"Aleichem sholom."

He waved me into a chair and proceeded to speak in Yiddish into the phone—something about a consignment of textbooks that had not yet arrived. "What kind of businessman are you?" I heard him say. "I have forty children waiting for those books, and you don't know where the shipment is. Next time I'm going to your competition." I looked around the office: pale-green walls; low freestanding bookcases stuffed with textbooks; school schedules on the bulletin board alongside his desk; and, on the wall behind the desk, a picture of the Rebbe. A wind had risen, and through the single window across from the desk I saw the rain slanting and blowing in waves across the parkway and splattering upon the panes, obscuring the trees and the cars and the people on the street. Rav Greenspan had put down the phone and was talking to me. Did I want a cup of coffee? Tea? It was good of me to come. He knew I was here for only a few days and time was precious. Deepest regrets about my uncle. A great man, a generous man. Did I mind it if there were teachers present from other departments in the school? Good. Was there anything I wanted or needed? There were no restrictions on what I could say; the yeshiva was not, God forbid, a prison. I could speak for twenty minutes or half an hour and then ask for questions. The children had been encouraged to come with questions. They were all eager to meet me. He looked at his watch. "It's time. The class should be ready. Are we ready? Good."

I followed him into the main office, past the receptionist, and out into the entrance hall and along a brown-tiled corridor to a flight of gray marble stairs. We climbed the stairs. Would I be interested in knowing how many students were in the school? Four hundred and fifty-two. Kindergarten through eighth. "The curriculum is the same as when you were here. Sacred subjects in the morning, secular subjects in the afternoon. Friday morning, secular; Sunday morning, sacred. The high school is on Ocean Parkway. No room for it here. We're growing. Every year we grow, thank God." Through small windows set in classroom doors I saw teachers, students, blackboards, pale-green walls. Rav Greenspan went on talking. He had recently seen a program on public television about the artist Jacob Kahn. Had I known Jacob Kahn?

Yes, I had known him.

"The program didn't mention that he was a follower of the Rebbe. He wasn't an observer of the commandments, but he had great belief in the Rebbe, as his father had before him, and from time to time he gave us prints and drawings we could sell through his dealer, a Mr. Douglas Schaeffer. That way he helped out the yeshiva. A fine man. It's good for us to have a world-famous artist as a follower of the Rebbe. It shows the children that the world knows of the Ladover Hasidim."

"Now all you need is a novelist or two, a rock singer, and Barbra Streisand, and you can conquer the world."

The lightheartedness I thought I had put into my witless remark was entirely lost on him. He turned a weight of sudden earnestness upon me. "You know Barbra Streisand? Can you get her for us?"

"What do you mean, 'get her'?"

"For a concert. Or to sing at a dinner."

"I don't know Barbra Streisand."

"If we could get someone like Barbra Streisand, I could put up the new building in a year. We need a new building. We have a property two blocks from here for a junior high school. Ah, here we are. This is the classroom."

We stopped in front of a door in a quiet corridor. Through the small window I caught a glimpse of a young, stunningly lovely dark-haired woman seated behind a desk, and rows of children's faces, and a tall wall of windows wet with rain.

"You should know," Rav Greenspan said, "that the teacher is not Jewish. She is one of the best teachers in the school. All our teachers are either Ladover or not Jewish. We do not have nonobservant Jews teaching here. They are bad examples for the children. Come, they are waiting for you."

He pushed the door open, and I followed him into the room. The door closed to the soft hiss of its hydraulic stop.

Every head in the class turned to look at me.

The teacher rose to her feet behind the desk. She wore an ivory-colored, long-sleeved, high-necked blouse and a dark-blue skirt. As if on signal, all the students immediately stood.

"Miss Sullivan," Rav Greenspan said. "This is Mr. Asher Lev."

"It's an honor to meet you," she said. She did not offer me her hand.

"Please take your seats," Rav Greenspan said to the class.

Only the quietest of shuffling sounds were heard as the students quickly sat down.

Miss Sullivan moved away from behind the desk and stood before the wall of windows, silhouetted against the gray light of the wet morning. Her black hair was combed straight back in a French twist.

Rav Greenspan stood in front of the class. "Children, good morning. I want to introduce to you Mr. Asher Lev, who is a very famous artist. Many of Mr. Lev's paintings are in museums in America and Europe. He grew up in this neighborhood and went to this yeshiva. He has agreed to come here this morning and talk to us about art and about his work, and to answer any questions you might have. Here is Mr. Lev."

Rav Greenspan moved away from the desk and went along the wall opposite the windows to the back of the room. He stood leaning against the wall and folded his arms across his chest. Standing there in the rear of the room, he seemed suddenly a dark and vigilant guardian presence.

I stood alone in front of the class.

There were about twenty-five students in the room, all girls; the boys' division of the yeshiva was in the adjoining building. They sat in four rows, each at a separate desk. In the fifth row were three adults, two of them women; the third was an elderly gray-bearded man in a dark suit, a dark tie, and a dark hat. I remembered seeing him in my Uncle Yitzchok's house during the week of mourning but did not know who he was. Rocheleh sat in the second row, near the wall of windows. Through the ponderous silence in the room I heard the sudden oncoming and receding blare of the horn of a passing car.

I saw them all looking at me, and I did not know what to say. It was warm in the room, and I had begun to sweat beneath my fisherman's cap. Outside, the rain continued to fall, and the corners of the windows were misted over. I looked at the rows of faces. Girls in ponytails and braids and short curls and side-parted loose hair, the long side held by a barrette. Thin faces, square faces, rectangular faces, owlish faces, round faces, cylindrical faces, triangular faces, pale faces, flushed faces. There was Rocheleh, waiting. One of the girls had red hair and sat low in her chair, as if afraid to be seen. She was watching me out of wide blue eyes. Eyes, eyes, waiting. Start as you would a drawing. Start with a point. A second point. A line. A clear and immediate truth.

"Good morning," I heard myself say, and cleared my throat and said it again. "Good morning," and somehow went on. "I once studied in this yeshiva, and I thank God for keeping me alive and enabling me to be with you today. I studied English and wrote compositions and stared out the windows a lot. But an artist is supposed to tell the truth, and the truth is that mostly I used to draw in my notebooks and get my teachers very annoyed at me." A whisper of subdued laughter skittered through the class. "My classmates thought I was strange. That was almost all I ever did. Draw, draw, draw. Does anyone here draw, draw, draw all the time?"

All were silent.

"But everyone draws sometimes."

A general nodding of heads.

"What sorts of things do you draw?"

Immediately hands went up throughout the room. I called on one after the other.

"A Pesach Seder."

"A succah, and the lulov and esrog."

"Dancing with the Torah."

"Playing with bows and arrows on Lag Bo'Omer."

"Houses."

"Gardens."

"Moshe Rabbenu on Mount Sinai."

"A Shabbos table."

"Noah in the ark."

"Very good," I said. "It looks like all of you draw. Now tell me this. Why do you draw?"

Again the hands shot up. Rocheleh sat quietly near the windows, watching.

"It's fun," one girl said.

"I like it," said another.

"The teachers tell us to," said a third.

Soft laughter spread through the class. Miss Sullivan smiled. Rav Greenspan stood leaning against the rear wall, his arms folded across his barrel chest. The two women and the man in the back row sat listening impassively. Rocheleh had not yet raised her hand. The rain fell in sheets on the parkway and it seemed as if night had come.

"Why do teachers do that?" I asked.

"It helps us remember things better," a girl in the front row said.

"Yes. What else does it do?"

Silence.

"Doesn't it do something else, when you draw? Think about it for a moment. Anybody."

Tentatively, from the second row, a girl in braids: "I think that sometimes it helps me express my feelings."

"How does it do that?"

"When I'm angry I use a lot of red."

"Does anyone else here ever draw their feelings?"

"Sometimes if I don't like someone I make the faces ugly," a girl not far from Rocheleh said.

The two adult women in the back row glanced at each other.

"How about if you draw someone you like?" I asked.

"I try to make them pretty."

"Does anyone else here ever draw her feelings?"

There was silence.

A trickle of sweat slid with an insect touch along my spine. I wanted to step to the blackboard behind me and scratch my back against it. The silence continued. A number of the children shifted restlessly in their seats. What else? Think. Think! Two points. A line. Form. Space. The two-dimensional plane. Color. A painting. The paintings on Uncle Yitzchok's walls. Cézanne, Renoir, Matisse, Bonnard, Chagall, Utrillo, Soutine.

"Are all drawings the same?" I asked.

"No!" resounded throughout the room.

"How are they different?"

"Some are better than others," the girl sitting directly in front of me said.

"How are they better?" I asked her.

"They're better. They're more real."

"They're truer," a second girl said.

"You mean they're more like photographs?"

"That's right," the second girl said.

"Does everyone agree that a drawing that's like a photograph is better than one that isn't?"

Amid the general nodding of heads I saw Rocheleh; she was the only one in the room shaking her head. But she said nothing.

"You mean a drawing like this"—I removed a stick of orange chalk from the box I had bought at the stationery store and drew rapidly on the blackboard a child's representation of a ram: awkward spindly legs, poorly proportioned head and body, scraggly horns—"is less true and less real than a drawing like this?" I drew, using a single unbroken line, a realistic contour of a ram, then quickly shaded its underside with the length of the chalk, giving it the appearance of three-dimensionality.

From the girls in the room came a universal "Yes!"

"But what about this kind of ram?" I drew with no shading a line abstraction of a ram, exaggerating the contours of its hindquarters in order to give emphasis to its power, and embellishing the soaring swirl and majesty of its horns. "Which is the truer ram?"

Silence. I saw their wide young eyes moving from drawing to drawing—the childish, the realistic, the abstract—and saw, too, the faint smile on Rocheleh's face.

"Aren't all three different ways of seeing the same object?" I said. "The first is a child's way of seeing. The second is a realistic way of seeing, the way a camera might see, for example. And the third"—I pointed to the abstract drawing—"well, what is the third? How would you compare it to the second?"

"It's stranger," a girl said.

"Why is it strange?" I asked.

"It looks strange," she said. "I've never seen a ram like that."

"Have you seen a ram like this?" I pointed to the second drawing.

"Sure. In the zoo."

"How many have seen a ram like this?"

Most of the hands went up.

"You've all seen this kind of ram?" I said. "This small? This color?"

A murmur of confusion ran through the room.

"What is this?" I asked, pointing to the drawing.

"It's a drawing," a girl said.

"Exactly," I said. "It's a drawing. It's the closest to the way the ram looks to our eyes on the outside. Now, what is the difference between this outside look at the ram and this third drawing of the ram?"

A girl in the fourth row—long dark hair, dark eyes, thin lips—raised her hand. "Is the third drawing an inside look at the ram?"

"What do you mean by 'inside'?"

She did not respond.

"Who made the drawing?"

"You did," she said. "Your inside."

"Yes. What do we call that sort of inside look? There's a very important word for it that you all know."

A tense silence and the restive straining for the key that unlocks the mystery. I let a moment go by.

"Anybody?"

I gazed into the rows of upturned faces. In the rear of the room the two women, the gray-bearded man, and Rav Greenspan all seemed riveted, eyes fixed upon me, anxiously waiting. Miss Sullivan stood silhouetted against the windows, her eyes wide, a faint, fixed smile on her lips. A ram. Had I seen a ram in the zoo while walking there with Devorah and the children? Of all the animals I might have chosen to draw, why had I chosen a ram?

Rocheleh raised her hand. Then the timid-looking redheaded girl near the back raised a hand, tentatively, and I nodded at her.

"It's an interpretation," she said.

"Yes," I said. "Exactly. It's an interpretation. Now tell me this. Who do you study who is a great interpreter? Not of drawings but of words."

There was another silence.

"You carry him around," I said. "You study him every day. He's the best and clearest of all the interpreters."

"Rashi!" half a dozen voices called out. One of them was that of Rocheleh.

"What's another word for interpreter?"

"Commentator," voices cried out.

"Is Rashi the only commentator?"

"No!"

"Who are some of the others?"

"Ibn Ezra."

"Ramban."

"Rashbam."

"Are they all the same?" I asked.

"No!"

"Do they all have the same ideas?"

"No!"

"What are they interpreting?"

"The Torah!"

"They are all interpreting the same thing. But they see parts of it differently, don't they?"

"Yes!"

"Why do we print them all in the same Chumash? Why don't we print only one of them? Why don't we print only Rashi?"

"The Chumash we use in our class has only Rashi," a girl said tentatively. "But my brother's Chumash has the others."

"The Chumash in the synagogue has all the others, too," the redheaded girl said from near the back of the room.

"Why do we print all the commentators?" I asked again.

"It's more interesting," a girl said.

"How can we choose which ones to leave out?" another asked. "You have to print all the good ones. My brother says that it's exciting to have all of them."

Thank God for your brother, I thought. "Very good. Yes. Art

begins when someone who knows how to draw goes from this"—I pointed to the second drawing—"to this." I pointed to the third. "When someone interprets, when someone sees the world through his own eyes. Art happens when *what* is seen becomes mixed with the inside of the person who is seeing it. If an exciting new way of seeing an old object results, well, that's interesting, isn't it? That's the beginning of serious art. Here, let me show you what I mean."

I erased the rams. I looked carefully for a moment at Miss Sullivan: high cheekbones, thin straight nose, oval features, dark eyes, dark hair combed back flat into a French twist. "Here are the different ways three great modern artists would have seen and drawn the same person. The first one is an artist named Matisse."

I wrote his name on the blackboard. Over the name I drew in a single continuous line with blue chalk the face of Miss Sullivan. It leaped, instantly recognizable, from the chalk onto the blackboard. There was a stirring throughout the room, and murmurs of surprise and recognition.

"The second is by an artist named Modigliani."

I spelled out his name on the blackboard and in red chalk drew Miss Sullivan, high-necked and with exaggeratedly high cheekbones and almond-shaped eyes, emphasizing through the cylindricality of her neck the charm and refinement I sensed in her bearing.

"The third artist is Picasso. How many of you have heard of Picasso?" Hands went up. "Good. Almost as many as have heard of Asher Lev." Rav Greenspan joined in the general laughter.

I wrote the Spaniard's name on the blackboard, and I drew Miss Sullivan in ochre as he had once painted Gertrude Stein: solid, sculpted, Iberian, a creature more stone than flesh but with eyes that penetrated into the farthest future. I looked over my shoulder and saw Miss Sullivan staring open-mouthed at the drawing. You thought of inviting me here, Miss Sullivan. The power of art, Miss Sullivan. On your young and lovely flesh.

"Three different ways of seeing the same person," I said. "It makes life richer to be able to see in so many different and exciting ways. Just as the Rebbe and Ladover Hasidus make Torah and Yiddishkeit richer."

I picked up the board eraser from the ledge and raised it over the first of the drawings. There were sudden gasps behind me, and someone cried out, "Oh, no!" I put the eraser down and turned to the class.

There was a long, uneasy silence. I was sweating heavily. A mist seemed to have entered the room, filling the air and blurring the faces and dulling the overhead fluorescents. I felt gritty with the chalk on my fingers.

"Maybe this is a good time to ask questions," I said.

A moment went by. A girl with glasses too wide for her thin face slowly raised a hand.

"When did you start to draw?" she asked.

"When I was about four or five."

"I mean to seriously draw."

"When I was about four or five."

I pointed to the girl who sat in front of Rocheleh. She had wispy brown hair and a fair-skinned freckled face. She wanted to know where my ideas came from.

"Everywhere. The street, the house where I live, the people I meet, this classroom. Everywhere."

A round-faced, heavyset girl waved a hand at me. "Are you a Ladover Hasid?" she wanted to know.

The pause was longer this time, heavier. Rav Greenspan shifted slightly on his feet. The two adult women glanced at each other. The gray-bearded man had removed a pad from his jacket pocket and appeared to be taking notes.

"I was born a Ladover Hasid," I said. "I studied Ladover Hasidus. In Nice, which is the city in France near where my family and I live, I pray in a Ladover synagogue on holidays and sometimes on Shabbos. We don't live within walking distance of the synagogue, and so we move in with friends whenever we go there to pray. I am a follower of the Rebbe. I believe in the future of Ladover Hasidus."

The girl said, before I could call on anyone else, "My father said you do things that are against the Torah. You make images that are bad, like what Rocheleh told us about yesterday."

A pronounced stirring of bodies and a murmur of voices, a palpable unease, washed through the room. There was a general subdued nodding of heads. Rocheleh threw the girl an angry look.

Miss Sullivan stood very still, her head slightly raised in what I thought might be a faint gesture of defiance. The gray-bearded man was writing steadily in his pad.

"The Torah says you should not make images for the purpose of worship," I said.

"It says, 'You shall not make for yourself a sculptured image, or any likeness of what is in the heavens above, or on the earth below.'" The girl was reading the verse from a piece of paper on her desk. She had come prepared.

"We may not make them for the purpose of worship," I repeated. "Doesn't the verse continue? Doesn't it say, 'You shall not bow down to them or serve them'? There were images in the First Temple, the temple of King Solomon. There were images in ancient synagogues. There are images in prayer books and in Pesach Haggadahs."

"Not the kind you make," a high voice called out from somewhere in the middle of the room.

"I'm trying to make new images."

"Why?" the same voice called out. It belonged to a thin, angry-faced girl with short blond hair.

"Because he's an artist," another girl said.

"It's against the Torah to make such images," another girl said.

"It's stealing time from the study of Torah," yet another called out.

"So is this English class," another girl said loudly.

Remarks flew about the room. The girls were talking to one another as if I were not there. I was losing control of the class.

Rav Greenspan moved away from the rear wall and stood just behind the fifth row of chairs. Miss Sullivan took a step away from the wall of windows toward the desk. The two seated women looked at each other nervously. The gray-bearded man stopped writing and glanced over his shoulder at Rav Greenspan.

My only weapons now: the stick of chalk and my trembling fingers and the image that leaped into my mind. I went quickly to the blackboard and began to draw a portrait. Silence invaded the room as soon as I completed the outline of the features, and when I drew the eyes, the stillness was so pervasive I could hear plainly the beating of my heart and the drumming of the rain on the windows. I finished the drawing and put down the chalk and faced the class.

"Is this also stealing time from the study of Torah?"

The silence went on. The girls sat staring at the face on the blackboard. I saw Miss Sullivan faintly smile. Rav Greenspan glanced at his watch, looked at me, shook his head, then looked at the blackboard. Everyone in the room was staring at the face on the blackboard: the face of the Rebbe as he had looked many years before. Across the length of the room, I saw the eyes of the two women and the gray-bearded man and Rav Greenspan, and read the sudden spontaneous longing that reached from them toward the portrait, and felt myself shiver.

A hand went up; wispy brown hair, dark intense eyes, thin pale lips, creamy complexion highlighted by touches of pink. "Rocheleh explained to us yesterday why you made those pictures of the cruci—the cruci—you know what I mean. What I don't understand is why you had to use that picture for suffering. My father says you could have used something else, something more Jewish, like the binding of Isaac."

There was a general nodding of heads. The gray-bearded man was writing in his pad. The two women smiled at each other. Rav Greenspan moved back to the wall and stood with his arms folded across his chest. I tried to imagine the discussions that must have taken place in the homes of these children the night before when they had told their parents I would be coming to the school next day. Asher Lev, Ladover Hasid. Asher Lev, troublemaker. Asher Lev, poisoner of children's minds. Why had they invited me? Why had they let me in the door?

"The binding of Isaac?" I said. "Is that really a theme for suffering?"

Using variously colored chalks, I drew a young boy bound on an altar upon a pyre of wood, and a bearded man towering above him, long-bladed knife in his upraised arm, and, vaguely visible in the background, the majestic head of a ram. I worked quickly, changing chalks, feeling the hardness of the blackboard, barely conscious of the flaking of the soft chalks, shading colors into one another by rubbing the bottom of my right middle finger across the surface of the slate board. I drew the boy with his eyes wide open, his thin neck arched back, throat exposed to the poised blade; the bearded man anguished and determined, his free hand clutching his chest in a gesture both pitying and purposeful—all of it frozen by the chalk and the work of my fingers. This is the Cave of Now, I told myself in strangely incoherent fashion. A drawing. A painting. Capture something forever. Can see it all at one time. No future, no past. Only a perpetual this-moment, only nowness. It was done and I turned and they were all staring at it—the students, Miss Sullivan, Rav Greenspan, the women and the gray-bearded man—staring at the drawing in colored chalks on the blackboard. I looked carefully at the drawing and saw the faces I had made and was suddenly bewildered and dismayed and wondered if Rocheleh had looked closely, too, and I moved in front of the drawing to conceal the faces as best I could. With swift movements of my fingers I redrew the faces. It took less than one minute. Then I turned to the class.

"The binding of Isaac is about a man who believes so deeply in the Master of the Universe that he is willing to sacrifice to Him his only son. What does that have to do with the theme of long and lonely suffering?"

Closed faces gazed at me; silent lips, silent eyes; and the rain on the tall windows of the room.

"That's the reason I made those paintings."

I doubted they understood what I was saying. Sixty-year-olds had not understood it over the years. And these were eleven-year-olds. I was sweating heavily. What a waste of everyone's time! I picked up the eraser and turned toward the blackboard.

A gasp went through the room like a wind, followed by a spontaneous, many-voiced "No!"

Startled, I put down the eraser and faced the class.

Rav Greenspan was coming quickly up the side of the room near the windows. He stood next to me.

"We thank Mr. Lev very much for his words and his art. The class is over."

I glanced at Rocheleh. She sat silhouetted against the windows; her face looked grainy, its features indiscernible. I nodded to Miss Sullivan and followed Rav Greenspan out of the classroom. In his office I retrieved my too-large raincoat and said goodbye to the receptionist. "Give us more paintings, Mr. Lev," she said, and winked.

I stood with Rav Greenspan at the door to the school. "Was that really worthwhile?"

"Oh, I think so," he answered cheerfully. "The teacher will continue to discuss it with the students. The two other teachers who were there will discuss it with the older grades. It was very worthwhile. Listen, are you sure you can't help us out with Barbra Streisand?"

I looked at him and shook my head.

"That's too bad," he said sadly. "We really can use some big-name help with that new building."

I stood on the front steps of the school and looked out at the rain. "Frankly, I don't understand why you called me and let me in the door."

"Mr. Lev, we called you and let you in the door because the Rebbe told us to. The elder gentleman who was in the class is Rav Shimon Seligson, from the Rebbe's office. Go in peace."

He patted my arm and walked away toward his office.

I hurried along the parkway in the rain. The windows of the stationery store and the cafeteria were misted over. I walked up our street under the trees and into the house. Devorah was at the desk in our room and did not look up when I entered. I went into the bathroom and washed the chalk from my fingers and then washed the sweat from my face. I could not get all the chalk from my fingers and from under my nails. The colors of the chalk stained the towel and the bottom of the sink. I scrubbed the white porcelain and watched the colors swirl and disappear down the dark opening of the drain.

That afternoon Avrumel returned from school with his right cheekbone bruised and his lower lip split. I was in the living room, looking out at the rain on the front lawn, when he came home with Rocheleh.

"Look at you," I said. "Where did you fall?"

He did not respond but went along the hallway and into his room. His face was very pale.

"A boy in the school hit him," Rocheleh said.

Avrumel came out of his room, holding his Shimshon doll.

"What happened?" I asked.

He went past me into the kitchen.

"What was it about?" I asked Rocheleh.

"He wouldn't tell me. He said the nurse took care of it."

"You don't know anything about it?"

"No. Is my mama writing?"

"Yes. Rocheleh, what was the reaction to the talk I gave?"

"There was a lot of discussion in the class after my papa left. Everyone liked the drawings you made of Miss Sullivan."

"What happened to the drawings on the blackboard?"

"I don't know. They were still there after class ended."

"No one erased them?"

"No. I liked the drawing you made of the Rebbe. Some of the students said you shouldn't have drawn it, because now it can't be erased. Papa?"

"Yes."

"Why did you put yourself and Avrumel into the drawing of the binding of Isaac?"

She had noticed it. Sharp-eyed, quick-witted Rocheleh. Who else had seen it? "I don't know. It was a surprise to me."

Behind her glasses her eyes took on a disbelieving look. "My papa draws things without knowing it?"

"Sometimes. Then the drawing tells me what I'm trying to say."

"What did my papa want to say with the drawing of Avrohom and the binding of Isaac?"

"I don't know. I need to think about it."

"I don't understand how my papa can make drawings without knowing what they mean."

"You want to understand everything at the age of eleven? Leave a little for later on. Don't you have homework?"

She went to her room.

I moved toward the kitchen. Avrumel was sitting at the table with his Shimshon doll. I poured milk into a glass and put it on the table in front of him. He waited until I sat down, and then he began talking to the rag doll. "Shimshon, you want to know what happened today? I'll tell you what happened today. During recess, one of the boys in first grade asked me if I was Avrohom Lev, son of Asher Lev, and I said yes, I was. The boy said my papa was a sinner. That's right, a sinner, and a man who shamed the Master of the Universe in public. My papa! What would you have done, Shimshon? I shoved him. He hit me. We rolled around on the ground until a teacher stopped us. That's what happened."

A moment went by. Avrumel picked up the glass of milk, put it to his mouth, wincing as the glass touched his split lip, and drank. He put the glass down. "If that boy talks to me that way again, I will hit him," he said to Shimshon. He drank some more milk. "No one will talk to me that way about my papa."

I heard footsteps in the hallway. Devorah came into the kitchen. "Rocheleh told me Avrumel was hurt."

I told her what had happened. "The sins of the father are being visited upon the son," I said. "We never had trouble like this in Nice."

"This is not France," she said. "This is Brooklyn."

Avrumel finished his glass of milk and got down from his chair, holding tightly to Shimshon.

"Are you all right?" Devorah asked him.

He looked up at her and did not answer.

"Ça va, Avrumel?" I said.

"Ça va, Papa," he said, and left the kitchen.

"I will call Rav Greenspan about this," she said.

"We should have gone home Tuesday the way we planned."

"The Rebbe asked you to stay. Did we have a choice?"

"No," I said.

My father returned from his office, took a look at Avrumel's face, was told by Avrumel what had happened, and marched off to the phone in his bedroom. While he was there, my mother came home. Avrumel told the story again in the kitchen, over a second glass of milk and some of my mother's cinnamon-and-sugar cookies, which he had some difficulty chewing because of the lip. My father returned from the bedroom. Avrumel went over to him. My father lifted him and held him. Avrumel's hands clasped my father around his neck. Wisps of my father's white beard flowed across Avrumel's cheeks and shoulders, enfolding him. Together, they went out of the kitchen.

"Wherever you go, your art causes trouble, Asher," said my mother, shaking her head.

"What a troublemaker I married," Devorah said, and flashed me a smile. "Why can't you make pretty pictures like Max does?"

"My mother used to ask me that when I was a child."

"I remember," my mother said.

"What did you answer?" Devorah asked.

"I answered that the world is not a pretty place, why should I paint lies?"

From a distant part of the house came the sound of my father singing. His deep, faintly nasal voice drifted through the halls and into the kitchen. He was singing a song I had never heard before, a slow, sweet, melancholy Yiddish tune about a deer that runs away from hunters and is lost in a dark wood. After a long journey the deer comes upon a clearing, where there is an old stone house with a softly glowing white light over the door. An elderly bearded man lives in the house. He has barely enough food for himself, but he takes the deer in, and the deer lives with the man and is happy. And it turns out that the man is the blessed and saintly Ba'al Shem Tov, the founder of Hasidism, the first and the greatest of all the tzaddikim.

Drawn by the sound of my father's voice, Rocheleh came out of her room and into the kitchen. The four of us, in the kitchen, listened to my father singing to Avrumel.

The next day Rav Greenspan called an assembly of the entire school, boys and girls. He announced that hospitality to guests is a commandment from the Torah. It was practiced by Avrohom our Father, and it would be practiced as well by all the students of the Ladover yeshiva. There were guests in the school from France, and they were to be treated as Avrohom our Father treated the three angels. That was the wish of the Rebbe, he said, who had called him on the telephone that morning. Did anyone have any questions?

There were no questions.

Rocheleh and Avrumel told Devorah and me about the assembly when they returned from school. Avrumel said that the boy with whom he had fought had come to school with purple marks around his left eye. In the rolling around on the asphalt, Avrumel's shoe had connected with the boy's eye. "I didn't mean to hit him," Avrumel said. "It just happened." The chance blow to the eye was not without its ensuing satisfactions. Avrumel was now regarded by many in his class as someone to be reckoned with, and there were even those who now looked upon him with a mixture of awe and caution. The fist—or, in this instance, the shoe—is not always decried by Ladover Hasidim.

I asked Rocheleh if the drawings I had made the day before were still on the blackboard. She said they had been erased before she got to school.

Later, I said to Devorah, "Why do you suppose they handled the fight that way?"

"What way?"

"An assembly. It could've been done in five minutes just with the two boys. Why the whole school?"

"I don't know."

"It strikes me as a little strange. The whole school called out for a little incident like that."

"The Rebbe telephoned."

"That's what I mean. Why did the Rebbe get involved with something as trivial as that?"

"Your father must have told him about it."

"I'm sure he did. Why? I was in school fights all the time. My father never interfered, not once. And to go to the Rebbe. Why didn't my father call Rav Greenspan?"

"What's troubling you, my husband?"

"I don't know, Dev. I'm ready to go home."

"In a week or so. Do you want the children to go back with the taste of fighting in their mouths? For the sake of peace. Another week or so. All right, my husband? For the sake of good memories and peace."

Zemiros and riddles filled the air of our Shabbos table that Friday night. Avrumel climbed onto my father's lap and fell asleep. He slept there, snoring lightly, as we chanted the Grace After Meals. His lip was healing, and his bruised cheek had turned a dull purple with dry under-the-skin blood. Devorah put him to bed and returned to the kitchen. Rocheleh, wearing one of my mother's aprons over her light-blue dress, helped Devorah and my mother with the dishes. My father asked me if I would like to study with him for a while, and we went into the living room and studied together one of the works written by the Rebbe's great-grandfather, reading the passages aloud and explaining them to each other. We studied the passage about one who is able to engage in the study of Torah and instead occupies himself with frivolous matters; such a one suffers severe penalties. In like manner, "he who occupies himself with the sciences of the nations of the world is included among those who waste their time with profane matters, insofar as the sin of neglecting the Torah is concerned.... Moreover, the uncleanness of the science of the nations is greater than that of profane speech...." We spent a good deal of time trying to understand the reasons for that. We studied that the sciences are forbidden because they lead to the defilement of the intellectual faculties in the divine soul, and then we came upon a passage that stated the study of science was permissible if "he employs these sciences as a useful instrument, as a means of a more affluent livelihood to be able to serve God, or knows how to apply them in the service of God and His Torah. This is the reason why Maimonides and Nachmonides, of blessed memory, and their adherents engaged in them." We studied that "all lusts and boasting and anger and similar passions are in the heart, and from the heart they spread throughout the whole body, rising also to the brain and the head.... But the abode of the divine soul is in the brains that are in the head, and from there it extends to all the limbs...." We studied about "the completely righteous man" in whom the evil inclination has been converted to goodness, who utterly despises the pleasures of this world and finds no enjoyment in the mere gratification of the physical appetites instead of seeking the service of God, because the physical appetites originate from the sitra achra, and whatever is of the sitra achra is hated by the perfectly righteous man. We read the words of the great sage Rabbi Simeon ben Yochai: "I have seen superior men, and their numbers are few. The reason for their title of 'superior men' is that they convert evil and make it ascend to holiness...."

My father looked up from the book and gazed off into space, his dark eyes glittering. He combed his long beard with his fingers and swayed slightly back and forth in his armchair and began to sing a Ladover melody. The words and music gently filled the living room, caressing the still air. The curtains were open, and I saw the lawn and the trees, tall and ghostly in the streetlights. A squirrel raced crookedly across the lawn, leaped upon the trunk of a sycamore, and vanished into its dark labyrinthine branches. I sat and listened to my father sing and closed my eyes and let the melody move against me, and it seemed to me at that moment that all was possible, that the world still held open the luminous doors of reconciliation, and I promised myself I would at least advance to the threshold and peer in and see what awaited me inside. I sat very still, listening to my father sing.

The next morning in the synagogue Avrumel sat with my father, huddled inside the cool white world of his large tallis. The Rebbe did not appear. My Cousin Yonkel was his usual surly self and barely acknowledged my presence. It was a warm spring day washed with brilliant sunlight and canopied by a clean blue sky. We walked home beneath budding trees. Rocheleh said the blue color overhead reminded her of the sky over our home in Saint-Paul. Avrumel, his bruises nearly healed, was walking with my parents. Devorah asked Rocheleh if she was homesick. No, she said. She liked it here. There were girls her age everywhere, her teachers were very good. "But I don't like the weather," she said. "It's like the weather of Paris."

"Without the beauty of Paris," I said.

"There is beauty here, Papa," she said. "Making new friends is beautiful. Being close to the Rebbe is beautiful."

Devorah smiled deeply.

"Yes," I said. "You're right. They are both beautiful."

Later that day, some of my parents' friends came over to the house, and we sat on the terrace, talking. The warm afternoon air, bathed in sunlight, carried faint hints of coming summer days. My mother, helped by Devorah, served cakes and juice. I listened and on occasion joined the talk, drifting in and out of the waves of conversation. It felt oddly comforting to be here, enfolded, accepted. One of those present was a computer engineer; another, a mathematician. Near me sat a professor of philosophy and a professor of classics. All either lived within walking distance of the synagogue or were spending the Shabbos with relatives or friends in the neighborhood. They were all followers of the Rebbe. We talked about Hasidus and Torah and the Ba'al Shem Tov and the Rebbe. The Ba'al Shem Tov asked: Why was evil, or the appearance of evil, created? So that after surmounting the most difficult of barriers man can enjoy all the more his coming into the presence of the Master of the Universe. We told stories about other Hasidic Rebbes. Menachem Mendel of Vitebsk claimed he was not a miracle worker, only the Ba'al Shem Tov could make miracles, could issue a decree and God would fulfill it; but he, Menachem Mendel, would pray for his Hasidim that they have children, good health, and a means of making a living. Someone told about Nachman of Bratslav, who believed in the virtues of solitude. A man should spend at least one hour each day alone in a room or a field, engaged in secret dialogue with the Master of the Universe. And a man should think only of what he has to do for God that day, and it will not be too burdensome for him. All a man has in the world is the now, the day and the hour where he is, because tomorrow is an entirely different world. Someone else told about Aaron Rokeach of Belz, who found it difficult to rebuke his people, always discovered good in them, no matter what they did, and who would not permit his synagogue to use electricity because the same current provided light for the nearby Catholic church.

The professor of philosophy, a man in his early sixties, trim and silver-haired, with keen blue eyes and a lively demeanor, asked me what I thought about Chagall being buried in a Catholic cemetery in Saint-Paul. I told him I thought it was shameful and scandalous; for the first time in two thousand years, Jews produced a world-class artist, one who helped shape the modern period—and he's buried in a Gentile cemetery because his assimilated family wanted him nearby and felt that the Jewish cemetery in Nice was too far away, or was too Jewish. I could not go to the cemetery in Saint-Paul and recite a chapter of Psalms over the grave, because entry into such a cemetery is forbidden to a religious Jew. I could see the cemetery from where I lived, and every time I looked at it I thought of Chagall buried there. It was an anguish. I saw my father watching me as I talked; his face wore a troubled look, as if he thought I might end up that way, too, if I continued my life as an artist.

The professor of classics, a handsome-looking woman in her fifties, asked me what I thought about the breakdown of the canons of aesthetic judgment in contemporary art now that Picasso was dead and modernism was over, and we talked about that for a while. Someone, I think it was the mathematician, mentioned having recently seen the film *Au Revoir les Enfants* and urged everyone to see it. I glanced at Devorah, who was sitting next to my mother; she stiffened perceptibly but remained quiet. I thought it curious that a follower of the Rebbe, in the course of a Shabbos-afternoon conversation, would recommend a film, even a film on the Holocaust. This was not the usual sort of Ladover Shabbos talk. They were interesting people. I could live with such people. Maybe I'll surprise all of you, after all. I was a little drowsy—the warm air, the sun, the play of light through the now densely budded sycamore—and I drifted away from the conversation.

In the evening my father and I returned from the synagogue, and my father chanted the brief Havdalah Service. Avrumel held the braided candle; Rocheleh, the spice box. Shabbos was over.

In our room a few minutes later, Devorah said that she would like me to take her to see *Au Revoir les Enfants*.

I said I didn't think it was a good idea, and whom could we get to watch the children.

"I asked your parents. They will be happy to stay with the children."

"You know what happens when you see movies like that, Dev."

"I cannot let them dictate my life to me, Asher. If I let them do that, they remain the masters and I remain defeated. They dictated my life to me for two years. If you don't want to go, I'll go alone."

We took the subway to the Manhattan theater where the film was playing. There was a long line on the street in front of the theater. The street was ablaze with neon lights and crowded with strollers and young people on dates. We waited in the line to get our tickets, then we waited inside the theater. There was a long line in front of the popcorn counter. Devorah looked pale and said nothing. We sat and watched the film.

The film is about Jewish boys who are brought to a Catholic

boarding school south of Paris near Fontainebleau during the Second World War. Their Jewishness is kept secret, and they try to blend in with the other students. But they are betrayed and, together with the priest who is the headmaster, are taken away by the Germans. The boys and the priest perish in the Holocaust.

I glanced repeatedly at Devorah in the course of the movie; her face looked white in the flickering lights reflecting off the huge screen.

She was very quiet during the subway ride home. The parkway and residential streets were dark and deserted, the trees like vaguely menacing sentinels. We let ourselves into the house. My parents and the children were asleep. I brewed up some coffee, and we sat in the kitchen.

"Memories," she said, her eyes blinking nervously. "The things we think we've forgotten."

"I wish we hadn't seen it."

"You protect me too much, Asher. Do you want me to hide from the world? I was hidden long enough."

"You don't have to keep punishing yourself because you survived and the others didn't."

"To remember is not a punishment, Asher. To remember is a victory against the sitra achra, against Hitler, may his name be erased. The film is a sanctification of the name of God. Why should I not participate in it?"

She sipped from her cup. She had removed her wig. Her long neck and cropped head and ashen features gave her the appearance of a concentration-camp victim. I stared at her and shuddered.

Later, in our room, Devorah lay in her bed with the lights on and her hand over her eyes.

"Dev, I wish you wouldn't insist on seeing those kinds of movies."

She turned away from me.

"Dev?"

"Leave me alone, Asher. Now I need to be left alone. Please do not turn off the lights."

She fell asleep with all the lights in the room burning.

. . .

I woke in the middle of the night and felt her sliding into the bed beside me. She was trembling, and her skin was hot and dry. The lights were on. Her face was flushed, and her eyes looked frenzied. I held her to me and listened to her talk.

"I can't remember the food we ate. I remember everything, but not the food. Isn't that strange?"

"I don't know, Dev. Is it?"

"I remember the smell of the cold air. Like stones. Like caves. Dear God, it was cold in that apartment!"

"Try to go back to sleep, Dev."

"There was no soap. We all had body lice. And scurvy. You see the things I remember. But I can't remember what we ate. I know we never had meat and almost never had bread. I remember the man who would bring us our food. I've told you this before, haven't I, my husband?"

"Yes. But tell me again."

"He was bald and had a cleft palate and sometimes he wore his pants unbuttoned in front. Eight months he brought us food, and one day he didn't come. We ate nothing. I told you this."

"Yes."

"Then an old woman came. 'I am from the resistance,' she said. 'Armand has been arrested. I will bring your food from now on.' She had a face like wrinkled paper. A pale-blue shawl. A ragged coat. White hair. She smelled like someone who did not bathe. Twice a week she brought us our food. But I can't remember what we ate. Why is that?"

"I don't know, Dev."

"I remember Max's father once gave the woman money to buy two kilos of butter on the black market. She had to walk a long distance. She returned with the butter wrapped in newspaper. We stood around watching Max's father undo the wrapping. And when the newspapers were all off, we saw it wasn't butter but an old shoe. Someone had substituted the shoe for the butter right under the old woman's nose. The old woman was furious and said she would go back the next day to the one who had sold her the butter, but Max's father said not to do it, he didn't want to start trouble, he didn't want anyone asking her who she was and was she buying all that butter for herself or for someone else. Max's father was nervous all the time. I remember that, my husband. Very clearly. A little man with a skullcap and a goatee standing in a dark corner and talking to himself. That used to frighten me, seeing Max's father like that, in a dark corner, talking to himself."

"What did he say?"

"I don't know. Whenever he did that, he would talk in a language I couldn't understand. After a while Max's mother would go over to him and take him into their bedroom. She would tell me children's stories from books she remembered by heart. I told you this. She had been a librarian in the children's section of the library in their arrondissement. Stories about a bull that refused to fight, and an elephant that could fly, and a little girl and her brother lost in a forest. Many stories. She would tell them to me again and again. You see how I remember all these details, but I can't remember what we ate."

"We'll ask Max when we see him."

"You know what I especially remember? Max always needed colors. He was preparing a portfolio for after the war so he could show it when he went looking for a job. He kept asking his father for money for colors. His father said he didn't have enough money for food, how could he keep giving him money for colors? Max said his father didn't care about him, didn't want him to be an artist. Once there was a terrible quarrel. It was after the business with the black-market butter and the shoe. I was so frightened. I was sure the neighbors would hear and call the police. Max didn't get the colors. You see all the things I am able to remember, Asher. But I can't remember what we ate. He is like a big brother to me, my Max. I am so tired, but I'm afraid to fall asleep. I was that way in the apartment. Always afraid to sleep. I thought the police would come and take away Max and his parents while I slept, and I would wake up and find myself all alone in the apartment."

"Shall I tell you one of your children's stories?"

She laughed softly. "You are so good to me, my Asher. I am sorry for all the misery I cause you."

"Oh, Dev, don't say that. I love you."

"What did you see in this wreck of a woman when Max brought me into your studio that day?"

"You mean what did I like about that beautiful young woman Max brought to interview me?"

"Yes. What?"

"That she was smart and looked ten years younger than her age."

"Thank you."

"That she seemed a good person."

"Thank you again."

"That she came from a Ladover family and, amazingly, knew about art."

"Max was a good teacher."

"That she looked at one of my drawings hanging on the wall and said it was an important work but she didn't like it."

"It is an important work, and I still do not like it."

"That she let me draw her face after the interview."

"That was a good drawing, and I did like it."

"And I was able to see her as my wife and the mother of our children."

"I would have been the mother of many more if there had not been the miscarriages."

"That is God's will, my wife."

"Is it? Is it? Why couldn't it have been God's will for at least one person in my family to survive? I would have someone of my own blood to talk to about what happened."

I held her. She was trembling.

"Isn't it strange that I can't remember what we ate? Two years of eating in that sealed apartment, and I can't remember a single meal. Asher, I am not sorry we saw the movie. It's a fine movie. Even though sometimes, sitting in a dark theater, I suddenly remember the dark apartment. If it's all God's will, my husband, there must be a plan. Don't you think there must be a plan?"

"Who knows? Maybe there's a plan."

"When I found out what happened to my father, I didn't think I wanted to live. When Max's mother told me my mother was also gone, I *knew* I didn't want to live. Living with Max's parents, going to the high school and then the Sorbonne, and then writing for the magazine—all that time, I didn't really want to live. When I met you I began to think there might be a plan. A person has to have a reason for living, and the best reason is another person. Together they can make a plan for their lives. What if we're carrying out a plan God has made? Do you understand me, my husband?"

I held her and felt her trembling and after a while she fell into an uneasy sleep. Lying awake and listening to her breathing, I tried to imagine her two years in that apartment and could not. From beyond the terrace door I thought I heard the sounds of mocking laughter and feet shuffling toward the tangled darkness of the sycamore.

In the synagogue two mornings later, Cousin Yonkel looked more dour than usual. From time to time I caught him glancing at me and thought I saw on his sallow features a burning rage odd even for him. I went over to him after the service and asked how things were, and he muttered something about "trouble with those disgusting idolatrous abominations" and stalked off. Cousin Nahum, looking embarrassed, murmured, "Good morning, Asher," and hurried away.

The parkway had little traffic. There were tiny leaves on the trees, fragile against the blue sky. On the way back to the house with my father, we stopped to pick up the Sunday *Times*. The front page was full of the raucous maneuverings of the American presidential campaign. France would soon be going through a national election. The powerful French right-wing nationalist party frightened Max with its racist rhetoric. Everywhere, disturbances in the ground of being. And here, among the Ladover of Brooklyn, in the heart of the Ladover world, the Rebbe was eighty-nine years old— and no one talked openly of succession, not a mention of it, not a word. Without a doubt the redemption would come first. But what if . . . ? Not a word.

Walking back to the house, my father told me he needed to be in Paris at the end of June on a mission for the Rebbe, and how nice it would be if we could go over together. I said the end of June was weeks away and we would probably be returning to Saint-Paul around the beginning of next week. He said, without looking at me, "All of you?"

"Of course."

"As you wish, Asher."

Later that morning, on her way out of the house to the university, my mother knocked on the door to the guest room, where I was sitting at the desk, staring blankly at my drawing pad. She stood in the doorway, looking lovely in a dark-blue suit and a creamy white blouse, an attaché case in her hand. My father had gone to his office, and Devorah was out somewhere, shopping.

"Can I interrupt you for a moment, my son?"

I told her she wasn't interrupting; I wasn't really doing anything.

"Your father tells me you are thinking of leaving soon."

"Devorah said she would talk to you about it."

"Doesn't it make sense for the children to finish the school term here? It is only a few more weeks."

"Devorah and I have to get back. We've got our work."

"I don't understand, Asher. You cannot do your work here? Devorah says she writes very well here. Do you need a studio? Can't you talk with Douglas Schaeffer about studio space in Manhattan? Or, if you wish, we can easily rent something for you in the neighborhood that you can use as a studio." She came into the room. Her face was flushed, and her brown eyes shone strangely; there were touches of high color on the planes of her cheekbones. "Perhaps the children can go to our summer camp," she said.

I stared at her.

"Do you have a summer camp for the children in Saint-Paul?"

"No."

"What do the children do all summer?"

"There are things to do. They swim in Max's pool."

"The children would love our summer camp. Think about it, Asher. Talk to Devorah."

She went up the hallway. I heard the front door close. I sat at the desk, staring at the empty page of the pad.

Devorah came home a while later, laden with packages. I followed her into the kitchen. She said my mother's suggestion was something to consider seriously. First we would talk to the children, she said. If they liked the idea, then we would decide one way or the other.

"Can Rocheleh go to summer camp?"

"I don't know." She was emptying the bags and putting food into cabinets and the refrigerator. "I will call your parents' doctor and ask him."

"Is there summer camp for five-year-olds?"

There was a Ladover day camp, she said. She had seen it advertised in the school.

"I've got to get back home, Dev. I've got work to do."

"This can be a very good experience for the children, Asher. There are not many children their age they can play with during the summer. And August is impossible with all the tourists in Nice and Saint-Paul. You don't really see it; you're in your studio all the time. This might be a blessing for the children."

"I promised Max I would work with him in Paris."

"You can go to Paris. What is preventing you from going to Paris?"

"Where will you be?"

"I don't know. Why don't we talk to the children first? We can't know anything until we talk to the children."

We ate lunch and afterward I went over to my uncle's house. Aunt Leah opened the front door. She wore an uncharacteristically disheveled look: the light-blue housedress she had on seemed lumpy, and her wig was awry. A strange coldness invaded her eyes when she saw me.

"What is it you want, Asher?"

I asked her if I could spend time with the art collection.

"Not today," she said.

"I won't be in anyone's way."

"Now is a bad time, Asher."

"I'll come a little later, then."

"All today will be a bad day."

"Are you feeling all right, Aunt Leah?"

"How can you ask if I'm feeling all right? My husband is dead, and he left me heartache. How can I be feeling all right? Please excuse me, Asher. I must go upstairs and lie down."

I returned to my parents' house and spent the afternoon in the living room, alternating between staring out at the lawn and reading Rilke's *Letters on Cézanne*. A passage reached toward me from the pages:

With regard to his work habits, he claimed to have lived as a Bohemian until his fortieth year. Only then, through his acquaintance with Pissarro, did he develop a taste for work. But then to such an extent that for the next forty years he did nothing *but* work. Actually without joy, it seems, in a constant rage, in conflict with every single one of his paintings . . .

I thought I heard a soft, distant whistling and looked up and saw no one. I went on reading:

. . . old, sick, exhausted every evening to the edge of collapse by the regular course of the day's work (often he would go to bed at six, before dark, after a senselessly ingested meal), angry, mistrustful, ridiculed and mocked and mistreated each time he went to his studio—but celebrating Sunday, attending Mass and Vespers as he had in his childhood . . .

I closed my eyes. A bird trilled softly from deep within the sycamore, then was silent. The book felt strangely insubstantial, as if it would float away. I held it tightly and opened my eyes.

. . . there was a conflict, a mutual struggle between the two procedures of, first, looking and confidently receiving, and then of appropriating and making personal use of what has been received; that the two, perhaps as a result of becoming conscious, would immediately start opposing each other, talking out loud, as it were, and go on perpetually interrupting and contradicting each other. And the old man endured their discord, ran back and forth in his studio . . . with green apples scattered about, or went into his garden in despair and sat. And before him lay the small town, unsuspecting, with its cathedral; a town for decent and modest burghers. . . .

Looking and receiving . . . appropriating and making personal use of . . . and before him lay the small town, unsuspecting . . .

Around the supper table Devorah talked to the children about the summer. Avrumel didn't know what day camp was and, when told, informed Shimshon that he wanted to go home for the summer and be with Uncle Max and swim in his pool. Rocheleh seemed frightened at the prospect of spending the summer away from us: what would happen if she had an attack? Both children said they wouldn't mind staying here at Grandmother's and Grandfather's house and finishing the school term in the yeshiva in Brooklyn.

"We have not decided anything yet," Devorah said to them. "We will think about it."

"At least stay until the summer," my mother said.

"If we stay, I can be in the school play," Rocheleh said. "My teacher asked me to take a big part. It's about Devorah the prophetess."

"Your father and I will discuss it," Devorah said.

In the synagogue that evening, Cousin Yonkel kept throwing me raging glances.

"What's wrong with your brother?" I asked Cousin Nahum. "He's looking at me as if I've done him harm."

"Ask my brother," Cousin Nahum said with a strange edge to his voice, and walked away.

"What's happening with my cousins?" I asked my father on the way home. "Suddenly they seem to have become my enemies."

He shrugged and did not respond.

I was alone in the house the next morning when the phone rang. The sound resonated shrilly throughout the empty rooms. The phone was on a stand in the hallway between the kitchen and the living room. I let it ring for a moment, then put down my drawing pad and went to it. The receiver felt oddly cold in my hand.

I heard a woman's voice. The voice said this was Alice Tomley of the law firm of Saperstein, Schneerson, O'Connor, and Diamond. She was calling for Mr. Diamond and wished to speak to Mr. Asher Lev.

"I'm Asher Lev."

Would I wait just one moment while she put Mr. Diamond on the line?

I waited. That voice on the phone. Eighteen years ago. Some things are never forgotten. Like Rocheleh's face on the night of her first attack: rigid with terror, white as death. Like the Sunday the Spaniard died. The king is dead, long live the king. The Rebbe, too, is a king. That voice. The Angel of Death. Muffled. Sibilant. The *s* sounds drawn out. A little like the sounds one of my teachers used to make scraping chalk along a blackboard. Who erased the drawings from the blackboard in Miss Sullivan's room? I should not have drawn the face of the Rebbe. Why did I do that? And Avrumel's face as the face of Isaac. Why?

"Mr. Lev?" The man's voice was clear, deep.

"Yes."

"Asher Lev?"

"Yes."

"My name is Moshe Diamond. Are you the nephew of the late Mr. Isaac Lev?"

"Yes."

"Mr. Lev, our law firm drew up your late uncle's last will and testament. I am calling to inform you that according to the terms of the will, you have been named the trustee of your late uncle's art collection."

"I beg your pardon."

"Your uncle has made you the trustee of his art collection. There are some stipulations that will have to be met. But you have been given very broad discretionary powers over the entire collection."

"What stipulations?"

"Mr. Lev, the details of this matter are best not discussed over the phone. A letter outlining the terms of the will insofar as the art collection is concerned will go out to you tomorrow. If you have any questions, please feel free to call me. It would be best for all concerned if you could come to our offices in a week or so to sign documents, though we could mail them to you if you are out of the country. I understand you live in France."

"Yes."

"When are you returning?"

"We're not sure yet."

"Well, as I said, it would be helpful if you could come over to the office in a week or so. I'll have my secretary get in touch with you as soon as we have all the necessary papers drawn up."

"Thank you."

"By the way, Mr. Lev, I am a great admirer of your work and

own two of your paintings, the Israeli soldier standing guard on the Temple Mount and the one that shows an old man putting up a mezuzah. It's good to talk to you. Goodbye."

He hung up.

I put the receiver down and stood there, staring at the phone and feeling the trembling of my hands. After some moments, I lifted the receiver and tapped in a number. A woman's voice answered.

"Schaeffer Galleries."

"This is Asher Lev for Mr. Schaeffer."

"One moment, please, Mr. Lev."

There was a very brief pause.

"Hello, dear boy. How is the weather?"

"The weather in Brooklyn isn't bad, all things considered."

"My dear fellow, are you still in Brooklyn? Have they made you a prisoner?"

"Doug, I need some advice."

I told him about the call from the lawyer. He let me go on without interruption. When I was done, there was a long silence.

"Doug?"

"I am here, dear boy."

"What exactly does it mean?"

"I think, Ash, it means that you can do nearly any damn thing you wish with your late uncle's art collection."

"He said there were stipulations."

"Did he tell you what they were?"

"No. He said there was a letter coming and he would like to see me in his office to sign some papers."

"Ash, take my advice and do nothing, say nothing, sign nothing. I will immediately call my lawyer and ask him how you ought to proceed. Trustee over that entire art collection, you say? Astonishing. Give me the name and phone number of the lawyer who called you."

"His name is Moshe Diamond. I don't have his number."

"Give me the name of the law firm. Do you remember that?"

"Yes." I told him.

"We will let the lawyers talk to each other. They are splendid at that. He gave you no indication at all concerning the stipulations?"

"No."

"I will call you first chance I have. Goodbye, dear boy. Astonishing news."

He did not call back that day.

In the synagogue that night, both my cousins turned their backs to me. My father saw, and shook his head. On the way home in the dark, I told him about the call from the lawyer and said, "You and Mama knew all the time."

"Yes."

"Why didn't you tell me?"

"My brother, of blessed memory, gave me and your mother the information in strictest confidence. How could we possibly tell you before the lawyer did?"

In the kitchen later that night, with the children asleep, I recounted to my parents and Devorah the details of the phone call from the lawyer, and asked my parents if they knew anything about the terms and stipulations of the will.

"Yes," my father said. "But I am not permitted to tell you."

The lawyers talked to each other for days. I roamed the neighborhood, read the Rilke book on Cézanne, did some drawing, visited the art museum on the parkway and saw the Jacob Kahn paintings that hung on its walls: swirls of densely textured abstractions: a painter in a struggle with his canvas. One afternoon I stood before one of his huge canvases and imagined him in paint-splashed trousers, stripped to the waist, paint on his white-haired chest, paint on his grizzled features, sweat on his face, sweat in his armpits, working. He looked at me briefly, and vanished.

Then a phone call from my uncle's lawyer brought me by subway to a skyscraper in Manhattan and paneled law offices and a carpeted conference room with a long glass-topped mahogany table and leather chairs and much solemn talk with sober-faced lawyers and many pieces of paper to sign. Douglas Schaeffer's lawyer, a trim, middle-aged man with a soft voice and a courtly manner, was there, together with Uncle Yitzchok's lawyer, Moshe Diamond, a tall, dapper man in his early forties who wore a charcoal-gray business suit, a pink shirt with a white collar, a dark-gray silk tie, and a dark-gray knitted skullcap. On one of the walls of his office hung his undergraduate degree from Columbia and his law degree from the Harvard School of Law. We sat at the long table in the conference room and he explained the stipulations. I had been given total control of the art collection. I could do with it as I saw fit. I could sell paintings and buy new paintings with the funds acquired from the sales; I could lose money or make money; I could keep it intact or dissolve it. But at the end of each year, any profits generated by the collection were to go to the Ladover organization.

The lawyers spoke in subdued voices. Sunlight shone through tall sealed windows. Across an expanse of rooftops I saw the maze of urban roads and bridges and the distant sheen of the East River and jetliners on the final approach to La Guardia Airport. Miles beyond lay Kennedy Airport and the plane home. I longed to be home, locked in my studio, if not to paint then at least to stare fearfully at the vast stretch of challenging canvas mounted against one of the walls, muted light falling upon it through the translucent overhead panes. Home! I had come for a funeral and a week of mourning—and now this!

"What happens if I refuse my uncle's request?" I asked Moshe Diamond.

He adjusted his tie, looked at his fingernails, and gazed out the window. "In such an event, the entire collection will go to your uncle's children," he said.

On the paneled wall opposite the wall of windows hung prints by Chagall, Miró, and Agam, along with the first print I made in Paris, with the help of Jacob Kahn, using carborundum. There was another copy of that print in Uncle Yitzchok's collection, and I wondered if he had acquired both and given one to his lawyer as a gift. I remembered Lucien Lacamp helping me carry the heavy load of artist's proofs of that print up the five flights of stairs in the apartment house on the Rue des Rosiers. We had sweated up that narrow wooden staircase beneath that load of heavy paper. I had made him a promise then and had forgotten it. One of the truly righteous Gentiles of the world. A forgotten promise. What had he thought of me? Truly a desecration of the name of God. Like the burial of Chagall in the cemetery in Saint-Paul. Desecrations unbalancing the world. So many things to correct. So many things to do to give a balance to the world.

I signed the Declaration of Trust. Moshe Diamond explained that I would have to file an account with the court, a formal document listing the appraised worth of each work in my uncle's collection. The appraiser would have to be an individual widely recognized by the art world. It was likely that the Internal Revenue Service would request its advisory panel to turn in its own appraisal. In any event, I would receive further details concerning the appraisal document at a later date.

There were more papers to sign. Each was carefully read by Douglas Schaeffer's lawyer before I put my name to it.

On the way out of the conference room, Moshe Diamond said to me, "Mr. Lev, may I speak with you a moment?"

He removed from the inside pocket of his jacket a sealed envelope and handed it to me. "Your uncle, may he rest in peace, specifically asked me to give you this in the event that you accepted the trusteeship over the collection."

I put the envelope into a pocket.

On the busy street outside the building I thanked Douglas Schaeffer's lawyer. How long would it take to appraise the worth of the collection? I asked him. "Weeks," he said. "Maybe months. It depends on who does the appraising." Yes, Douglas Schaeffer could act as the appraiser. No, the court did not have to approve my choice of appraiser. "Douglas will certainly help you with that, if you wish."

"Thank you."

"Is it a valuable collection? Douglas was a little vague as to what it contains."

I told him what was in the collection.

He stood there in the middle of the crowded Manhattan street and listened, and his eyes widened.

"Your uncle was a Hasid?" he asked.

"Yes."

"A strange sort of Hasid."

"A complicated man, as I'm discovering."

"How do your cousins feel about this?"

"Probably cheated and certainly very angry."

"Well, if that's the case, you might want seriously to consider moving the entire collection to a safe place as soon as possible. People who feel cheated and angry sometimes do things they later regret."

"What's involved in moving it?"

"I'll look into it for you. Well, good luck, Mr. Lev. I hope this trustee matter doesn't keep you away too much from your real work. I'm one of your admirers. I think your painting of the legless man in that township outside Cape Town is a masterpiece."

"Thank you."

"I read somewhere that you had trouble getting your drawings out of South Africa."

"The customs people gave me a bad time."

"Did they?"

"They said they were false and subversive works."

"Like the French frontier police who thought that some of Picasso's Cubist drawings were plans of the country's defenses."

"I never heard that."

"Yes. When he worked with Diaghilev in Rome. Well, goodbye, Mr. Lev. Good luck with the collection. Call me anytime you feel I can be of help."

He walked off into the crowd.

It was nearly one o'clock. I went into a crowded dairy restaurant and ordered fruit salad. I took the envelope from my pocket. It was a white business-size envelope; my name was on the front, handwritten in black ink. I opened it and removed a single sheet of cream-colored writing paper, at the top of which was embossed my uncle's name in block letters, ISAAC LEV. The text of the letter was handwritten in Yiddish:

My Dear Asher,

If you are holding this letter in your hands, then two things have taken place. I have gone to the True World, and you have consented to accept the responsibility for the future of my art collection. The Master of the Universe, in His infinite wisdom, has called me to Him, and I accept His judgment with faith and humility. I have asked that you take responsibility for the care of my collection of art because I do not trust my children to do it.

They are not bad children, but they have no understanding of the true value of such a collection. Whereas, my Asher, you will know what to do with it. You will know that such loveliness, though born of the soul and mind of the Gentile world, can be made to enhance the name and presence of the Master of the Universe. Ever since my visits to your apartment in Paris and your home in the south of France, where I saw on your walls your own art collection, I have lived with the hope that perhaps there are not two realms, the sacred world of God and the profane world of Gentile art, but that great art can also be for the sake of heaven. It is my wish, my nephew, that as you deal with these works of art you will always bear in mind the Master of the Universe. May these works also be transformed into "the work of My hands, to glorify Me." My Asher, for all the years that I have been blessed with the ability to gaze joyously at the works of human hands, I thank you. I wish you the greatest of the creations of God, wisdom and a good heart, as you deal with the loveliest of the creations of man. I ask that you not show this letter to anyone, not even to your parents. It is a covenant between the two of us, a covenant for the sake of heaven. Your uncle, who loves you and has always admired and loved the work of your hands.

And he signed his name in Hebrew.

I reread the letter, folded it, unfolded it and read it again, put it back into the envelope, and put the envelope into the inside pocket of my jacket. On the subway ride back to Brooklyn I looked into the window opposite my seat and saw my uncle gazing back at me, happily smiling and smoking a cigar. "Art can also be for the sake of heaven," he said inside the dark and dusty window. He waved the cigar at me and vanished.

I got out at the Kingston Avenue station and walked beneath trees suddenly rich with young leaves to my parents' home.

The children were in their rooms. My father returned from the office and came into the kitchen, where I was sitting with Devorah and my mother. I told them about my conversation with Uncle

Yitzchok's lawyer. My parents did not seem surprised. Devorah stared at me in astonishment.

"What did you tell him?" my father asked.

"I accepted."

"You accepted?" He looked startled. "What did you accept?"

"To become the trustee of the art collection."

"Asher," my mother said. Her face was pale.

I looked at them. "What's wrong?"

"Was that wise?" my mother asked.

"I don't understand. The lawyer said I had a choice."

"You had a choice," my father said. "But you did not choose wisely. There will be no end to the trouble this will cause." He shook his head. "In certain matters my brother was not wise."

"Can Asher change his mind?" my mother asked.

"Asher can change his mind anytime he wishes," my father said.

"I don't want to change my mind," I said. "It's a privilege to be able to oversee such a collection."

My parents fell silent.

In the synagogue later that evening, Cousin Yonkel sat stiff with anger, his bony face pale. Cousin Nahum would not look at me. After the service Cousin Yonkel walked stiffly over to where I stood near my father. Cousin Nahum followed behind him.

"I need to talk with you," Cousin Yonkel said.

"Do you want to talk here?"

"Here, there. What difference does it make? The whole world will know soon anyway. I hear you saw the lawyer today."

"Your father's lawyer?"

"No, the lawyer for your hero, Picasso, that shining example of human decency. Of course my father's lawyer. What did you decide?"

"If you know I was there, you know what I decided."

"Asher," Cousin Nahum said. "Don't be that way."

"You had no right to make such a choice," Cousin Yonkel said.

"Your father gave me the right."

"It is our property. You are stealing from us."

We were not far from the podium near the center of the synagogue. There were always people in that synagogue, between as well as during the times for services. Some now stood around, talking; others were at the long tables, studying. Our conversation was beginning to attract attention.

"Perhaps you should talk somewhere else," my father said.

"You shouldn't have accepted," Cousin Yonkel said heatedly. "My father was wrong. What a man does in a weak moment, others should correct, not take advantage of."

"The letter he wrote me is not the letter of a weak man."

"What letter?"

"Never mind."

"Show me the letter."

"It's a personal letter addressed to me."

"You deluded him! You enticed him! You stole his thoughts! He was never the same person after he returned from his visits to you in France!"

"That's ridiculous."

"Asher," my father said. "Do not say another word."

"What's the matter with your brother?" I asked Cousin Nahum.

"I agree with Yonkel," Cousin Nahum said in a low, trembling voice. "You should have turned it down."

"You are stealing from our family!" Cousin Yonkel said shrilly. "Do you hear me?"

"Yonkel," Cousin Nahum said. "This is really a family matter. It shouldn't be discussed in front of all the people and the congregation."

"All the people will soon know of it anyway. I'm taking this to court. Let a judge decide the matter. We will see who is right."

"You see what you've done?" Cousin Nahum said to me.

"What *I've* done? It was your father's wish!"

Cousin Yonkel pushed his gaunt frame up close to me. His eyes flared. "You are a troubler of Israel!" he shouted, using the Hebrew term hurled by King Ahab at Elijah. "Wherever you go, you make trouble. When you lived among us here, you made trouble. In France, you made trouble. You come back here, and again you make trouble. Why don't you go away and leave us in peace? Who needs you here? Wherever you go, you cause heartache."

"Yonkel, I ask you not to say anything you will later regret," my father said sternly.

"With all respect, Uncle Aryeh," Cousin Yonkel said. "How

much can a person bear? Is there no end to this? We were a good
family until my father, may he rest in peace, returned from his
visits to your son. He deceived our father. He was like Satan in his
ear." He turned upon me. "You are from the sitra achra!" he
screamed, suddenly no longer able to restrain himself. "You are an
evil man! An abomination!" He looked wildly around. "Stand
back from this Satan! Stand back!"

He pushed me roughly away from him. I felt the strong thrust
of his arm against my chest but did not move. There was a stirring
in the group around us, raised voices. I caught a glimpse of my
father's face; he looked aghast. Cousin Nahum moved toward his
brother in an attempt to restrain him. Cousin Yonkel was suddenly
pushing at me hard with both hands and pulling his arms away
from people trying to hold him, and there was a roiling mass of
faces and bodies, and I was shoved from behind. Arms flailed
around my head, fingers grazed my cheek, and all the time I heard
Cousin Yonkel screaming, "Destroyer of Israel! Stand back from
him!" An elbow smashed into my nose and the knuckles of someone's hand struck my right eye. There were shouts: "Stop it! This
instant! Stop! Desecration of God's name!" The crowd backed
quickly away and dispersed. My cousins were gone. Both of my
nostrils were bleeding. The warm blood trickled into my beard.
Someone brought me a small packet of ice wrapped in plastic. I
held a handkerchief to my face and sat in a chair awhile with the
ice against my nose. Older students from the yeshiva kept coming
in and out of the synagogue to stare at me. My father kept asking
me if I was all right. After a while the bleeding stopped. My eye
seemed unimpaired. I walked home with my father, breathing
through my mouth and feeling the stiff, congealed blood in my
nostrils. I kept hearing Cousin Yonkel shouting, "Stand back from
him! Stand back!"

The children were in their rooms. I lay down on my bed. My
mother and Devorah came in from the kitchen.

"Your father just told us," my mother said.

"My God, look at you!" Devorah said.

"Just like the good old days," I said. "Back to my lovely childhood."

"Asher," my mother said.

"I'm very tired," I said.

They went out of the room. I lay on the bed, breathing slowly through my mouth, feeling the air drying my palate and throat. I swallowed saliva and went on breathing through my mouth.

In the days that followed there were many phone calls. Some were from Moshe Diamond's law firm and from Douglas Schaeffer's lawyer. Twice Douglas called me and we talked at length. One call was from a lawyer I didn't know, asking if I wanted him to represent me in a lawsuit against Mr. Jacob Lev for defamation of character—he had heard about the scuffle in the synagogue. I hung up on him.

I remember I did a lot of waiting and walking: waiting at home for the phone to bring me answers to certain questions; walking through the neighborhood and drawing people and objects seen and felt. I stayed away from my cousins. In the synagogue I kept myself far from them. But it made little difference: I could feel Cousin Yonkel's hate even when my back was to him. Once I went over to my uncle's house and asked Aunt Leah if I could see the art collection. She closed the door in my face.

The doctor who examined Rocheleh said that he thought she could probably attend overnight summer camp. She would have to restrict her physical activities, bring along her special pillow and her medication, and the camp authorities would have to be informed of her condition. He would let us know definitely when the lab results came back. Rocheleh said she did not want to be away from us for the entire summer—she was not always the adult she made herself out to be—and wanted to go home and be with Uncle Max. My parents listened, concealed their disappointment, and said nothing. Avrumel came home from school one day and informed us that he had been made captain of his class sports team for the Lag Bo'Omer games. No, he said, he did not want to stay in New York for the summer and go to the Ladover day camp; he wanted to go back home and be with Uncle Max and swim in Uncle Max's pool. And Shimshon wanted that, too.

I took the subway into Manhattan one day and spent part of the morning signing papers in Moshe Diamond's office and talking to him about my cousins. Yes, he said, they could cause all sorts of nuisance-type mischief: they could contest the will; they could charge me with unduly influencing their father against them; they could try to get the courts to enjoin my use of the collection. But none of it would amount to anything. The will could not be broken. Yes, he agreed with Douglas Schaeffer's attorney: it was probably a good idea to move the collection to a safe storage area. One never knew what people might do in times of great anger and stress. Why tempt them? " 'One ought never place an obstacle in the path of a blind man,' " he quoted.

Later, I walked over to Douglas Schaeffer's gallery, and we spent a while talking about the collection. I was on my way out when he asked me what I was carrying. I said a drawing pad, and he asked if he could see it. I handed it to him. He sat at his desk, slowly turning the pages. He looked up at me.

"These are extraordinary," he said.

I said nothing.

"How do you do this? You are seeing as if with three eyes."

Still I said nothing.

"Do you have any more of these?"

I nodded.

"We'll have that show in the fall," he said. "If there are no paintings, it will be drawings."

I told him I would think about it and took the elevator down to the street and walked around looking at galleries. In some I was quickly recognized, and when people started coming over for my autograph I excused myself and fled. I saw work by Jasper Johns that was splendid, and drawings by Larry Rivers, Robert Rauschenberg, and Jim Dine that were admirable. In a dairy restaurant I ordered fruit salad and sat there, eating and drawing. When the drawing began to attract attention, I closed the pad. I heard someone say, "I think that's Asher Lev, that guy over there in the fisherman's cap." I paid the check and took the subway home.

Alone in my parents' home later that afternoon, I noticed that the room Devorah and I lived in was becoming crowded with books. Many were new books bought from the neighborhood Hebrew bookstore on Kingston Avenue: children's books and works on Hasidus; others were popular paperback novels; some were from the local public library. Devorah tended to fill empty spaces with books: end tables, the tops of dressers, the edges of desks, on occasion even a chair. She would arrange and rearrange the books with exacting care, lining up the spines so none jutted out: sentinel rows of books. It was her way of taking possession, of declaring that she planned to occupy a certain space for a length of time.

I asked her that night how she had managed to take books out of the public library. She was using my mother's library card, she said. Perfectly legal, perfectly in order. She had been spending a great deal of time in recent days alone with my mother in the den or out on the terrace. What did she and my mother find to talk about so much? Our families, she said. "I'm discovering what an important lineage you have. You've never ever mentioned your genealogy to me. Your mother is telling me about her and your father's families, and I'm telling your mother about my family. Only I can't tell her a lot about mine. I barely remember anything about my parents. I don't remember what they looked like or the sounds of their voices. There aren't even any photographs of my parents. But you have a lovely family, Asher, an important family."

"Did my mother mention any artists in my family?"

"No, she didn't."

"That's because there aren't any. I'm a freak."

"Poor Asher."

"Asher Lev, artist and freak. Ask any Ladover. They'll tell you: Asher Lev, artist and freak. Asher Lev, troubler. Stand back from Asher Lev."

"Are you very tired, my husband? Do you want to go home?"

"Yes and yes."

"The doctor called earlier and said that Rocheleh's tests came back and confirmed what he told us. There is a new medication he wants her to try. She can go to the overnight camp if she wants."

"But she doesn't want."

"She discovered today that some of her school friends are going to that camp."

"I have to go to Paris, Dev."

"There is no reason you cannot go to Paris, Asher."

Avrumel returned from school the next day and said that Rav

Greenspan had come into his class and shown a movie about the day camp. The Rebbe appeared in the beginning of the movie, urging the children to go to the camp. There were pictures of the camp: colorful tents, rolling grounds, and grassy fields somewhere in Staten Island. Every morning at eight the campers traveled there by bus, and they returned by five in the afternoon. Pictures of boys playing games, hiking, swimming, and learning Torah. The swimming pool was very large. "Larger than Uncle Max's," Avrumel said. The Rebbe came on again at the end of the movie and gave a blessing to all the children who would attend the camp. Shimshon thought the camp looked nice, Avrumel said. I saw my parents glance at each other and exchange the faintest of smiles.

"The children have friends here," Devorah told me later. "There is family here. There is community here."

She was right.

Two days later, in the early afternoon, a truck pulled up in front of my Uncle Yitzchok's house, and three men climbed out. I went with them to the front door. Aunt Leah opened the door and without a word stepped back and let us come inside. Her eyes cold and her face sullen with anger, she gave me the keys to the study and the attic. Then she went off into the kitchen.

I watched as the men carefully removed my uncle's entire art collection from the study, the master bedroom, and the attic, and put it all into the truck. They took the paintings, drawings, prints, gallery announcements, publications, files. They did not remove the micrographic drawings in the living room. I glanced into the dining room and saw that the painting I had once made of Uncle Yitzchok and his family was gone. The painting was not listed as part of his collection; apparently, Uncle Yitzchok had left it to his family. On the wall was a faint outline, the residue of its lengthy presence in that room.

The day before, I had bought two lovely silver mezuzahs in the Hebrew bookstore. When the study and attic were empty of art, I quickly affixed the mezuzahs to the doorposts, reciting the appropriate blessing.

The truck pulled away from the curb and turned down the street toward the parkway, heading for the lower Manhattan storage facility recommended by Douglas Schaeffer. I wanted to say goodbye to Aunt Leah, but when I called her name she did not respond. I went back to my parents' house.

Max Lobe phoned from Saint-Paul. When were we returning home? What did I mean, I didn't know? What was going on in Brooklyn? Everything was fine, the house was fine, the studio was fine, Saint-Paul was fine, only John Dorman wasn't fine, he had been in the hospital again, this time with bronchitis and a kidney problem. He, Max, was thinking of going to Tokyo for the opening of his show. Yes, he had been invited. The Japanese were eager for him to come. Devorah got on the phone and talked to him. Then the children talked to him. Avrumel said he was probably going to stay in New York for the summer and go to a camp. Shimshon liked the idea, he said. He handed me the phone. "Uncle Max wants to talk to you again, Papa." I took the phone.

"What is happening over there?" Max said.

"It's very complicated. I'll tell you when I see you."

"And when will that be, my friend?"

"I'll call you in a day or so."

"Are you well?"

"Yes."

"Rocheleh is all right?"

"Yes."

"John thinks you have all been kidnapped and are being—how do you say it?—brainwashed."

"John is a writer of fiction."

"I will tell him you said it. Goodbye, my friend."

I hung up the phone and went back into the kitchen. They were all sitting around the table, finishing supper. I took my seat and resumed eating. "What is happening over there?" I heard Max say, and could see him saying it, his round face troubled, his bald head glistening.

"I have to know what we're doing this summer," I said.

"I want to go to camp day with Shimshon," Avrumel said.

"Day camp," Rocheleh said, rolling her eyes toward the ceiling.

"The Rebbe said we will have a nice time in day camp."

I looked at Devorah. Out of the corners of my eyes I saw my parents looking at their plates.

The telephone rang. Rocheleh went to answer it. We heard her talking on the phone. Then there was a brief silence. She returned to the kitchen.

"It is the office of the Rebbe," she said in an awed voice.

My father put down his napkin and began to rise.

"It is for Papa," Rocheleh said.

They all looked at me. My father slowly sat back down.

I went out of the kitchen to the phone.

"Hello," I said.

"Asher Lev?"

"Yes."

"Asher Lev, the Rebbe would like to speak with you."

"When?"

"Tonight. Eleven o'clock."

"All right."

"If you have not been to the mikvah today, Asher Lev, I suggest you go before you see the Rebbe."

He hung up. I put the receiver down and went back into the kitchen.

A warm wind blew through the dark street and moved through the branches of the trees. I walked in the shadows of fluttering young leaves. The street was deserted, most of its homes dark. The yellow lights of the streetlamps fell benignly upon tree trunks and branches and cars parked for the night. Somewhere overhead a jetliner whispered through the smoky black sky. I turned up the path to the Rebbe's home. The two tall dark-bearded men on the porch nodded at me. One of them opened the door, and I stepped inside.

The house was silent. I entered the waiting room and was about to sit down when my father came out of the Rebbe's office. He motioned me over to him. I saw his eyes darken with concern as I went slowly past him. He closed the door behind me.

The Rebbe sat behind the desk. He wore a dark caftan, a dark tie, and an ordinary dark hat that shaded his eyes. He beckoned to me, and as I moved toward him I saw him watching me, saw the eyes glittering within the shadows beneath the brim of the hat. He seemed wraithlike, spectral, a blurred and nebulous presence. His face was stark white: white as the sheets of drawing paper in my pad, white as the primed canvases that waited for me in my studio in Saint-Paul, white as Rocheleh's face when she coughed and could not breathe. No face could be that white. It had to be a trick of the chandelier, or a failure of my tired eyes to register properly the refraction of the room's light.

The Rebbe was talking to me, but I could not hear him. I looked at him for a long moment and still did not hear him. He raised his hand and motioned me into one of the chairs near the desk.

". . . your family?" I heard him say. "All are well?"

I nodded.

"And little Avrumel? Avrumel is well?"

"Thank God."

"And how are you, Asher?"

"I have problems. An artist's problems."

"Your work comes to you now with difficulty?"

"Yes."

"Jacob Kahn, may he rest in peace, suffered from such problems. He told me once all artists endure such obstacles. Only those of lesser mind and heart are able to work all the time, he said. But it was not a consolation for him to know that."

"Nor is it a consolation for me."

"In a book I read once on the greatest of your artists, it said that even he, Picasso, had periods when he was unable to paint. This is such a time for you, Asher?"

"Yes, Rebbe."

"I am deeply sorry for your suffering. An artist who is unable to do his art is like a Hasid who has lost his Rebbe and like a Rebbe who, may God protect us, has lost the key to the gate through which he must pass to the Master of the Universe. But the Bratslaver Rebbe taught that obstacles are given us in order to make our desire even stronger. The more a thing is hidden from man, the more he desires it, and the greater the chance that he will one day discover it. I pray you will soon overcome your obstacles."

"Thank you, Rebbe."

"All have obstacles, Asher Lev. All. Even a Rebbe."

I sat very still and said nothing.

"They want more from me than I am able to give. I am, after all, only flesh and blood. I, too, had a beginning and will one day have an end."

I felt a trembling move heavily through me like a sudden shaking of the earth.

"Your Picasso, he lived in disorder. An artist may choose disorder in order to create his own order. I understand that, Asher. But a Rebbe may not leave behind disorder. God created order. In order there is life. In disorder there is the possibility of death. I speak to you this way, Asher, because you are a man of understanding. I do not speak this way to all who come here. You understand?"

"Yes, Rebbe."

"Then listen to me. There is an ordered future for us. This I know with certainty, for I see it in visions and dreams. The number three is our future, and the third will save us. I ask you to consider this, my Asher. The third will save us. Few here understand you. Most despise you and your work. They see the surface and do not understand what lies beneath. But they will one day understand that three is our future, and the third will save us. One day soon I must give a sign, and only the third will be our future, our orderliness, our permanence, our anchor, our certainty in this world of chaos that surrounds us. We are the world's permanence, my Asher, its gravity. Without us all would fly off into space, God forbid. Do you understand me? I see it in your eyes, Asher Lev. Yes. Perhaps you begin to understand. Then listen to me. Let your family remain here for the summer. Your children's teachers tell me that they are happy here. Can it hurt them to remain here awhile longer with their grandparents? And I am told your Devorah is also happy here. You are already here longer than you planned. Perhaps there is a greater plan that keeps you here. Consider that with care. I give you my blessing, Asher Lev, son of Rav Aryeh and Rivkeh Lev."

He raised his right hand in a faint waving gesture. I rose unsteadily and went from the room.

My father was not in his office. The two tall dark-bearded men looked at me closely as I emerged from the house: I had just been with the Rebbe; surely some of his sanctity clung to me. I walked quickly home beneath trees strangely still in the raven night.

The weeks began to go by with a patterned regularity. On the holiday of Lag Bo'Omer, which celebrates the end of a terrible plague that struck the students of Rabbi Akiva in the Land of Israel during the Roman occupation, I went with Devorah to Prospect Park and watched Avrumel's team roundly defeat all opponents in a variety of sports. Little Avrumel, his face sweaty with excitement, his red hair and freckles making him stand out on the field even amid a tangle of bodies, was the hero of his team. "Freckles," I heard some call him in English. "The Red One," others referred to him in Yiddish.

Some days later, Devorah and I and my parents went to the school and saw Rocheleh perform in a play about the prophetess Devorah. Pale-faced, garbed in a flowing saffron robe, and without her too-large glasses, she spoke her lines in a clear, high, penetrating voice, and dominated the stage and the auditorium. "Who is that?" I heard someone behind me ask during the lengthy applause at the end. "She is the daughter of Asher Lev," was the answer. "Asher Lev, the painter?" "Yes." "I don't believe it. Such a lovely child from such a wicked man." I saw Devorah's face stiffen, but she did not turn around.

The festival of Shavuos came and went. The air was warm and fragrant with flowers. The Rebbe was present in the synagogue both days of the festival, and spoke on the first day about the Revelation on Mount Sinai and the Torah as our permanent heritage and the importance of continuity, and I had the impression as he spoke that he was looking at me, but I could not be certain.

I walked around a lot and made many drawings, but I showed the drawings to no one, not even to Devorah. There were more calls from the lawyers, and much talk about the Internal Revenue Service and their appraisers, and complete silence from my cousins, who no longer spoke to me and shunned me when they saw me on the street or in the synagogue.

The summer drew near. Devorah was buying clothes for the

children. Their closets and dressers filled with clothes, and it began to look as though they had lived in this house all their young lives. She and my mother were together often. With my mother's help, Devorah bought herself dresses and two lovely wigs, both in chestnut brown, the original color of her hair, one a short, softly waved coif, the other a brush cut. Often I saw her on the terrace, deep in conversation with my father and mother. She seemed finally to be filling the space left when her parents were torn away from her that July day in Paris.

One morning I took the subway to Manhattan and walked in sun and shade to the tall building that housed Douglas Schaeffer's gallery. He greeted me warmly. I told him I would be leaving for Europe soon and gave him three drawing pads for safekeeping.

"The printer should have the bon à tirer of that print," he said. "You remember you asked me about that?"

I remembered, and thanked him.

He began looking through the pads. I asked him if certain of his artists who lived in Paris would be at home for the summer; I would like to see them when I got there. He seemed not to have heard me. I repeated the question. He glanced up from the pads, annoyed, and said, "Please, dear boy. Please." It was as if the drawings were no longer mine and I was now an intruder. I went out of the office.

Standing before the elevator, I heard the gallery door open and close behind me, and I turned and there was Douglas Schaeffer.

"We will show them in the fall," he said.

I said I wanted to think about it.

"Dear boy, you can think about it all you wish, but we will show them in the fall. Give my best wishes to Max." He went back into the gallery.

A week later, I said goodbye to my parents and Devorah and kissed Rocheleh and Avrumel. Devorah, accustomed to my comings and goings, seemed to be treating this as merely another of my journeys from our home in Saint-Paul. "Your papa will be back in two weeks," she said to the children. "Wish him a safe journey." My father took my hand in his firm grip and reminded me again that he would be in Paris on Thursday and we would spend Shabbos together at the Ladover yeshiva. "Travel in good health," he said. My mother embraced me and kissed me. "Have a safe journey, my son," she murmured, her face warm against mine.

I climbed into the taxi. They all stood in the doorway, waving at me. It was a Sunday afternoon, and the street was quiet. The taxi turned into Brooklyn Parkway, and after a while we were riding through a neighborhood of broken streets and shattered buildings and then along the Interborough Parkway, past the exit to the cemetery where my Uncle Yitzchok lay buried and onto the Grand Central Parkway to the airport.

The airport was crowded with tourists. There were lines everywhere. The plane left two hours late.

I spent much of the trip rereading Rilke's letters on Cézanne, and drawing. I read Cézanne's words about his life in the little town of Aix: "Ça va mal.... C'est effrayante la vie!" And I read this:

> ... artistic perception had to overcome itself to the point of realizing that even something horrible, something that seems no more than disgusting, *is*, and shares the truth of its being with everything else that exists. Just as the creative artist is not allowed to choose, neither is he permitted to turn his back on anything: a single refusal, and he is cast out of the state of grace and becomes sinful all the way through.

And Cézanne, in the last letter he wrote, laments his poor health, and adds: "Je continue donc mes études."

To his last days, he continued learning. I fell asleep reading the book.

BOOK TWO

✦ ✦ ✦

3

✤ ✤ ✤   The airliner descended through rough air and dense clouds and landed on a wet runway in a gray and gritty dawn. At a newsstand inside the terminal I saw the headline in *Le Figaro:* AIRBUS: L'ACCIDENT INEXPLIQUÉ. An Airbus had gone down during an air show in France: three dead, about fifty hurt. Inexpliqué.

A taxi took me through nearly empty early-morning streets. I saw shopkeepers sweeping down the sidewalks. Traffic was light all the way to the hotel. A weary receptionist registered me; a sleepy bellhop took me up in the elevator.

My Paris is resonant with private memories: the roundup and the sealed apartment; painting the crucifixion canvases; marrying Devorah, the wedding small and simple, with Max and my parents and some friends; Rocheleh born; Lucien Lacamp climbing the stairs to our Rue des Rosiers apartment; Jacob Kahn suddenly here from New York; my show last winter and Paris at its worst: arrogant and dismissive, pouncing. They had been right to scorn. Too much art, too little heart. The Paris of Asher Lev.

I lay down on the bed for a few minutes of rest, and when I woke it was noon and there was sunlight. I washed and unpacked and made some phone calls. Waiting for one of the calls to go through, I fell asleep with the phone in my hand. I slept again and woke hours later, with the sun now a huge motionless orange-red disk in the cloud-studded western sky and the lingering twilight embracing the city like a tender lover.

I sit for a time on the narrow ornamented balcony of my hotel room and gaze across gabled rooftops and tall chimney pots at the stationary sun. A summer twilight seems never-ending here, like a suspension of duration; darkness glides across the sky with the silken slowness of an infinitely languid tide. I sit with the drawing pad on my lap, looking at air dove-gray with fumes from the interminable traffic below and the early-evening streets crowded with tourists and the vast spread of the city beneath the slowly paling sky. Abruptly I am on the street in front of the hotel, with no memory of how I got there, and I set out along the Rue de Beaune to the river.

At the Restaurant Voltaire I turn right and walk parallel to the river, past elegant old apartment houses and the terraces of cafés. There are many people on the streets, and the cafés are crowded. I cross the river on the Pont des Arts, the long buildings of the Louvre to my left. Hot, water-scented winds blow across the dark-surfaced river. I turn left and walk on slowly and go past the Pont Royal. From time to time I stop to gaze over the stone parapet at the river walk below, with its occasional strollers and lovers and the houseboats moored for the night. Along its banks the river is scummy with a greenish-brown detritus of waterlogged scraps of paper, bottles, crushed cigarette packs, plastic containers. It is nearly dark when I start across the Pont de la Concorde and notice the gendarme standing alone in the middle of the bridge.

Armed with a machine pistol, wearing the peaked cap, with the dark-blue trousers of his uniform smartly rolled over the tops of his polished boots, he seems more sculpture than man, a modern equivalent of the equestrian statue of Henri IV near the Pont Neuf. As I walk past him, a light spattering of rain sweeps suddenly across the bridge. A second gendarme stands at the end of the bridge. I turn into the Quai Anatole France and see three others. They are all armed with machine pistols, and they stand very still, like statuary resonant with contained violence. The words of the Rebbe in his office that night. What? All around us is chaos, the world needs a center. Across the road from the bridge, the stone façade of a huge building is bathed in soft amber light and bears the words ASSEMBLÉE NATIONALE.

The light rain ends, leaving a film of water on the street. I walk beneath the trees to the Pont Royal and cross to the Quai Voltaire. There are few pedestrians and automobiles now on this street. I sense someone behind me. I walk on, and there is still someone behind me. I hear a low, sustained whistling, and I turn and see a short, stocky, bald-headed man in a sweatshirt and baggy trousers and sandals. He steps smoothly into the shadows of a tree and is gone.

An emblazoned tourist boat appears suddenly on the river, its cyclopean prow light and upper-deck halogens cutting huge swaths of light out of the night. A blare of musical instruments, horns of some kind, rises from somewhere on the street. It stops, then begins again, horns climbing in unison to a crescendo, as if heralding the advent of royalty. Half a dozen people have stopped at the parapet near the Pont Royal, and I go over and look down.

Along the river, on a stone bank that looks like an ancient quai, stand five men and two women. A flight of stone stairs leads from the street to the quai. The river runs dark and silent alongside the stones. Stairs and quai are lit by electric lamps. The men and women stand in a semicircle in the light, holding large curved antique-looking trumpets. They put the trumpets to their lips, and once again a resonating flourish of ascending horn tones rises from the quai and ends abruptly on a sustained high note. It seems a rehearsal for some medieval pageant. I wonder what contemporary personage merits such a greeting and in what sort of craft he or she will arrive at the quai.

The Pont Royal affords a clearer view of the quai than the parapet along the street. I walk onto the bridge and stand at the stone railing and gaze down at the musicians. They stand inside their circle of light, and the river and the night run dark all around them. I feel the presence of someone behind me, and I turn but see no one.

Light-spangled tourist boats glide beneath the bridge. The left bank is dark in the distance and lighted to high noon where the boats turn their floodlights upon the stone façades of the seventeenth-century apartment houses and the awnings of elegant restaurants and hotels. I search for certain windows in the whitestone building over the Restaurant Voltaire where Jacob Kahn lived before moving to the south of France. I imagine him standing there, looking out at the river and the Louvre. Over the right bank, river birds wheel in and out of the darkness, wings flashing silvery white in the boat lights. Distant streaks of lightning play over the city, splintering the darkness and flickering through the undersides of swollen clouds. A fine rain begins to fall. On the quai below, the trumpet players stand looking up at the sky. Tourist boats keep gliding along the water beneath me. I walk off the bridge and go past the Restaurant Voltaire and along the Rue de Beaune.

The street is dark and deserted. The rain begins to fall hard. All along the narrow street, doorways are closed and shops and restaurants are shuttered. There are no lowered awnings or open courtyards. All is sealed to the outside. I walk quickly in the rain, and then the rain is suddenly torrential, and I run in the dark through the pelting summer storm along streets deep with rivulets and between cars parked on the sidewalks and see the rain coursing through the gutters and falling in silvery streaks through the haloes cast by streetlamps. I enter the hotel and stand dripping in the lobby.

The night clerk shakes his head and clicks his tongue sympathetically and hands me my key. I hear a distant clap of thunder. Inside the elevator I watch the rain drip from my clothes and shoes to form puddles at my feet.

In my room I get out of my wet clothes, towel myself dry, and put on pajamas. From the doorway to the balcony I watch the rain. It falls into the darkly reflecting mirrors of puddles on the glistening asphalt of the street. A motorcyclist speeds past the hotel in a blare of engine noise. The city is a wonderland of lights, resplendent and jeweled. Across from the hotel, the wide dark windows of the Maeght Gallery reflect the shifting colors of the street: the changing greens and reds of traffic lights; the whites and ambers of passing automobiles; the neon signs left on for the night: a blurry kaleidoscope of wet-night colors. In a distant apartment building a dark window suddenly fills with light, and a woman begins to remove her clothes. A man appears and draws the drapes. I stand in the doorway to the balcony, looking out at the rain and the night.

The hotel stood next to a Catholic church and seminary. Church bells woke me. The bells seemed just the other side of my walls; I could feel the bed vibrating. After a while, the bells fell silent. In the stillness of my room they seemed to go on moments longer, echoing between the walls.

I opened the balcony doors. Chill pearl-colored mist hung in the morning air. The rain had stopped, but the streets were still wet. Tires hissed on the asphalt. Dark-gray rain clouds lay across the city, rendering rooftops and chimney pots an impressionist blur. A police siren sounded distantly, rising, falling, rising, falling, abruptly silent. I washed and dressed and put on my tallis and tefillin to pray the Morning Service.

I prayed slowly, trying to concentrate on the words. Two mornings ago with my father and raging cousins in the Ladover synagogue in Brooklyn; now in a hotel room in Paris. A week in Paris: visit the new Picasso Museum; go to the printer to work with Max; find the widow of Lucien Lacamp; Shabbos with my father in the yeshiva. Then Saint-Paul: a week to check the house and mail and spend time with Max and John. And back to Brooklyn. Why had I let the Rebbe talk me into this? Foolish. But how spurn the order of the Rebbe? Unthinkable. As soon blaspheme the Master of the Universe. How gaunt the Rebbe's hand had appeared jutting out of his tallis and beckoning to me, beckoning. Three will save us, the third is our future. The Spaniard was good at riddles. Most of his life he painted riddles. I was done praying. On the street a car horn blared, receded. I removed my tefillin and tallis and started from the room, when the phone rang.

I let it ring three times, my hand on the doorknob. The ringing echoed dully inside the room. I closed the door, went to the desk, and lifted the receiver.

"Hello," I said.

"Asher Lev?" a man's voice said.

"Yes."

"The notorious and legendary Asher Lev?"

"Who is this?"

"You don't recognize my voice? It's Shaul Lasker."

"Shaul!" He was the head of the Ladover yeshiva in Paris. I had seen him during the week of mourning for my uncle.

"Sholom aleichem," he said.

"Aleichem sholom."

"How are you, Asher?"

"All right, thank God."

"And the family?"

"Thank God."

"Everyone is back in sunny Saint-Paul?"

"Everyone is still in Brooklyn. The children are going to La-dover summer camps in the States."

"A smart move. You're going back to Brooklyn?"

"In a couple of weeks."

There was a slight pause. "You saw the Rebbe recently?"

"Yes."

"You were alone with the Rebbe?"

"Yes."

"How is the Rebbe?"

"As well as can be expected, thank God."

"Does the Rebbe leave the house?"

"Very rarely."

There was another pause. "What will be?" he asked quietly.

"The Rebbe expects at any moment the final redemption."

He sighed. "Amen. You'll be with us for Shabbos?"

"Yes."

"You know your father will be here."

"Yes. Give my regards to your family."

I hung up the phone.

The room was suddenly strangely silent. I sat there looking at the attaché case on the desk and the suitcase near the polished wood armoire and the disarray of the slept-in bed. For a long moment I felt a vague emptying sensation, and nothing in the room seemed to have anything to do with me: I was outside everything, looking. How crowded the room seemed. Its walls covered with pale-blue flowery paper. A blue carpet on the floor, a maroon easy chair in a corner. The ceiling off-white, stippled. The bed wide, the desk narrow. Against the wall across from the bed stood the antique armoire, its wood surface lacquered to a high sheen, thin cracks showing in the polish like fine hairs. On the wall over the bed, illuminated by the pale light that came in through the balcony doors, hung a splendid reproduction of *Women Bathing* by Fragonard: the meticulous play of washes and impasto; the deliberate eroticism of the bare buttocks facing the viewer. I sat at the desk awhile, looking at the painting, then went out of the room.

The elevator brought me down to the lobby. There were fresh flowers in the vase on the coffee table near the sofa: red, yellow, and blue petals in a field of lacy ferns. The clerk nodded to me as I left my key on the counter. I drank a glass of orange juice in the small restaurant bar and went out of the hotel.

The morning was cool and gray. I walked toward the Métro. About fifty feet beyond the hotel, an old woman lay asleep on a stoop on the street. She wore a pale-blue cotton kerchief, a dark-red windbreaker, and navy-blue pants. The soles of her bare feet were blackened; her ankles were swollen. She slept on her left side, her sunken face turned toward the sidewalk, hands tucked under her cheek, knees drawn up. People went by and averted their gaze. I could see them looking at her and not seeing her. I stood there a long moment. The shriveled face. Like the Indian woman I had once drawn on the reservation in South Dakota. I went on past her toward the Métro.

Graffiti scarred the walls of the Rue de Bac station: echoes of the recent national election. MITTERRAND DEHORS. The train rolled in smoothly with its startling absence of metal-on-metal noise. Inside the car, graffiti soiled the posters and direction maps: swirls of reds and blacks. The train was not crowded. It started up and was immediately inside the tunnel.

Following the directions given me by the hotel concierge, I took the Balard line to the Concorde station, changed for a Château de Vincennes train, and got off at Bastille. I climbed up the stone stairs of the Bastille station and emerged into a boulevard of torn pavement, towering construction cranes, and thundering jackhammers. Crowds of pedestrians clogged the sidewalks; cars and buses jammed the streets. A reeking fog of diesel and gasoline fumes lay upon the boulevard. The air was heavy with impending rain. I looked around for street signs, crossed the boulevard, walked a block, and was lost.

A smartly dressed middle-aged woman, cradling a tiny poodle in her arms, came toward me. I asked her if she knew where the

Picasso Museum was. Her eyes, heavily lined and blue-shaded with makeup, stared past my head as if I were not there. She inclined her head slightly and murmured something to the poodle, caressing it with her free hand, and I smelled her perfume as she hurried past me.

I stepped into a café. The chairs were on the tables, and a man was sweeping the floor. Two waiters stood against a wall, smoking and talking. I asked one of them if he knew where the Picasso Museum was. He pursed his lips and looked at the other waiter, who rolled his eyes and shook his head.

Outside on the street, a thin, dark-haired, olive-skinned man standing behind piles of newspapers and magazines in a small kiosk directed me in Arabic-accented French to the Boulevard Beaumarchais. Weaving cautiously through the traffic, I crossed a wide street. On the boulevard I went past a jackhammer crew that was shredding a sidewalk. The noise struck me like blows to the head. A light rain began to fall.

The street was lined with old cafés and inelegant shops. I went into an optician's store. Behind the counter stood a middle-aged man. He wore a white smock and had thick black hair and wide, kindly eyes. I asked him if he knew the location of the Picasso Museum.

He looked surprised. "Is there truly a Picasso Museum here?"

"Yes."

"But I have never heard of it. I am so very sorry."

I went back out onto the boulevard.

On a corner under the awning of a café stood a gendarme. "The third street to your left," he said. "And then you go straight straight straight to the museum. You will see it."

I walked quickly in the light rain, hugging the windows of shops and the awnings of cafés, counted what I thought were three streets, and turned into a narrow cobblestone street called Rue des Minimes. After two blocks it led into a wider, perpendicular street named Rue de Turenne and vanished.

I stood in the rain looking up and down the Rue de Turenne. It was deserted.

I was lost in Paris.

I thought to give it up and return to the hotel. But I wanted to see the Spaniard's collection. More than three hundred paintings and sculptures, thirty sketchbooks, eighty-odd ceramics, sixteen hundred prints, fifteen hundred drawings. The government had collected it from his heirs in place of inheritance taxes and, in 1985, had put much of it up on the walls of a restored seventeenth-century hotel for all to see. I would see it if I could find it.

A man had suddenly appeared on the street—from where? a doorway? an alley?—and now stood in the rain, peering into the window of a clothing store. He was old and bearded and wore a dark coat and suit and a wide-brimmed dark hat. He stood gazing into the store, the brim of his hat touching the window.

I went over to him and said in French, "Excuse me, do you by any chance know where the Picasso Museum is located?"

He took a small shying step away from me and went on looking at the display of suits, shirts, and ties in the window.

I looked at him a moment. He went on gazing into the window. I said to him, this time in Yiddish, "Please excuse me."

Slowly he turned away from the window and fixed his eyes upon me. Dark, deeply wrinkled eyes and thick gray eyebrows and pale features above the line of white beard.

"You know perhaps where the Picasso Museum is? I was told it is in this neighborhood."

He looked me up and down. His eyes paused briefly on my beard. "From where does a Jew come?" he asked in Yiddish.

"From Saint-Paul-de-Vence."

His dark eyes narrowed. "Originally?"

"Originally from Brooklyn."

"From where in Brooklyn?"

"Crown Heights."

"You are a Ladover?"

"Yes."

"What is a Ladover Hasid doing in Paris looking for the Picasso Museum?"

"It's a long story. Do you know where it is?"

"Go to the corner and turn left and continue walking."

I thanked him and went on along the street in the rain. As I neared the corner, I turned and saw him standing in front of the clothing store, still looking at me.

The museum, a beige-and-graystone building, was on the corner of Rue de Thorigny and Rue Parc Royal. About a dozen tourists stood around in the broad open cobblestone courtyard. I followed signs to a wing of the building, bought a ticket, and went back through the courtyard to the main entrance.

A tall wide marble staircase rose in a straight majestic sweep beneath an ornately decorated ceiling. On the landing at the head of the stairs, entwined garlands, naked cherubs, and robed statuary of heroic proportions stood out in relief upon creamy white walls. I entered the first of the galleries.

The room was large and richly lit, the ceiling tall. Paintings greeted me like old friends: I had seen them so many times before, in retrospectives, in reproductions. The Spaniard at work making his magic. There was the portrait of the young girl he painted when he was fourteen. There was Casagemas, a suicide, awaiting burial, the wound to the temple startlingly bluish and ugly. So that's where that painting had been all these decades—in his own collection! And the self-portrait painted in 1901: wide weary eyes staring from pale features glazed with misery and fatigue. He was twenty years old when he painted that: the artist gazing darkly into the mirror of his future.

I walked slowly through the first-floor galleries and down to the galleries on the ground level and down farther into the basement. Self-portraits; Cubist paintings; constructions; an oil painting of a seated woman done in the massive style of ancient Roman statuary; two women running on a beach; two hideously distorted figures engaged in the act of kissing; monstrous biomorphs at the edge of a sea; a crucifixion horrific with twisted forms placed on the canvas like the pieces of a puzzle; still lifes; bulls and matadors and gut-ripped horses; the power and mystery of the Minotaur; portraits of Olga, Dora Maar, Marie-Thérèse; the sculptures of the goat and the man with the sheep; a painting in neoclassic style of two robust loincloth-clad youths on a wall by the sea, one of them playing the flute of Pan. Paintings of the artist's son as Harlequin; the artist's son as Pierrot; the artist's son seated at a table, drawing; the artist and his wife and son at the edge of a sea.

I stood a long time at the painting of the artist and his wife and son by the sea: the artist supine on the sand and nude, his left hand covering his sex; his infant son touching his father's ear with a finger of his left hand; his wife placing a gentle restraining right hand upon the child's shoulder. Beyond the yellow beach lay a dark, menacing sea and sky. I felt myself a voyeur on that beach, straining toward that family's every word and act. I gazed intently at the face of the child, and I saw it was Avrumel; at the face of the woman, and saw Devorah; at the face of the artist, and saw myself—the three of us on that beach, with sea and sky meeting in a distant, menacingly dark horizon that cut directly across the back of the woman's head.

From somewhere behind me came a soft whistling. A man slipped silently into the space to my right. He was short and bald save for a fringe of disheveled white hair that ran around the back of his head like a garland. His forehead, flecked with small brown spots and deeply furrowed, moved from a high ridge of bone to the thin curving white lines of the eyebrows and the black smoldering eyes set in wrinkled sockets. Twin trenches came down from the sides of the broad nose and formed vague semicircles around a mouth set in a disdainful smile. He wore a black shirt and dark-red trousers. He stood gazing at the picture, enveloped in an aura of pulsing energy, faintly luminous, magnetic, chilling. The room seemed to be emptying of visitors. We stood alone, looking at the painting of the artist and his wife and son on the beach.

"Well, what do you think of this one?" he asked in his Spanish-accented French.

"I am still reading it and learning from it."

"Learning?" He raised an eyebrow. His tone was shaded with disdain. "What are you learning?"

"The man's sex is concealed, as are the woman's breasts and sex. The child's finger that probes the man's ear is perhaps an echo of the man's hidden member. The man lies on the sand as if dead; only the woman and child are in motion. The sky is threatening; the sea is dark. The mother of this child protects and castrates simultaneously. It is a picture both tender and terrifying. Of course, I am not dealing at all with its formal properties, which I think are flawless."

There was a lengthy pause. He stood very still, staring at the picture.

"Are you finished?" he asked sullenly.

"This is the first time I see the original painting."

"You disappoint me, Lev. Where did you learn to read pictures? In Brooklyn? From Jacob Kahn? Perhaps he did the best that could be done with someone born in Brooklyn."

I felt the heat rise to my face. "What difference does it make where someone is born?"

"You don't think it makes a difference? Málaga, Barcelona, Paris, Brooklyn? All are the same?" He peered intently at me for a long moment, his teeth bared. A musky scent rose from him, and the smell of turpentine. "That is amusing, Lev. Very amusing. Too bad there is no painter here able to capture the look on your face that accompanies your little piece of wisdom. Max Jacob might have enjoyed it. Perhaps Guillaume would have given it a paragraph or two. Barcelona and Brooklyn as sources for serious art. Amusing. All right, look at them." He pointed a paint-splattered hand at the woman in the picture. "This is what you should see. You give them a baby to make them happy, to bind them to you, and they forget you are alive. You die in every way except as the supporter of their baby. It makes no difference what you give them. In the end, they leave you without balls. When the baby grows up, he also tries to cut off your balls. That's the way the world is, Lev. Did they teach you that in Brooklyn?" He gave a brief, snorting laugh. Then he looked around. "You like this collection?"

I nodded.

"You know what a painter really is, Lev? A painter is a collector who wants to create a collection for himself, and he does this by painting himself the pictures he loves by other artists. This is a good collection."

"All women aren't as you describe them," I said.

His eyes narrowed. "How would you know? How many women have you had? They are all that way; they are good at concealing it, though some are more clever than others. You know about concealing things, Lev. But you are not yet really good at it. You wear your heart on your face. Your uncle was good at it. He was very good at it. Cézanne was damn good at it. All the anxiety concealed behind those apples. I would not care a damn about

Cézanne if it wasn't for that anxiety. Your leader is an expert at hiding things. His riddles. Truth has to be given in riddles. People can't take truth if it comes charging at them like a bull. The bull is always killed, Lev. You have to give people the truth in a riddle, hide it so they go looking for it and find it piece by piece; that way they learn to live with it. You tell people God is a murderer, they can't take it, they become angry, they kill you like you're a bull. Why are you shaking your head? You don't think God is a murderer? What do you know about God? You think in Brooklyn you really learn about God? In Spain is where you learn about God. God killed my little sister. That's right, Lev. A little girl, suddenly sick and dead. Everything He touches is destroyed. Casagemas, Apollinaire, Eva, Max Jacob. How do you worship Him, Lev? He's the true destroyer. Satan works out in the open, cards on the table. He gives it to you straight, no games. God plays at sweetness and goodness, and kills you. Who's worse, Satan or God? Satan at least has the decency to show us his real face. So I pay God back with my paintings. I tell the truth in my paintings, but I conceal it. He knows it's there, and He has to wait sweating as people figure it out and it sinks in. I paint pictures like this, and people come along and slowly learn to read them. That's how I pay Him back for His sweetness."

"Why does the horizon divide the woman's head?"

He looked at me. I felt myself held in the diabolic lure of his eyes. "You don't like it? Too bad." *Tant pis* was the French, uttered with derision. "Figure it out for yourself, Lev. It's time you learned to work with riddles."

A burst of white light filled the room: people had entered the gallery and someone had set off a forbidden flash to photograph the painting of the family on the beach.

The light erased the presence of the Spaniard.

I stood there trembling and taking deep breaths.

Max Lobe once told me that it took him days to recover from a museum encounter with the Spaniard: he felt bereft of talent, an obsequious courtier, inadequate, drained. I, on the other hand, always felt myself soaring, charged with his malevolent energy. I could ride his demoniacal imagination to the brightest and hottest of stars.

I continued on slowly through the galleries to the room that contained his collection of pictures by Matisse, Cézanne, Rousseau, Renoir. Matisse's *Marguerite* was there! What had the Spaniard ever seen in Rousseau? What had his eyes caught in the imagination and painstaking renderings of that naïf? It eluded me.

A short while later, in the museum bookshop, I asked for a copy of the catalogue. They were out of the English translation. I bought the French edition and stood near a wall, turning its pages. I found the reproduction of the 1930 oil painting *La Crucifixion* and began to read the commentary on the facing page. I read until "Picasso assemble comme dans un puzzle différents motifs des compositions anciennes, d'où la complexité de l'oeuvre, qui est un véritable dictionnaire du vocabulaire plastique," when I heard someone say, "Isn't that Asher Lev?" I hurried out of the building into the wet streets and headed for the Métro.

Near the Métro I changed my mind and decided to walk. I walked for nearly an hour from the Rue de Turenne and the Rue des Francs Bourgeois toward the Rue des Rosiers, where I had once lived with Devorah and Rocheleh. I kept taking wrong turns and asking for directions from gendarmes. Buildings were splashed with graffiti. MITTERRAND DEHORS. AU LIEU D'AVOIR DES IDÉES BIEN ARRÊTÉES, LE PEN FERAIT BIEN D'ARRÊTER D'AVOIR DES IDÉES.

I went past a Hebrew bookstore, its display window stocked with candelabra, wine cups, spice boxes, rams' horns, books. The sign in the window read EN VENTE ICI MEZOUZOTS ET TEPHILIN KACHERS. I walked on down the street and turned the corner into the Rue des Rosiers.

Near the corner I took a table on the terrace of the small café that had a kashrut certificate in its window. COMMUNAUTÉ ISRAELITE ORTHODOXE DE PARIS. STRICTEMENT KACHER. A waiter stepped out of the interior of the café. He looked to be in his fifties and combed his thinning hair sideways across his head. I ordered a salad, vegetable soup, and lemon tea.

"We have an excellent strudel today," the waiter said.

"Another time."

He went back inside.

Diagonally across the street from me, on the corner, was a large restaurant, its terrace crowded with tourists. Flower boxes with green shrubs separated the terrace from the traffic on the street. Waiters in red jackets with white towels on their arms came and went. The restaurant's huge deep windows followed the corner and faced the street on both sides of the turn. Behind the windows, long salamis hung from hooks; there were shelves of wine bottles, breads, racks of smoked meats and Norwegian salmon; neon lights advertised Smirnoff and Cinzano.

A waiter emerged from the restaurant, carrying a tray. He set it down on a small folding table and began serving a young couple seated near the curb. A small scrawny black dog with floppy ears and a white diamond-shaped patch on its head loped along the street and came to a stop at the table, where it stood gazing hopefully at the tray. The young man and woman, eating, looked at the dog but did not see it. After some while it went away, its tail drooping. The waiter hovered over the young couple. His face was lean, bony, clean-shaven. He had close-cropped gray hair and a military manner. Standing near the table of the young couple, he raised his eyes and saw me. His closed features did not change expression. He went back inside the restaurant.

My waiter brought my food. I sat eating and looking out at the street. The sidewalks and curbs were still wet from the morning rain. Behind the wrought-iron grillwork of narrow balconies, the windows of the four-story gray and yellow houses gazed at one another dully across the asphalt street. A tall bearded man in a dark-gray suit and a dark hat walked past me, carrying a brown attaché case. His curled earlocks swung against the sides of his face. From the window of our Brooklyn apartment my mother and I would watch my father starting out for his office or beginning one of his journeys for the Rebbe, carrying his attaché case, limping slightly and finally vanishing beneath the densely branching trees along the parkway. The apartment then forlorn without him and my mother turning to her books and I at my desk in my small room with my pencils and crayons and drawing pads. On the Rue des Rosiers the bearded man with the attaché case turned into the kosher butcher store, and I could no longer see him.

I paid for the meal and walked down the street past clothing stores and a kosher fast-food place and the butcher shop, into the courtyard of an apartment house. The nameplates on the wall inside the entranceway did not have the name I was looking for.

I crossed the street and walked back up past the large restaurant. Through the plate-glass window of the Hebrew bookstore I saw a short, stout, gray-bearded man in a skullcap standing behind the glass counter, reading a book. I opened the door and stepped into the tinkling music of an overhead bell. The man behind the counter looked up from his book. I closed the door, and the bell sounded again.

"Is it permitted to look around?"

"But of course, of course."

The store was small and densely stocked with religious articles and books. Glass shelves held skullcaps, prayer shawls, tefillin sacks, mezuzahs, neck chains with six-pointed stars. Along the walls stood glass cases filled with jewelry, candlesticks, Havdalah candleholders, spice boxes, books. There were books nearly everywhere—on shelves on the walls, in stacks on the floor, on a chair in a corner, on the edge of the counter, on angled shelves in the window.

Near the door was a shelf laden with coloring books and little boxes of crayons. The books contained pictures drawn from the Bible: Abraham gazing at the heavens and discovering God; Isaac bound to the altar, Abraham standing above him, a long knife in his upraised hand; Jacob receiving the blessing of Isaac; the wayside tomb of Rachel; Joseph in the garb of an Egyptian prince; the death of Jacob; Moses at the burning bush; the Israelites at the parting of the sea; Moses receiving the Torah on Mount Sinai; Moses gazing at the Land of Canaan from afar.

Above the shelf of coloring books was a shelf of artbooks: Chagall, Agam, Bak, Bergner, Rivers, Newman, Rothko, Tobiasse. I took down from that shelf the book titled *The Unorthodox Art of Asher Lev.* It had been published three years before by a New York house specializing in artbooks. The color reproductions, remarkable in their fidelity, and the text, written by a noted New York critic, were on heavyweight, glossy paper. Holding the book in my left hand, cradling it, feeling its substantial weight, I turned the pages, looking at the reproductions. Nearly twenty-five years of

Asher Lev lay between those covers: paintings, prints, pastels, pencil and charcoal and pen-and-ink drawings, watercolors, gouaches, sculptures. The trees and houses of my Brooklyn neighborhood; the rowboats in the lake in Prospect Park; pigeons on Brooklyn Parkway; old ladies gossiping on the parkway benches; old men walking, talking, gesticulating; a homeless woman asleep on a Manhattan sidewalk; a Hasidic young man eyeing a streetwalker on a Manhattan corner; Hasidic teenage boys with earlocks and skullcaps at a game of baseball; a Portuguese fisherman painted during one of the summers I spent in Provincetown with Jacob and Tanya Kahn; my mother at her desk behind books on the Soviet Union and the papers of her students; my father walking along Brooklyn Parkway with his attaché case; a black man dead on a New York street, the passersby looking at him but not seeing him. There were fine reproductions of *Village Burning, Old Man Journeying,* and *Village Death,* which had been in one of my earliest shows at Anna Schaeffer's gallery. I didn't even know where those canvases were now. America? Japan? Switzerland? West Germany? Brazil? France? The two *Brooklyn Crucifixion* paintings were in the book, each on its own full page. Some of the later paintings had caused an even greater furor than had the crucifixions. The author of the text quoted the *Time* magazine critic who claimed that I was using my art to attack in a mean-spirited way the religious tradition in which I had been raised and which, he claimed, I unconsciously detested. *The Sacrifice of Isaac, The Deceit of Rebekah, The Death of Moses, The Song of Devorah.* Huge canvases, positive and negative space constructed with fastidious care; weeks of preparatory drawings, some of which were reproduced in the book; weeks of work to lay on the colors; fusions of geometric and biomorphic forms. The subject was not literature but color, texture, space, forms. How some of the religious press had railed against those paintings! Blasphemy. Perversions. Satanic sensuality. Deliberate desecrations of the name of God. Anna Schaeffer would send me press clippings along with accompanying notes. "The voice of the religious is heard again throughout the land." "It appears the Baptists have joined your compatriots in Lev bashing." "How safe you must feel in the south of France. Come to New York and see what it is like to show Asher Lev. Some poisonous clippings enclosed. When may we expect your next show?" "This old woman is both exhilarated and exhausted by the tumults you cause. Your parents were in to see the show. Your mother embarrassed. Your father in a barely contained rage. Enclosed clippings show some Catholics share their sentiment and have joined the anti-Lev chorale. Entire show sold out. What next?" She had died soon afterward.

Burdened by memory, I closed the book and put it back on the shelf. The bearded man behind the counter had been watching me go through the book and now seemed disappointed that I was not buying it.

"Tourist?" he asked.

"Yes," I decided to say.

"From where?"

"America."

"From where in America?"

"New York."

"Brooklyn?"

"Yes."

"I have relatives in Brooklyn." He mentioned some names.

"Brooklyn is a big place."

"They are Ladover Hasidim."

"There are thousands of Ladover in Brooklyn."

"You are a Ladover?"

"Yes."

"You heard of this Asher Lev? I saw you looking at the book." He had clearly not opened the book. There was a full-page picture of me facing the title page.

"I've heard of him."

"You know him?"

"Slightly."

"I have heard that he converted."

"What?"

"He became a Christian."

"Where did you hear that?"

"I heard it. Who else would make such paintings?"

"You've looked at the paintings?"

"Feh! Why would I want to see such paintings? They are a desecration of the name of God."

"Why do you carry the book?"

"My wife gets it for the store. She says he is a very important painter and people buy books about him. What can one do? One must make a living. We have, thank God, eight children. Always my wife is in the store. But today her mother took sick. For me, you understand, this is time stolen from the study of Torah." His earnestness shone in his pale-blue watery eyes. "This Asher Lev, his father is the Rebbe's right arm. A great man, the father. I heard he recited Kaddish for his son when he converted. As the prophet says, 'I reared children and brought them up, and they have rebelled against me.' A father is not to be blamed for the actions of a son. Such a heartbreak no one should know, especially a great man like Rav Aryeh Lev. Tell me, you can maybe learn?"

"What?"

"You look like a man who can learn Torah. I have in the back some exceptional holy books."

"Not now."

"I have an excellent set of Rambam."

"Another time maybe."

"I am also a Ladover. But I have never been to Brooklyn. Not enough money for traveling. It is a dream of mine one day to go to Brooklyn and see the Rebbe. My father, may he rest in peace, knew the Rebbe when he lived in Paris during the war. You saw the Rebbe recently?"

"Yes."

His eyes went very wide, and he seemed suddenly to come to attention. "And?"

"The Rebbe, thank God, is well."

"He should live long and remain well. How are you called?"

"It's not important how I'm called."

"Go in good health."

"Thank you."

The bell tinkled as I opened the door and died abruptly as the door swung shut behind me.

Cool air brushed my burning face. Asher Lev, convert. A new wrinkle. I had not heard that one before. That was how some rid themselves of certain problems. In my sealed world, a problem person who crossed over to the outside was briefly mourned and soon forgotten: an enemy all knew how to handle. They stood away from such a person. But a problem person who chose for whatever reason to remain inside became a feared and troubling liability, and ultimately a demonic presence. They didn't know how to relate to you, because you were inside and outside simultaneously; you blurred the lines of separation; they didn't know what to tell their children. Asher Lev, convert. Asher Lev, troubler. The air felt glacial on my hot and raging flesh.

I walked quickly past the restaurant, crossed the street, and entered the kosher butcher shop. The bell over the entrance sounded loudly as I opened and again as I closed the door.

The shop was clean. Beige tile walls glistened in the ceiling fluorescents. The floor was covered with sawdust. Long hooks and saws hung from overhead metal rods. The cool air smelled of raw meat. A tall, big-bellied, heavy-shouldered man stood at a counter over a long slab of meat, a gleaming cleaver in his hand. He had a graying beard and wore a dark hat. A long, blood-splattered white apron covered his shirt and trousers. A second bearded man, thin and tall and also wearing a white apron, was weighing ground meat on a sheet of waxed paper on a scale. The tiny curling threads of red meat glinted oddly in the bright light. In a corner near the huge wooden door to the walk-in refrigerator, a young aproned Asiatic man sat on a stool, flicking feathers from slain chickens into a tall green plastic garbage can.

There were three customers in the shop, all of them women, two of them elderly. The third, a thin, gray-eyed woman in her late forties or early fifties, with high cheekbones and oval features, looked startlingly like Devorah. All wore wigs.

I went over to the man at the scale.

"Excuse me," I said in Yiddish. "Maybe you can help me."

He peered at me nearsightedly from across the counter.

"I need information about someone in the neighborhood."

"You are from around here?"

"I used to live over the café."

"Yes? I don't remember you. You used to buy here?"

"We moved away before you opened the shop."

"Aha. Where do you live?" He had turned and was looking at the scale.

"In Saint-Paul."

"Saint-Paul-de-Vence?"

"Yes."

"Very nice." He removed the ground meat from the scale, placed it on the counter, and put on the scale a sheet of waxed paper containing lamb chops. "Saint-Paul. Sunshine. The Riviera. Very nice. There are Jews in Saint-Paul?"

"Not many. Listen, the wife and children of Lucien Lacamp, who used to live upstairs—where do they live now?"

"I have no idea," the man said, peering at the scale. "You are an acquaintance?"

"I am a friend."

"They are no longer upstairs?" one of the elderly women asked the man at the scale.

"Which Lucien Lacamp?" asked the second of the elderly women.

"How many Lucien Lacamps do you know?" the first one asked.

"This is the Lucien who worked in the restaurant?" asked the second woman.

"Yes," I said.

"Wait," said the man at the scale, looking at me closely. "This is one of those killed in the explosion?"

"The same one."

They all stood there in silence, regarding me intently. The man with the cleaver paused with the instrument in midair and stood gazing at me.

"You should ask Mrs. Levy," said the second woman. "She is wise and knows everything that goes on in this neighborhood."

"Who is Mrs. Levy? Where does she live?"

"I am Mrs. Levy," the second woman said. "You should ask me."

I stared at her. There was an odd glint to her eyes, a strange tightness to her false-toothed smile. Her wig was slightly askew.

The bearded man at the counter put down the cleaver and proceeded to use a saw on cartilage and bone. The one at the scale removed the lamb chops and began to wrap up the ground meat.

"Mrs. Levy," I said. "Where do the wife and two children of Lucien Lacamp live?"

"Wife and one child. The older child died."

"I am sorry to hear that."

"She had the asthma. They live now on the Rue d'Aboukir in the Second Arrondissement." She gave me the number of the house.

"Thank you," I said. "I am in your debt."

"When you see Mrs. Lacamp, tell her Mrs. Levy sends warm greetings. The old woman with the bad heart. Tell her. She will remember."

"I will tell her."

I went out of the shop through the sound of the overhead bell and stood on the sidewalk a moment, taking deep breaths. At a storefront snack bar across the street I bought iced tea in a can. I walked toward the Métro, sipping the tea. Weak light shone from a milky sun. The streets were crowded. Inside the Métro, on the wide and crowded platform, I felt myself suddenly jostled, and I turned and saw a short, squat, bald man in a long gray coat and gray scarf and dark beret. The train suddenly entered the station. I rode to the Rue de Bac station and walked to the hotel past the barefoot old woman, who was still asleep on the stoop in the street.

In my room, weary to near-exhaustion, I slept for more than an hour and woke thinking Devorah was next to me. "Come into me, my husband," I heard her say, and I held her and loved her and was at peace—until the sudden clanging of the church bells jolted me awake. I lay a moment, dazed and disoriented, thinking I was home in Saint-Paul, listening to the tolling of the village bell.

In the bathroom I splashed water on my face and looked at myself in the mirror. The outline of my face traced with my finger into the mist covering the mirror in the bathroom in my parents' home: small, doll-like, long erased now. After the death of Apollinaire, the Spaniard had hated mirrors. He would not render the face they revealed. He hated mirrors, he hated death, he hated women. How could so much vindictive hatred, so much crude sensuality and vain egoism, be the source of such a torrent of awesome primal creativity? No, not entirely true. Sensitive, too. And generous. And a man of meager needs. Gilot should not have the final word on him. Besides, I knew of two or three great contemporary Talmudists with that kind of complex and contradiction-faceted being: cruel and generous, benevolent and pitiless. See how good I am being to you today, Spaniard. Chagall would not have been so kind.

I took the elevator down, left my key with the clerk, and went out of the hotel.

It was late afternoon. Air and sky were an oppressive and un-relieved gray. Traffic streamed through the streets; tourists crowded the sidewalks. The old woman, now awake, sat on her stoop, talking to her blackened feet and throwing furious glances at passersby.

I crossed the wide street to the Galerie Maeght and entered to the tinkling of the overhead bell. The owner of the gallery was in the Côte d'Azur for the week. I did not recognize the blond-haired young woman who sat behind the desk, reading a fashion maga-zine. She glanced up. Her eyes, picture-logged from the photo-graphs in the magazine, barely focused upon me. She gave me a vague smile and returned to her reading.

On the walls of the two large rooms of the gallery were draw-ings and watercolors by Saul Steinberg. It was cool and pleasant in the gallery. I was the only visitor. The art hung challengingly on the walls, inviting inspection. Curious cats, grinning crocodiles, hapless men. Gamblers, terrorists, dancing couples. Gaudy cars, vacant landscapes, Cubist cities. From white rectangle to white rectangle, his line traced a journey through the absurdities and emptiness of modern life. Sharp observation, exaggeration, wit, a blurring of the boundary between fiction and reality. Ambiguous, troubling, unfathomable. Riddle after riddle. Draftsmanship de-void of sentiment. The passionate Spaniard and the dispassionate Rumanian—both in one day. The gifts of Paris.

I bought a catalogue from the blond-haired young woman be-hind the desk and asked for the price of the watercolor of the figure on the precipice. She told me, and I said I would buy it. She began to make out the papers, and when I gave her my name she looked up at me, startled. I paid for the painting and gave her the

Saint-Paul address for shipping. Afterward I walked over to a nearby café to get something to eat.

On the balcony of my hotel room, I sit with my drawing pad propped on a knee and draw the faces of the living and the dead. I draw the face of the old woman on the stoop in the street, the dark vacant eyes and thin bloodless mouth and pointed nose, all her features like a foreshadowing of death; and the faces of two people, a man and a woman, walking past her: the flicker of shame, like the shame on the faces of those who were the first to liberate the death camps and stared at the unutterable horror and then stood looking at the ground at their feet and the sky overhead, and were possessed suddenly of a profound humiliation at belonging to a species capable of such unspeakable acts—and then the masks falling into place, for shame is among the most unendurable of sentiments. The mask of the old woman's face, and the masklike faces of those who go past her. I draw the faces of blacks and whites in Brooklyn passing one another on the streets, staring through and around and past each other, their faces like masks, each bodiless to the other. I draw the raging face of my Cousin Yonkel, and then the emptiness he turns upon me, the bloodless mask of a face concealing a dark torrent of fury and contempt. I draw the face of the woman with the poodle, a face painted and rouged to camouflage the fearful dawning of old age, the death-in-life face of one contemptuous of the needy stranger. I draw the face of the old Jew as I asked him in French about the Picasso Museum: cold, sealed, vacant, a mask—concealing what? fear of the stranger? contempt for any seeker of a museum of art? I draw the face of the Spaniard, cold with disdain and suddenly empty of all expression, a grotesque mask, as he talks of death. I draw the expressionless face of the butcher with the cleaver and the masklike face of the Asiatic man plucking feathers from dead chickens. Then I draw the face of Lucien Lacamp, squarish, stolid, bones and angles, straight nose, cool eyes, close-cropped hair, a soldier's lean face; Lucien Lacamp, a parachutist in the French Foreign Legion, wounded by a Russian mortar shell fired by Berbers in a skirmish near Oran, the fragments leaving him with cratered legs and a deep gouge between his shoulder blades about one inch to the left of his spinal column; Lucien Lacamp helping me put in the racks I needed for my prints, building my stretchers, stretching my big canvases, playing with Rocheleh, carrying the artist's proofs of my first carborundum print back from the printer and up the stairs. The forms baffled him. "I do not understand it," he kept saying, looking at the print. "It is an enigma. Such shapes do not exist. But the colors. Ah, the colors. They are formidable, the colors." And I draw his face dead amid the smoldering rubble of the restaurant explosion. Lucien Lacamp. One of the righteous of the Gentiles. I draw the face of Jacob Kahn, the smile he wears as he says, "Only the French could have given the Spaniard a museum like that," and the dark, poignant sadness in his eyes as he adds, "Even the Spaniard lost it a number of times. Chagall lost it. I lost it." I draw him in his final moments of life in his home near Saint-Paul, and again in his first moments of death. The withered grayish-green face gone completely slack. Jacob Kahn, my teacher, my master. Then I draw the face of Anna Schaeffer; she gazes at me coolly, regally, from the drawing pad. "What are they doing to you in Brooklyn?" she says. "Brooklyn is making mud of your mind." She had little patience for the vacuous world of the philistine, and no comprehension of the subtle texturing of religious consciousness. She saw in both those worlds—the bourgeois and the religious—bigotry, small-mindedness, the clawing of the benighted; greed for money and zealousness for God. She loved her artists and their art, her collectors and curators and art connoisseurs. "Do not disappoint me, Asher," I hear her say from the page of my drawing pad. I draw her during her last days in her apartment in New York. I draw her in her hospital bed. I draw her in her open coffin—something I would never have seen in my Brooklyn world, where such funerals are forbidden.

Above the rooftops of the city the day has slowly waned. By its final light I draw a picture of Devorah: the pale slender face, the curve of shoulder and breast, the roundness of thigh and leg. I draw her with Rocheleh. I draw her with Avrumel. I draw Avrumel hugging his rag doll, Shimshon. "How goes it, Avrumel?" "It goes well, Papa." I draw Devorah in her bed in Saint-Paul, the arching of her neck, the wide-open eyes, her tongue moist on her lips as she holds me in the final moments of one of our together-times. She calls it that on occasion: together-time. "Together-time tonight, Asher," she would sometimes whisper to me in the presence of the children. The Spaniard was not the only one who could draw good erotica—though I always concealed mine and rarely showed it even to Devorah. I am not a Neanderthal troll; but neither am I a bloodless angel.

It is dark. The city hums and throbs with its streams of traffic and nocturnal lights. I pray the Evening Service and lie in my bed and feel inside the room the heavy presence of the living and the dead. I finally fall asleep, imagining Devorah beside me, her arms gently encircling my neck in the warm and rocking embrace of a together-time.

4

✤ ✤ ✤ I woke from turbulent sleep to the banging and clanging of the bells. Troubled by dreams I could not remember, I dressed and prayed the Morning Service. I had something to eat at a café across the street from the hotel. At the table next to mine a middle-aged German couple sat talking in low voices about the Airbus accident and the train disaster at the Gare de Lyon. I went back upstairs to my room to use the bathroom and for the address book in my attaché case. I was looking through the address book when the phone rang.

The operator said it was a person-to-person call for Asher Lev from the United States. I said I would take the call, and thought, Something must be very wrong for Devorah to be calling me at three o'clock in the morning.

"One moment, please," the operator said.

"Hello," a man's voice said in English. "Is this Asher Lev?"

"Yes."

"Asher Lev, the artist?"

"Yes." Was there another Asher Lev?

"Asher Lev, the Rebbe wishes to speak with you."

The Rebbe! At three o'clock in the morning! When did he sleep?

I waited, my heart hammering. I was seated at the desk, and found myself staring at the drawing I had made the night before of Devorah in her bed in Saint-Paul. I couldn't remember having left the drawing pad open when I had gone out earlier. Still waiting, I flipped the pages. The Spaniard. Jacob Kahn. Anna Schaeffer. Devorah and Rocheleh. Avrumel and his Shimshon doll. Devorah and I in a together-time. I closed the pad.

"Asher Lev." I heard the voice, distant, tremulous.

"Yes, Rebbe."

"You are well?"

"Thank God, yes."

"Your wife and children are well. Your parents are well."

"Thank you, Rebbe."

"Asher, I speak to you as if you were here before me. I see you clearly. Distance is an illusion if one trusts in the Holy One, blessed be He. You understand?"

"Yes, Rebbe."

"I want to tell you something. Listen to me. You are now on a journey. We are told that when Jacob set out to journey from Beersheba to Haran, he stopped at a certain place for the night and had a dream. What did he dream? A stairway was set on the ground and its top reached to the sky, and angels of God were going up and down on it. Some were going from the earth to the heaven, others from the heaven to the earth. The great Moshe Chaim Ephraim of Sudlikov once said that this comes to teach us the following. A man does not always remain at the same stage. He is always ascending or descending. When he reaches the top, he must concern himself with the probability that he will fall. When he reaches the bottom, he must strive once again to climb to the top. That is the nature of man. When the soul of a man is in its darkest night, he must strive constantly for new light. When one thinks there is only an end, that is when one must struggle for the new beginning. This is true, Asher Lev, not only for the individual but also for the community. I wish you a safe journey up the ladder, Asher. Do you understand me?"

I did not respond.

"Asher, do you understand my words?"

"Yes, Rebbe."

"I wish that your journey will be to a light not only for yourself but for all of us. I wish that it will be a journey for the sake of heaven. I give you my blessing, Asher Lev."

The line went dead.

I hung up the phone.

For some minutes afterward I sat at the desk, staring down at the phone and the drawing pad. There was a strange tingling sensation in the tips of my fingers. The sounds of traffic came distantly through the closed doors of the balcony. Finally I locked my drawing pad in my attaché case, put the attaché case in the armoire, and took the elevator down to the lobby. I walked quickly in the gauzy mist of the Paris morning to the Métro.

Narrow cobblestone streets encumbered with traffic and tight with sidewalk cafés. Flower stands, fish stands, meat hanging raw and bloodied from hooks in butcher shop windows, sides of sheep, cuts of pork, rows of plucked, pink-skinned chickens. The warm and inviting aromas of food from the cafés mixing with the hot and repellent stench of diesel exhaust from the trucks. A dirt-blackened man sits on the sidewalk, propped against an apartment house wall, with a coal-black dog asleep beside him. On the man's lap is a sign that reads NOUS AVONS FAIM AIDEZ-NOUS. Cracked and peeling seventeenth-century apartment houses, their gray and yellow outer walls misshapen and bulging, lean precariously toward one another over the streets as if on the point of collapse.

An alleyway overarched by a yellow stone building brings me to a small bare inner courtyard and a short flight of iron stairs. At the end of the iron landing is a heavy wooden door that opens smoothly to my push.

I am inside an enormous, high-ceilinged room. Drawing tables, chairs, printing presses, stacked cans of color, tall piles of paper, laden drying racks. Men and women in stained aprons, hands blackened with ink, are working the presses. An entire wall is covered with decades of old lithographs, some so well known they are used as decorative tiles for bathrooms. Two of my prints are on that wall. Along the adjoining wall stands a ponderous cutting machine operated by a man who feeds it stacks of thick cardboard, which it guillotines with thudding sounds. At the tables, draftsmen are bent over opaque plates and color transparencies. In a far corner of the room, another flight of stairs leads up into darkness. Crossing the room, I see the workers looking at me, and I acknowledge their greetings with a wave of my hand. I climb to the landing at the top of the stairs, push open the heavy iron door, and step inside. The door swings closed behind me with a loud clanging noise.

About half a dozen men are standing at a long, cluttered table. Max Lobe, in protective goggles, is bent over a thin, flat sheet of metal, a lighted blowtorch in one hand, a scraper in the other. The noise of the closing door startles them, and they turn. Max Lobe cuts off the flame and removes his goggles.

"Asher Lev!" he calls out. "It is you, my friend!"

He puts down the scraper and the blowtorch and hurries toward me.

"Hello, Max," I say.

He embraces me and kisses my cheeks. He is short, roundish, robust. I smell his cologne. "How are you, Asher? You are so late, I almost despaired. Come see what I am doing. I am still unable to give it the shape I wish. How is my Devorah? And the children? You must tell me what I am doing wrong. The truth. Do not waste our time being gentle. Be like your Jacob Kahn. Here, stand here."

I move through the room, shaking hands with the others as I approach the table. One of the printers, a genial young man with shell-rimmed glasses and ink-smeared hands, offers me his elbow instead, and I shake it and we laugh. A tall, thin young man is introduced to me as a poet. He wears round silver-framed glasses. A wispy blond beard covers his long, pale face. His hand is limp, his fingers moist.

"Enchanted," he murmurs. "An honor to meet you."

Max is wearing a red-and-white-striped shirt and sharply pressed light-blue trousers. His round, smooth face and bald head glisten in the overhead lights. The printers have moved off discreetly and are talking among themselves. Max smooths his brush mustache with a stubby finger. "I am not happy with it; it does not sing. The texture is not quite right, but I am afraid if I play with it more it will cause the paper to crack. The first proof is on the wall there. Tell me what you think, my friend. The truth, as always."

On the white wall beyond a lithographic press gleaming beneath a fluorescent lamp is a print. Against a smoky background of blue and purple grays, bold strokes of black and red hover over an indistinct smear of ochres that vaguely resembles a cloud in which are suspended blurred numbers painted in primary colors. The thick paper is densely textured; it swells and dips and bulges; ridges and valleys lie beneath the fields of color; splashes of viridian and cobalt blue streak the surface; a thin swath of cadmium red gashes the upper-right-hand corner like a brief cry of danger.

"What do you think?" Max asks. His anxiety is as gray and tangible as the rain now falling on the rooftops outside the tall windows of the print shop.

"It is formidable."

He laughs uneasily. "You sound better when you say that than most Frenchmen I know. But I see in your eyes that there is something wrong. Tell me what you think about the red in the corner."

"The blacks and reds are a Clavé combination."

He blinks and says nothing.

"And the Clavé combination, striking as it is, is borrowed from Picasso."

"Dead, he still haunts us all, that Spaniard," Max says, with some bitterness. "Can you imagine him still alive?"

"Yes, I can. I do, often."

He stands gazing at the print, his thick shoulders sagging. "One has to be as good as you are, my friend, in order to endure him. I am not that good. I can live without such kings."

"To get back to the work," I say, indicating the print on the wall. "One should not use blacks and reds without giving them a center that attaches to black and red. Certainly the texturing should have a center."

"I tried to build it up, but it cracks the paper."

"Possibly it isn't necessary to build it higher, but to play a variation on what you have already done. Right now it's like the six days of creation without a focus. Maybe you ought to consider doing this."

We return to the metal plate on the table. The printers stand in a tight quiet knot, watching us out of the corners of their eyes. Max and I talk for some while in the technical language of art—linear accents, surface patterns, passage, movement patterns, multiple centers of interest, distribution of space, bridging tension points,

space and surface control, techniques of texturing, color movement, graphic balance. Max puts on his goggles, strikes a match,
and touches the flame to the blowtorch. The torch spurts into life
with a hard popping sound. I talk to him quietly as he works the
carborundum over the surface of the plate, softening it with the
flame, then spreading, smoothing, leveling, gouging, pitting, raising, lowering, streaking—so the thick paper will be alive with a
textured surface that is a unity with its colors and forms. We work
together a long time, and we are deep in it, lost in the working of
it, and then Max has caught it and I can sense him moving into it
alone, his face moist with concentration, and I step back and watch
him for a while, and there is much pleasure in that for me. I find
myself at a long table before a large sheet of empty drawing paper,
and I motion to one of the printers and he quickly brings me a box
of charcoal sticks, a bottle of India ink, and a reed pen, and I stand
there suddenly drawing and very soon there is a sliding away of the
time span between thinking and drawing and I feel the warm
sensation of self-transparency as the charcoal and the pen move
across the surface of the paper. I am drawing variations of the
number three: one double curve floats alone; another interlocks
with a third; a fourth wears an ordinary dark hat; a fifth leans
against a sixth, which is tall and stalwart. Variant forms, the ink
flowing from the pen as if from a brush and shaping often surprising marks, and quickly drying into a range of subtle textures
and values. And the center a face swiftly drawn and molded in
charcoal, the face of Avrumel, and a child's hand, barely visible,
clutching a Shimshon doll. I look at the drawing and it is done, and
I sign it and date it and put down the stick of charcoal and step
away from the table—and bump into one of the printers. He
apologizes softly, profusely. On the pale face of the poet, who
stands beside him, is a look of rapture. His eyes are wide and round
behind his round silver-framed glasses. They have all been standing bunched behind me, watching. Max has been watching me, his
blowtorch still spurting flame, his goggles on the table near the
metal plate. Avrumel, I hear myself silently calling. Avrumel. And
he replies, Here I am, Papa, and I hear his eager laugh. A vast and
overwhelming sadness takes possession of me.

Max turns off the blowtorch and puts it down. His face is pale and moist. "Enough for now," he says in a faintly tremulous voice. He seems troubled. "We will pull another proof after lunch." He gazes at my drawing. In his eyes are conflicting emotions: admiration, awe, dejection, envy. "How do you do that?" he murmurs. "I have seen you do it a hundred times. How? It is . . . incredible."

Outside the tall windows of the print shop the gray rain falls steadily on the rooftops and the chimney pots of the city.

"You were very helpful, my good friend," Max says. "I thank you."

"How long will you be in Paris?"

"I fly back this evening if there is no strike. I try not to stay too long in Paris. It reminds me too much of gendarmes and sealed apartments." He looks at my drawing and slowly shakes his head. "I have no idea what it means, yet it touches me. . . . You are having a problem with little Avrumel?"

I do not respond.

"What is it? You are concealing something from Max Lobe?"

Still I am silent.

He says, after a moment, "My friend, if I can help you with something . . ."

Everyone in the shop is silent. We hear the rain on the windows. For some reason I suddenly recall the horn players on the quai and the gendarme on the bridge and Jacob Kahn in his apartment overlooking the Louvre and the riverboats.

"There is mystic significance to the number three?" asks the poet in a hushed tone.

"I don't know," I reply.

"Of course," he murmurs after a moment. "I understand." He gazes at the drawing. "I understand perfectly."

I go over to the sink in the corner near the table and wash my hands. The white porcelain is smeared and stained with ink. The soap foams on my hands. I wash off the soap and dry my hands with a paper towel. Stains remain on the fingers of my right hand and along the edge of my left hand where I brushed across the paper for shading.

Max is inviting everyone to lunch. The printers are washing their hands. The poet says to me, "Where do you live now?"

"Saint-Paul."

"Ah, yes? Saint-Paul-de-Vence?"

"They call it Saint-Paul now. The village fathers don't want the world to think they belong to Vence."

We leave the printer's shop and walk along the narrow street. The rain has eased.

"You have a family?" the poet asks me.

"A wife, a daughter, and a son."

"Ah, how nice. I myself do not believe in marriage. An unhappy marriage results in quarrels that drain away one's creative energies. And a happy marriage results in laziness and a fear of disequilibrium. I believe that without disequilibrium there is no genuine art. Excuse me for asking, but are you truly a member of this group of—how are they called?—Hasidim?"

"Yes."

"How interesting! I read about it in *Le Monde,* in an article that appeared during your recent show in Paris."

I said nothing.

"May one ask if Asher Lev is working on something new?"

"At the moment, no. I am between things."

"I understand," he says. "I understand perfectly."

We stop at the entrance to the restaurant. I shake hands with the printers and the poet, and they go inside. Max lingers in the doorway.

"You cannot join us?"

"You know I can't eat in here."

"Where do you eat?"

"I have an arrangement with a café near the hotel."

"There is a kosher café near your hotel?"

"The owner provides for me. I repay him with a print or a drawing."

"That is a wise restaurateur. Like the owner of the Colombe d'Or. Yes. Very wise. Goodbye, my friend. John Dorman looks forward to your company once again. He is not well. You are staying only for a week after next Sunday? Too bad. You leave for ten days and are gone, it seems, forever. When I see you, you will tell me everything that is going on in Brooklyn. I should have gone to that funeral in your place. Me they would have sent back immediately."

"We'll talk next week, Max."

"What are you doing with that drawing? Shall I bring it down with me?"

"I'm giving it to André. I need the bon à tirer of an old print. An exchange."

"Which print?"

I told him.

"You are exchanging that drawing for a bon à tirer? You really are not well, my friend."

"I'm repaying an old debt, Max."

We shake hands, and I walk along the busy streets in the light rain. On the crowded nearby boulevard I stand waiting at a covered taxi station. Empty taxis come along and go by without stopping. The drivers do not even glance at me but sit behind their wheels, staring straight ahead. Are they all off duty? I wait a long time in the light rain. A taxi pulls up for a red light. I go over to the driver and through the partially open window ask him if he's free. He is olive-skinned, unshaven, thickly muscled, and wears a tight dark shirt and dark pants. He wants to know which arrondissement, and I tell him, "Eighteen." He motions with his head, and I jump into the back of the cab as the light changes.

I will not enter that apartment house again; enough to see it now from the outside. A pilgrimage of sorts to the dark core of the Other Side. A gray cement building, one of four on the block, each seven stories high. Narrow streets, paved now, cobblestoned when Max and Devorah lived here for the two years of their tomb-time, as Devorah once bitterly labeled it. Rue Gustave Rouanet on one side, Rue du Ruisseau on the other. A school on the street opposite the entrance to the building. A church on the corner diagonally across the street from Devorah's room. Housewives and children. Stores and shops and the heavy stir of traffic.

I have been inside the building once, with Devorah. Narrow entranceway, long dimly lit corridors, slow rattling elevator. We did not go up to the apartment. Who lives there now? Do they know what once took place within those walls? Imagine if every apartment and home had its history written on its doorposts. An unendurable notion. Max has never been back here, not once, since the day he left Paris. He says very little about that tomb-time. Nor has he ever drawn or painted it. Max and his decorative bursts of color. His swirling reds and blacks and floating clouds and rectangles and upside-down letters and numbers. Max says he paints to celebrate life. But you can only be a true celebratory modernist if, like Matisse, Dufy, Chagall, you really mean it. Max paints to conceal the terror of his tomb-time, and his lightheartedness is seen by the discerning as drawn too taut, with minute cracks showing here and there; an unconvincing and derivative decorativeness. He is a fine colorist, and very popular; important collectors have him on their walls. But he is not in museums, and that embitters him. I tell him often that he should paint the darkness he feels, not the false light that he covers it with. "You paint it," he responds. "You are a specialist in darkness." I tell him, "I didn't live through it." He says, "We all lived through it, everyone; all of humanity lived through it. Was Picasso in Guernica? Did Guido Reni see with his own eyes the slaughter of little children in Bethlehem?"

On the July day of the roundup, Devorah came home from playing with a friend in the schoolyard and noticed cars and trucks parked up and down the street. But it meant nothing to her. She was four years old.

They lived on the third floor. Inside the front door she pushed the button for the temporary light. The entrance hallway was silent and deserted, and this, too, meant nothing to her. The door to the apartment was open, and from the corridor she saw the two gendarmes and the two men in ordinary clothes, and her parents in the living room stuffing things into suitcases. She was about to call out, "Mama!" when her mother spotted her in the doorway and shouted in a voice that jolted her like an electric charge, "What are *you* doing here? What do you *want*? There is *nothing* for you to see here! This is *not* a circus or a zoo! *Go home to your parents!*" The voice was a wall of energy; it had a force of will that bent her response to it. Her mother stared at her with raging features; her father had his back to her and did not turn. The men looked at her and at each other. She whirled and fled.

She fled to the next-door corner apartment house of her Cousin Max. Fearful of the slow elevator, she raced up the stairs to her relatives' apartment—just in time to be scooped up by them as they were fleeing the apartment before the arrival of the gendarmes. The concierge, an elderly man, a Gentile, rushed them to an empty apartment on the seventh floor. There they waited in dread—Max, his parents, and little Devorah—until the concierge returned to tell them that the police had arrived, found them gone, sealed their apartment, and left. He and Max's father then conferred in low voices in a corner. Devorah went to a window to look out at the street; perhaps she could see her parents. Max's mother quickly pulled her away. She began to cry, softly. Max, ten years older than Devorah, tried to comfort her in his awkwardly gallant way. Everything would be all right. He was sure she could stay with them. He would protect her.

Later that night the concierge led them back downstairs through the eerily silent corridors and stairwell, took off the wax seals and the wire placed on their apartment door by the gendarmes, quickly removed the mezuzah from the doorway with the claws of a hammer and handed it to Max's father—who subsequently lost it; it was never found—and closed the door behind them. A few days later, a man from the French resistance brought them food.

Five small rooms. The dimmest of electric lights. Who paid their very low electric bill? They never found out. No heat. Two bitter winters. Metal shutters fastened across the windows, angled downward so they could see only slitted views of the street. For two years no glimpse of the sky.

Late one morning, about a year after the roundup, cars and trucks filled with German soldiers suddenly appeared at the corners, sealing the street, and they knew it was over, someone had betrayed them. They waited in terror for the knocks on the door. But it was only the German commandant of Paris coming to be photographed distributing oranges to French children in the nearby school. And one night American bombers struck at the nearby railroad yard and lit the sky to high noon, and two blocks away a row of houses disappeared beneath an errant cluster of bombs, and they felt the walls of the apartment shaking and the windows rattling and plaster falling from the ceiling, and she cried again and Max held her awkwardly to him, patting her shoulder, soothing her with promises of his dauntless protection. Darkness and terror for two years until August 1944, when the great bell of Notre-Dame peals the liberation of the city. Crowds in the street, shouts, distant gunfire. Devorah and Max open the door to the apartment and do not wait for the elevator. They race down the stairs together, he holding her little hand—she is six years old—and burst out onto the street, the air warm and the sky cloudy, and feel their eyes pierced and blinded by the hazy late-afternoon light.

Max went to art school, struggled for ten years, and began to sell. That was when I met him, in the sixties, through the Ladover representative in Paris. He came up to my studio apartment to look at the crucifixions. "I heard of you all the way from New York," he said. "Now I know what the tumult is all about." He came often, alone. Then he came with Devorah. By then Anna Schaeffer had arrived on one of her regular European jaunts, and the crucifixions were on their way to New York. Devorah has never seen them except in reproductions. She does not want to see them. "The reproductions frighten me enough," she told me once.

The taxi driver was looking at me in his rearview mirror. "Is this the place you wanted?"

"Yes."

He was waiting for me to pay him and leave the cab. He kept looking at me in the rearview mirror.

A woman emerged from the apartment house, accompanied by a girl and a boy. She hesitated near the entranceway and looked up at the cloudy sky, squinting. She took the hands of the children. The boy reached up to her, and she lifted him and held him tight. Clearly, as though she were sitting beside me in the taxi, I heard her say to the boy, "There is a plan. With all my heart and soul I believe there is a great plan."

They went together up the street and turned the corner.

I told the driver to take me back to my hotel. He drove away from the apartment house and out of that neighborhood.

The rain continued to fall. On the stoop in the rain sat the old woman, beneath a large brown sheet of plastic, staring with raging eyes at passersby. I ate a late lunch near the hotel and, through the rain-streaked window of the café, watched the traffic and the

people on the puddled streets. When I returned to the hotel, the
concierge told me my wife had called about half an hour earlier. It
was now close to three o'clock in Paris: nine in the morning in
New York. I took the elevator to my room and called the overseas
operator.

Devorah answered. "Asher? How are you, my husband?"

"Is everything all right? How was the first day of camp?"

"Everyone is well. Rocheleh loves the camp."

"And Avrumel?"

"He's fine. He's learning to play baseball."

"Baseball."

"Are you all right, Asher? You sound tired."

"Jet lag. I spent the morning with Max at the printer's. He sends
his love. What else is Avrumel doing?"

"He studies Torah, he plays all sorts of games, he eats. It's a
good day camp. He went on a long walk yesterday evening with
your father. Your father says he'll take him to his office on Sundays
now and then."

"Have you heard anything more about Uncle Yitzchok's will?"

"Your Cousin Yonkel came over to the house last night and said
you exerted undue influence on his father and that's why he left
you the collection. Asher, are you all right? You sound exhausted."

"I went over to look at the apartment house."

There was silence. The line seemed to have gone dead.

"Devorah?"

"I'm here, Asher."

"They painted the outside of the entranceway, so it looks a little
better than the last time I was there. Otherwise, nothing has
changed. How is my mother?"

"She's wonderful. We have beautiful talks together."

"Take good care of Avrumel."

"Of course."

"Goodbye, Dev."

"Goodbye, my husband."

In the silence that followed I could hear clearly the rain on the
panes of the balcony doors. I was seated at the desk, and I looked
at my drawing pad and found I had drawn in it, on a single page,
in contour, the face of the Spaniard and the face of the Rebbe, both

in profile and facing one another. The Rebbe had on his ordinary hat, the Spaniard his beret: two kings gazing upon each other on the page of my drawing pad. I could not remember removing the drawing pad from the attaché case, and I could not remember making the picture.

I closed the drawing pad and lay down on the bed. The quilted spread was soft against my back, the rounded pillow hard beneath my head. I covered my eyes with my hand. The museum swam into view, wet in the morning rain; and the old ladies in the butcher shop and the cleaver in the butcher's hand; and Max Lobe brushing the violet-blue flame of the blowtorch across the surface of the metal plate and the large gallery across the street from the hotel with the Steinberg drawings and watercolors; and the quai in the rain and the gendarmes near the bridge and the lights of the tourist boats on the façades of the elegant old buildings. It all moved back and forth across my vision, slide upon slide, layered like transparent geological strata. Then I was drifting into sleep and someone was tapping on the wall. I was asleep, and the tapping moved to the door. I walked sleepily to the door, and it was one of the bellhops with a package. "Pardon, Monsieur Lev. Very sorry to disturb you. The concierge directed me to deliver this. The messenger said it was very urgent. Pardon. Good afternoon."

The package was long and tubular. I opened it carefully and removed the protective sheets of tissue paper and pulled out what looked like a print and, suddenly fully awake, saw it was the bon à tirer from the printer.

I spread it out on the bed. The colors and forms leapt from it, the complementaries vibrating upon the surface, vying with the texturing for control of the picture plane. The words were in my handwriting in the space at the foot of the sheet of thick handmade paper: *bon à tirer*. Ready for the press. Approved by me for the final printing. I had signed and dated it: Asher Lev 17 February 1970. The first print I had made in Paris after being sent away by the Rebbe—ordered away, exiled—from my Ladover world in Brooklyn because of the raging reactions to the crucifixion paintings. A twenty-copy run. Anna Schaeffer had said the price would have to be high if the print was to pay back the cost of the paper and the printing and return a profit. The price was outrageous, and the entire print run swiftly vanished into museums and private collections—including, as I had recently discovered, the collection of my late Uncle Yitzchok. Ten years later, all my artist's proofs of that print vanished, too—stolen from the moving van somewhere between Paris and Saint-Paul. Accounts of the theft made the papers. This was the print I later elaborated into the large oil painting *The Sacrifice of Isaac,* which my father abhors even more than he does the crucifixions, and which now hangs in the Stedelijk Museum in Amsterdam.

I sat on the bed looking at the print and running my fingers over its densely textured surface. Jacob Kahn had come to Paris earlier that year, 1970, at the invitation of the Ministry of Culture. The French wanted him to work on the walls and ceiling of one of their historic public buildings, a seventeenth-century Baroque Parisian edifice; give its vaulting interior the touch of an authentic twentieth-century master, one of the few remaining giants from the legendary School of Paris. While he waited for a government committee's routine approval of his preliminary drawings, we worked together on the carborundum process.

Carborundum is a metallic powder that can be mixed with a resin and dripped onto a surface wet with that resin. It hardens to the consistency of metal and it retains ink. Jacob Kahn, then in his high eighties, white-haired, robust, the fingers of his hands callused with decades of sculpting yet strangely delicate when drawing or applying color, mixed and poured and talked about Picasso in the Bateau Lavoir, and about Braque and Picasso working together in the early Cubist days, and Matisse and the Fauves and "that crazy Lithuanian painter, Soutine, saved from destitution by that clever American doctor, Barnes." He talked about Marc and Bella Chagall and what he thought really caused Bella Chagall's sudden death in upstate New York. He talked about Dadaists and Surrealists and the coming of the Nazis to Paris and his flight south to Marseilles and across the Pyrenees to Spain and then the ocean voyage to New York. He had been told that French police brought the Gestapo to his studio. The Germans had melted down all his sculptures. Decades of labor gone into the fires. He had sworn he would never return to Paris. But how could he refuse such an invitation? Indeed, wasn't it true that a nation, like a person, must be given the opportunity to repent, else there would be no end to the cycle of human hate and suffering?

He talked about the carborundum process. A painter named Henri Goetz had discovered it some decades ago. Joan Miró and others used it. You worked in layers: the background, the drawing, the forward planes. Each had its own sheet, its own carborundum texturing, its own colors. The process yielded a remarkable variety of embossings and reliefs. Different thicknesses of carborundum resulted in different textures. Any material that was flat and held the resin could receive the carborundum. The paper that would receive the print was thick, each sheet handmade. "Some experiment with this for years before they can get it to work for them," Jacob Kahn said, working the blowtorch, his grizzled features running with sweat. It was summer in Paris. We worked with printers standing around us, shaking their heads in disbelief. They murmured with delight as the paper took the ink and the carborundum texturing and emerged crosshatched, indented, ridged, undulating with life.

Then I worked on my print, with Jacob Kahn watching and guiding. "What I am not able to understand is why Picasso never discovered this," he said to me one morning as I mixed and poured the powdery metal. "That Spaniard discovered and changed everything else. No, you do not want to lay it on so thickly there, Asher. It will unbalance the color dynamic. Be gentle with it. It is metal, but it must be treated gently and with patience." How the art magazines had picked up on that—Jacob Kahn and Asher Lev working together in Paris on a recently discovered process for the making of prints! They had all thought Jacob Kahn would be dead by then. He had undergone major surgery in New York the year I was sent away by the Rebbe. "The Rebbe prayed for me and predicted I would recover," Jacob Kahn told me one afternoon as we stood over a worktable at the printer's. "I am giving all my artist's proofs of this print to the Ladover. It will bring them a small fortune, and I will have repaid all my obligations to the Rebbe. Debts of that kind are too heavy to carry. What are you doing, Asher Lev? If you put it on that way, they will need to frame it in a box. You will need a thicker paper, and Anna will tell us again about her outrageous costs. How are you finding life in Paris? It is not so easy to be a Jew here, is it? It is not Brooklyn."

The designs were approved, and he completed the building and returned to America.

A year later, he was back in France with Tanya—to stay. "They make me feel welcome, the French. They give me space for my sculptures, walls and ceilings to paint, and churches to make stained-glass windows for. They hint they will build me a museum one day. How can I refuse? Besides, I find the art world of New York unendurable. There was passion in the time of the Abstract Expressionists. Now . . . now there is greed and—what is the word?—glitz. And chaos. If the chaos were hot, I could create in it. But this chaos is cold with the touch of money. Why should I remain in New York?"

They lived in Paris for four years, in the apartment overlooking the Seine and the Louvre, the night boats brushing their tall windows with halogenic gold. Devorah and I visited them often when he was not away somewhere working on a church. He did some fine work of his own during those years, in Paris and Petra Santa— three huge oil paintings in his easily recognizable style, and two monumental sculptures, one of which is in the sculpture garden of the Israel Museum in Jerusalem. But the fire seemed to have gone out of him. Then he was sick again. Suddenly he needed warmth, he needed sunlight. "I do not want to die in the cold mists of Paris," he said to me in the apartment on the morning of their move south to Saint-Paul. The large rooms were echoingly bare, the high walls starkly vacant. He looked shrunken, his eyes dark and brooding, his walrus mustache drooping over his dry lips. He turned away from me and stood gazing at the murky waters of the river. Along the Quai Voltaire, trees were turning green after a cruel winter. In a low boat that glided slowly beneath the bridges stood a young woman in a billowing yellow dress, hanging her laundry on the stern deck. Houseboats hugged the banks. An elderly couple sat on the deck of a moored barge, eating breakfast. Fishermen were playing their rods and lines along the banks, and book dealers were opening their stalls along the quais. "I want to die in Cézanne's light," he said, "and be buried under the sun. You will come and visit me, will you not, my Asher? You will say a prayer over my grave?" He had died in the southern light and now lay buried beneath that sun.

I put tissue paper above and beneath the print, rolled it carefully, and inserted it in the tube. It was nearly five o'clock. I took the elevator down to the lobby and went out of the hotel.

The rain had turned to the sort of mist Jacob Kahn had moved south to avoid. The old woman lay on the stoop under the plastic cover. I walked toward the taxi station on the Boulevard Saint Germain.

The taxi took me into a neighborhood of torn-up streets. The driver, dark-skinned and unshaven, looked to be a recent arrival from North Africa or the Middle East. "It is not far from the monument," I heard him say. I did not know which monument he meant. "This is very bad for taxis," he added as we bounced along the rutted streets.

A Parisian late-afternoon summer rush hour. Darting cars, blaring motorcycles, buses, pedestrians, gendarmes, a miasma of exhaust fumes hanging in the humid air. Gazing out the window as we sat stalled in traffic, I saw a well-dressed middle-aged man sail serenely past us on a bicycle, retaining in the thrust of his chin and the tilt of his head a cool and urbane dignity. The taxi driver kept turning into the wrong streets. "This is a shit of a city," I heard him mutter. "I don't know what I'm doing here." His French began to yield to his Arabic as he struggled through the neighborhood's one-way streets and broken pavement. Scrawled boldly on the blotched stone façade of a yellowish apartment house were the words MITTERRAND DEHORS. How many times had I seen those words? Mitterrand out. Election this fall in the United States. Election this fall in Israel. My father traveling to Israel because the Ladover are involved in politics there. And in the world of the Ladover? The next Rebbe would not be elected. The next Rebbe would be chosen. By a sign from the present Rebbe. The sign would have to be given soon. What would it be and how would it be given? I thought I knew what the Rebbe wanted. It terrified me.

The taxi came to a stop.

"Rue d'Aboukir," the driver said. "There is the number."

I paid him and climbed out of the taxi.

"Your package," the driver called out.

I reached in, retrieved the tube, and thanked him. He drove away.

The street was a narrow, one-way, traffic-clogged tunnel lined with stores and old six-story apartment houses. I stood in front of the building that bore the address given me by the old woman in the butcher shop. The address was on the narrow streetside edge of a pale-gray marble wall that, together with a store window, formed an alleyway leading to a door. A naked mannequin gazed back at me through the section of the window that faced the street. Smooth and lovely curves and the vacant face and dead eyes. The two other mannequins in the window were fashionably clothed. I went down the alleyway and through the door and found myself inside a long corridor that led to a small courtyard open to the sky and another corridor and a flight of narrow winding wooden stairs. The air was cool and smelled of raw earth and mold. On the wall of the corridor beyond the courtyard were rows of mailboxes. Scrawled on a piece of paper and inserted into one of the plates so that it lay slightly askew was the name Lacamp.

They lived on the top floor. There were no elevators in these old houses. I began to climb the stairs.

The gloomy wooden stairway curved upward into shadows and creaked beneath my feet. On the final landing I stood awhile before the door, sweating, waiting for my breathing to ease. Once I had climbed five flights of stairs day after day and thought nothing of it. Often I had carried Rocheleh up those stairs. Once Lucien Lacamp had carried Rocheleh—

I heard voices beyond the door. A woman's voice; a child's voice.

I tapped on the door. Immediately the voices fell silent.

I waited. No one came to the door.

I tapped on the door again.

"Who is there?" a woman's voice asked after a moment. She sounded frightened and seemed to be talking with her mouth against the door.

"Asher Lev. A friend of Lucien's."

There was silence. Barely audible sounds rose from the shadowy stairwell: a man's voice, a child's cry.

"Asher Lev," I repeated. "From the Rue des Rosiers."

"Asher Lev, the artist?"

"Yes."

"Ah, yes? Is it truly you?"

"Yes."

The door opened. She stood in the doorway, blinking nervously. She looked past me at the landing and the stairwell, as if fearful there might be others concealed in the shadows.

"I apologize for disturbing you." I saw her peering at me myopically, suspiciously. "You don't recognize me?"

She regarded me closely. "Ah, yes, I do, I do, of course. Yes." She drew her housecoat tightly to her thin neck. She was a birdlike woman in her mid-forties, with sallow features, dry yellow hair, and darting eyes. A wide-eyed girl of seven or eight clung to her housecoat. "I remember you, of course. Come in, monsieur, come in, please."

I stepped into the apartment. She closed and locked the door with exaggerated care. Her hands fluttered tremulously. "Please sit down. Please. A cup of tea? Coffee? A cold drink? No? Georgette, this is Monsieur Asher Lev, a friend of your papa's. Now you will go and play quietly in the other room."

The little girl gave her mother an imploring look.

"Georgette," her mother said.

The girl left.

"Yes," the woman said. "Of course, I remember. The artist with the big paintings."

"That's right."

"Always the paintings have to go out through the balcony doors because the stairway is not large enough for them. Lucien makes jokes about that. Asher Lev of the balcony paintings, he used to say."

"He would attach them to ropes and lower them carefully to me in the street. Once or twice you watched him do it."

"Ah, yes. I remember. He said you were a little crazy. Always drawing and painting, painting and drawing. He said you were a kind man, not like some other artists he knew."

We were sitting in worn rattan chairs in a small and dingy room that was a living room, dining room, and kitchen. The kitchen section lay behind three thick unpainted wooden beams that seemed to be holding up the ceiling. The floor and walls were bare. The low ceiling buckled slightly in the area of the kitchen, where it received the heat of an ancient two-burner stove. Through the open doorway near my chair I caught a glimpse of the adjoining room: two narrow beds, bare floor, bare walls, a dresser, a mirror, a chair. The little girl sat on the floor, playing with a rag doll. Tall doors with thin dirty curtains and unwashed panes led out to a narrow balcony on which were two black metal chairs, a metal table, and pots of dry earth containing the rotted stalks of long-vanished flowers. Across the street stood yellow stone houses: grill-work on the windows and narrow balconies; dormer windows projecting from sloping blue-painted roofs; TV antennas and chimney pots protruding into the milky sky. Devorah and I and Rocheleh had lived in a similar apartment on the Rue des Rosiers, but with carpets on the floors and the Danish furniture Devorah favored and paintings on the walls—hers the Paparts and Coignards and Lobes; mine the Lipchitz and Henry Moore and Jacob Kahn drawings and work of my own and the paintings of young Parisian artists I had begun to collect. The apartment had a room for Rocheleh and one additional room, where I worked; Devorah and I slept in an alcove behind the studio. In the spring and summer, each time Lucien and I needed to lower one of my paintings to the street, a path would have to be cleared through the balcony garden of pansies, geraniums, daffodils, and marigolds cultivated by Devorah.

"Your Lucien was a very good man. I trusted him."

"Others have said the same thing. I loved him. But God chose to take him away. I remember you wrote to me when it happened. He was working in the café, bringing someone an espresso—and poof! We aren't Jews, you know. The bomb was meant for Jews. But God chose to take him away."

"What do you do now?"

"I wait on tables in a restaurant. I remember when you moved from the Rue des Rosiers. You live now in the south?"

"Near Saint-Paul."

"Saint-Paul-de-Vence?"

"Yes."

"It must be nice in the south. How is your daughter?"

"She is well, thank you. We also have a son."

"A son. How nice. Thanks to God. A son."

"I heard only yesterday about your older daughter. I am deeply sorry. May God give you comfort."

Her nearsighted blue eyes misted over. The thin, sallow features of her squat face—the flat nose, the small, bow-shaped mouth—seemed to melt. She wiped at her eyes with the palms of her hands and smoothed her lap. "Poor child. What could God have had against her? An innocent child. Pneumonia, the doctor said."

"Not asthma?"

"Ah, no. She had not the asthma. Pneumonia. One day she is alive and laughing. The next day she is sick. And the day after she is dead and gone to God. Poof! Just like that. Lucien is with her now. I have one daughter, and he has the other. It is the will of God."

Through the open doors of the balcony I could hear the sounds of the evening traffic below.

"We visit their graves. It is a comfort. My little Georgette and I, we speak to them, we bring them flowers, we pray. You are a religious man. You know that is a great comfort."

A comfort. Uncle Yitzchok. Jacob Kahn. A comfort.

"He was a good soldier, a good Frenchman, a good husband. Not like the others. You know what I mean? He did not chase women or come home drunk. But God took him away."

You had to take him away? He wasn't a Jew. The bomb was not meant for him. It was a mistake You made, wasn't it? How? A half-blind, half-dead clerk would not make such a mistake. Lucien. Once I woke in the cold of a winter night to odd sounds in the Rue des Rosiers apartment—deeply drawn gasping breaths—and thought I was dreaming and went back to sleep. In the morning it occurred to me to ask Rocheleh if she had had a bad dream, and she said no, she woke and couldn't catch her breath for a minute because the air was so cold. They turned the heat down in the building after eleven at night. I gave Rocheleh another blanket.

In the evening about ten days later, Lucien was putting in a new bank of deep-angled shelves in my studio, and I was working on a series of drawings that would later become the basis for my print and painting *The Deceit of Rebekah,* and Devorah was wading through a pile of children's books and was at the moment reading, if I remember correctly, *Le voyage à la recherche du temps* by Lucie Ledoux—or was that published later?—when I hear the sounds of someone gasping and choking and find Rocheleh on the floor near her bed, where she has been playing with her doll; she lies there arched, rigid, clutching her throat, her eyes wide with terror, her face a bluish white. I ask her if she has swallowed anything, and she manages to shake her head no. Devorah has come rushing into the room by then and Lucien is putting Rocheleh on her bed and Devorah is calling for a taxi but it is pouring outside and she cannot get through to the taxi company, the line is busy. She tries another and another. They are all busy. Rocheleh is gasping for air, strangling. Devorah begins to phone for an ambulance. Lucien says we should not wait for an ambulance, he has seen this sort of shallow breathing before, we should bring her immediately to the hospital. I pick her up and hold her to me, her grating breaths like a metal saw scraping at the back of my neck and the roots of my teeth, and throw Devorah's raincoat over her, and Lucien accompanies me as I carry her down the five flights of stairs and out into the rain-soaked street, and he takes her from me and runs with her, and I follow, rivulets of rain coursing through the cobblestones, our shoes splashing through the deep puddles, rain in our mouths and eyes, and all the time the stiff, arched little body and the choking sounds. She may have the asthma, the doctor in the hospital said. There were forms to fill out. Where did I live? the nurse at the receiving desk wanted to know. Was I a citizen of France? A permanent resident? What kind of medical insurance did I have? And Lucien on the bench in the waiting room, wet, patient, soldierly, unwilling to leave me alone in case I needed help with the doctor, the nurse, the intricacies of French hospitals, the paperwork, the despair that suddenly settled upon me. One minute well, the next minute ill. One minute alive, the next minute dead. Lucien. Uncle Yitzchok. Poof! A fourth-level bureaucrat on the take could do better at running things. Master of the Universe, why are they so angry at me for the art I make? You are the cruelest artist of all!

Then the weeks of tests. Frightened little Rocheleh and dread-filled Devorah. Chest X-rays, sinus X-rays, pulmonary function study, allergy tests. The nights in the apartment now like the sealed apartment during the war, Devorah and I often awake and waiting for sounds, from inside the apartment now, from Rocheleh. Wheezing, coughing up mucus, waking and asking us to open the window, she needed air. It turned out that she was allergic to cigarette smoke; Devorah immediately stopped smoking. She was allergic to her rag doll; we got rid of it; she wept bitterly. She was allergic to cheese and aspirin. She was allergic to oil paints, the chalk of pastels, the dust of charcoal. I rented a two-room apartment in our building, two floors below ours. Lucien helped me move my studio.

Lucien. One of the righteous Gentiles of the world.

I took a deep breath of the stagnant air in the apartment, and I said to his widow, "Your husband was a good man. When I came to Paris I was a stranger in your country. Even though I had lived and worked here before, I had never truly gotten to know your country and its ways, because I believed I would soon return home to New York. But then I came here to live, and I met your husband and we became friends. He was a help to me, and I was made desolate by his death. He was not a Jew, but he died the death of many Jews. Once your husband helped me carry copies of my first print up the stairs of our building. And once he helped me carry my daughter to the hospital in an emergency. Surely he told you of that incident. I could not repay him for that second kindness because he was a proud and religious man, and I would not insult him with an offer of payment for an act of mercy. But for the first kindness, the carrying of the print, for that I had promised him a picture, and with all that happens in life, I had forgotten my promise and did not give it to him. I was reminded of that while in New York recently, and it weighs heavily upon me."

The widow of Lucien Lacamp sits listening to me, her eyes wide and soft and intent, her small mouth slightly open.

"I have brought you a picture," I tell her. "It is of much value.

You can make use of it now or later, as you wish. What you must know about the picture is this: the longer you wait with it in your possession, the greater will be its value. If the picture is worth this and this now"—I quote an amount of money—"it will be worth possibly ten times that in about ten years, when your daughter will be ready for university."

Her face fills with astonishment.

"Inside the tube with the picture is the name of a man in New York. He is called Douglas Schaeffer. He is a great dealer in art. He is the one you must get in touch with whenever you decide to make use of this picture. He will tell you what to do. If you change your address, you must notify this man. From time to time I will send you an additional picture, so that soon you will have a collection of pictures. Perhaps you will want to go to the library and take out a book or two about art and how to care for such a collection. Here is an envelope with some money so that you can have the picture in the tube properly framed. The best place to put a picture is on a wall. Pictures require walls in order to breathe and remain alive. I wish you and your daughter a good life. I will remember always the great kindness of your husband."

I stood. She got quickly to her feet. She looked dazed.

"I must go. I would like to say goodbye to your daughter."

"Of course," she said, and called, "Georgette, come here."

The girl came hesitantly into the room and reached for her mother's hand.

"Monsieur Lev wishes to say goodbye to you."

"Goodbye, Georgette. I am sorry you lost your big sister. My people in New York have a great leader, and if he were here now, I am sure he would give you and your mother a blessing for a long and healthy life."

I stood in the doorway to the apartment.

"Treat the pictures as though they are living beings. They will grow together with you and your daughter. Goodbye, Madame Lacamp. Goodbye, Georgette."

I walked down the poorly lit creaking wooden stairway and through the courtyard to the street. It was drizzling. The twilight air was gray and dim. A taxi pulled up, and I climbed in and gave the driver the name of my hotel.

I draw the face of Lucien's wife. I draw the face of the daughter, Georgette. I draw the face of Rocheleh. I draw the face of Avrumel. He went on a long walk with your father. I draw the face of Devorah. Your father says he'll take him to his office now and then. Again I draw the face of Avrumel.

Avrumel in my father's office. The Rebbe's office close by. One day he follows my father into the Rebbe's office. Or my father says, "I must see the Rebbe about a matter, come with me, I don't want to leave you alone." And the door is opened and the Rebbe sits at his desk in the hushed room that is softly lit by the chandelier rescued from a Ladover synagogue destroyed during the civil war in Russia that followed the October 1917 Revolution. My father approaches the desk. Avrumel hangs back near the door, awed, wishing for the comforting presence of his Shimshon doll, which my father urged him to leave at home so it would not be lost or forgotten. Now he wishes for the hand of his mother, the presence of his father. Ça va, Avrumel.

The Rebbe becomes aware of Avrumel's presence and raises his arm in a beckoning gesture.

"Come closer," the Rebbe says. "Come here to me, Avrumel."

Avrumel, fearful, does not move.

"Avrumel," my father says gently. "The Rebbe is talking to you."

"Avrumel," I hear myself say. "When the Rebbe calls you, you must go to him. Go over to the Rebbe."

Avrumel moves toward the small dark-garbed figure behind the desk, his little heart beating so loudly he is fearful it can be heard like a drum in the room.

"Here," the Rebbe says. "Stand next to me. A fine-looking boy. Your grandfather tells me you like riddles. Yes?"

Avrumel nods uncertainly. Up close, the age of the Rebbe strikes him profoundly. He has never been so close to anyone so old: even Uncle John, John Dorman, who is the oldest person he knows, is not so old. The long flow of silver-white beard. The eyes gray, clear. The skin above the beard and around the eyes webbed with a million tiny connecting lines. Wisps of white hair cascading from below the dark hat and across the dark lustrous front of the satin caftan.

The Rebbe reaches out and gently pulls Avrumel close to him. "One day, when I have more time, I will tell you some riddles. Your grandfather informs me you are going to our day camp. What do you do in the day camp?"

"I play."

"What do you play?"

"Games."

"What games?"

"Running games. Jumping games. Baseball."

"You like baseball?"

"Yes. I like to hit the ball."

"Very nice. And what else do you do?"

"We study. We listen to stories."

"What kind of stories?"

"Stories about the Patriarchs. Stories about Rebbes. Stories about the Messiah."

"What stories do you hear about Rebbes?"

"The story about the Rebbe who couldn't sleep if there was money in his pockets and he always gave the money to the poor every night before going to bed. And the story of the Rebbe who wouldn't talk for twenty years. And the story of the Rebbe who loved orphans, and when he died, he was buried with music at his funeral."

The Rebbe glances at my father, who is behind Avrumel. Their eyes lock briefly. Then he turns again to Avrumel.

"Do you have a favorite story?"

"Yes."

"Which is it?"

"It's about an artist named Hersheleh Kutin."

"Yes? Tell us."

"Hersheleh Kutin was a great artist. He did paintings for rich people. But he didn't live like a rich person. People didn't like him because he wouldn't give money to charity. Some people hated him. When he died, no one cried for him. But the week he died, the poor people of the town went to the butcher and the baker for their food for Shabbos—and they were very surprised. For years the butcher and the baker were giving the poor people meat and bread for free. Now they suddenly stopped. Because Hersheleh Kutin, the artist, was paying for it secretly, and now he was dead. And the people were sorry they had said bad things about him. My papa told me the story."

The Rebbe gazes intently at Avrumel. My father runs his hand over his beard and is very still.

"What class will you go to after the summer?" the Rebbe asks after a moment.

"I will begin first grade, God willing," says Avrumel proudly.

The Rebbe nods slowly. He glances at my father, then looks again at Avrumel. "You like it here with us in Brooklyn?"

"Yes, I like it. But I won't like it when it gets cold and it snows. We don't have snow in France where we live. Cold and snow are very bad for Rocheleh."

"Where I grew up in Russia, we had snow nine months of the year," the Rebbe says. It is very rare for the Rebbe to talk of his childhood in Russia. My father stirs slightly and runs his fingers through his beard.

"My mama says she doesn't like snow because it reminds her of the winters in Paris during the big war when she had to stay locked up in an apartment with her Cousin Max."

The Rebbe gazes a long time at Avrumel, nodding, his dark hat moving slowly up and down.

"I think I will tell you a riddle," says the Rebbe. "I just reminded myself of one, and I think I have a little time. Would you like to hear a riddle?"

"Yes," says Avrumel eagerly.

"An old Jew was once walking along a road to a city, when the road suddenly divided and went in two different directions. There was a little boy standing at the side of the road, and the old Jew asked him which road he should take. The boy said, 'This road is very short but also very long. The other is very long but also very short.' And then the little boy ran off, leaving the old Jew all alone. What do you think the boy meant, and which road should the old Jew take to the city?"

There is a brief silence.

"The long road that is short," Avrumel says.

Another silence follows. The Rebbe and my father are both looking at Avrumel. "Tell me why," the Rebbe asks.

"Because the short road that is long can lead him to a river or a mountain, and the man may not be able to cross even though the road is short. But the long road will bring him to the city even though it is long. And because of that, it is really short. My papa once told me that a long way that is sure is better than a short way that is not."

Now I gaze at them: the Rebbe, my father, my son. The Rebbe seated at his desk, Avrumel standing beside him, my father behind Avrumel. They form a tableau of arrested time. I have them before my eyes. I have drawn them on the page in my pad.

Now I slowly turn the page—and they are gone.

Outside my hotel room, it is still drizzling. The evening has begun its slow glide across the vast gray Parisian sky.

The following day I walk to the new Musée d'Orsay and wander through its nineteenth-century world. I look carefully at Courbet's *A Burial at Ornans* and *The Artist's Studio*. I take a taxi to the Pompidou Center and gaze up at its gaudy oil refinery look, at the crisscrossing white steel rods and exposed brightly colored pipes, ducts, girders, vents. I watch the jugglers in the plaza and draw an elderly bearded sketch artist sketching a fire-eater, and I ride the glass-enclosed tubular escalator to the roof garden and stand there a long time, looking out at the city. Kings, wars, a revolution, uprisings, barricades, riots, military occupation, treachery. Disorder and frequent sorrow the mulch for creativity. Like Florence. Is a Brooklyn tranquillity—community, continuity, serenity of soul in a sacred world—a killing acid?

I wandered through some parts of the Pompidou. I took a train to the Louvre and visited old friends. I made swift pencil drawings of the Avignon Pietà, Delacroix's *The Massacre at Chios*, Géricault's *The Raft of the Medusa*, Tintoretto's *Susanna at the Bath*, El Greco's *Christ Crucified*, Rembrandt's *Pilgrims of Emmaus*, da Vinci's *Mona Lisa*. Old familiar friends. Just to keep the eyes working and the fingers nimble. I had copied them many times before. Run the eyes across each minute detail of the facture; keep the circuit to the fingers clear and clean, and render what the eyes see. Old and dear friends. Jacob Kahn took me through the Louvre the first time. Old and dear and dead friend. My drawing of the *Mona Lisa* begins to draw a crowd. People gather around me, peering over one another's shoulders. Someone says, "I think that's Asher Lev." A guard approaches, looks at the drawing, nods approvingly, and saunters away.

I walk back to the hotel, past the quai with the trumpet players in the rain, past the apartment house on the Quai Voltaire where Jacob and Tanya Kahn once lived, past the street where rain like grapeshot caught me three days before. What were they doing there, those trumpeters? Whom were they heralding?

When I returned to the hotel there was a message from Shaul Lasker. My father had arrived safely.

The next morning I took a taxi over to a studio on the Rue de l'Université and spent some time helping a young artist select paintings for his first one-man show in Paris. I had met him in Nice two years before at a party given by Max Lobe. He was in his mid-twenties, very talented and very unsure of himself. "This one is good? You are sure, maître? It is not too facile? And this one? The fête galante in the style of the Fauves? Yes, of course, an Expressionist satire. You like it? I am happy. But this one you do not like. The linear perspective is a cliché? It is intended as irony. Yes, I will put it aside for the time being. I thank you, maître. Will it be a good show, do you think?" He smoked and sweated and paced. His girlfriend was in the studio. She had long shiny raven hair and was lovely. She kept staring at me. They were both French, he from Paris, she from Lyons. I wished him good luck and said goodbye to the girlfriend. Outside, the air was cool and wet. I returned to the hotel.

Later that afternoon, I packed my bags, checked out of the hotel, and took a taxi to the Ladover yeshiva.

5

❖ ❖ ❖   The taxi rolled past the apartment house in which I had created the two crucifixion paintings, turned into a wide tree-lined boulevard, went on for two more blocks through heavy afternoon traffic, and came to a stop. I paid the driver. He helped me with my bags, climbed back into the taxi, and drove away.

I stood on the sidewalk in front of a cream-colored four-story stone building. Stone front stoop, wooden entrance doors, tall windows, ornate grillwork on the narrow balconies. It looked like any of the other buildings on the boulevard. Once there had been a small sign over the doorway: LADOVER YESHIVA DE PARIS. But it was removed in 1982, during the time of the terrorist bombings of Jewish institutions in Paris.

Parked at the curb was a police car with two gendarmes in the front seat. I saw them watching me.

The front doors opened, and two young men in dark suits and dark hats and white open-collared shirts came out and let the doors close behind them. They wore short dark beards and were of the same height. I heard them talking in Yiddish and saw them break off their conversation when they noticed me. I imagined them looking at me, saw myself through their eyes: baggy chinos, creased photographer's jacket, fisherman's cap, red beard.

The two young men came over to me.

"Can we help you?" one of them asked in American-accented French.

"I'm here for Shabbos," I said in English. "Is Rabbi Lasker inside?"

The young man nodded. The other stood looking at me curiously.

"Where are you from?" the first one asked in English.

"Brooklyn."

"No kidding. Crown Heights?"

"That's right."

"No kidding. What street?"

I told him.

"Hey, I live one block away, but I've been in the Paris yeshiva for two years. My father wrote me the parkway is all torn up."

"That's right. They're repaving."

"I know you," the second young man suddenly said. "It comes to me. Aren't you Asher Lev?"

"Yes."

"That's a familiar face, I told myself. I know that face."

"Asher Lev," the first young man said. "I once read a book about you."

"I knew I recognized your face," the second one said. "The minute I saw you, I knew."

"I have to tell you right off that I don't like what you paint," the first one said. "I have to be honest with you."

"Did you see the article on your father in today's *Le Monde?*" the second one asked. "They interviewed him about Russian Jewry and *glasnost.*"

"I didn't see it."

The gendarmes sat in the police car, smoking; they had lost interest in me as soon as the two young men and I had begun talking.

"It's a good article," the second one said. "There's a good picture of your father and the foreign minister."

"We'll give you a hand with your bags," the first young man said. "Tell me something. How do you get away with painting crucifixions and nudes and all that other stuff? Doesn't the Rebbe tell you not to do it?"

"It's a long story."

"In the newspapers and magazines where I see your picture, your beard isn't so gray," the second one said. He picked up my large bag; the other took the attaché case.

I followed them along the cement walk to the double doors and into an office on the right side of the entrance hallway. They put down my bags.

Shaul Lasker sat behind a cluttered wooden desk, his ear to the telephone. He got quickly to his feet and shook my hand across the desk, his ear still to the phone. He gave me an upright index-finger signal to indicate that the conversation would be brief, pointed to a chair, and sat back down. The two young men wished me good Shabbos and left. I took a narrow slatted wooden chair and waited.

The office was small and had three wooden chairs, a single tall window, and the desk. The walls were painted the same pale-green color as the walls in the Ladover yeshiva in Brooklyn, where Rocheleh and Avrumel had attended classes and I had taught an art class weeks back. I shuddered, thinking about that class. A fiasco. But a lovely-looking person, that Miss Sullivan. I would have liked to be able to paint her. Silhouetted against the rain-splattered windows of the room. The softness of her against the cold grayness of the rain. And the geometrics of her form: the head held a certain way, the arms in this position, the legs here, the torso slightly curved. . . . All right. Enough. You're in a yeshiva. So much for the Spaniard in Asher Lev. I wondered who had erased the picture of the Rebbe I had drawn in chalk on the blackboard. A large bulletin board took up most of the wall across from where I sat. Tacked to it were lists, schedules, announcements in French and Yiddish, and a recent letter from the office of the Rebbe, typed in either Yiddish or Hebrew; I could see the headquarters letter-head and the signature of the Rebbe, but I was too far away to make out the words. A large framed color photograph of the Rebbe hung from the wall behind Shaul Lasker's desk. It showed the Rebbe in a dark suit and tie and dark hat and had been taken about twenty years before.

Through the tall window of the office I saw the boulevard and its leafy trees and the police car at the curb with the two gendarmes and the afternoon traffic on the street. In two hours it would be Shabbos. What time was it now in New York? What was Avrumel doing? Playing baseball? Studying Torah? Listening to a story about one of the Rebbes?

Shaul Lasker was talking to me. "You look tired, Asher. Are you all right?"

"I'm okay. How's my father?"

"He's terrific, thank God. He runs around like he's in his forties. You called home since you got to Paris? What do you hear about the family?"

"They're fine, thank God."

"What's next from you? Paintingwise, I mean."

"I don't know. I'm between things now."

"Dawn between things or dusk between things?"

"I don't know that, either."

"The life of an artist, eh? Glamour, romance, security, the fast track. Come, I'll show you where you're staying."

He picked up the heavy bag, and I took the attaché case and followed him out of the office. He was my age, short, stocky, goodhearted. His brown beard turning gray; his brown velvet skullcap slanted forward at a jaunty angle, the way my father used to wear his when I was a child, before my mother's illness, before her brother's accidental death, before my father began his rise through the Ladover hierarchy. A wave of memory rose before me: my father's anger over my poor schoolwork; the hot humiliations of classroom mockery over my endless drawing. I followed Shaul Lasker through the entrance hallway to the courtyard and then into a long corridor. We went up a flight of curving metal stairs, our footsteps echoing, and stopped at a door. He put the suitcase down and fished in a pocket for the key.

"We only have one spare room in our apartment," he said, "and I gave it to your father. Otherwise you'd be staying with us."

He opened the door.

The room was small and narrow and furnished with a single bed, a small desk, an empty bookcase, a bureau, and two wooden chairs. A tall window looked out on a cement yard and small flowered lawns and the backs of buildings. On the wall over the desk hung a framed color photograph of the Rebbe. He looked the way he did when I was a child and he would go walking in the night beneath the trees of Brooklyn Parkway and I would be awake and standing at the window of our living room, looking down at the lamplit world below.

"The back door is always left open on Shabbos," Shaul Lasker said, putting the key on the desk. "You can leave the key with the caretaker when you go out. And now I need to get ready for Shabbos." He went to the door. "I'm sorry you can't stay with us in the apartment. Eight children, thank God, they take up a lot of room. I'll see you later in shul, Asher." He closed the door quietly behind him.

I stood there in the sudden silence inside the room.

Someone knocked on the door. It was Shaul Lasker, looking sheepish and holding a white envelope.

"The most important thing I forgot," he said in Hebrew, and handed me the envelope. "Your father asked me to give it to you." He turned and walked away.

I closed the door and looked at the envelope. It was from the office of the Rebbe.

I went over to the desk and opened the envelope and removed the letter. It was handwritten. The writing—Yiddish and Hebrew in black ink, slightly tremulous but bold and clear—slanted across the creamy white paper, the personal stationery of the Rebbe. There was the Hebrew date in the upper right and the indication of this week's Torah reading. And then the body of the letter:

To My Dear Asher Lev, Greetings and Blessings:

Your father, may he live a long and healthy life, will bring this letter to you, with the help of Hashem, blessed be He.

You and your family are very much in my mind and heart. I see before my eyes your pale and weary face and I know what an artist endures inside himself no matter how cheerful his demeanor and how loud his laughter. And you, dear Asher, endure not only the torments of your art but also the burden of your responsibility to the Ladover. We have hurt you, yet you love us. We have exiled you, yet you are tied to us. "Though He slay me, yet will I have faith in Him."

All men of wisdom know that there are endless worlds and spheres, and in each sphere there are tens of thousands of heavenly creatures, beings without end, without number, all emanating from the single act of creation. The mouth cannot utter it, the mind cannot fathom it. And among the heavenly beings themselves there are gradations and categories without end, higher and higher—and all are possessed of wisdom, and all acknowledge their Creator. But our little world, our suffering world, in its closeness to the lowest of the spheres and with its mixture of good and evil because of the sin of Adam and Eve— how does our world continue to exist? What creates harmony between the upper and the lower worlds? That, my Asher, is perhaps the most difficult riddle of all.

Asher Lev, our teachers tell us that this harmony is the special creation of individuals who engage in certain deeds for the sake of the deeds themselves. Such deeds rise as a song, as the greatest of art, to all the spheres. And when the heavenly beings hear this song they take upon themselves gladly the yoke of the Kingdom of Heaven, and they exclaim in unison, Holy! Holy! Holy!—and there is peace in all of creation, and peace to all of Israel, and the beginning of an end to the exile.

Asher Lev, in the name of my father and my father's father before him, in the name of the sacred Rebbes who speak through me and act through me, I give you my blessing for wisdom and strength. May the final redemption come soon for the people of Israel and for all the world. Amen.

And he signed his name.

I sit in the silence of that small room, with its dim light and stagnant air, and read the letter again. *What creates harmony between the upper and the lower worlds? . . . deeds for their own sake . . . rise as a song, as the greatest of art . . .*

I fold the letter and slide it back into its envelope. I open my attaché case and insert the letter into the drawing pad and close the attaché case and leave it on the desk. I haul my suitcase onto the bed, open it, and begin to prepare for Shabbos. The Rebbe's face gazes down at me from the wall over the desk.

The synagogue of the Ladover yeshiva in Paris was a near-duplicate in miniature of the large Ladover synagogue in Crown Heights. Double doors led to it from the main entrance hallway, diagonally across from Shaul Lasker's office. Dark wood paneling, chairs, prayer stands, long tables, the curtained-off women's gallery in the rear, the center bimah, the lectern, the dark wood Ark in front with its deep-purple velvet curtain, and, against the wall to the right of the Ark, the tall dark leather chair with its own prayer stand, but without the sectioned-off area in which the Rebbe sat. As I entered through the double doors, I half expected to see Cousin Yonkel close by the bimah, staring at me with rage in his eyes.

My father stood near the dark leather chair to the right of the Ark. Before him were about a dozen students of the yeshiva and a group of older men, some white-bearded. All wore dark suits and dark hats; some had on ties. My father saw me enter and beckoned me over to him. Heads turned. The group before him stirred, moved, divided. A path opened for me and I went through, feeling their eyes upon my face. My father embraced me. I felt the strength of his arms, smelled the soap he used, saw the white hairs of his long beard, the thick arcs of his eyebrows, the lines in his forehead and around his eyes, and the care with which he had knotted his dark tie beneath the collar of his starched white shirt.

"It is good to see you, Asher," he said quietly. "Your mother sends her love. Devorah and the children are well."

"How is Avrumel?"

"Avrumel is very well, thank God."

I stepped back into the crowd, and my father resumed his conversation with those around him.

They were talking about the Arab riots in the territories occupied by Israel. One of the students asked if the Rebbe had said anything recently about making peace with the Arabs by returning territory. "The Rebbe says we must give back nothing," my father said. "It is the sacred land promised by God to the Patriarchs. We have no right to give back any of it."

Shaul Lasker stood nearby, looking at my father. They were all looking at him and listening intently. Someone asked how Russian Jewry was affected by *glasnost*, and my father said more was going on now in the Soviet Union than most people knew, and he could not talk about it but there was reason for hope. Someone asked about relations between blacks and Jews in Crown Heights, and he said it was uneasy but there had been a decrease in street crime since the start of the Ladover night patrols. Someone asked my father if he could repeat for them the Rebbe's talk on the previous Shabbos, and my father said the Rebbe had not been in the synagogue the previous Shabbos. A hush fell upon the group. Glances were exchanged. There was an uneasy shuffling of feet.

An old man stepped up to the lectern in front of the Ark and began the Afternoon Service. It is a brief service and was soon over. One of the yeshiva students who had helped me earlier with my bags, the one who didn't like what I drew and painted, began to lead the service that welcomes the Shabbos.

There were about eighty men in the synagogue. Our voices filled the room: chanted words warm and ascending through the innumerable spheres to the celestial beings and thereby uniting all of creation. The greatest of art. I heard clearly from time to time my father's strong and slightly nasal voice rising above the others. He prayed with his eyes fixed upon the prayer book on his stand, swaying slightly back and forth. In his dark suit and white shirt and dark tie and hat, he appeared an austere and regal presence. I noticed the way people would glance at him, the subtle cues they would take from his motions and demeanor. Far away from the presence of the Rebbe, beyond the aura of the Rebbe's luminescence, my father suddenly seemed bathed in a light of his own. I turned away from him after a while and gazed fixedly at my prayer book.

In Shaul Lasker's apartment later that evening, in air still thick with the aromas of recent cooking, we stand around a dining-room table laden with food and crowded with children as my father chants the Kiddush. Then we wash our hands and Shaul recites the blessing over the braided breads. The children speak French and Yiddish and are clearly on their best behavior in the presence of my father. They are all awed by him and begin to relax only when he starts telling stories about the deeds of the Rebbe during the early years of the Second World War. He tells them how the Rebbe helped get the great artist Jacob Kahn out of Paris the day before the Gestapo came to his studio to arrest him; how an art dealer arranged a meeting between the Rebbe and Picasso, and they met in Picasso's studio on the Rue des Grands Augustins, and to this day no one knows what they talked about; how the Rebbe, before he left Paris, established a secret Ladover yeshiva that operated all through the war. Then my father suddenly asks for a length of previously tied string and one of the children brings it to him and he proceeds to play cat's cradle with the younger children. During the main course—roast chicken, peas and carrots, noodle pudding with raisins—he gives the older ones a riddle to solve. "Listen carefully and see if you can find the answer," he tells them, his eyes shining with pleasure. "An old Hasid called his sons together and told them that he wished them to divide his property in a certain way after he departed for the True World. The oldest son was to take one-half; the next son, one-third; the youngest son, one-ninth. Soon afterward the old Hasid was called by the Master of the Universe to his eternal rest. The sons wished to obey their father, but they discovered that their father's property consisted of seventeen goats, and seventeen cannot be divided by one half or one third or one ninth. They didn't want to kill any of the goats and divide it, because each goat was much more valuable alive than dead. And so they went to the Rebbe, and in his wisdom the Rebbe immediately solved their problem. What did the Rebbe tell them?" They puzzle over it excitedly and unsuccessfully for the rest of the main course, and then, over tea and sponge cake, my father turns again to the older children. "I have another riddle for you. Are you ready for another riddle? All right. There was a Hasid who owned a little lamb, a big cat, and a big dog. It is known that big cats can do great harm to little lambs, and big dogs can do great harm even to big cats but will never hurt little lambs. The Hasid cared for his animals, was with them always, and prevented them from quarreling and, God forbid, harming one another. Now it happened that one day there was a terrible storm, and the river rose outside the home of the Hasid and threatened his life and the lives of his animals. The Hasid had to get himself and his animals to the other side of the river, where there was a hill that would protect them from the rising water. But he had only one little boat, and in that boat he could only take with him one animal at a time. How did the Hasid get the animals across the river in such a way that they did not harm each other when they were left on the riverbanks without him?"

I listen to him, sense clearly the light and ease that surround him, the soft and certain grace in which he is bathed, and I wonder where it all was when I was growing up and sitting at Shabbos meals with him and my mother in our apartment in Brooklyn. Was I so preoccupied with my own self that I never saw it? Had he pushed the softness away because he needed to appear strong in the face of my mother's illness and during all the hard journeying years that followed? I loved him, but we never showed each other love. Why? That was perhaps the most bitter riddle of all.

Miriam Lasker—trim, blue-eyed, wearing a lovely pale-blue dress, her head covered with a kerchief—moved efficiently back and forth between the kitchen and the dining room, helped by the two oldest girls. No one started a course until she took her place at the table. She participated in the conversation: Torah talk; tales about the Rebbe; concern about the nascent power of the right wing in the recent French elections; the efforts of the Ladover movement to influence the forthcoming elections in Israel. She had majored in political science in Brooklyn College and thought the movement would do best in the small development towns of Israel, especially among the alienated religious Sephardim. Years back she had worked as a buyer for the Printemps department store on the Boulevard Haussmann, but now she was home all the time with the children. Shaul had told me earlier that she was once again pregnant—in her second month with their ninth child. I looked at her and thought of Devorah and the crippling of her life during the years of terror in the sealed apartment with Max Lobe and his family, Devorah and the miscarriages, Devorah and the tenacity with which she wrote her children's books, Devorah and her passionate caring for Rocheleh and Avrumel.

We join my father in the singing of zemiros. Then my father leads us in the Grace After Meals. Miriam and the children clear the table. I sit in the living room with Shaul and my father, and we talk about the Torah portion of the week. The children are going off to bed. I am very tired.

Shaul says he'll walk me back to the yeshiva.

"You don't have to do that."

"I need the walk."

"We will walk tomorrow afternoon," my father says to me. He

is sitting on the couch, a midrashic text open on his lap. He looks wide awake. A transatlantic flight, two days of meetings with government officials, a night of talk and heavy eating—and still alert. His labors seem not to enervate but to strengthen him.

I walk with Shaul beneath the trees of the boulevard. The night air is cool. A distant beam of light probes the sky, moving slowly back and forth in a wide and indolent arc. The streets are nearly empty. Even Paris seems at rest this Shabbos.

Shaul says, "Not to speak of it on Shabbos, but what's going on with your uncle's art collection?"

"How do you know about that?"

"There was a little piece on it in the *Herald Tribune.*"

"It made the papers?"

"I knew about it before it made the papers. We all know about it. We don't know the details."

"Devorah told me over the phone that my Cousin Yonkel was going to try to break the will."

"How can he do that?"

"He claims I exerted undue influence on his father."

"Are you allowed to say how much the art collection is worth?"

He's an old friend. I tell him.

He stares at me in astonishment. "Master of the Universe!" he says in Hebrew, and adds in Yiddish, "I don't believe it."

"Believe it," I tell him in English. "My uncle, may he rest in peace, was a very clever man."

"A lot of good can be done with that money."

"My Cousin Yonkel wants to build jewelry stores with it. He wants to colonize northern New Jersey and maybe even go into Connecticut. A Lev's jewelry store in every major shopping mall from Summit to Hartford. Then go national. Franchises. A household word. Lev's. Like McDonald's."

"It's a desecration of the name of God if it goes to a goyishe court."

We are standing in front of the yeshiva. At the curb is the police car with two gendarmes inside. They are smoking and watching us. I say good night.

"Asher?"

"Yes."

"Have you recovered from the art show?" His voice is low, resonant with the concern of a friend.

"In the daylight I've recovered. At night it's another story."

"Can I do something for you? Do you need anything?"

"I'm all right. Good Shabbos, Shaul."

"Good Shabbos, Asher."

I left him on the sidewalk in the shadows beneath the trees. The caretaker gave me my key, and I let myself into the room. I had left on the bathroom light. Inside the room I undressed by the light of the bathroom and the lamp in the yard outside, and washed up and climbed into bed. A wedge of light shone through the partially open bathroom door onto the wall near the desk. I could make out clearly the picture of the Rebbe on the wall. The room was very small. I recited quietly the Krias Shema. The light from the bathroom seemed unnaturally bright, and I got down from the bed and closed the door. The room was dark save for the dim yellowish light from the lamp outside. I lay in the bed with my eyes open, thinking of the halogens on the Seine, and Jacob Kahn looking out the window of the apartment house, and Lucien running through the rain carrying Rocheleh, and Avrumel playing baseball. The darkness began to teem with the living and the dead, and I got down from the bed and opened the bathroom door again. I lay in the bed with the light from the bathroom on the floor and the wall, trying to fall asleep.

The light was blinding, they said. There was no sunlight that day, still the light was blinding. They left the building, Max holding her hand, and stood on the street that was crowded with joyous people and stared up at the sky, and felt the light as pain. Tears flooded Devorah's eyes. Max stood with his eyes toward the sky, breathing deeply, his round face flushed with the effort to open his eyes wide. And then he laughed with joy. Devorah still remembers that laugh.

They walked through the throbbing streets. Horns and bells and people weeping with happiness. The sun shone briefly, and Devorah found herself touching things the light fell upon—the sides of buildings, the windows of shops, the white cotton shirt that Max was wearing, her own threadbare and too-small pale-blue summer dress. She looked at herself in windows in the sunlight and was frightened by her appearance. Ghostly white faintly freckled features, dark haunted eyes, frizzy braided brown hair; a weighty sadness surrounded her like a visible presence.

She had gone to sleep in darkness for two years, and that night she needed light. She went to bed with the lights on. Max's mother saw the light in the crack of the doorway and tapped on her door and Devorah said she needed the light and Max's mother said nothing and from then on Devorah went to bed with the lights on.

The next day Max's father went back alone to the apartment where Devorah had lived with her parents. Others lived there now. Then he went to the police to inquire about Devorah's family. The police seemed surprised that Jews had managed to survive concealed in the neighborhood for two years. They had no information about Devorah's family.

The news came in bits and pieces. Each piece of information had somehow to be conveyed to Devorah, and each was greeted by her with increasing disbelief and horror, and each was a separate blow. The sadness grew within her until she seemed to exist only as a dark nimbus of melancholy, and even Max could no longer cheer her with his talk and his drawings. Once he showed her a drawing and she looked at it and he left it with her, and when he came back for it he found it torn to shreds. It was a very long time before he left her alone again with one of his drawings.

Her father had perished in Auschwitz, as did her other relatives; her mother, in Budy, a small camp for women near Auschwitz. The official who informed Max's father about the death of Devorah's mother seemed embarrassed and unusually ill at ease. Pressed by Max's father, he grew annoyed. Max's father probed other sources he knew, some that had been in the French Resistance, and, when he discovered the truth, wished he had not pursued the inquiry. He told no one in his family, not even Max.

One week before Devorah and I were to be married, he showed up unannounced at my studio. He was a thin, nervous man, given to pulling on his gray goatee and staring past the person to whom he was talking. He was sorry he had not informed me he was coming. He had been in the neighborhood. He had not planned to come up. It was truly an impulse. He needed to talk to me. Of course, if I was too busy he could return another day.

I asked him inside, found him an empty chair amid the clutter of the studio, offered him a cup of coffee.

We sat surrounded by my work. He told me about the death of Devorah's mother.

The village of Budy was located about four kilometers from Auschwitz. Its schoolhouse was the center of a small slave-labor farm camp comprising about four hundred women, many of them Germans, others French Jewesses. Most of the Frenchwomen were from intellectual circles: some were artists; not a few had studied at the Sorbonne. Surrounded by barbed wire, the schoolhouse served as the living quarters for the women, all of whom worked in the fields outside the village.

Max's father blinked and rubbed his hands together and stared past me. This was very difficult for him, he said. If I did not want to hear any more, he would understand. I told him to go on. He tugged nervously at his goatee.

The SS men who guarded the camp, he continued, would incite the German prisoners to mistreat the Jewish women. Many of the German women were prostitutes. The SS found in such spectacles a pleasant way to pass the time. The result was perpetual conflict between the two groups of women. One night a hysterical German woman accused a Jewish woman, who was returning from the lavatory, of threatening her with a stone. Guards heard her screams and rushed into the building. Together with the German prisoners, they began to beat the Jewish women. Some of the Jewish women were thrown down the stairs; others were flung out the windows to their deaths. The guards drove the Jewish women from the schoolhouse into the yard. They used gun butts, bludgeons, bullets, and axes. The victims were repeatedly struck, hacked, dismembered. There were no survivors. The official SS report stated that the prisoners had rebelled and the rebellion had been put down.

Devorah's mother had been a graduate of the Sorbonne, with a degree in fine arts.

I sat there and listened. I felt the draining of the power in my fingers and then the boiling rage. Max's father sat quietly for a while, blinking and tugging at his goatee. Then he stood up, thanked me politely for the coffee, and left.

I did not tell Devorah about her mother's death in Budy until a few years after we were married, and only after I read about the incident in a book on the Holocaust. I did not want her to find out about her mother from a book.

For a long time afterward, even lights would not help her to sleep. That was when she began seriously to write children's stories.

I should not be thinking of such matters on Shabbos. It is forbidden to disturb the joy of the day of rest with such dark and baleful thoughts. But memories of the Holocaust often come unbidden to mind. They dwell in a realm of their own, and are not subject to the laws and whims of humankind.

When I finally told Devorah about the death of her mother, she sat in silence a long time. We were still in the apartment on the Rue des Rosiers. Rocheleh was asleep. A wind blew through the narrow streets, rattling the wooden shutters on the windows. I remember the frozen look on her face: horror caught in stone. She stirred finally and said, incongruously, "Did I ever tell you that it took Max's father weeks before he was able to find a mezuzah to put back on the doorpost of their apartment? Weeks. A Ladover found one for us." Then, after a long moment, she said, "Do you think there's a plan to all this, my husband? Do you think there could be a plan?"

That was all she said then about my account of her mother's death. She took off her clothes and went to bed and lay in the light, trying to fall asleep.

As I lie now, years later, in the Ladover yeshiva in Paris.

The next morning in the synagogue, my father leads the Additional Service. His head covered with his prayer shawl, his long white beard protruding from behind the silver-lined rim of the shawl, he chants the words of the Kedushoh in his strong nasal voice. "He is our God, He is our Father, He is our King, He is our Savior, and He will redeem us again, and in His mercy will let us hear again, in the presence of all living beings, the promise, 'Indeed, I have redeemed you again in the end as I did in the beginning, in order to be your God. I am the Lord your God.'"

The congregation joins my father in song, and the voices rise and swell. The redemption must come. And soon. How long can this life be endured? My father sways back and forth at the lectern, a luminous presence before the Ark.

Later, around the Shabbos table in the Lasker apartment, triumphant children announce that they have solved the riddles. My father listens to their breathlessly delivered solutions and pronounces them correct. There is jubilation. The children sit proudly, basking in the light of my father's approval. "I didn't help them," Miriam Lasker says to me. Shaul says, "Don't look at me. I'm terrible with riddles." We eat and we sing and I lead the Grace After Meals. My father says he will walk back with me to the yeshiva.

On the boulevard we walk awhile in silence. Sharp bright sunlight throws broken shadows onto the sidewalks. A warm wind stirs the trees. The afternoon traffic is light, and there are few pedestrians. We walk along together.

"Is there anything in the Rebbe's letter you want to talk to me about?" my father asks.

"No."

"The Rebbe especially asked me to tell you that he thinks of you very often."

"Please tell the Rebbe that I thank him for his good wishes."

"The Rebbe is very preoccupied these days. We live in a dangerous world. Jewish life in America is threatened by assimilationists. Israel is beset by secularists from within and by enemies from without. The Rebbe prays and visits the grave of his father, of blessed memory, and makes plans and sends us out as his eyes and ears and hands. Tomorrow, with God's help, I go to Israel. We are developing strategies for the coming election there."

"What about the election in America?"

"We have our policies for the American election as well."

"A solid Republican bloc, like the last time?"

"We will vote for those we believe are best for us and for America. We will not vote for the homosexuals or the abortionists or for those who care more for the criminal than the victim."

"What will you do in Israel?"

"There are people I must see for the Rebbe. We will form alliances. We will make promises, which we intend to keep. The world will be surprised by the outcome this time. The world will have to reckon with us."

"You'll make a lot of people very angry."

"I am not concerned with those people. They like us only when we are powerless and merely colorful. But when we make our rightful bid for power, then they begin to hate us. It is not for them to tell us whether we are or are not entitled to a stake in the game of power. Our power is, after all, for the sake of heaven."

He follows me into a side street off the boulevard. "Where are we going?"

"I want to look at something."

We continue up the steep cobblestone street. It is lined with old apartment houses. The sidewalks are narrow. I stop in front of a five-story building with tall windows and balconies and a beige façade stained dark beneath its eaves and around its drainpipes. There are flowers on the balcony of the fifth-floor apartment and curtains on the windows. Who lives there now? Do they know what once took place within those walls? The street, bathed in afternoon sunlight, dozes in summer languor.

"Do you see the apartment on the fifth floor? Yes, that one. That's where I painted the crucifixions."

My father gazes upward, and his face hardens. He stands very still, looking up at the windows of the apartment. A small black dog lopes past us and heads down the street toward the boulevard. A lovely young woman goes by, dressed in brightly colored loose-fitting summer clothes, wheeling an infant in a carriage and leaving in her wake a whiff of scented air. My father stands staring up at the fifth floor of the building. He seems to be trying to penetrate the wall and uncover the demonic forces concealed in the apartment, the powers of darkness that moved me to so malevolent an act of creation. And I . . . I am so flooded with memories of that time of anguish, suddenly so keenly aware of long-forgotten instances of hesitation and decision: the texturing here; the brushstroke modulations there; the laying down of color fields; the balancing of forms; the fearful chances; the nightmarish dares; the smell of my armpit sweat; the sheer exhausting terror and joy of it all—that I am irrevocably convinced I will never again be able to embark upon another such act of creation.

"Anna Schaeffer asked me to take a long walk. Later she told me she had to have the paintings taken out through the balcony. They were too large for the staircase and the front door."

He looks at me somberly and shakes his head. "I want you to know that I try to understand you, Asher. It is very difficult."

"Well, at least Avrumel won't be an artist. He has no talent for it."

"Avrumel has other talents."

"Devorah tells me you'll take him into your office with you on Sundays."

"Why not? He enjoys watching people come and go. It will give Devorah and your mother more time to be together."

"Will Avrumel be able to meet the Rebbe?"

"Of course. Why not? It was the Rebbe who suggested that Avrumel might like to spend time with me in the office."

We stand there awhile longer, looking up at the apartment. Then we go back down the street and turn into the boulevard. We walk along together.

"Thank you for the time you spent with us in Brooklyn," my father says. "Your mother and I got to know Devorah and the children. We are grateful to you, Asher. I am only sorry it had to be my brother's death that brought us together. Who knows? Perhaps it is the will of God."

Perhaps there is a plan, Devorah says from somewhere in the summer wind around us. Asher, do you think there is a plan?

In front of the yeshiva building is the police car with the two gendarmes inside. They watch us.

"People tell me I am wise," my father murmurs, gazing down at the sidewalk near his feet. "But about this"—his arms describe an encircling gesture that takes in the two of us—"and about your art I have no wisdom at all."

He embraces me briefly, then steps back and turns and walks quickly away in the shadows of the trees.

Half a block down the boulevard there is a wooden bench, empty in the sunlight. I walk over to it and sit down. Dappled sunlight filters erratically through the trees. The sun casts a long flat broken shadow of me at my feet, and I sit gazing at it. I close my eyes and, a moment later, open them. The boulevard is suddenly filled with dark-garbed Ladover Hasidim on their way to the synagogue and the Rebbe. I feel myself begin to shiver, and I close and open my eyes. A motorcycle roars by on the nearly deserted boulevard, its helmeted rider bent forward into the warm wind.

I walk back to the yeshiva in the shadows of the trees.

Alone in my room after the Evening Service, I lay awake in the small room, the air still and dark. Whispers of boulevard traffic drifted in through the open window. After a long while I fell asleep.

There came a faint tapping on the door. I thought it a half-dream and sought to sink deeper into sleep. The sounds persisted: the tip of a finger striking a low tap tap tap on the wooden door. In the darkness I crossed from the bed to the door and saw dimly silhouetted against the night light in the hallway the figure of my Uncle Yitzchok in his dark suit and dark hat, rotund and cheerful and chewing on a long cigar. "A good week to you, Asher," he said. "May we come in? I bring you an honored guest."

I stepped back and opened my eyes wide and found myself in my pajamas in bed. A crushing weight of terror moved suddenly upon me. I reached over and turned on the desk light. The attaché case on the desk and the picture of the Rebbe on the wall and the room in shadows beyond. I went to the bathroom and climbed back into bed and snapped off the light.

I heard the soft sounds of slippered feet on the floor. Then, silence.

There was someone in the room, sitting at the desk, watching me.

A long and tremulous sigh came out of the darkness and, a moment later, the gentlest of voices.

"How I wish . . . How I wish . . . Asher . . ."

The voice faded.

It was the Rebbe! The Rebbe was in this closed and narrow room, sitting at the desk in the darkness! I knew then, with all the certainty born of my childhood years of listening to wonder tales, that the Rebbe had just made a miracle journey, a kfitzas haderech—he had traversed three thousand miles in a single stride, using the mysterious powers given a Rebbe by the Master of the Universe to venture across vast distances effortlessly in the wink of an eye.

I lay very still, trembling, my eyes closed.

"You are well, my Asher?"

"I am tired, Rebbe."

"I watched you all this week in Paris. Your work with Max Lobe, the woman and her child, the artist you went to see, your comings and goings. How can you not be tired?"

"It's not that kind of tired, Rebbe."

"Fatigue is from the Other Side, Asher. It sunders our partnership with the Master of the Universe and prevents us from participating in the daily act of creation. It is food for the Angel of Death, this melancholy, this hopelessness."

I was quiet.

"Listen to me, my Asher. There may be much time or little time. In such matters I am not prescient. Certain decisions must be made quickly, else all the work of our hands may, God forbid, come to nothing. Fatigue is a wall to climb, not an emptiness in which to wallow. You are wise, Asher Lev. Slowly you begin to unravel the riddle. Your answer may save us and return you to your work."

I trembled and was still.

"It is frightening, my Asher. Of course. How precious your son is to you. But you will consider it. If I am called to the True World and this matter is still not resolved, I will go to my grave with sorrow."

"God forbid!" came another voice from the darkness.

"Uncle Yitzchok?"

"Yes, Asher."

"Did you hear?"

"Of course, I heard."

"Asher," the Rebbe said. "It is sometimes possible for a man to acquire all of the world to come by means of a single act in this world. Consider that, my Asher. You will redeem all that you have done and all that you are yet to do."

I was quiet.

"You will return home for the summer. It is likely I will give the sign sometime after the summer, during the holy days or the festivals. You and your family should remain with us until after the festivals. Consider my words carefully, Asher. There is not much time."

I said nothing.

"We must return now, Reb Yitzchok. We are away too long. The power of the miracle journey must not be abused."

There were soft rustling sounds, a quiet shuffling of feet, an emptying of the air, and sudden patches of deepest blackness inside the darkness. And silence.

I was alone in the room.

I lay very still in the silence, listening. The room was quiet; it seemed sealed off from the noises of the world. I turned on the desk light. There was the attaché case and, on the wall above it, the picture of the Rebbe. I went again to the bathroom, climbed back into bed, and turned off the light. It took me a long time to fall asleep.

The next day, after the Morning Service in the yeshiva synagogue, I said goodbye to my father and Shaul, packed my bags, and took a taxi to the Gare de Lyon. It was raining hard. A sweating, gray-haired porter looked at my ticket and brought me to the proper track. I boarded the fast train to Nice.

The train begins a slow glide out of the Gare de Lyon, slips through railroad yards, picking up speed, and slides smoothly past houses with red-tiled roofs and graystone walls. The rain falls in a sudden torrent, and people scurry for cover. Automobile wipers arc frantically; the tops of tall buildings vanish into the mist. I lean back in my seat and close my eyes and immediately see the little room in the yeshiva and sense the presence of the Rebbe and my uncle in the darkness. The rhythms of the train lull me to sleep. I wake, dazed. It is still raining. We are an hour out of Paris, rocketing on the nonstop run to Lyons.

The car is about half full. Orange-and-brown seats, dark-green carpeting, indirect lighting, wide double-paned windows, orange curtains. All of it glistens, new-looking. Smooth, silken, gently undulating motion on welded tracks running through cultivated fields, and red-roofed farmhouses in the distance, and villages, trees, power lines, and a flat line of horizon below a vast milk-white sky.

I sit alone in the row of single seats to the right of the carpeted aisle. Across the aisle, and two seats forward, are two girls and, opposite them, a woman, handsome, well dressed, in her early forties. The girls, about eleven or twelve, are identical twins. One is reading; the other is bent over a pad on the table between the facing seats, drawing. They are blond-haired and wear red-and-white-striped shirts and dark-gray jeans, with pink bows in their hair. The woman is watching intently the drawing coming slowly to life on the table.

Outside my window drenched fields flash by, then a glistening highway. There is a sudden blurring run through a small station, trees, ponds, villages with stone houses and tiled roofs. The train slows and enters Lyons and glides to a stop in the station. A few passengers enter the car through the sliding end doors. The girl continues drawing. Small stubby fingers, wide blue eyes, creamy white face, freckled nose, hair pulled back tight on her forehead, tongue pushing against her cheeks and lips, the way Max works, as if the energy from the fingers were being echoed by the actions of the mouth.

The train is moving again, soundlessly, through railroad yards and past trains laden with factory-new automobiles and on past tall smoking chimneys and tarpaulin-covered freight trains and clusters of villages on distant hills. I fall asleep and wake with a trembling start and find myself staring at a wet six-lane highway and an enormous smooth-surfaced lake that mirrors the gray sky and at a canyonlike gouge in the stony earth that is a quarry studded with cranes and earth-moving trucks and then, a moment later, a billboard with the words HOTEL MERCURE. There are dense woods right up to the tracks and then far-off hills and soaring thunderheads limned with shafts of silver light and a road sign that reads VIENNE and a dark narrow curving river and rain suddenly slanting hard against the window.

The twin who is the reader gets down from her seat and goes along the aisle and through the automatic sliding doors to the ladies' room. I have my drawing pad open on the small drop table in front of me, and I begin to draw the remaining twin, who still sits opposite the woman, drawing. I draw her sitting in her seat drawing.

Once, soon after we settled into the house in Saint-Paul, Rocheleh came silently into my studio and sat in the soft green chair near the door, watching me draw. I saw her enter and sit in the chair, and then I was deep inside the work and forgot she was there until I heard the choking breaths and looked toward where she was sitting and saw her bathed in the beams of muted sunlight, her face bluish white, her hands to her throat, her eyes wide open and terrified.

Afterward she said she had thought it would be different in Saint-Paul, somehow the air in the studio would be cleaner than the air in the studio in Paris, and I said I had deep inside me thought that, too, else I would not have permitted her to remain in the studio that long. I thought I hoped I prayed, Papa. I prayed to the Master of the Universe. Why didn't He answer me? Why did we move to Saint-Paul if I can't come into your studio here, either? Avrumel would come in and sit down and watch me work. He would sit against the wall, hugging his Shimshon doll, beneath the color reproductions of Manet's *Olympia,* Delacroix's *The Massacre at Chios,* and *Madman* by Géricault. Once he asked me why there was no picture of the Rebbe in the studio. I told him that in my studio I was with myself alone and with no one except myself telling me what was right and what was wrong. He said, "Not even Mama?" and I said, "Not even the Master of the Universe." He was four at the time and did not understand what I was saying. Avrumel. He came in often afterward, clutching his Shimshon doll, sitting quietly, watching me work. He seemed with his repeated presence to be trying to make up for what he knew was Rocheleh's inability to enter her father's studio and watch him paint.

I was drawing the girl drawing. The second girl returned to her seat and resumed reading. Passengers went along the aisle toward the café car up ahead and returned with trays of food. The automatic doors kept sliding silently open and shut. It was still raining heavily, and clouds touched the tops of the trees. We hurtled into a notch between two hills, and I could hear us inside the tunnel of our own sound. A station flashed by, platforms and signs suddenly tilting toward me and gone.

I got up to go to the bathroom. The sliding doors would not open. I moved back and forth and sideways until my foot found the contact beneath the carpet. The doors opened silently. In the café car I ordered a green salad and a cold drink. The car was crowded. I ate off a paper plate with plastic utensils, standing at a window table and looking out at the landscape. We sped alongside a lake and through fields and near a village and then a field on fire, white smoke rising in the rain, and a grimy old stone house with cracked graystone walls and a red-tiled roof and broken windows through which I glimpsed dark interiors.

I returned to my car. The sliding doors opened and closed without difficulty. I sat in my seat, watching the girl drawing.

A conductor came quickly up the aisle, anticipating the automatic opening of the doors, and the doors would not open and he nearly ran into them. He did a little dance in front of the doors, searching for the contact. They slid slowly open. He reached up and did something to the top of the right door and then went on through to the next car. The doors remained open. Stiff gusts of sultry air blew into the car, bearing the hot scents of sodden fertilized fields. The girls looked up and wrinkled their noses. The woman shook her head and laughed. Small stations kept rushing by. There was a river and hills terraced with vineyards and, along a macadam road, an Esso service station. I fell asleep and woke and saw, as in a speeded-up motion picture, train stations—Donzère and Pierrelatte—and fields of corn and a huge green-and-gold expanse of tall sunflowers, and without thinking I reached up and touched my ear. The train slowed and stopped in Avignon.

The twin girls and the woman collected their luggage and left the car. I saw them met on the platform by a tall flaxen-haired man in his forties and an elderly couple. They all looked neat and decent and untroubled. I thought of the Spaniard and his brothel painting and began to draw from memory the faces of the whores. But I was tired, and besides this was not the Avignon of that painting. The station was long and wide, with glassed-in waiting areas and platforms with high arched roofs and the pipe supports showing. Devorah's parents were taken to a train station that July and sent out of Paris to Auschwitz and Budy. There must be a plan, my husband. The train started up and a sign glided by: 200F LA NUIT CENTRE VILLE TOUT COMPRIS. I fell asleep again.

Through sleep I sensed the train slowing as it took a long curving length of track that tilted it steeply to the left. I opened my eyes to an expanse of brilliant blue water. In the distance was a curving shoreline and glistening white houses and boats. The train picked up speed and shot through Debeaux. I saw an old cemetery with a wrought-iron fence and weather-worn leaning tombstones. Uncle Yitzchok, was that really you last night in my room with the Rebbe? What do you want with Avrumel? You want me to give him up so the Ladover will be assured of continuity and leadership deep into the next century? The Rebbe will not transfer the mantle of leadership to my father, even though he merits it, unless he is assured that Avrumel will follow? Because my father is too old and no one knows how many years he has left? And his death, God forbid, without immediate automatic succession would give rise to dissension? Is that it, Uncle Yitzchok? You want Avrumel? You want me to give him to the Rebbe so the Ladover can continue to conquer the Jewish world? Send him to live with my parents? Have him attend the Ladover schools in New York? Prepare him for his future role as king when the time comes for him to take my father's place? Aryeh Lev, Rebbe. Avrumel Lev, future Rebbe. And skip over Asher Lev, artist and troubler, who is no more fit to be a Rebbe than he is to be a lawyer or a shoemaker. Is that it? We were suddenly inside a long tunnel, hurtling through a sheath of darkness enveloped in the tumultuous noise of our motion and then abruptly bursting forth into sunlight and a spreading city of tall apartment houses and crowded streets and warehouses and soccer fields and suddenly another tunnel and then sunlight and a sign that read À VOTRE SERVICE and through a station, Marseille Blancard, and a range of mountains up ahead and a warehouse with an enormous sign, ALARM SERVICE, the train now curving back on itself so I could see the first cars.

We stopped briefly at Toulon and started up again. I sat gazing at the Mediterranean world where I now lived—sunlit pastel-colored houses, palm trees, wave-lapped pebbled beaches, earth-red cliffs hugging the shoreline, sailboats, motorboats, yachts, stone jetties, the masts of hundreds of moored boats looking like the pikes of a medieval army, and overhead a sky so clear and blue and of such surpassing loveliness as to be simultaneously a joy and an ache.

We are in Antibes. The train runs parallel to the beach, and there are high waves. A motorcyclist in shorts, sneakers, and a crash helmet speeds along on the road between the tracks and the beach. The train stops in Antibes. I look out the window and think of the night-fishing painting by the Spaniard. I once studied it with Jacob Kahn. The train begins to move.

I sit back in my seat. There is Nice in the distance, blue and dreamlike, a jetliner coming in on its long slow gliding approach to the airport, and way out to sea tall banks of brilliant white clouds, and the long length of curving beach, and signs reading SIESTA and TOP FUN. I put my drawing pad back into my attaché case.

We enter Nice and are soon in the station. It is late afternoon.

I climb out of the train with my bags and take a deep breath of the hot, humid, sea-scented air. A porter appears. I follow him along the platform and up the escalator and through the crowded terminal. There are tourists everywhere. A middle-aged suntanned woman hurries past me, cradling a small dog in one arm and holding in the other a plastic bag on which is a picture of a beautiful dark-haired woman and the words, white against black, JE SUIS BIEN DANS MA VILLE. The porter finds a taxi, and I give the driver my Saint-Paul address.

The driver is an Arab. He maneuvers the taxi smoothly along the crowded boulevard. There are bathers on the beaches and in the water. On the sidewalks and along the curbs, puddles of water reflect the palm trees and the sky. Pastel-colored hotels line the boulevard and face out to the sea. Later, with the night, the hotel lights and beachfront lamps will come on, the perfect curve of the coastline will blaze like a fiery necklace, and the fabled nightlife of Nice will begin. I almost never go to Nice at night.

The driver winds along the crowded autoroute to Cagnes-sur-Mer and then on the fast road to Vence and Saint-Paul. We drive through the toll booths and onto the four-lane highway, and then beyond the traffic circle to a two-lane road and more hills and another circle and a valley to the right and a group of young cyclists. Was I from around here? the driver asked. We were going to my home, I said. I'd been away a few months. Was I originally from France? he asked. From the United States, I said. But living in France the past twenty years. Anything special going on in Nice these days? He said there was a storm here yesterday that knocked down trees and power lines. He said I looked like a decent sort of fellow, and some indecent things were going on. I said what sort of indecent things, and he said the hotel owners were organizing a secret list of those who had left town without paying their hotel bills. They were going to keep them out of Nice. He said he had a cousin who drove a taxi in New York. You could never get away with anything like that in New York. But this was France. You could get away with it in France. It was a plain case of discrimination against Arabs. Had I been here for the national elections? No? This Le Pen was a fascist, and it wouldn't be surprising if someone took a shot at him one day. He said I wouldn't believe the kinds of people who rode in his taxi: Mafia people, drug pushers, whores, pimps. He said he had a younger brother who was going to play the trumpet in the jazz festival at Cimiez. He said the drivers from Belgium were idiots who didn't know what a steering wheel was. He went past the Restaurant les Oliviers and almost missed the turn that led to the house.

He pulled into the gravel driveway and helped me with the large bag. He was olive-skinned, unshaven, and had a dark mustache. I asked him where he was from, and he said Beirut. I paid him, and he drove off.

I opened the gate with my key, carried my bags through, left them on the gravel path, and pushed the gate closed. It was heavy and clanged into place and clicked loudly shut. A hot wind blew through the white pines that lined the path. I brought my bags to the end of the path and left them there and walked to the building that was my studio and unlocked the metal door and let myself inside.

Hot still musky dim air, heavy-scented with linseed oil and pigments. I stand very still and breathe deeply. It is an intoxication, a celestial wine, this air. Everything untouched, as I left it, my own clutter and disorder, the chaos of my making. There is the green chair near the door, where Rocheleh once sat. I thought I hoped I prayed, Papa. I draw open the opaque overhead blinds, and sunlight filters through the translucent glass ceiling bricks and falls upon the disarray of brushes, paints, knickknacks, boxes, tools, sketches, drawings—all of it scattered on half a dozen worktables mounted on trestles. On a wall hangs a large photograph of Picasso taken when he was in his mid-eighties, robust, smiling, his eyes jet black, piercing, alert. Below the photograph is a reproduction of the Spaniard's *Guernica*. Against the opposite wall, catching the light, stands a huge umber-washed canvas. Nearby is where Avrumel would pose. I look again at the green chair. There is where Avrumel would sit with his Shimshon doll, silently watching me work.

I close and lock the studio door and pick up my bags and cross the brick-paved courtyard. The garden looks lovely. Brilliant oleander and nasturtium, the pink and orange petals catching the light of the sun. Trumpet-shaped red and orange blossoms in abundance on the vine near the entrance to the house. New ageratum and marigolds. Everything neat and trim and clean. As if I have merely been away on a shopping trip to Nice for art supplies and meat and bread, and Devorah is inside with Rocheleh and Avrumel.

I let myself into the house.

The air is warm and musty. I open the kitchen windows. The curtains, the old wooden table and chairs. Like friends, these furnishings. I'll call Max and John and let them know I'm back. I'll call Devorah and let her know I'm here. In the morning I'll go to the post office and see about the mail. Then I'll walk up to Jacob Kahn's grave.

I go through the dining room, and there is the picture of the

Rebbe on the wall between the windows and amid the many paintings of my own collection. I carry my bags up the winding staircase. Passing Avrumel's room, I glance inside, and there is his old Shimshon doll on his bed where he left it months ago.

I am home.

BOOK THREE

✦ ✦ ✦

6

✤ ✤ ✤ The bedroom is dim with stagnant air. I open windows and shutters and stand awhile, gazing at the village and the valley.

The air vibrates with light. Late-afternoon sunlight brushes a brilliant pink across the village wall. All through the green valley are clusters of small red-tiled houses. The sea is a faraway sliver of polished metal that joins the pale-blue sky along a vague line of horizon.

When we first moved into the house, Devorah would sit for hours looking at the light on the village and the valley. She could not get enough of the light.

I unpacked and left the Rilke volume on my night table. Using the bedroom phone, I called Max and was told by his caretaker that he was at a party in Nice. "Welcome, Monsieur Lev," the caretaker said. "We missed you. The wife and children are well? Monsieur will find everything in good order. I have seen to it myself." He was a retired customs agent, and he ran Max's domain with a nineteenth-century sense of service to people and property.

I called John Dorman. Holding the phone in my hand and listening to it ring, I looked out the rear bedroom window and could see the red-tiled roof of his house. Maybe he'd gone to the party with Max; he did that sometimes. More likely, he was in a drunken stupor. I hung up the phone.

Later, I walked up the road to the village and the café at the foot of the wall and sat on the terrace beneath the awnings and the ancient trees. It was cool here, and crowded. Waiters sauntered over to welcome me back and ask about Devorah and the children. The owner came out and shook my hand. Tourists stared. The waiters knew what to bring me for supper. I ate quickly, watching some of the men of the village at their bowling game on the red clay earth of the playing field outside the café.

Afterward I walked through the village to the cemetery and stood outside the open gate with the dark metal cross over the entrance and gazed across the lines of tombstones at the marble tomb of Chagall. The sun touched the crests of the nearby hills and sent long shadows into the cemetery. Crowded with old and new tombs and studded with tall cypresses, the cemetery stood hushed in the approaching twilight, its host of crosses clear and sharp in the bronze sheen of the sunset. After a while I walked back to the house and sat on the terrace, watching the night come, with the lights of the valley like motionless fireflies in the advancing darkness. I fell asleep in the chair on the terrace and slept a long time and was awakened by the racketing noise of a motorbike on the road. The air was soft, cool, scented with flowers. I went inside.

It was nearly midnight. Sitting on my bed and looking out at the lights of the village, I picked up the phone. It was answered by Devorah on the second ring. She sounded as if she were on the bed beside me.

The family, thank God, was well, she said. She had talked with Rocheleh by phone before Shabbos. She liked the camp very much. How was my father? Did I have a good Shabbos? Was the house all right? How were Max and John? She had gone rowing in Prospect Park with my mother and Avrumel. It was very hot in New York. My mother was fine. She was right there.

"Asher? Are you well?"

"Yes."

"Your father?"

"He's in Israel, rounding up votes. We had a good Shabbos together in the yeshiva."

"I'm glad, Asher. Devorah and I are having a fine time being together. It is like finding a daughter."

"Has anybody heard anything more from Cousin Yonkel?"

"Nahum told me after shul yesterday that your Cousin Yonkel

is going to try to have you removed as trustee. He is going to take you to court."

"Can he do that?"

"I don't know, Asher. It saddens me that there is such a fight in the family."

"It saddens me, too. I don't know what to do about it. Is Avrumel around?"

"Here he is."

"Papa?" The high voice, breathless. I imagine the red hair, the freckled face.

"How are you, my son?"

"I am fine, Papa. We went rowing today. I helped Mama row."

"That's great."

"And guess what, Papa."

"What?"

"When Grandfather comes back from Israel, he will take me with him to his office on Sundays. Grandfather says I can maybe even see the Rebbe."

I was quiet.

"And I play baseball in the camp. Every day. Where are you, Papa?"

"At home."

"Did you find Shimshon?"

"Yes."

"Will you bring him back with you?"

"Sure."

"Here's Mama."

Devorah came back on. "I miss you, my husband. Did you get everything done in Paris that you needed to do?"

"Yes."

"I am really having a wonderful time with your mother."

"How is the book coming along?"

"Very well, thank God. It's quiet here now. A good place for writing."

"Take care of yourself, my wife."

"Goodbye, Asher. Travel well."

In the silence that followed, a motorbike moved laboriously

along the road like a truculent mosquito. The village stood on its hill, bathed in the nighttime glow of halogens. I thought I saw Jacob Kahn in the window of a village home, gazing out at me. After a while I fell asleep.

The village bells woke me, clanging sweetly in the morning air. I lay in my bed and felt the sounds softly against my ears. Soon the bells fell silent; the bedroom began to fill with a strangely foreboding stillness. I felt the stillness all through the house, and after a while I got up and dressed. I prayed the Morning Service and walked up the hill in the morning sunlight to the café for breakfast. It was early; the storekeepers were washing down the streets in front of their shops, and there were only a few people in the café. One of the waiters came over, a short round man in his fifties who had once been a painter, and we talked for a while about the forthcoming Léger exhibition in the Fondation Maeght outside the village. He had it on the best authority: it would be formidable. A new look at Léger from his very early days to just before his death. He himself was not one of the great admirers of Léger. But it would be a formidable exhibition.

Afterward I went to the post office and mailed a tubular package to the widow of Lucien Lacamp in Paris. It contained the drawing of the girl drawing I had made the day before on the train. There were other postal matters to settle. The line behind me grew long. Finally I was outside the post office in the shade of a green pine. Two gendarmes stood talking on the sidewalk in front of the pharmacy across the street. There were cars and motorbikes on the road, and the streets were beginning to receive the first waves of tourists. I walked out of the village to the sculpture at the road juncture and turned right and started up the steeply climbing road to the Fondation Maeght.

Up the climbing road in sunlight that is bright and warm now and on past the Fondation Maeght to the gravel road with the wrought-iron gate and the two sculptures in polished white marble—a mother and child and the trumpeting Gabriel—on the grass inside. The voice of the housekeeper, a woman from a nearby village, answers my ring. It comes through the black metal box mounted in the stone pillar to the right of the gate. "Ah, Monsieur Lev, welcome back, welcome back. How good to hear your voice. Ah, no, I am sorry; Madame is away today." The gate slides open, and I step through. A moment later, it slides shut.

I walk along the curving path bordered by lantana and rose of Sharon and mandarin trees and up the grassy lawn to the knoll and the lone cypress and the grave of Jacob Kahn. The pale-gray marble slab, flat on the grassy earth, glistens in the sunlight, giving off sparkles of light as if inlaid with precious stones. The inscription on its polished surface reads:

JACOB KAHN
1884–1983

The pale-brown stucco-and-wood house lies beyond the garden and terrace where he would sit with Tanya and listen to the wind. It was the one clear sense left him toward the end, his hearing, and he would sit with his head inclined toward the wind and say there were subtleties to the mistral and the sirocco that one hears only when there are no other senses to distract one, faint nuances that reminded him of certain color patterns he had seen in Matisse at one point and on occasion in that madman Soutine and often in the work of the Spaniard. It moved differently through the white pines and the apple trees, a surge of cadmium red in one and a subtle earth green in the other, and in the slender leaves of the olive tree a wash of cerulean blue like a cool, caressing hand. Among the silver-barked cherry trees the wind played in a flow of dark purple, and it was bright yellow in the juniper hedge and orange among the marguerite. He was so old, so brittle, and a dry fetid odor rose from him, and he needed his Indian blanket—the one I had bought him as a gift during a trip to Arizona—he needed it even in the sunlight.

Tanya always sat nearby on the terrace, reading another of her novels in Russian. Émigrés and old friends brought them to her: recently released Jews; Russian writers; diplomats on trips to the West. She was more than fifteen years younger than her husband, a woman of striking appearance, high cheekbones, silver hair drawn back into a bun, dark-eyed, aristocratic. Before the Russian Revolution her family had been wealthy Odessa merchants with connections everywhere. She would read as Jacob Kahn and I talked.

"What are you doing these days, Asher Lev?" he would ask each time I saw him, and I saw him often in those years, two or three times a week. I was a son in their home; sometimes Devorah would come along and bring Rocheleh.

"This and that," I would answer, and we would talk technical matters for a while.

It was difficult for him to speak for long periods of time in any one language. He would move from English to Yiddish to French to Russian. At first, the language he used would be appropriate to the years of his life he was describing to me: an account of his early life in Russia would be told in Yiddish; his years in Montmartre with Picasso would be recounted in French; his years in America were relayed in English; to Tanya he often spoke Russian, which I did not understand. Then he began to move from one language to another within sentences, and there seemed no clear connection between subject and word. His talk was layered with language as his canvases were with paint.

"I do nothing any longer," he said to me once. "I hear Chagall is still able to paint. But I do nothing. The eyes do not see. The legs will not stand. The hands refuse to work. Only the ears are still able to hear. No matter. I have done what I was put here to do. I have a right to my fatigue. It is an earned fatigue."

He sat—the blanket with its dance of Indian colors and forms tight around him—with the sun on his astonishingly withered face, the walrus mustache sagging and the dry white hair loose and uncombed on his skeletal head and the brownish blotches on his pale pink skin and the hooded eyes shiny with the watery glaze of age.

He said to me another time, "Do you remember when the Rebbe first brought us together? I had no hope it would succeed. You could draw, yes. You had an eye. But many can draw. It is not a rare gift. And you were such a child. Thirteen years old, and a naïve child. I think the Rebbe expected you to fail. I wonder if the

Rebbe does not regret having brought us together. Have you ever considered that, Asher Lev?"

"I have, yes."

"I think of that often these days. Because soon you will be my future."

"Enough."

"Oh, do not think it was all done out of the goodness of my heart, Asher Lev. Artists are not kind. Artists are selfish and calculating. If you had only a talent for drawing, it would have ended quickly. But you possessed the capacity for rage. Even the Rebbe could not see the anger in you. I saw those demons. They were the source for your art. I saw that right away, during the first weeks we were together. I gave you years of my life because I saw in you my future."

"You are talking too much," Tanya said to him, raising her eyes from her book. "You should rest."

He said something to her in Russian, and she shook her head.

"She wants me to rest," he said to me in his hoarse, throaty voice. "What for? I have already had more time alive than most people who have ever lived. I will talk with my student, who is my future."

Tanya responded to him in Russian, and he laughed and coughed and wrapped the Indian blanket tighter around himself. He was so gaunt, there was so little of him inside the blanket, that the folds and ridges of wool seemed to be wrapped around bones and air. I sat in a short-sleeved sport shirt and khaki pants and sandals and my fisherman's cap. He turned to me. "You know what she said? 'It is your funeral.' How right she is, my Tanya! Will you say a prayer for me, Asher? I do not believe in God, you know. But a prayer cannot hurt. Oh, yes, he is a clever man, the Rebbe."

Another time he asked me, "Do you ever go back there? To Brooklyn?"

I shook my head. I had not told him about that phone call.

"Not at all?"

"I went back once."

"It is all over between you and Brooklyn?"

I said nothing.

He nodded soberly. "You do not answer. That is called ambivalence. I am glad you save it for Brooklyn and do not put it into your art. Ambivalence in art is like piss in coffee."

"Kahn," Tanya said, looking up from her book. "Old age should not become an excuse for vulgarity."

He ignored her. "They will not let you alone, you know. Wait. A time will come and you will need them or they will need you. They will make demands. When they need you, they will call you. What will you do then, Asher Lev?"

"It will depend upon what they want."

"You think so? My father, you know, was a Ladover, a follower of the Rebbe's father. I remember my father singing and dancing in our little synagogue in Kiev, frightened of the Communist bastards all around us. Me, I believed in nothing except my art. Still, when they called on me—" He broke off and stared into the late-afternoon sunlight.

"When was that?"

"Long ago."

"What did you do?"

"I took you on as my student, Asher Lev." He turned his eyes upon me. A wan smile played over his dry lips. "It is difficult to say no to them. They touch something deep, very deep. They deal in eternity, the roots of the soul."

"They are charlatans," Tanya said. "They take advantage of one's natural feelings of self-doubt and guilt. You will excuse me, Asher. I do not number you among them."

"Our Asher is among them and not among them. Is that not right, Asher?"

I was quiet.

"Listen to his silence, Tanya. He does not answer. The silence is a mark of his ambivalence. Look at him. Ambivalence covers him like a mist. Oh, they will call on you one day, Asher Lev. One does not require an overabundance of wisdom to foresee that. I know the Rebbe from our days together in Paris. Yes, yes, sooner or later demands will be made."

Devorah asked me once, on our way back from one of our evening visits, "Why do you see him so often? Most of the time when you're with him he sleeps."

"He's my teacher," I said.

"But you rarely talk now."

"I don't need words to talk with him."

"Was he really so close to Picasso and the others?" Earlier Jacob Kahn had talked ramblingly of the Bateau Lavoir days.

"He was in some ways Picasso's equal and in other ways his student. What Picasso was to painting, Jacob Kahn was to sculpture."

"What does he mean when he says you are his future?"

"I don't know."

She was silent. We walked on down the hill and past the sculpture and onto the main road. She took my arm. "We won't talk about it, my husband. Some burdens are best borne in silence."

Jacob Kahn said to me one afternoon, "Do you think about women?"

"Often," I said. "Devorah, Rocheleh."

He laughed dryly. "I have been remarkably faithful for an artist, considering what has come my way." I saw Tanya look up from her book. "And now, the older I get, the more I think about them. I always believed it would be the other way around. How life surprises you. Have you seen the Spaniard's *347 Suite*? An astonishment. What he could no longer do with his penis he did with his pen."

"Kahn," Tanya said in a mildly scolding tone. "You talk like a schoolboy or a dirty-minded old man."

"I was at the museum in Antibes yesterday," I said. "How he treated his women!"

"Flowers need to be fertilized," he said in Yiddish, and added in French, "To create a rose, one needs shit."

"Kahn," Tanya said.

"Women were his demons, his shit."

"You are embarrassing our guest."

"Our guest is forty years old, Tanya. Our guest knows about demons. What are your demons, Asher Lev?"

I walked over to him one afternoon and the housekeeper's voice over the black box sounded faint and strained and as I came up the walk the gardener gave me a sidelong appealing glance. A red Peugeot was parked in the driveway near the garage, and I knew the doctor was there. Tanya sat in an armchair in the spacious living room, her large brown eyes uncharacteristically fearful, but all of her carefully composed. He had been sitting in the garden, she told me, and had suddenly lost consciousness. One of the servants had carried him upstairs to the bedroom. Tanya had called the doctor. We waited together in the living room. The walls of the house were covered with his private collection: a small museum of modern art. After a while the doctor appeared, a dapper man in his fifties, gray mustache, gray hair, kind eyes behind rimless glasses. Failure of the heart. Congestion of the lungs. Madame must make the necessary preparations. In the meantime, there was the remote possibility of temporary recovery. One could not be certain. Madame surely understands. It is not given to us to be on this earth forever. And at such an advanced age, the congestion, the weakness of the heart . . . Madame will call if any change is observed.

I sat with him in the dim light of the bedroom. His hand lay lightly on mine, dry, cold, pallid. Death gazed dully from his features; its bloodless mask was upon him. Once he had hacked at marble and wood, his hammer and chisel ringing clear and loud, the chips flying, muscles and veins bulging in his arms and neck, sweat streaming down his face. Now there seemed nothing beneath the blanket. He looked unsubstantial, wraithlike.

He opened his eyes. "Asher Lev."

"The doctor says you should not talk."

He coughed and murmured something in Russian. Tanya, seated beside me, responded softly. He said to me in Yiddish, "Say a chapter of Psalms for me, Asher. It cannot hurt." I recited a Psalm from memory. He closed his eyes and lay breathing shallowly, stirring from time to time. Pencils of reddish light filtered into the room through slits in the shutters. He was talking in Russian, calling out. Then he lay quietly and said in French, "Do you see them sometimes, our teachers, our friends, our enemies?"

"Sometimes," I said in French.

"The Spaniard I see often. We have long talks. There were many good things about him, if he was your friend. . . . But he was a devil." He said in Yiddish, "You are a devil, Asher Lev. A pencil or a brush in your hand, and you are a devil. Do not let your work become too easy for you. You are like the Spaniard. You need demons in order to remain a devil. These eyes see it."

"He no longer knows what he is saying," Tanya Kahn said in English.

"I am now very tired," Jacob Kahn murmured in Yiddish. "I have earned my rest."

He lay still, his breath coming in short, shallow wheezes.

Tanya called me early the following morning. Jacob Kahn had died a short while before. The doctor had just left. Arrangements had to be made. Had Jacob talked with me about arrangements?

I spoke with her briefly and hung up the phone. Devorah was awake in her bed, her face pale. She was in her seventh month of pregnancy with Avrumel. I said in Hebrew the verse from the Book of Job, recited when one learns of a death. " 'The Lord has given, and the Lord has taken away. Blessed be the Name of the Lord.' " And I wept.

The authorities had made an exception and had granted permission for Jacob Kahn to be buried on his own property: the only cemetery in Saint-Paul was Christian; the Jewish cemetery in Nice was too far away. Picasso lay buried on his own property. And, after all, this was Jacob Kahn. The windows of great French cathedrals shimmered with his luminous colors and forms. His sculptures adorned public places in a dozen European cities.

It was a large funeral. The minister of culture flew down from Paris. The mayor of Nice was there, along with the mayors of Saint-Paul and Vence. Jacob and Tanya Kahn had no living children. Four distant relatives were present, none of whom I had ever met before. There were many painters, sculptors, writers, and people from the village. I heard French, English, Russian, Italian, Spanish, German. There were curators, dealers, printmakers, radio reporters, television crews, journalists. Chairs were set up on the terrace. The brief service was conducted by the young rabbi from the small Ladover synagogue in Nice. I delivered the eulogy, and I do not remember what I said, though I remember having to stop a few times to take deep breaths. I was one of the six pallbearers who brought the coffin to the knoll. It felt strangely light, as if the body had already begun its dissolution. It was a hot morning, hazy with a tentative sun. A sirocco blew in from the sea, and I could hear it in the cypress. Can you hear it, maître? The wind in the tall climbing tree. My voice said, " 'You who dwell in the shelter of the Most High . . .' " I stood between Tanya and the young rabbi and gazed into the open grave, the raw earth gaping, the coffin lowered, the people hushed. " 'I will be with him in distress; I will rescue him and make him honored; I will let him live to ripe old age, and show him My salvation.' " I shoveled earth onto the coffin and heard it strike with loud hollow sounds. All the inside of me felt raw, empty, a numbing ache. I turned away.

Tanya lived alone in that huge house. Everywhere were his sculptures and paintings. I saw her often. She lived in her books and memories. "I am the widow of a great man. There are not many of us around, you know. We are a special breed. I miss him terribly, though I would not want him to remain alive as he was in his final months. You must not stop your visits, Asher. The servants have been instructed to let you in whether I am home or not. Do not look so sad. Our Jacob Kahn lived a long and worthwhile life. What more can this world give us?"

I visited frequently. I would join her in the garden. Sometimes Devorah and the children came with me. Once we brought Avrumel over alone—Rocheleh was in school—and Tanya let him go into Jacob Kahn's studio. He was, I think, about two years old. Surprisingly, the dusky air of the studio was still tinged with the cold smell of chipped stone. Avrumel stood amid the blocks of raw marble, the sculpted figures, the huge paintings, the tools and worktables and clutter, his little mouth and eyes rounded with awe.

Jacob Kahn bequeathed his estate to Tanya. He left me a small bronze sculpture of the two of us dancing together with a Torah scroll. He had made it when I was his student. He came to see me once during the festival of Simchas Torah, and we danced together among the tumultuous crowds in the street outside the Ladover synagogue. I put the sculpture on a pedestal in our living room, beneath the picture of the Rebbe.

I continued to visit. I would stand at the grave and recite chapters from the Book of Psalms. I spoke often with Tanya. This past spring, a few weeks after my Paris show, she called and asked me to come over. I climbed the hill and rang the bell and spoke into the black box.

We sat in the large light-filled living room, surrounded by Jacob Kahn's sculptures and paintings. He seemed to hover in the air. I felt his presence and imagined his eyes, his grizzled features, his walrus mustache. I heard his voice.

"How do you feel, Asher?" Tanya asked gently.

"I can't remember when I've felt worse, though I'm sure I have."

"How is Devorah?"

"She worries about me."

"And the children?"

"I thank the Almighty, they are well."

"I have read all the newspapers and journals."

I said nothing.

"What will you do now?"

"I don't know."

"I recall Jacob Kahn saying often that one should never take too seriously one's critics. Critics are among those an artist must teach."

"It's possible that I have nothing more to say."

"Asher Lev, that is nonsense."

"If an artist has nothing more to say, he should quit. Good critics are almost always cruel, but they are rarely stupid. And those who write about my work are among the best."

"Kahn once said to me that an artist does not create art for the critics but for himself." She had taken to quoting her husband, a tendency, I had read somewhere, of the widows of great men. "For whom do you create, Asher?"

"It's not a bad idea to listen to the good critics."

"You have been severely hurt, Asher. That is all the more reason for you to continue."

I was quiet.

He seemed everywhere in that spacious room, filling its corners, radiant among the dancing motes in the shafts of light coming through the large windows. Outside was the garden and the terrace and the lawn with some of his large sculptures, and beyond was the knoll and the lone cypress and the grave.

Tanya Kahn leaned toward me. "Listen to me, Asher. After we fled Paris and the Germans melted down all the sculptures in his studio, he was in despair. He could not work. It was a darkness that drained from him every drop of his energy. You used to see him that way, but only on occasion. When we came to America he was that way for nearly a year. He would say to me again and again, 'The salt has gone out of the soup. Stone is no longer stone. Blue is no longer blue. Red is no longer red. Yellow is no longer yellow. It is all the color of an open grave.' Then he went to see your Rebbe. And he began to work again."

"I didn't know that."

"Oh, yes."

"What did the Rebbe tell him?"

"I have no idea. I asked him once, and he would not tell me. I never asked him again. Can I bring you a cup of coffee or tea, Asher? It is April, but it is still quite chilly. It is true, this is a darkness that can be conquered. It is inconceivable to me that Asher Lev will be defeated by his critics, great as they may be."

Two days later, my mother called to tell me Uncle Yitzchok was dead.

Now I stand on the knoll before the grave of Jacob Kahn, the cypress tall against the blue morning sky and the wind warm on my face. It is the only sense left me, I hear him say. There are colors in the wind, Asher Lev. Find your demons again and return to your work. Colors wait for you in the wind. Things were too comfortable for you. An artist needs a broken world in order to have pieces to shape into art. Isn't that right, Asher Lev? Comfort is death to art. Asher Lev, artist. Asher Lev, troubler. Asher Lev, my future. His voice weaves through the wind, and I add to it the words of the psalmist. " 'Protect me, O God, for I seek refuge in You. I say to the Lord, You are my benefactor; there is no one above You. . . .' " The wind is red and black in the trembling cypress.

I walk back down the steep road past the turnoff to the Fondation Maeght and then to the towering modernist sculpture at the juncture with the main road. Cars are parked all up and down the road, and the road is crowded with tourists. A green-and-white Mercedes tour bus goes by in a cloud of diesel fumes; curious faces peer at me through tinted windows. Near Max's house a dog comes loping out of some roadside shrubbery; large and black and sleek, it sniffs at my heels and follows me for a while, then turns and ambles off in the direction of the village.

Passing the gate to Max's house, I see Jameel, the Arab gardener, working inside on the fruit trees, and Max's cream-colored Peugeot under the green plastic awning alongside his studio. I catch brilliant glimpses of the pool through the shrubbery and the trees: a still mirror of water reflecting the warm blue of the sky. How they love that pool, Avrumel and Rocheleh! Avrumel in the pool, his white skin flashing, his red hair catching the sunlight. His skin needed frequent applications of sunscreen lotion; he burned easily. Rocheleh was good in the water, sure strokes of her thin arms, smooth kicking of the pale legs, her long light-brown hair trailing after her like some living creature. The water was fine exercise for her, but she was not able to swim quickly for too long; her breathing would become labored. The water on their faces and dripping from their hair and swimsuits, making little puddles where they sat in the sunlight beside the pool. And Devorah, wearing a light summer dress, sometimes nearby under one of Max's shade umbrellas. She never went into the pool unless she was entirely by herself or with me.

Through the front gate I see Jameel moving among the lemon trees. Max is probably inside the studio now, working. Easels and canvases lined up like soldiers, Max naked to the waist as he moves among them, laying on colors. He is really a fine painter; never seems to have much difficulty getting started, locating and entering his precise arena of creativity. His colors are lush, sensuous; he deserves his success.

I walk on a few feet and turn left into the side road that branches off from the highway. The back of Max's property is directly across the side road from our front gate. I let myself in and walk slowly in the hot sunlight along the gravel path to the house. Inside, I open windows and shutters and let air and sunlight invade the mustiness. I wander through the rooms. Here Devorah sat nursing Avrumel. Here Rocheleh played with her puzzles. Here I conceived the idea for a certain painting. Here my father and I sat and talked. Here John Dorman told me about his and his wife's many years with the Communist Party in New York. Here Avrumel got too close to the back of the electrician and, as the electrician turned to move away from the floor socket, his screwdriver struck Avrumel's eye. The blood and the pain. He nearly lost the eye.

I called Max and got his answering machine and told the machine I was home. I looked at my watch and decided to call John Dorman. I sat on my bed and looked out the window at the ramparts of the village and dialed John's number. The phone rang a long time before it was picked up. A slurred voice said in English, "Better be a good reason for this."

"John? This is Asher Lev."

"Who?"

"Asher Lev."

"Don't know any Asher Lev. Goodbye."

"How are you feeling?"

"If I'm on the phone, I must be okay. Hey, is this really Asher Lev?"

"Yes."

"Sonofabitch. Your people have damn strange burial customs, Lev."

"Didn't you get my letter?"

"Must've got it if you sent it. Having a little trouble remembering things. Is the missus with you?"

"No."

"The kids?"

"I came back alone."

"Sonofabitch. You should've stayed and sent back the missus and the kids. Too quiet here without them. You going to be around awhile? Damn strange burial customs you people have. Two months to put someone away. Suggest you tip off the *National Geographic.*"

He hung up.

A moment after I put down the phone, it rang. I picked it up and heard Max's soft voice. "Hello, my friend. How are you? Come over later and I will have Claudine serve us a nice lunch on the terrace. How did you come down? The train, yes? Clever. The strike is delaying the flights. I waited two hours in the Paris airport. A misery. I must return to my work. I am—how do you say it?—cooking with the gas."

I hang up the phone and lie back on the bed. The beds, the dressers, the mirrors, the carpets, the chairs, the beamed ceiling, the stippled white walls, the windows and the view of the valley and the village. Everything is the same and everything is different. Before we left, I saw Brooklyn distantly through the shimmering world of Saint-Paul. Now everything in Saint-Paul is coated by the months in Brooklyn. I close my eyes and see Avrumel walking with my father up the steep road that leads past the Fondation Maeght to Jacob Kahn's home. I see Rocheleh and my mother climbing the narrow medieval streets of the village. I see Devorah and my mother sitting on the lounge chairs alongside Max's pool. I see my father talking to Max about the future. "Without the future there is no present," my father is saying. "Without the future there can be no hope for redemption, and without hope for redemption there is nothing. A man must plan for the future." Max smiles politely. That is the sort of talk, he once told me, he used to get from his own father. "They talk about redeeming the world for the future," Max said. "I have more modest goals. I wish only to redeem a canvas for today."

The sunlight coming through the window has angled and is now on my eyes. I peer into its golden world, see the lazy motions of the motes: dust specks flashing in sunlit life. I get up from the bed and stand in front of my dresser mirror. Asher Lev. I am tempted to make another outline drawing of myself, perhaps with one of Avrumel's crayons, leave behind in the mirror a ragged doll-like dwarfed image of Asher Lev. Instead, I leave the house and cross through the baking sunlight and the cool swaths of shade to my studio.

The large closed room is silent. Its smells, intoxicating to me, are deadly to Rocheleh. Master of the Universe, how You run Your world. To me You give this gift so I cannot live without the scents in which the gift finds life; to Rocheleh You give a curse so she cannot go anywhere near those scents. If there is wisdom here, it escapes me. Unless You wish to show irrevocably that the gift is mine alone; that there is no future for it in my family; that it begins and ends with Asher Lev. Is that it? Asher Lev, artist. Asher Lev, troubler. Asher Lev, dead end.

I stand in the silence of the sunlit studio and look around at the cluttered worktables and walls and splattered floor and at the huge empty canvas still waiting for me, at the brushes lying idle and the pigments and turpentine and oils left abandoned where I had placed them before the Paris show—everything stopped as in a snapshot; as Devorah had once described to me her own and her parents' lives: suddenly halted one July day in 1942: frozen in memory: her mother shouting at her to get out and go home, this wasn't a circus or a zoo: stopped and frozen and gone, all her early childhood, all the possibilities of love and family: halted, aborted. Paris is noted for beginnings and endings. Read any history book.

Abruptly the studio is tomblike, its odors stifling. I go out the heavy metal door, close and lock it, leave through the front gate, and cross the road to the rear gate of Max's home. The gate clicks open. I walk past the caretaker's cottage and the large spread of vegetable garden toward the studio and hear Max call to me from the terrace.

"Asher, over here. How are you, my friend? Come and sit down. Claudine has made for us one of her miracles."

Claudine emerges from the house. She is a trim, redheaded middle-aged woman from one of the nearby mountain villages. She carries a wooden bowl filled with salad. She greets me and says how good it is to see Monsieur again and Monsieur has lost weight and how are Madame and the lovely children. She goes back into the house.

Max and I sit alone at the table beneath the shade umbrella. The pool shimmers in the sunlight. All around its flagstone border is a riot of flowers bounded by shrubs and trees. I can see the edge of my property, a small stand of willows, jutting above the shrubs beyond the pool to my left, and beyond that the valley, deep green in the early-afternoon sun, and the rise of the hills that lead to the sea.

"The print turned out splendidly," Max says. He wears tan shorts, a red-and-white-checkered short-sleeved shirt open to the second button, and brown loafers with no socks. A delicate gold chain encircles his plump neck. The fringe of gray hair around his bald head is trimmed and combed. His gray mustache lies neatly groomed upon his upper lip. "You were of enormous help to me, my friend. I cannot understand how I know you all these years and have never before asked you to show me the carborundum process. I saved for you the first copy after the bon à tirer. It will be my gift to you."

"Thank you, Max."

"It is an astonishment to me that the stone will press against the paper in such a manner and will produce such lovely textures and not destroy the paper. Please eat. Claudine is right; you have lost weight. What is troubling you, Asher? Tell me what happened in Brooklyn."

We sit on his terrace alongside his pool, eating the meal served by Claudine. Across the calm surface of the pool flies a humming-bird, halting in midair and hovering, drinking from the water, then swiftly flying off. I hear the traffic on the road: motorbikes, tourist buses, cars. What can I tell him? I say something about Devorah and the children wishing to stay on beyond the week of mourning because they wanted to be with my parents, they liked the community, the children wanted to spend the summer in La-dover camps, Devorah enjoyed being with my mother.

"And you, my friend. What about you?"

"What about me?"

"You enjoy New York?"

"I can take it or leave it."

"Were you able to work?"

"I did some drawing."

"It is—how long?—about four months since you have made a painting."

"One need not work all the time, Max."

"It depends upon the reason one is not working, does it not? Have an orange, my friend. They are from my own trees, and they are excellent. Did I tell you I will be leaving in two weeks for Stockholm? Yes. They are giving me an opening. A very fine gallery. And then Oslo. Splendid people. Have some of these grapes. They are very good."

We finish our lunch and Max goes off to his studio and I sit alone by the pool, gazing into the water and watching a dragonfly sail lazily over the surface, fragile wings beating silkenly in the hot afternoon air. After a while, I leave through the rear gate and cross the road and go into the house. It is the heat of the day. A nap is called for. But I cannot sleep.

I am inside my studio later that afternoon, staring at the large, empty, umber-washed canvas, when someone rings the bell on the front gate. Through the gate telephone I ask who it is. "John Dorman," a voice says. I push the button for the front gate and open the studio door and stand in the sunlight, waiting for him. He walks up the path between the cypress trees in his shuffling loose-limbed gait. He wears baggy tan trousers, a frayed short-sleeved white shirt, and sandals. He is tall, and his head is topped by a dry strawlike mat of thinning uncombed white hair. A green plastic eyeshade throws a viridian shadow across the upper part of his face. We shake hands.

"Came over to see if it was really you. How you doing?"

"I'm all right. Come inside out of this heat."

"You've lost weight, and there's more gray in your beard. What did they do to you in Brooklyn?"

He enters the studio and I close the door. He stands amid the clutter, looking around. His pale eyes take in everything, pausing for a long moment over the large empty canvas and then moving on to the tables and walls.

"You were gone a long time, Lev." A tone of reproach edges his phlegmy voice. His skin is flushed. A faint odor of whiskey rises from him. "Missed you all. Strange way to bury someone." He keeps looking around, avoiding my eyes. "Do any work in New York?"

"Drawings."

"You got them here?"

"I left them with Doug. I've got some Paris drawings."

I bring one of the pads over to him, and he sits down in the green chair Avrumel uses when he is inside the studio and begins to leaf through the pages. I stand in front of the huge umber-smeared canvas. The canvas is an ocean, dark and heaving, and I dread entering it because it runs with treacherous currents. The tips of my fingers tingle with a sensation of numbing cold. I put my hands under my armpits. Cold fingers in the summer in southern France! John returns the drawing pad.

"Damn good. This one here—are they trumpeters?—first-rate. Your work scares the hell out of me, you know that? Why do your people put up with you? Instead of asking you to stay longer, they should want to throw you out sooner."

I do not respond. We stand there together awhile, looking at the canvas.

"How's the writing, John?"

"Coming along."

He has published nothing since *Dream of a Gifted Child,* one of the great novels of the thirties. He writes every day and puts everything into a black metal box in his bedroom. He came to Paris with his wife after the Second World War, and when she died he moved to Saint-Paul. He drinks steadily and is often ill. I know very little about him. He is shy and gentle and the children love him and call him Uncle John. Once, during a mild drunk, he told me he stopped publishing because he had lost two worlds: his neighborhood, from which his family moved when he was twelve, and the Communist Party, with which he broke after the Hitler-Stalin pact. I remember Avrumel was sitting on his lap and staring up at him when he told me that. Afterward Avrumel asked me, why did Uncle John have tears in his eyes when he talked to me?

Later, I walk with John to the front gate and he says, without looking at me, "Quiet here as the tomb without the missus and the kids. You tell her." Sunlight shines through the eyeshade and throws a green shadow across his large sad face. "Tell her to come back and bring the kids. Tell her that, Lev."

He goes out the gate and along the road and onto the gravel path toward his house. There is much traffic along the road. I return to the studio and sit in the green chair, looking through the drawings. I remove from the pad the drawing of the trumpeters, spray it with fixative, put tissue paper under and over it, carefully roll it up, and insert it into a mailing tube. I address the tube to the widow of

Lucien Lacamp and walk in the afternoon heat to the village post office and mail it off. I walk back through crowds of tourists to the house.

The next day I busy myself with correspondence: commissions, collectors, museum curators, an inquiry from a European dealer asking that I authenticate a print bearing my signature. I walk through and around the house, checking the plumbing. The house, built before the French Revolution, stands on an acre of land five minutes by foot from Saint-Paul. Max found it after Devorah wrote him about an especially bad asthma attack suffered by Rocheleh. "Sunlight, Asher," Devorah murmured. "Sunlight." Phone calls, letters, photographs, real-estate documents, architectural plans journeyed back and forth between our apartment on the Rue des Rosiers and Max's home in Saint-Paul. I flew down to see it and described it to Devorah. Max oversaw the renovations. "The house will perhaps help to erase the memory of the years in the sealed apartment, yes?" Max said to me once over the phone in the course of a conversation about carpenters and plumbers. There was little chance it would do that; but it was nice to think that it might.

The house had borne up well under our two-month absence.

That afternoon Claudine went shopping in the village and came over to the house and used our pots and dishes and utensils to prepare supper, as she had been taught to do by Devorah. John and Max joined me on the terrace. Afterward we went over to Max's house and sat near the pool and watched the sun set. There were glasses and a bottle of Dewar's Scotch on the table. A reddish dusk spread across the valley. The sky paled and emptied of light. The road lamps came on: beads of light winding through the valley and climbing the hillsides to the distant crests, winking in the darkness like stars. Musky scents rose from the valley, carried by the night breeze. We sat there some while, silent in the darkness. Max went into the house and turned on the underwater lights. A soft blue-white glow spread outward from the pool and shone upon the flagstones and the flowers and the undersides of the motionless leaves. From nearby came the rhythmic pulsing of cicadas and the deep monotonous thrum of frogs. Max and John, faintly brushed by the lights, seemed ghostly and unsubstantial.

I asked Max if he would be doing much traveling in the fall. He said he would probably be going to Japan for openings of his shows in Tokyo and Kyoto. "And there is a possibility I will also go to China. Yes, China. Imagine. I did not even know the Chinese cared for Western art. Now they are interested in the art of Max Lobe."

John drank from his glass and said he hated traveling; he had done more than his share of traveling when he was young. He and his wife running around to clandestine Party meetings; secret passwords; covert operations; organizing workers; dodging the goons hired by owners to break strikes. "We almost got ourselves killed a few times. Only time I ever had all to myself was when I took seven months off to write the novel."

"You wrote the novel in seven months?"

"Before I was married. Lived in a small room in the Bronx with a regiment of cockroaches and bedbugs. Near the zoo. Wrote day and night. How was Paris, Lev?"

"It was fine. How can Paris not be fine?"

"Have to get back there one of these days. Miss the old whore. Haven't been since your show."

"My show," I said.

There was a lengthy silence. I turned away from the pool and looked out across the dark valley.

John poured Scotch into his glass. "When do you go back to Brooklyn?"

"Thursday."

"You told me Sunday," Max said.

"I've taken care of everything I needed to do. There's no point to hanging around. I'd rather be with Devorah and Avrumel for Shabbos."

"Where is Rocheleh?" Max asked.

I told him.

"It is all right for her to be in an overnight camp?"

"Rocheleh knows how to take care of herself."

"Avrumel in day camp playing baseball," John said. "Would like to see him swinging a bat."

"Devorah says he's pretty good."

"Not surprised," John said. "Great kid, Avrumel."

There was another silence. John drank from his glass. His hand raising the glass to his lips trembled slightly. A motorbike went along the road, its staccato noises shattering for a moment the still night.

"New York hot as hell in the summer," John said. "Used to sleep on the fire escape. Air like a furnace. Asphalt would melt."

"We used to go away summers," I said. "My parents have a little place in Massachusetts."

"My, my," John said. "You hear that, Max? A place in the country. Didn't know you were a capitalist, Lev."

"A capitalist yet," I said in Yiddish.

"Not only didn't we have a place in the country, Lev, we didn't even have the idea of a place in the country."

"It's a bungalow, John. A small cottage. In the middle of a lot of other bungalows. A Hasidic bungalow colony."

"Asher Lev, capitalist," John said, drinking from his glass. "Knew there was something about you I didn't like. Cannot figure out how you snagged such a decent woman like your missus."

"Blame Max," I said. "Max introduced us."

"It was one of the few smart things I have done," Max said, smiling.

"Maybe she took pity on me because I was in such bad shape. I had just finished the crucifixion paintings."

"We ain't going to talk about those paintings," John said. "Not tonight."

"I hope not, John."

"Because, tell you the truth, never told you this before, I don't much care for them. Jews shouldn't paint crucifixions."

I said nothing.

"Goddamn cliché is what it is. Bad taste if you're a Jew. Too much Jewish blood spilled on account of that crucifixion. Jews should leave it alone."

"What should I have used?"

"Don't know. Your problem, Lev. But crucifixion definitely a cliché. Also upsets too many people. Got to know your limits."

"John, I clearly heard you say we would not discuss those crucifixions," Max said.

"You heard right," John said. "End of discussion."

"Are there any limits to what you would write?" I asked.

"Never write a novel about the life of Jesus. Not my business.
What the hell do you know about crucifixions, Lev? Got no right
to steal other people's experience. Becomes phony if you use it.
Takes genius to absorb other people's experience and use it right."

"I didn't know how else to depict torment, John."

"Easy way out, steal someone else's experience." He poured
more Scotch into his glass and drank.

"That was not the easy way out, John. The easy way out would
have been not to paint it at all."

"Goddamn easy way out is how I see it," John said.

"The discussion that is not supposed to be going on is going on
a long time," Max said.

"Right," John said. "My fault. Absolute end of discussion. Feeling a little tired anyway. Come on, I'll walk back with you, Lev.
Won't hold your past against you. Good night, Max."

"Good night, John. Asher, are you really leaving on Thursday?"

"Yes."

"Tomorrow night I have a party in Nice with the mayor that I
must attend. It is a political matter having to do with a new
museum. But I will see you before you go."

We left him sitting by the pool and went past the vegetable
garden and the caretaker's cottage and out the back gate. A car
sped by, heading up the road toward the village. We crossed the
road. The road lamps bathed us in amber light. We came up to
John's gate.

"How about a nightcap?" John asked.

I told him no, thanks; I was ready for bed.

"You sure?"

"Yes."

"See you, Lev. Thanks for the American notebooks. Cannot
stand these French notebooks. Lines and boxes make my eyes jump
all over the place. Good night."

I watched him go through the gate and up the path to his house.
Later, in my bedroom, getting out of my clothes, I glanced out

a window and saw him at the table in his kitchen, writing. I washed and got into bed and reread some more of the Rilke. I turned off the light and recited the Krias Shema and lay awake in the darkness. The sounds of an occasional car and motorbike drifted through the night. I heard odd noises inside the house, strange stirrings along the dark hallways. I lay in bed a long time, trying to fall asleep.

The bells woke me. I dressed and prayed the Morning Service and walked to the village for the newspapers. The air was winy and still cool in the early-morning sun. There were only two people in the terrace of the café. One was a local carpenter whose wife had died during the past winter and who often ate breakfast here before beginning his day's work. The other was John Dorman.

He was sitting at a table, bent over one of the American spiral notebooks I had brought him, and writing. His long thin frame described an arc of sorts over the notebook and seemed to be embracing it. His left hand held the pen; his right arm was curled around the top of the notebook; his green eyeshade hovered over the pages; his eyes tracked myopically the journey of the words. I stood near the entrance to the terrace, watching him. He wrote steadily, pausing occasionally to sip from a cup of coffee, which a waiter kept refilling.

I did not want to disturb him and took a distant table. I ate my breakfast and read the papers. The Paris train crash toll now at fifty-six. The South African army killed three hundred Cuban and Angolan troops. Ethiopian warplanes killed more than five hundred Tigrean rebels. The presidential campaign in the United States. *Glasnost* attacked by the Soviet Communist Party. Movie stars, directors, rock stars, jazz musicians visiting the Côte d'Azur. More Arab disturbances in the West Bank and the Gaza Strip. Secretary of State Shultz expected to visit Israel. Where was my father? Probably visiting Ladover Hasidim all over Israel. Meeting with politicians. Vote for the Rebbe's party and you will receive the blessings of the Rebbe. My father and then Avrumel. A matter of time. Give them Avrumel. I saw Avrumel sitting in the green chair in my studio, clutching his Shimshon doll, watching me paint. It isn't that I can't paint any more, Avrumel; I could paint all day and all night. It's that I don't want to continue painting in the same way over and over again like a computer. But why do I have to keep pushing against the boundaries? Why the eyes always to the future? I could paint this way the rest of my life and sell everything. Only a few really care about frontiers, about the future. Why bother with it? Why?

"Why what?" someone said. I glanced up, startled, and saw John Dorman standing at the table, tall and thin and red-faced, looking down. "You're talking to yourself, Lev. Sure sign of the beginning of the end. Why didn't you join me?"

I told him I hadn't wanted to disturb his writing.

"Appreciate that. Join you? Did three good pages."

"Do you want a cup of coffee?"

"All coffeed up for the morning. So much coffee, the hands are shaking. See? You going back up soon, or you going to sit and read about the cheerful planet we inhabit?"

I finished my coffee and paid the bill. We walked together out of the village. The sun slanted sharply from the east onto the road, bright and hot. A tourist bus went by. Somewhere in the distance a dog barked. We stood at John's front gate.

"Have something to give you later," John said. "Bring it over."

I watched him go up the path to his house, tall, ungainly, slightly stooped.

I wandered about the house for a while, moving from room to room. In the living room I stopped to look at the picture of the Rebbe that hung amid the many paintings on the wall. I spent the rest of the morning in the studio, looking through drawings and gazing from time to time at the huge waiting canvas. Any of the drawings would have made a fine painting. But I wouldn't do it. What had John Dorman once told me during one of his drinking bouts? He had quoted a toast by Sean O'Casey. "May the best of the past be the worst of the future." Keep everything always off balance. No boundaries. No repetition. The opposite of what the Rebbe wants. The Rebbe seeks fixed boundaries, perfect balance, eternal repetition. Asher Lev caught between the two. Like the paper between the press and the carborundum. Crush it and texture it. Put colors on the texturing and make a work of art. But Asher Lev is not a sheet of paper.

A while later, I walked in the hot sunlight to the home of Jacob Kahn and stood before the grave and the lone cypress and quietly recited a chapter of Psalms. The housekeeper greeted me and let me into the house, and I spent some time with Tanya. She regretted having missed me when I had come over earlier in the week. Why had I been away so long? Yes, she had received my letter; still she could not understand why we had stayed on in Brooklyn. There were still some legal problems involved in settling the Kahn estate. Yes, even after so many years. Entanglements with cold-hearted bureaucrats. But the minister of culture had assured her all would be well in the end, and there was a strong likelihood of a Jacob Kahn museum in Paris. "You look pale and you have lost weight. Go and bring back your family, Asher. I miss your wife and your children. You are not nearly so pleasant to talk to as they are. You have your head too much in your work. Like Jacob Kahn."

I was eating a makeshift late lunch on the terrace, when the front-gate bell sounded and I went to see who was there and it was Max. He was carrying a plastic shopping bag. I opened the gate and let him in.

"Isn't it kind of early for your party, Max?"

"The party is actually cocktails and a dinner. I go to pick up a lady friend. This is for Devorah and the children. Little gifts."

I took the shopping bag.

"Have a good trip, my friend. I will see you after all the holidays, yes? Do not let those people in Brooklyn ruin you. Bring back your family."

He stood for a moment, awkward and uncertain, the afternoon sun in his eyes. He reached up and embraced me and kissed both my cheeks above the hairline. I felt his lips wet and warm on my face. Then he turned and walked quickly back across the road.

Toward evening John came over carrying something inside a small plastic bag. He fished inside the bag and removed a soft-cover book: *Letters to His Son Lucien* by Camille Pissarro. "This is for you. Damn good stuff. Have a safe trip back. Best to the missus and the kids."

We shook hands. I watched him walk slowly back up the road toward his house.

I slept little that night. In the early morning I closed down the house. Claudine and Jameel would care for it, as they had before. Personal mail would be forwarded to my parents' home by Max. The rest would pile up in the post office, to be picked up when we returned. I stood in the living room, looking at the picture of the Rebbe.

The taxi was outside the front gate. I buzzed the gate open, and the taxi came up to the house. I brought my bag and attaché case outside. The driver put them into the trunk. I was locking the front door of the house when I remembered Avrumel's Shimshon doll. I went upstairs and found it on Avrumel's bed. There was no room for it in my already overstuffed valise and attaché case, so I carried it in the taxi and through departure and onto the Airbus. People kept looking at me. The Airbus was crowded. I did not put the doll into the overhead bin, because I was afraid I would forget it. I held it on my lap.

I flew through the day, reading *Letters to His Son Lucien* by Camille Pissarro.

7

✤ ✤ ✤ The water gives way to land and small Long Island towns and roads swarming with traffic. A sulfurous stench invades the cabin. Refineries somewhere. The Airbus lands on time.

At passport control, the officer in the glass cage looked at me and at the Shimshon doll, checked his big book, and returned my passport. The baggage area was crowded and noisy: a maelstrom of tourists. I waited at the carousel for my one bag. All the baggage carts were taken. I carried my bag and attaché case and the Shimshon doll to a customs counter. The customs officer looked at me and at the doll and asked me to open my bag and attaché case. The bag open, I felt embarrassed by the sight of my exposed clothes, as if I were on view in a public toilet. What were the pads for? Drawings? Was I an artist? He was a smooth-shaven, pink-faced man with a barrel chest and small gray eyes and black hair combed back flat and parted on the right. There was about him the look of lighthearted efficiency that let you know he had all the time in the world in which to find out if you were trying to get away with something. He told me to close the bags and asked for the doll. I watched him inspect the doll, squeeze it, shake it, turn it upside down. He called over another inspector, and they stood talking quietly, their backs to me. The people in the long line behind me waited silently. Finally he handed me the doll and waved me on.

As I was leaving the customs area, two men in dark suits approached me and flashed badges. One asked was I carrying more than five thousand dollars in cash. I said no. The other said would

I show them what was in the pockets of my jacket. There was nothing in the pockets of my jacket except two drawing pads, some pens, and my wallet with my passport, my credit cards, and one hundred dollars. They looked briefly at the drawings and returned the pads. They were very polite and seemed vaguely disappointed. They told me to go on, and I went through the exit doors, carrying the bag, the attaché case, and the Shimshon doll.

A dense but orderly mass of people stood outside the doors. I began to move through the crowd. Someone tapped me on the shoulder, and I looked into the blue eyes of a tall blond-bearded young man. He had on a dark suit, a tieless white shirt, open at the collar, and a dark hat.

"Asher Lev?"

I nodded.

"Sholom aleichem. My name is Baruch Levinson."

"Aleichem sholom, Baruch Levinson."

"The Rebbe's office asked me to pick you up. It's an honor for me. Come."

He took the large bag. I followed him through the crowd and out the door into blazing sunlight and steaming air. Holding the Shimshon doll, I waited for him on the crowded traffic island. Children went by and looked at me with the doll in my hands. I put the doll on top of the valise but was afraid someone might snatch it, and after a minute or two I picked it up and held it. Baruch Levinson pulled up in an old two-door car, and we loaded the bags and drove out of the airport.

"How was your flight?"

"Fine."

He slipped expertly into the dense and rushing traffic of the Van Wyck Expressway.

"Where were you, if I may ask?"

I told him.

"Is Paris as nice as everyone says?"

"It's an unusual city."

"I'd love to go there. But who has the money? A wife, five kids. It eats up everything. Were you gone long?"

"About ten days. You're not from Brooklyn."

"You can tell from the accent? I try to hide it, but it comes out.

I grew up in Chicago. We just moved here to be close to the Rebbe and so I could study in the yeshiva."

"You saw the Rebbe recently?"

"The Rebbe is in the country."

"What do you mean, the country?"

"The mountains. In the yeshiva we heard the Rebbe's doctor said he shouldn't stay in the city because of the heat. Everyone is predicting this will be a terrible summer."

The traffic moved smoothly along the Belt Parkway past the exits to the beaches. There was no air-conditioning in the car, and the windows were wide open. Hot, moist air blew stiffly into my nostrils the smells of baking asphalt and gasoline fumes. We slid beneath the massive, rising girders of the Verrazzano-Narrows Bridge. Avrumel is in the Ladover day camp on the other side of this bridge, somewhere on Staten Island. Baruch Levinson turned off the parkway at the Prospect Park exit.

"What is the doll you're carrying, if I may ask?"

"It belongs to my son. He forgot it."

"You bought it in France?"

"It was a gift. You can get them in Crown Heights."

"It's cute. I think I'll get one for my son."

He turned into the street skirting Prospect Park. Traffic was heavy. Heat shimmer rose from the car engine when we stopped for lights. People sat on stoops in undershirts or stripped to the waist and moved slowly in the heat.

"There was an article in yesterday's *Times* about you and your uncle's art collection."

I said nothing.

Baruch Levinson drove past the library and turned into Brooklyn Parkway.

"I read some articles about you once. I took a course in modern art where I went to college, the University of Chicago. You know, Rothko, Pollock, de Kooning, Newman, Avery, Gottlieb, Motherwell, all those guys. I still remember the names. Good course. Some women, too. And some contemporary artists, you know, people working today. We did a couple of your paintings and some prints, talked about them in class, slides and stuff, you know."

"Which paintings?"

"Which paintings? Let me see if I remember. Yeah, the crucifixion ones and *The Sacrifice of Isaac*. I like your stuff. I hope you
don't mind me talking like this. If it's, you know, embarrassing, I'll
shut up."

"You majored in fine art?"

"Yeah. I thought I'd be a painter, you know? Then I met this
Ladover guy in Chicago, and he turned me on to Ladover ideas
and things, and here I am, born again, you might say, a ba'al
teshuva, back to my roots. I really like your work. So did the
professor teaching the course."

"Thank you."

Brooklyn Parkway was still torn up. Long stretches of the road
had been stripped of asphalt, leaving a washboard surface. Here
and there the innards of the broad street lay exposed: sewage pipes,
telephone cable, electrical lines, raw red clayey earth. Huge construction equipment obstructed traffic. Road barriers funneled
traffic through temporary cattle-chute lanes. We drove past the
Ladover yeshiva. There was the usual small crowd in front of
the synagogue, people milling about, coming and going. The car
turned into the street where my parents lived and stopped in front
of the house. There was my Uncle Yitzchok's house, its blinds
drawn.

Baruch Levinson unloaded the bags. I said I would bring them
in myself. He shook my hand. "An honor to help you, Mr. Lev."
He drove off.

I started up the path to the house. The air was hot. I was
halfway up the path when the front door opened and Devorah
came rushing out. She wore a yellow summer dress, an apron, and
a pale-orange kerchief, and she looked as if she had lived in this
house all her life.

"You look lovely, my wife. Brooklyn agrees with you."

"It feels good to be here, Asher."

"Max and John and Tanya send you their love and want me to
bring you all home."

Devorah stands near the sliding glass door of our room, watching me unpack. She seems to have put on a little weight, there is

high color on her face, her eyes are bright, the gray irises sparkling—or is it a trick of the afternoon light? She is telling me what has happened during my time away. Avrumel loves the day camp, though he gets into fights now and then with one of the boys in his group. Rocheleh telephoned the other day to say that she had been given the part of Moses' sister in a play about the early life of Moses. My mother was busy on her book and right now was at a meeting with the Rebbe's staff. Yes, the Rebbe would be away all summer. Doctor's orders. He was up at the Ladover community in the mountains.

"How do you call it? In Massa . . . ?"

"Massachusetts."

"Yes. And how are you, Asher? How was your trip?"

I tell her about the trip: the visit to the Picasso Museum; working with Max on the carborundum print; Lucien's widow; the Shabbos in the yeshiva; the few days back home in Saint-Paul.

"When is my father returning from Israel?" I ask.

"We don't know. Mama will be back soon from her meeting. Maybe she'll bring news."

Mama. She says it in the most natural way. I cannot recall her using that word before in connection with my mother. She said "your mother" whenever she talked to me about her, and avoided calling her anything when she spoke directly to her. I was away ten days. Now, Mama.

"Mama and I thought it would be a good idea to spend the weekend in the country," she says.

"What about Avrumel and the day camp?"

"It won't hurt him to miss a day."

I shut the valise and open the attaché case. "You might want to look at these." I hand her the three large-sized drawing pads. She stands there holding them close to her.

"One of the men from the yeshiva will drive us up in the morning."

"Fine."

"I missed you, my husband."

"And I you, Dev."

"I enjoyed being with your mother. But I missed you very much."

I move to her. She puts the drawing pads on the desk. I hold her and kiss her. She clings to me, faintly trembling. The house is not air-conditioned, and her face is moist with heat. Small wrinkles seem to have invaded the corners of her eyes. She puts her hands on my face and I feel her fingers in my beard. Devorah. A sealed apartment in her childhood and a two-year brush with the Angel of Death and her family gone and Max her only solace and an artist for a husband and children's books for her fantasy life and a hunger to create families wherever she lives and now a new family for her in Brooklyn.

"Would you like a cup of coffee, Asher?"

"Sure."

On the way to the kitchen I leave the old Shimshon doll on Avrumel's bed, propped up on the pillow next to the new Shimshon doll. Side by side, old and new, one doll appears exhausted and frayed, a worn mirror image of the other. I sit in the kitchen drinking coffee with Devorah and talk to her about Max and John.

I am on the terrace outside our room, dozing in the late-afternoon sunlight. I slip in and out of a troubled sleep as sounds drift through the stifling air: a child's high voice; a man complaining in Yiddish about the heat; the leaves of the sycamore stirred by an occasional hot breeze; the music of George Gershwin on a radio somewhere; a Hebrew song about the armies of God.

A noise wakes me, the sound of the sliding door being quickly opened. I hear "Papa!" and Avrumel is suddenly all over me. "My papa is back!" He climbs onto the recliner, and I hold him. He wears a baseball cap and shorts and a T-shirt and his freckled face is tanned and he smells of sunlight and chlorinated water—the pool he swims in.

"How are you, Avrumel?"

"Ça va bien, Papa!"

It is so good to hold his lithe strong vibrant little form. My son.

"I am learning to play the baseball," he says, his freckled face close to mine.

"Uncle Max and Uncle John send you their love."

"Thank you, Papa. We are going to the country tomorrow. It is a long ride. Grandmother says maybe we will see the Rebbe."

He leaves, and I am alone again on the terrace, still feeling his presence and hearing his high eager laughing voice, and I close my eyes and he is still there, and I open my eyes and he is really there, all over me again, holding his old Shimshon doll, his face radiant.

"I thank my papa for bringing me Shimshon!" And he plants a kiss on my face and runs off, holding the rag doll to him, the doll looking as if Avrumel's joyously enthusiastic clutching will squeeze the stuffing from it.

I lie back on the recliner and close my eyes. The ground yaws and I feel myself on the Airbus, reading Camille Pissarro's letters. I hear repeated distant ringing, and then silence. A moment later the door to the terrace slides open. Someone wants me on the telephone, Devorah says. I get out of the recliner, and as I walk through our room I notice that on my bed is the new Shimshon doll Devorah bought Avrumel to replace the old one he forgot. It lies propped against my pillow, no longer needed, abandoned.

The voice on the telephone sounded deep and nasal. "Is this Asher Lev?"

"Yes."

"You'll be with us for Shabbos?"

"What?"

"I understand you will be here for Shabbos."

"Who is this?"

"I'm sorry. My name is Yehuda Birkov. I'm on the Rebbe's staff. You'll be with us in the mountains for Shabbos?"

"Yes."

"The Rebbe would like to talk to you. Right after Shabbos." I said nothing.

"Hello?"

"All right. Yes."

"Be well." He hung up.

I was lying on my bed on top of the spread and next to the Shimshon doll, when I heard my mother calling from the entrance hallway. "Hello! I'm home! Is Asher back?"

I got up, and the doll fell to the floor. I picked it up and put it on a chair and went out into the hallway. My mother kissed me and said it was good to see me back safely; she was happy I had decided to return today rather than Sunday. How was my father? Did he look all right when we were together in Paris?

"I worry about your father. It is not pleasant now in Israel."

"Is Papa anywhere near the demonstrations?"

"I almost never know exactly where your father is when he travels. I am going to change into something comfortable, and then we will have supper. It is good to see you again, my son. Doesn't Devorah look wonderful? She has put on weight, and there is color in her face. You see, even in Brooklyn one can get sunlight and air. And Avrumel! Did you see how tan he is?"

We ate supper together in the kitchen, and afterward I went for a walk with Devorah and Avrumel. Then I was very sleepy. I got into pajamas and stood before the mirror in the bathroom and heard myself say in Hebrew, "Blessed art Thou, O Lord our God, Master of the Universe, who revives the dead," and I had no idea why I said it.

I climbed into my bed and was immediately asleep.

Sometime during the night, I woke and felt Devorah in bed beside me, whispering. I held her to me with love, I held her to me with tenderness. She clung to me with a strange ferocity and I heard her say in French, "I love you, my husband. God brought you to me. I love you."

In the morning Devorah and I and my mother were at the table when Avrumel entered the kitchen, his baseball cap on his head, his old Shimshon doll tucked firmly under an arm.

"Sit down and I'll make you an orange juice," I said to him. I squeezed a fresh orange into a glass, put in a teaspoon of sugar, and filled the glass with cold water.

"That's the way Grandfather makes it," Avrumel said.

"Drink it," I said. "All the vitamins will go out of it if you let it stand too long."

Baruch Levinson, the blond-bearded Chicagoan who had driven me in from the airport, showed up about an hour after breakfast in a newer, roomier car—one that was, he said, more appropriate for the women and a long drive. He had borrowed it from a friend.

He would remain in the colony with another friend over Shabbos and bring us back on Sunday afternoon.

The roads out of Manhattan were dismal with traffic. Jet-lagged, fatigued, my head more in Paris and Saint-Paul than on a crowded highway with my family, I sat next to Baruch Levinson in a fog of discomfort, slipping in and out of dazed sleep, waking in fits and starts to new roads and countrysides, as if I were moving through discontinuous corridors of time. I heard dimly the conversation in the back seat, where my mother and Devorah sat, with Avrumel between Devorah and the door behind Baruch Levinson, who kept humming Ladover melodies as he drove. On the Taconic the traffic thinned, and he went hurtling along the highway. Once I woke with a start from hallucinatory sleep and saw an old European car draw alongside us, the Spaniard in the back seat, smoking a cigarette. He rolled down his window and looked at me. I felt his eyes scourge my face. The car sped past us. I was suddenly bathed in sweat, my heart thundering. After a while I fell again into a half-sleep and saw Jacob Kahn walking quickly across the dunes in front of his summer home in Provincetown and on into the waves, his head of thick white hair flashing in the sunlight.

We stopped at a roadside restaurant for some drinks and to use the bathrooms. I went with Avrumel into the men's room. He stood at a low urinal in his shorts and Ladover day camp T-shirt and his Mets baseball cap. The bathroom was crowded. A thick-chested, huge-muscled, bearded man in jeans and a teamsters cap took the urinal beside him. He glanced at Avrumel.

"How you doing, young feller?"

"Fine, thank you."

"Mets ain't doing too well this year."

"God will help them."

The man looked startled. He chuckled. "You bet He will!" He shook himself down and went away.

Outside, we stood on the hot tarmac in the blinding sunlight, drinking Cokes and waiting for Devorah and my mother.

"Papa, will we be there soon?"

"Another hour or so."

"It is a long trip."

"America is a big country, Avrumel."

"Bigger than France?"

"Much bigger."

"I like America."

"What do you like about it?"

"That I am with my grandfather and my grandmother."

"What else?"

"I like the day camp and the yeshiva and that we live near the Rebbe. I like baseball and the pool."

"There's more to America than baseball, Avrumel. There are many poor people and people who sleep on the streets, and there is terrible crime."

"If I go to school in the yeshiva here, will I learn about America?"

I stared at him, and before I could respond, my mother and Devorah came out of the restaurant. They wore light long-sleeved summer dresses and sunglasses, and their heads were covered with kerchiefs. They looked strikingly like mother and daughter.

We walked through the parking lot to the car. The lot was crowded. Shimmering waves rose from the baking asphalt. Avrumel and I walked a few feet behind Devorah and my mother.

"Avrumel, who talked to you about going to the yeshiva in America next year?"

"Grandmother."

Baruch Levinson sat behind the wheel of the car. The motor was running and the air conditioner was on. We climbed inside.

"Ready to roll?" he asked cheerfully.

My parents' cottage was in a private Ladover summer colony in the Berkshire Mountains of Massachusetts. The colony stood along a sandy beach on the western rim of a lake. There was a dense wood of oak and pine and white birch behind the colony, and off in the distance beyond the lake were green hills and tall trees and wide fire lanes running along the slopes to the crests and looking like the raked side lanes of Brooklyn Parkway. All the cottages, save that of the Rebbe, were identical bungalow-like, one-story structures: white clapboard exteriors, red-shingled roofs. Cement walks wound among them to their front doors. Some of the cottages had small flower beds in front. The Rebbe's dwelling, set a distance from the others, was the size of two cottages and had a front porch and a rear raised screened-in deck. The synagogue, too, was the size of two cottages, and it stood about fifty feet from the house of the Rebbe. A tall oak shielded the Rebbe's large cottage from the afternoon sun.

In the summer weekdays the colony was crowded with women and children; husbands, working in the city, would come up for Shabbos. Now women and children stood watching as we pulled up to our cottage. They murmured words of greeting to my mother and Devorah. Baruch Levinson, sweating, helped us with our bags, wished us a good Shabbos, and drove off. Avrumel went down toward the lake.

Devorah wandered slowly through the cottage, looking at the furniture, the small kitchen, the bedrooms. The air had a moist, earthen, cavelike smell. Always, when entering a new place—a store, a house, an apartment, a room—she moved with caution, giving the impression of deep interest in her surroundings but actually looking for windows and doors through which light might come. She gazed out our bedroom window at the lake. I could see Avrumel on the beach, talking to some boys his age.

In the early evening I went with Avrumel to the synagogue for the Shabbos Service. The Rebbe did not appear. Some of the children apparently knew Avrumel from the yeshiva and the day camp, and they clustered around him after the service. Later, I walked back with him to the cottage under a jet-black sky jeweled with stars. The air was cool. I used to walk with my mother beneath that sky. She knew many of the constellations and would try to point them out to me—the Bear, the Swan, Orion—but I only learned to make out the Big Dipper. There it was now in that vast star-laden sky, and I stopped and looked up at it and felt myself seized at that moment by an immense and nameless dread. The sky slowly turned. I became light-headed, dizzy.

"Papa?" Avrumel said.

The Big Dipper wheeled toward me, its stars blazing. It would scoop me into itself.

Avrumel tugged at my arm. "Is my papa all right?"

I looked at him. He wore his Shabbos clothes: a shirt, a tie, a dark-blue summer suit. A black velvet skullcap covered his red hair.

"The Big Dipper contains all the evil deeds that people do during the day," my mother had once told me. "And during the night it spills those deeds into a special place in the heavens, the Place of Evil Deeds. But there is also the Little Dipper, and that contains all the good deeds. The good deeds are fewer, but they weigh more in the eyes of the Master of the Universe. The Little Dipper spills the good deeds into the Place of Good Deeds. Blessings come to the world when the good deeds outweigh the evil."

I was very young when she told me that. I had not thought to ask her what might happen if the evil deeds ever outweighed the good ones.

She told me all that about the Big and Little Dippers on one of the many nights when we were up here alone and my father was in Europe on a journey for the Rebbe. "Your father is trying to give a balance to the world, Asher. He is trying to fill the Little Dipper with good deeds, fill it to the top, so it will outweigh the evil deeds in the Big Dipper." I remember thinking it was an awesome task for one man, all that balancing and outweighing of the good over the bad, and my father seemed to me at that moment a being of heroic dimensions, one altogether beyond the normal and the human, a celestial creature moving with ease among the stars, gathering the good deeds of mankind and pouring them into the Little Dipper. I knew I would be frightened by his presence when he returned to earth.

Later, we sat around the table in the cottage, the four of us, and ate the Shabbos meal and sang zemiros. At times during the meal my mother fell silent. She would sit with her eyes wide open, staring, as if a lever had been pulled inside her, sealing off her feelings. Her face sagged; the light went out of her eyes. I knew those moments: sudden retreats into herself as she thought of my father journeying for the Rebbe. She looked old, limp, doll-like: all her features intact but the life gone from them. Apparently Devorah now recognized those moments, too; she knew to bring my mother back with a gentle remark about a current event, a quote from something the Rebbe had said, an observation about the children. During the meal, they would talk for long periods of time, just the two of them, as I sat by, watching or talking with Avrumel. I thought I might make a painting of them one day. I would have to do it from memory. My mother would not sit for it. When I was young she would let me draw her often, but I had not been near her with a pencil and drawing pad since the day she saw the crucifixion paintings. How would I capture her face in those moments of withdrawal? There was something in her face then: a strange flickering in the otherwise dead eyes. Some sort of odd life in the midst of emotional death. How would I render that? We were chanting the Grace After Meals, Avrumel swaying back and forth in his chair, saying the words loudly, as if he had known them from birth. There I was, in the midst of the Grace After Meals—thinking of how to do a painting of my mother! Truly a desecration of the Shabbos. I abandoned the painting and concentrated on the words.

The Rebbe did not come to the synagogue the next morning. It was a warm, sun-filled day, the sky clear and blue. The placid lake darkly mirrored the sky. After the service many walked past the Rebbe's cottage, men, women, and children, walking in silence, and there were glances, but nothing was said, and people wished one another a good Shabbos and went off to the afternoon meal.

I fell asleep after the meal and woke and saw Devorah under a tree near the edge of the beach, looking through my drawing pads. My mother was somewhere with friends. I found Avrumel on the beach with some of his classmates and asked him if he wanted to go for a walk, and we went into the woods behind the colony and I showed him where I had played as a child and had skimmed stones across the surface of the lake and where my mother and I used to go rowing and the clearing in the woods where I would play alone. Beyond the stand of white birch were lines of oak and pine and silver spruce, and one of the oaks had an enormous low branch, and often I would climb up and lie on it and gaze through the canopy of leaves and branches and imagine myself becoming weightless and rising from the leaden pull of the earth through the leaves to the light beyond. Rising and flying free from the weight of the world. I told Avrumel that, and he looked at the branch and the tangle of leaves overhead and said he didn't want to climb onto the branch, he was afraid he would fall off. I said he was too young yet to climb trees, but one day he might find it was an exciting thing to do.

We left the clearing and started back through the woods, skirting the houses, and as we passed the back of the Rebbe's cottage, I saw the Rebbe on the screened-in deck. He was sitting in a recliner. Nearby stood a dark-bearded man, staring out through the screen at the lake. The few boats on the water were from the private homes on the far side of the lake. Distant summer sounds drifted toward me: birds, voices, the lapping of water, the whispery rustling of leaves. There was the languorous feeling of the slowing of the world.

I lingered behind and Avrumel continued on alone and went into the cottage. I looked across the lawn to the tree under which Devorah sat. Two of my drawing pads were on the grass at her feet. She was looking through the third.

I went into the cottage and fell asleep on my bed. Devorah woke me about an hour later and asked me if I knew where Avrumel was. I said he was probably playing with his friends and I would see him in the synagogue for the Afternoon Service. I washed my hands and face, and left.

He did not appear in the synagogue. After the Evening Service I walked back alone in the darkness beneath a waning moon that sparkled like shards of glass on the black surface of the lake. A man came toward me on the path, bearded, in his twenties. He said, "Ah, the air is good here," and wished me a good week. Another stood on the path, gazing up at the sky, and, as I went slowly past him, murmured, " 'The heavens tell of the glory of God.' "

I stopped near him a moment in the darkness beneath the arc of stars and stood looking up at the sky. I imagined my father striding among the stars, filling the Little Dipper. Images from childhood. I walked back to the cottage.

Devorah was in the kitchen with my mother. Wasn't Avrumel with me? I said he hadn't been in the synagogue, I thought he would be home by now. Devorah said he wasn't home. I said he might be walking along the lake and went out to find him.

The lake was silent and dark. Yellow lights shone in the homes along the opposite shore. Lake and woods and star-filled sky formed a single continuous darkness. I could not make out anyone along the shore. Passing the rear of the Rebbe's cottage, I heard voices and looked at the screened-in deck and saw the Rebbe in the recliner, wearing a dark suit and tie and an ordinary dark hat. In the wicker chair beside him sat Avrumel. A tall dark-bearded man stood on the top step of the wooden stairway that led from the deck to the beach, his back to the screen door.

Avrumel and the Rebbe were talking in French. I could not make out clearly what they were saying.

The man on the stairs saw me and stood very still as I approached.

"I am Asher Lev, the boy's father."

The voices on the deck were suddenly silent.

"I know who you are," the man on the stoop said.

"Papa?" I heard Avrumel say. Then, "That is my papa!"

The Rebbe said in Yiddish, "Come inside."

The dark-bearded man opened the screen door, and I went up the stairs and onto the deck. The Rebbe beckoned to me. The yellow lights of an overhead fixture shone dimly on his dark clothes and gave his aged face a pale luminosity.

"A good week to you, Asher Lev."

"A good week, Rebbe."

"I came to say good Shabbos to the Rebbe, Papa," Avrumel said.

"You've been here all this time?"

"The child said to me his father was Asher Lev," the Rebbe said, "and I asked him to come inside. He is a bright child."

"My grandfather told me I could come with him to his office and sometimes I might see the Rebbe," Avrumel said.

"God heard your grandfather's words and hurried to make them come true," said the Rebbe. "How are you, Asher?"

"I am well, thank God."

"How was your journey? You did what you had to do?"

"Yes, Rebbe."

"You were with your father in Paris." It was a statement, not a question. My father called the Rebbe daily from wherever he was. The Rebbe knew every detail of my father's work.

"Yes, Rebbe."

"And in Saint-Paul, everything was in order?"

"Yes."

"The matter of the art collection has become unpleasant. You know of it?"

"About my cousin and the lawsuit? Yes. I'm told there isn't anything he can really do."

"He has made of this a great desecration of the Name of God. The Other Side has taken hold of him."

Near the door, the dark-bearded man stirred and was still.

The Rebbe brushed his hand across Avrumel's cheek. "The child tells me that in Saint-Paul there are two people he loves. Who are these people?"

"Devorah's cousin, Max Lobe, who is an artist. And an elderly American writer named John Dorman."

"The child also tells me that he loves to sit and watch his father paint, but that his father does not paint any more."

"My papa draws a lot," Avrumel said in his high, eager voice.

"If I remember correctly, we have talked of this before," the Rebbe said. "Jacob Kahn had such troubles. All have such troubles, such indecisions and waverings. Even, sometimes, a Rebbe."

The man near the door took a small step toward us, then, at a gesture from the Rebbe, stepped back and was still.

"Asher," the Rebbe said. "Listen to me carefully. Choices must be made very soon. Do you understand?"

"Yes, Rebbe."

He sighed and sat back in the recliner. I made out his eyes peering at me intently from the shadow cast by the brim of his hat. He beckoned me closer to him and I leaned forward and saw the old wrinkled brittleness of his flesh and thought of him when I was a child and felt my love for him. He was talking into my ear, almost whispering. I felt his breath moving against me, puffs of warm odorless air. "Asher Lev, listen to me. All the future of the Ladover depends upon three. When two of the three are gone, the third will save us. This you now understand with perfect clarity. I wish you a good week, and I give you and your son my blessing."

He closed his eyes and was still. The dark-bearded man approached and motioned us to leave.

I went with Avrumel down the stairs and along the rim of the lake toward the cottage.

"Is the Rebbe sick?" Avrumel asked.

"The Rebbe is well," I said. "But he is old."

"Will the Rebbe die soon?"

"With the help of God, the Rebbe will live many, many more years. What did you and the Rebbe talk about?"

"We talked about Rocheleh and you and Mama and Shimshon and what I learned in the yeshiva. And about baseball."

"Baseball?"

"The Rebbe knows about baseball."

I laughed softly in the starlit darkness.

"I told the Rebbe about Uncle Max's pool and about the trips we take to Nice and to the mountains and how good the air is for Rocheleh and how nice the goyim are to us."

"What did the Rebbe say?"

"Mostly the Rebbe listened."

"Did he say anything?"

"He said I was smart and he saw something in me."

"What?"

"I don't know. He used a word I don't remember."

We walked on together. The air was cool, sweet-smelling, redolent of honeysuckle. I heard the lake lapping softly against the rowboats tied to the dock.

Later that night, when Devorah and I were alone in our room, I said, "What did you think of the drawings?"

"I do not understand them. You have never made drawings like these before."

"Is there anything about them you like?"

"I want to look at them again."

"Dev, did you see the Rebbe alone while I was away?"

She looked surprised. "The Rebbe asked to see me, yes. He wanted to know where Avrumel would go to school next year."

"What did you tell him?"

"That, with God's help, he will go to the yeshiva in Nice."

"What did the Rebbe say?"

"He gave me a blessing. We did not talk long. Asher, I am very tired."

"Let's go to sleep," I said.

There was a fierce rainstorm during the night. Devorah woke and lay frightened in her bed. Flashes of lightning ripped through the sky. I went into Avrumel's room. He was asleep, his arm around Shimshon. My mother came into the hallway, bareheaded and wearing her robe. Was Avrumel all right? I told her he was asleep and she returned to her room. From my bed the mountains were like bloated creatures rising toward the sky in the blue-white lightning. The rain fell upon the house and the lake with a fierce waterfall sound. I slept and woke to a dawn of sunlight and sparkling air. There were puddles of rain on the beach and silvery beads on the leaves in the woods. I dressed and went to the synagogue for the Morning Service.

Later, I took Avrumel and Devorah and my mother out on the lake in a rowboat. I showed Avrumel how to work one of the oars, but it was too much for him; he wearied of it quickly. I rowed slowly along the lake, remembering the rowing in Prospect Park as a child, my mother at the oars and me drawing. Young, so young. And white birds in the water. Had there ever really been such an Edenic time in our lives? I gave the oars to Devorah, and she rowed us awhile. Avrumel sat in the bow with Shimshon, trailing his hand in the water. My mother had her face to the sun, her eyes closed. Small birds skimmed the surface of the water and rose in soaring flocks. Many Ladover were swimming in the section of the lake where a wooden partition extended from the bathhouse on the beach deep into the water, separating men from women. Others were in boats on the lake; they hailed us as we went by. Devorah tired and I took the oars and rowed deep into the lake and there were little waves now and I could hear them against the gunwales. Rowing back, I looked over my shoulder from time to time to get my bearings, and once I saw the Rebbe standing behind the screen of the rear deck of his cottage, gazing out across the water, and

when I looked again he was gone. In the afternoon we drove back
to the city.

The following Wednesday, my father returned from Israel and
immediately closeted himself with his staff. I was with him in the
synagogue Thursday morning and at home during supper, which
he ate quickly: there was a meeting he had to attend. The next
Monday he flew down to Washington and was gone two days.
Then he was taken by car to Massachusetts to see the Rebbe. He
returned the next day.

I felt weary watching him. He seemed indefatigable. During my
walks with him to and from the synagogue, and as we all sat
around the table for his hurried meals, he told us something of his
work in Israel: the splinterings and maneuverings of the religious
parties; the campaigns of the secular parties; the real possibility
that the party of the Ladover—in Israel the Rebbe's followers
numbered in the many thousands—would win seats in the Knesset
and the political power that came with that. He seemed ecstatic at
the prospect of such power, the influence it would give the Ladover
as the secularists devised strategies to form a coalition government,
the bargaining and agreements that would inevitably follow with
the secular parties that needed the Ladover votes, the ability the
Ladover would then possess to push through the Rebbe's policies:
no return of the conquered territories; an emended Law of Return
to exclude from automatic citizenship those Jews converted to
Judaism by non-Orthodox rabbis; increased government funding
for religious education. Much work needed to be done. He would
be returning to Israel soon. Victory was a distinct possibility. The
Rebbe and his followers would emerge triumphant.

My father was seventy years old, and he talked with the ease and
lightness of someone half his age about his journeys and his work,
while my mother sat quietly, listening to him. I saw the same look
in her eyes I had seen all the years of my growing up: the window-
watching, night-haunting dread. But he saw only his work, his
dream, the giving of himself to the Rebbe and the Master of the
Universe. Devorah sat and listened and watched, and for the first

time began to understand, I thought, what lay behind the crucifixion paintings.

On the Sunday at the end of the first week of August, we all rode with my father to Kennedy Airport in a borrowed station wagon driven by Baruch Levinson. We waited in the King David Lounge of the El Al terminal for his flight to be called. The lounge was crowded, and I saw people glancing at me and my parents and whispering to one another. Devorah noticed that, too. Avrumel sat on my father's lap, holding the Shimshon doll by a tattered arm.

My father said to me, "The Rebbe told me that he and you and Avrumel had a long talk."

"The long talk was mostly with Avrumel," I said.

"The Rebbe told me he likes baseball," Avrumel said.

Devorah and my mother laughed. My father looked as if he wanted to ask Avrumel, "What else did the Rebbe tell you?" But that would have been somewhat unseemly in public and in front of me and Devorah—there was no telling what Avrumel might come out with—and my father chuckled and remained silent.

A few minutes later, his flight was called.

"Travel in good health and return in good health," my mother said to him.

Avrumel, his Mets baseball cap awry, his Shimshon doll momentarily abandoned on the leather armchair, clung to my father with both his arms and kissed him. "The Rebbe told me he sees greatness in you," my father said to Avrumel, and kissed him in return.

I shook his hand. How strong his fingers were! Like the sculptor's grip of Jacob Kahn years ago. Devorah wished him a safe journey. He went out the door of the lounge, tall and broadshouldered, carrying his attaché case and limping slightly, towering above most of the others there. We watched him go, all the years of separations trailing behind him like some dark and stubborn cloud.

The drive back home was through Sunday-night summer traffic. For a while we crawled along the Grand Central Parkway and the Interboro Parkway. Then Baruch Levinson left the Interboro and drove along rutted roads through garbage-littered streets and destroyed neighborhoods. Avrumel fell asleep on my mother's lap. I sat in the front seat, looking at the rancid streets and thinking of the sunlight on the green valley and Max Lobe and John Dorman and our closed home in Saint-Paul.

My father remained in Israel until close to the end of August. He did not write; but every day he phoned his office and someone from the office would call us and ask to speak with my mother. If my mother was not home, the man on the phone would call back. Early every Friday morning my father would call and talk with my mother. He was well. The work was progressing. How was Avrumel? How was Rocheleh? How were Devorah and Asher? Always in that order. The Arab uprising? God would help. How was the weather in Israel? Hot, very hot. And in Brooklyn? The same. Very hot.

My mother would put down the phone after talking with my father and sit for a moment, her eyes closed, wispy ghosts of past nightmares clinging to her like visible mist. Afterward she and Devorah would go off somewhere and talk.

I grew up in New York, sometimes suffering the heat of its summers, but I do not remember anything like the heat of that summer, the summer of 1988. Humid heat and no rain, week after week: the asphalt on the streets soft with it; the air dense and insect-ridden with it; my skin wet with it; Devorah's face flushed with it; the house sultry with it. There was no air-conditioning in my parents' home, and the window fans stirred futilely the swampy air. I wandered through the city in a daze, often losing track of time. I met with Douglas Schaeffer about my show of drawings, which he had scheduled for the fall; I met with lawyers about the attempts of my Cousin Yonkel to have me removed or enjoined as trustee of his father's art collection.

I went to museums and galleries. I saw old artist friends in their Greenwich Village lofts; rode the subway trains; breathed the fetid tunnel air that blew through the stations; went for walks along Brooklyn Parkway, watching men at work over the hot, torn roadbed and thinking often of Saint-Paul, and the terrace of the café in the shadows of the trees, and the ramparts of the village wall, and the graves of Jacob Kahn and Marc Chagall, and Max Lobe painting his lined-up canvases, and John Dorman alone in his house with his memories and whiskey bottles, and the red-tiled Cubist houses set among the green fields and cypresses of the long valley and climbing to the hills and the sea.

Early every weekday morning Avrumel went off to his day camp, and late every afternoon he came home. When I had been away in France, Devorah would go with him mornings and, afternoons, bring him home. After my father left, I took to walking Avrumel to the bus pickup station in front of the yeshiva, and then to meeting him there in the afternoon. We would leave a few minutes before eight, which was soon after I returned from the Morning Service in the synagogue. He carried with him only a little bag with a light sweater and his bathing suit and towel. He wore tan-colored shorts, a Ladover day camp T-shirt, sneakers over socks, and his Mets baseball cap. Shimshon he always left in his room on his bed. Reclining on the pillow, the torn and tattered doll looked oddly enough as if it were in command of that room, a sort of drowsing royal personage waiting to be awakened and served. At odd moments of the day, if I was home, I would poke my head into the room to see if it had somehow moved from its place on the bed, if it needed something, if it had a request. This strange behavior, I told myself, gave me something to do, broke up long empty stretches of time, was the result of the heat, came about because I was feeling myself confined, entombed. One day, alone in the house, I heard myself talking to the doll. "How would *you* do it? A half year here, a half year there? A year at a time? And what of the loneliness?" I felt the blood in my head and a loud buzzing in my ears. Flies seemed to be circling before my eyes. I fled from the room.

Later, sitting on the terrace, I made a drawing of the doll. Then I made a drawing of the Spaniard holding the doll. I liked neither drawing and destroyed them both. I went out for a walk and watched the construction along the parkway.

Douglas Schaeffer said to me, during one of my visits to the gallery, "You look awful, dear boy. What good are you going to be to anyone if you become ill? Why don't you go off to the country for a while? This is a simply terrible summer to be in the city."

I told him Avrumel was in a day camp, my father was in Israel, my mother was in a perpetual state of panic over his safety and wanted to be near JFK Airport in case, God forbid, anything happened to him and she needed to get over there fast, and Devorah was busy giving little talks to women's groups all over the city about the Ladover movement's attitude toward feminism.

"But what does all that have to do with *you*, dear boy? I am talking about *you*. Why don't *you* get away?"

I shrugged. Where would I go? Off alone to the cottage in Massachusetts? And do what? Talk to whom? Eat where?

He shook his head sadly, touched his bow tie, smoothed his hair, and returned to the subject of my show. After his initial comments about the drawings—the look that flooded his eyes when he first saw them, unusual for him: he had his mother's laconic self-control and was sparse with praise; it was simply assumed by him, as it had been by his mother, that the artists of the Schaeffer Gallery were among the finest working today—after his first brief comments, we talked only business: catalogue, invitations, critics, curators, collectors, prices, advertising, taxes, hanging days: the clanking apparatus of the art world. I chose one of the drawings and told him we would show it but not sell it; I wanted it to go to the widow of Lucien Lacamp. He made a note of this in his book.

Afterward I took the elevator down and walked through the cool marble lobby and the glass front door into the inferno of the Manhattan summer.

I meet with lawyers in large offices furnished with polished mahogany desks and tables. They talk in low voices. Expensive art hangs on the walls: Dubuffet, Dufy, Chagall, Coignard, Papart. I listen to terminology I barely understand. Probate petition. Combined verification. Oath and designation. Oath of trustee. Valuation process. Liquidity problems. Douglas Schaeffer's lawyer is present. I sign papers. My uncle's lawyer tells me he has heard I am going to have a show in New York in the fall. How could he have heard that so soon? Perhaps from one of the secretaries in the gallery. Perhaps he and Douglas belong to the same club. New York is a big city, but the successful travel in small circles and learn

quickly what wares each plans to offer as a grab for a share of the
city's wealth. Everything is in order, my uncle's lawyer tells me.
My Cousin Yonkel has tried again to enjoin me from touching the
collection and has failed. I may now do with it as I wish, provided
I adhere to the basic stipulation of the will: all profits are to go to
the Ladover organization.

Douglas Schaeffer's attorney accompanies me down to the burning street. I thank him for his help.

He asks me what I plan to do with the collection, and I tell him
I don't know.

"That's a great deal of money, if you sell it. Douglas and I would
like to handle it for you."

"Of course."

"Good luck with the show." He offers me a moist hand and
walks off into the crowd on the street.

The heat is stifling. Sunlight strikes the sidewalks and streets.
Traffic barely moves. Gasoline fumes choke the hot and humid air.
I stand there sweating in my fisherman's cap and Ladover T-shirt.
BRING MOSHIACH NOW, the T-shirt says in black letters against a red
background. It is the shirt that Avrumel often wears to his day
camp, but many sizes larger, and now on the street it is the object
of curious stares and indulgent smiles. Earlier, the lawyers had
looked at it and kept their faces blank.

I take the subway uptown and get out and walk along Broadway
and down a side street past the building that once housed Jacob
Kahn's studio. An elderly black doorman stands inside the air-
conditioned lobby, gazing out the glass door at the melting street.
Not the same doorman who was there before. I go down the slope
of the park to the stone parapet that overlooks the highway and the
river. The surface of the water is slate gray and smooth, and seems
to be swallowing all the sunlight falling upon it. I think of the
night boats on the Seine and the light-flooding halogens and Jacob
Kahn looking out the window of his apartment on the Quai Voltaire. A hot wind blows across the river and the waves of the wind
are washed in red and I hear Jacob Kahn say do not concern
yourself that others will not understand you the drawings are a
beginning I see how you achieve the texturing of the carborundum
process by using charcoal and a pencil the rhythms come from the

very paper itself, and I stand there looking out at the blistering sunlight on the dark surface of the river. In strange slow motion I see cars on the highway and people on the grass beneath the trees and children in the nearby playground. The many times I have been to this place during my years of travel to the studio of Jacob Kahn! It seems askew today; strangely out of focus; familiar and unfamiliar; uncanny. I feel suddenly cold.

A solitary bird screeches high above the river, and I turn, startled, and see it soaring into the sky, a large glistening white bird, swiftly flying and gone.

I take the subway home.

We visit Rocheleh in her camp in the Pocono Mountains of Pennsylvania. It is parents' day. The grounds and bungalows and buildings bulge with visitors. The lawns are jammed with cars. Baruch Levinson has brought us up—me, Devorah, my mother, Avrumel—in another of his borrowed cars. Rocheleh is tanned, exuberant. She shows us around the camp. She has been away about a month and seems to have grown a year. We enter her bungalow: beds neatly made, clothes carefully arranged. On her shelf I see a large slim illustrated book called *Superstuff* and notice that it is published by the American Lung Association for children with asthma. Rocheleh says one of her bunkmates, who has asthma, loaned it to her. Devorah and I leaf through it: information on what to do in case of an attack; how to discover one's asthma triggers; how to iron the title of the book onto your T-shirt; a board game called "Breathe Easy." And riddles. Why do you sometimes feel like a frog when you get asthma? You think you're going to croak. What happens to an elephant with asthma when it stands in the rain? It gets wet. How do you give medicine to an asthmatic gorilla? Ve-e-e-ry carefully.

We meet Rocheleh's counselor—the daughter of a Ladover elder—and her junior counselor and new friends. We see the playing fields, the lake, the synagogue, the mess hall. Beneath the veneer put on for the visitors, there is about the place an unkempt East European look, like the desultory appearance of many of the Hasidic stores in Crown Heights. But no one really cares. Western neatness counts for little in this world of the spirit. The children appear healthy. They are studying Torah. They look happy. My mother is repeatedly congratulated by parents for the success of the camp; the Ladover camp program was conceived by my parents years ago. She is regarded by many with awe, like a queen.

In the late afternoon Rocheleh walks with us over rolling grassy fields to the car. I cannot get over how splendid she looks. Her thin body has begun to change: arms and legs filling out; chest no longer flat; her long skinny neck suddenly not birdlike but now lending her a supple grace. Devorah cannot take her eyes off Rocheleh's luminous face.

"I miss Uncle Max and Uncle John," Rocheleh tells us.

"They send you their love," I say.

"But I'm happy to be here."

"Do you play baseball?" Avrumel wants to know.

"Of course we play baseball."

"The Rebbe likes baseball. He told me so."

Rocheleh looks at him.

"The Rebbe said I have greatness in me," Avrumel says.

Rocheleh rolls her eyes. My mother smiles. Devorah looks embarrassed.

"Did the Rebbe say you have humility?" I ask him.

"Asher," Devorah says.

Departing cars are rolling off the fields and heading for the dirt road out of the camp.

"We have to go," I said.

"I miss you, Papa," Rocheleh says. I kiss her. She is warm and soft. I smell the sun on her. Rocheleh.

"Grandfather asked especially that I send you his love," my mother says.

"Take care of yourself," Devorah tells her. "Don't forget to take your medicine."

"Mama, I am not a child."

"The Rebbe asked me if I wanted to study in the yeshiva next year," Avrumel says to Rocheleh. "The yeshiva in Brooklyn."

We all look at him. Red hair, baseball cap, tan shorts, Ladover T-shirt, Shimshon doll. Avrumel.

"What did you answer?" I hear myself ask.

"I said I like the yeshiva in Brooklyn, but Shimshon wants to go
to the yeshiva in Nice."

"Shimshon is wise," I say. "We really have to go."

It was a long ride back to Brooklyn.

Devorah still needs light to fall asleep. The sliding door is left
slightly ajar to let in whatever air the night will offer us, and the
light attracts insects. They crash and dive against the screen door.
In the mornings I wake drenched. Because of the heat, Devorah
and I have very few together-times.

During the day the street bakes in the heat. The lawn beyond
the terrace is turning brown. The sycamore droops. It is early
afternoon. The air is thick with insects that seek out the shade,
where they sail about in swarms at the mouth and eyes, forcing me
into the sunlight on the terrace. I sit on the terrace in a stupor and
hear the door slide open behind me. Devorah emerges and asks if
I will come inside, she wants to talk to me; it is too hot to talk on
the terrace in the sun.

We are alone in the house. Avrumel is in day camp. My mother
is at a meeting with the Rebbe's staff.

We go into the living room. Devorah wears a pale-yellow summer dress and a pink cotton kerchief over her graying hair. Her
oval features are moist with heat. In one of the small windows a
fan hums, stirring the dormant air. My father refuses to put in
air-conditioning. It is a luxury, he says. Better to give the money to
the poor. Outside the large picture window the street looks deserted. Shards of stark-white sunlight break through the motionless maples and sycamores, dappling the sidewalk. A car passes
slowly along the street, stirring dust, leaving fumes in its wake. I
feel my shirt clinging to my body, and the sweat under my velvet
skullcap.

Devorah wants to know why I keep wearing T-shirts. There is
a strange edge to her soft voice. Her delicately boned hands are
restless.

"What's wrong with these T-shirts?"

"There are nicer shirts in your drawer."

"For whom should I be wearing nicer shirts? In Saint-Paul I wear nicer shirts?"

"This isn't Saint-Paul, Asher. A grown man shouldn't go around in T-shirts that announce the Messiah."

"The announcement is only for children?"

"It's not seemly."

"What isn't, Dev? The T-shirt or the announcement?"

"Will he come sooner because you wear this T-shirt?"

I watch her nervous eyes, the movement of her hands. There is fear in her mouth. She nervously scratches a knee. How fragile she seems—and yet what nightmares she manages somehow to overcome! Surely those years in that sealed apartment were in a real sense an ordeal by torture for her and Max and his family. An Austrian philosopher named Jean Améry, tortured by the Gestapo because of his activity with the Belgian resistance and then deported to Auschwitz because he was a Jew, wrote that anyone who has been tortured remains forever tortured and can never again be at ease in the world. One's faith in humanity is broken and can never be acquired again. Devorah tried to reacquire it by going to the Sorbonne for a degree in literature; by writing children's stories; by marrying me and having children of her own; by making Max Lobe and John Dorman part of her family; by embracing my parents and the Ladover; by hungering to uncover the Divine Plan that had taken her from entombment in Paris to Asher Lev to Saint-Paul to the heart of the Ladover world in Brooklyn. It isn't my shirt that is on her mind now.

"You don't really want to talk to me about T-shirts, Dev. What's wrong?"

"It came over me a few minutes ago that I wanted to see your drawings again. But I couldn't find them."

"Douglas is having them photographed for the catalogue."

"It occurred to me that Avrumel is in almost every one of them. Isn't it strange how you can look at a drawing and not really see it, and then go away from it for a while and see it very clearly."

"That happens often."

"I realized it on the way back from the camp last Sunday. I fell into a kind of half-sleep in the car and began to see your drawings.

Very clearly. Avrumel is in nearly all of them. It is not just my imagination, Asher, is it? Avrumel is on a bridge in Paris, looking at a gendarme; he is on a sidewalk, looking at a homeless woman; he is in a museum, talking with Picasso; he is in a print shop, watching you work with Max on a print; he is in the Louvre, watching you drawing; he is on a train, watching twin girls reading and drawing; he is on our terrace, watching Jameel water the flowers."

"There are no figures in those drawings, Dev."

She gives me a hard, nervous look. "Asher Lev, I am your wife. I gave birth to your children. I have deciphered your drawings and paintings in the past, and I do it now again. I had a good teacher: you. I am not talking about what you tell the world. I am talking about what you are telling yourself. I can read your drawings, my husband, though your language gets more and more difficult, and these took me a longer time than usual. It is a new syntax, isn't it? A new iconography. But I can read it."

"I am not aware of Avrumel anywhere in those drawings, Dev. You're seeing something in a piece of art that isn't really in it. It's not an uncommon occurrence. There's even a name for it. The Stendhal syndrome. The French writer Stendhal visited Florence, I think it was in 1817, and saw the frescoes in the Church of Santa Croce, and suddenly he felt his heart begin to beat irregularly and—"

"Asher Lev, there are times when you are infuriating. I am talking to you about our son, and you are telling me about art in Florence."

"Avrumel is not in those drawings, Dev."

"I am not talking about his face, Asher. I *feel* him in those drawings. Why is he there?"

"Dev, I am telling you, those drawings have nothing to do with Avrumel."

I feel her eyes on my face: searing. I know she cannot hear the pounding of my heart or see the flashing hues that float before my eyes. She shakes her head and closes her eyes a moment.

"I don't understand it, then," I hear her murmur. "They are an enigma to me, all those drawings. That makes me very sad, Asher."

She sits limply in the armchair, disconsolate, her face sagging. I feel my heart turn over. But I say nothing. She dabs at her mouth and forehead with a handkerchief and then rises and goes out of the room.

I sit very still, bathed in the torrent of sweat that suddenly begins to pour from me. I feel weak in every bone and muscle of my body and cannot move, and I see with astonishment the trembling of my fingers and hear clearly the loud and stormy beating of my heart.

The sky is white. I look at it through the leaves of the sycamore on the back lawn and am reminded of the huge primed canvas in my studio in Saint-Paul, white as summer lightning, before I covered it with an umber wash. White is fearful to gaze upon for too long: it is the color of shrouds; it is all-color, the prism fused, undifferentiated, linked wave to wave and particle to particle. The sky is white the afternoon my mother comes out onto the terrace and asks to talk to me. I close the copy of the proofs of the catalogue to the show that I have been going through, looking for typographical errors and for the presence of Avrumel.

Carefully, hesitantly, my mother sits down in the lawn chair next to mine. In her mid-sixties, wearing a long-sleeved cotton summer print dress of a light-pink color, with an off-white kerchief over her short silver hair, she displays the beginning of a frailty that is beyond the fragility that colored all the decades of life I shared with her and can still remember. There are more frequent visits to doctors now; her eyeglasses are changed often; she is on regular medication of some kind. Something about her heart and the chemical levels in her blood. She will not talk about it, suppresses it, remains toward me and Devorah her old self, willed to strength. Now she sits gazing across the lawn at the sycamore and through its branches and leaves at the bleached sky. On the other side of the hedge is my late uncle's house. I have seen neither my aunt nor my cousins since my return from the mountains; they have a summer home on the shore of Lake Mohegan, about an hour's drive from New York. My mother is talking to me. She has just spoken to the Rebbe, she says. My father is in Hebron and is, thank God, well. The Rebbe talked with my father just an hour ago. The Rebbe asked about me and sent me his blessing. The Rebbe especially asked about Avrumel.

I tell her Avrumel was all right as of this morning when I walked with him to his day-camp bus station in front of the yeshiva.

"The Rebbe asked if you will consider sending Avrumel to the yeshiva here for the coming year."

"Why?"

"The Rebbe feels it is important."

"Rocheleh, too?"

"The Rebbe mentioned only Avrumel. But if you wish, then Rocheleh too."

"We have a fine yeshiva in Nice."

"It is not the same. There is the community here."

"Who will Avrumel live with?"

"With us, of course."

"He doesn't want to stay. He wants to go home."

"Asher, since when do you ask a child where he wants to go to school?"

"Rocheleh can't stay here."

"There are children with asthma in our yeshiva. You think there are no people with asthma in New York?"

"New York is not a good place to have asthma. Too many die from it here. The statistics are not good."

"We cannot build our lives around sickness, Asher. We must have faith in the Master of the Universe."

"I can't work here."

"Why not? Once you worked here. All your early life you worked in Brooklyn and in Manhattan."

"This is not my early life. I've lived that life already. I don't want to repeat it."

"Parents sacrifice for their children, Asher."

"Why is it so important for Avrumel to go to school here? Especially now. He's only five."

"It is the beginning of the roots of his soul, Asher. There are no more important years than these. I am telling you what the Rebbe said. And what your father said. The roots of the soul are formed in these early years. Children come to our yeshiva from all over Europe, Australia, South Africa, South America, Turkey, Israel. Parents send them so they will be in the heart of the Ladover world, and close to the Rebbe. Is that not something you would want for Avrumel?"

"I want Avrumel near me. I want to watch him grow up. I want to be able to talk to him every day. I want to be able to teach him about the value of art. I want him to be able to watch me paint. I don't intend to give away my son."

She seemed astonished. "What do you mean, give away? Who is talking about giving away? I am talking only of this coming year."

"We came for a week of mourning and we've stayed four months. Now we're talking about another year. What will we be talking about after that year? The next year and the next and the next?"

"You are making it sound as if some sort of conspiracy is taking place. Is that what you think, Asher? This is a plan, a conspiracy? A conspiracy for what, my son? For Torah? For love? It's nothing more than grandparents whose years are numbered wanting to spend as much time as possible with their son and his family whom they have never truly seen and come to know. That is what this is, Asher."

Nothing about her face, always open, always so easy to read, gives the faintest hint of a concealed purpose behind her request. Aging grandparents wanting a year of life with their grandson, or their grandchildren; eager to make up for all the years of neglect; hungry for reconciliation and family peace before their lives ended and they slipped into the True World. And as an added incentive, the concern of the Rebbe that the grandson receive a proper Ladover education. All the purest of innocence. Or is it the deepest of concealments, one about which she herself is not aware? Can motivations be so hidden that even the holder is ignorant of their force? What if she both knows and doesn't know at one and the same time? What if the entire community knows and doesn't know? The Rebbe, whom we all love, will soon remove himself to the True World. And afterward? What of afterward? Splinterings? Chaos? Who would lead? My father is the natural choice. But how long will he live? And after him? Again, God forbid, splinterings and chaos? Therefore, afterward, after my father: Avrumel. Then don't give it to my father, give it to someone else, someone equally worthy. You would deprive your father of such a destiny? You would remove the line of your family from such a linking with the Master of the Universe? You are prepared to live with such a decision the rest of your life? Think of the pain you have caused your father. Personal redemption is now offered you, a tikkun, a balancing, a transforming, a healing, a repairing, for all that pain. Asher Lev, artist. Asher Lev, father of a Rebbe. A Ladover redemption and a Ladover immortality. And my mother knows nothing of all this, sees it nowhere within her, has it so deeply buried I can detect not a glimmer of it anywhere in her wide brown eyes, her high-boned cheeks, her long bony delicate fingers. She knows her way through the byzantine convolutions of Kremlin power, writes of the Soviet mind as if the Russians were our next-door neighbors, and yet does not perceive the hot bright core within the Rebbe's request. Most destinies come to us in simple declarative or interrogatory sentences: "Let there be light." "It is not good for man to be alone." "Am I my brother's keeper?" "Some time afterward, God put Abraham to the test." "Asher's bread shall be rich." There is destiny in this simple question: "Will you consider sending Avrumel to the yeshiva here for the coming year?" A simple sentence. Like some of the drawings of the Spaniard. Simple—and boiling as a caldron of fiery stars. And my mother knows nothing of this? How is that possible? A riddle! She is either all innocence or all guile. But she is incapable of guile. All of her is visible on the surface of her. That was why I was able to see all the years of her suffering. That was the reason I painted the crucifixions. If she is lying to me now, then the crucifixions are a lie, all my own life these past twenty years, lived in the shadow of the crucifixions, has been a lie. No, she knows nothing of what is beneath the Rebbe's suggestion about Avrumel.

"Does Papa know you're talking to me about Avrumel?"

"No."

"Let Papa talk to me."

"I don't know when your father will return."

"Whenever he returns, let him talk to me."

Her lips stiffen; her face locks, wilts. She looks at me a moment, as if to say something more, seems to think better of it, and sits back in the chair. Then she nods and slowly rises and leaves the terrace through the sliding screen door.

I stare through the greenish-black underside of leaves and branches at the hot white sky. In the insect-infested shadows of the sycamore stand Max Lobe and John Dorman, looking at me angrily, accusingly, in silence.

I close my eyes. "We're on a different track here," I tell them. "A different train, a different destination." "Then get off," John Dorman says. "Sometimes it's my train, too," I tell them. But it makes no difference: they stand there in the shadows of the sycamore, looking at me.

Odors waft across the lawn: roasting meat, charcoal smoke. Afternoon summer sounds: indistinct voices, the song of a bird, the barking of a dog. I am alone in the house. Devorah is at a meeting. How solidly she has settled into the Ladover community, embracing it as family. Have I kept her from family all these years? There was no community on the Rue des Rosiers, and only Max and John in Saint-Paul. We had little to do with the glitter and pleasure seeking of Nice society. Max went to its parties, and sometimes John; mostly, we stayed home, me painting, Devorah writing and caring for the children. In our apartment on the Rue des Rosiers, she would sit up nights at the kitchen table, writing. She wrote her master's thesis on the kitchen table of Max's parents' apartment—that once-sealed apartment—where she lived before we were married: "Vardaman's Fish and Addie's Coffin in William Faulkner's *As I Lay Dying*." Accepted by the faculty of the humanities; special notice taken of her facility with the English language—a gift to her from Max's mother, who, from the mid-twenties to the early thirties, had lived in New York, returning to her native France because of the havoc wreaked on the American branch of her family by the stock market crash and the Depression. Devorah wrote the thesis on those French pads that John disliked so much. Lately she has stopped writing. I've noticed that. She doesn't talk about it. She would write every day. Now? Nothing, for weeks. A temporary halt, as with my painting? White canvas, white paper. Curious how white the sky is, heat pressing against it and bleeding it of color. A vast arc of white paper crushed by the burning air. The hottest summer in the one hundred and thirty years that the world has been keeping records. Catastrophes everywhere. News stories about the strange disappearance of fish in one-fourth of the lakes in the Adirondacks; forty percent of the counties in the United States drought-ridden disaster areas; floating sewage on long stretches of East Coast beaches; huge holes in the ozone layer. Disaster and apocalypse heralding the redemption. Sound the trumpets! And the Rebbe, he should live and be well, very tired now and ready to give a sign. Press the hot metallic world against the white paper of the sky and see if the sky yields new textures, new fields of vision, or cracks and shreds apart. Max working the carborundum process, his face sweaty with the effort; a new success for him; another triumph; more dealers made happy. And why not? He earned his triumphs during those years in that sealed tomb of an apartment. Buried alive. Alive and not-alive. And Devorah: alive and not-alive. No vision of the sky for two years. A grave. Max painting his way out of that grave; Devorah writing her way out of that grave. Devorah suddenly in a living community and the feeling of the grave now gone. Uncle Yitzchok in his grave has made it possible for Devorah to emerge from her grave. Ironic. Am I right, Uncle Yitzchok? Am I right? From the other side of the hedge that separates my parents' house from the house of my aunt comes a rustling sound, and I think I see my uncle in the hedge, deep in the tangled cluster of thin branches and leaves, but no one is there. Beyond the hedge is his house and, a few doors down, the house of the Rebbe. Will my parents move into that house one day? The questions one thinks about! The sky is white, veined here and there with wispy threadlike pale-gray lines. Lucien carrying the large, heavy packs of white drawing paper up the five flights of stairs as I follow, my heart pounding. Thin and barely visible gray lines lacing the white surfaces of the paper. "What is the maître planning to draw on these? More pictures to trouble the world? The maître's last drawings were formidable." Sketches in oils went onto those sheets of paper until I saw the painting clearly and then put it on a huge canvas, Devorah watching in tense silence as I brought it to life, her astonished eyes telling me how much she disliked it; and my father showing up at the apartment during one of his trips through Europe for the Rebbe and staring in trembling anger and bewilderment at the finished painting, his face white, and saying, "What have you done? He did not kill him," and I replying, "There is a midrash that states he did," and my father saying, "But it is only a midrash. This is what you will show the world? Abraham slaughtering Isaac?" And I replying, "It's how I feel about it." And he finally excusing himself and leaving and never returning to that apartment all the rest of the time we lived there, because he was genuinely fearful of what he thought he might find on my easels and walls. Uncle Yitzchok came to the apartment twice during diamond-buying trips in Europe, and once years later to our home in Saint-Paul a few weeks after Avrumel's ritual first haircut at the age of three; he gazed in silence at the walls, puffed on his cigar, stayed overnight, and left the next morning, saying not a word about what he saw. Douglas Schaeffer came to the apartment on one of his periodic trips to his European artists and stared at the painting that had disturbed my father, murmured something about "your bloody devilish masterpieces," and with Lucien's help had it removed through the balcony doors and shipped to New York, where he called it *The Sacrifice of Isaac*—I had wanted to name it *Legacy*—and made it the centerpiece of my next show and sold it to the Stedelijk Museum in Amsterdam. I was glad to be rid of it. Why had I painted it? I don't know. My eyes and hands painted it.

I am on the street outside my parents' house, with no memory of how I got here. I have forgotten my sunglasses; the white light stings my eyes, bringing tears. The air is heavy with moisture. African jungle heat on the paved streets of New York. I turn into the wide traffic-choked street that leads to Brooklyn Parkway. The sidewalks are filled with bearded dark-garbed men, pregnant kerchiefed women, baby carriages. Gasoline fumes cloud the stagnant air. The bookstore is crowded. The food shops are jammed. It is the last Thursday of August; people are shopping for Shabbos. The parkway is dusty with construction. They are still working on the road—thready-muscled men in hard hats using massive equipment: bulldozers, asphalt scrapers, earthmovers, jackhammers—tearing up this stretch of the parkway to replace antiquated conduits and pave it anew. The rush-hour traffic crawls through

the construction areas. I walk beneath the dusty trees and the white
sky to the camp bus stop in front of the yeshiva to pick up Avrumel.

How weary he looks, strangely subdued, his T-shirt and shorts
grimy, his sneakers mud-caked, his baseball cap battered. We walk
together, he beside me, tense, his eyes to the ground.

"How was your day in camp?"

"It was all right, Papa."

He is in a hurry, eager to get off the street. Unusual for him.
Always he stops to look at the progress of the construction, the
machinery, the new holes cut into the earth. Or something else
catches his attention: the slow advance of an aged person across the
width of the parkway; the faint rumble of the subway beneath our
feet; a jetliner sailing by overhead; a booming radio in the hands
of a lithely moving black teenager.

"Why are you in such a rush?"

"Want to talk to Shimshon."

"Did something happen in camp today?"

"Nothing happened."

"Something happened. What was it?"

"Nothing, Papa."

"Avrumel."

"A boy in my group was hurt."

"Badly?"

"He fell with his mouth on a rock."

A sudden sensation of ice on the backs of my knees. "Is he all
right?"

"They called an ambulance and took him away."

"How did it happen?"

"We were playing baseball."

"Who was it?"

He gives me a name I do not recognize. "He is one of my
friends. We all said a chapter of Psalms for him. There was a lot
of blood."

I put my arm around his thin shoulders. He feels deeply; too
hard, perhaps. I want to hold him. At such moments he senses the
edge of the blade that from time to time pierces the fabric, enabling

us to catch a fiery glimpse of the Other Side, its black and boiling nothingness.

"Why did God do that to him?"

Another riddle. "I don't know."

"I will ask Grandfather when he returns."

"Grandfather may not know, either."

"Then I will ask the Rebbe."

Nearly six years old. A frenzy of feeling.

"There was blood on the rock and the grass and all over the counselor." He keeps his eyes on the ground. "I will ask the Rebbe. Will we see the Rebbe again soon?"

"I don't know."

"I want to talk with Shimshon, Papa. Can we go faster?"

We walk home quickly together. I get him a fresh T-shirt and shorts. As I throw the soiled clothes into the hamper, I see the caked blood in the dirt and grime and feel again the stiletto thrusts of coldness on the backs of my legs.

The house is quiet. We are home alone. I bring him a glass of milk and his favorite cookies. Later, I glance in the door of his room and see him sitting on the floor, talking softly to Shimshon. He tells Shimshon about the accident and listens for a moment. He nods and asks how such a thing could happen, and leans forward, listening. I do not hear Shimshon's reply.

The heat continued into the next week: blazing rainless days, black swamp-air nights. A sulfurous haze settled over the city. On Monday I took the subway into Manhattan to see Douglas Schaeffer about the show and sensed everyone close to the edge, saw people talking to themselves on the streets. Douglas told me that three of my collectors had begun a bidding war on two of the drawings. A most pleasant way to begin the show, he said.

Afterward I came out of the gallery and walked through the sun and shade of Fifty-seventh Street and saw a show of small-scale canvases by the Spaniard, and a show of drawings by Jackson Pollock, one of them, the half man–half beast in the colored *Psychoanalytic Drawing*, looking as if it had stepped right out of the *Guernica*. There was a show of splendid unsettling drawings by

Philip Guston: allegories of pessimism and doubt—old shoes, piles of junk, light bulbs, hooded men. In a show of drawings by Richard Diebenkorn, I marveled at the skill with which the artist put pieces together as in the most intricate of puzzles to achieve fragile balanced works. At the Pace Gallery, I stood a long time before a barely readable drawing by Malcolm Morley—tremulous, quivering lines—called *Ghost Drawing of the Barcelona Cathedral.*

I came out of the Pace into the sunlight. A block from the gallery, an old man with a dirty white beard lay very still in the middle of the sidewalk. He was dressed in torn brown trousers and a grimy shirt. A policeman and two uniformed men from a rescue squad were working over him. A small, silent crowd had formed. I stood amid the crowd and reached into a pocket for my drawing pad and made a swift sketch of the fallen man. His face was blackened with dirt above the line of his beard; his eyes kept darting about, wide with terror. That look of terror seemed to rise from him and hover in the poisonous air of the street, and from time to time I saw it in the crowded subway I rode back to my parents' home.

Rocheleh returned from her camp that day. How lovely she looked: two months away and suddenly grown, the beginnings of womanhood touching her fragile being. She bubbled over with stories about the camp: a canoe trip along the Delaware; overnight cookouts in the woods; the friends she had made. The young woman who had been her division head was the daughter of the Bonrover Rebbe in Borough Park, a Brooklyn neighborhood crowded with Hasidic sects, not all of them friendly toward the Ladover Hasidim, whom they considered too hospitable toward modernism, too eager to evangelize, too quick to use the media, too adept at the trappings of contemporary communication, and therefore probably too prone to produce an Asher Lev. That young woman had been like a mother to her a week ago, Rocheleh said. During a sports competition, Rocheleh had participated in a swimming race, which she lost; immediately afterward she suffered a mild asthma attack, so mild the infirmary elected not to call us about it. The division head was with her all the time. Avrumel listened to his sister's stories, pretended not to be interested, and held whispered conversations with Shimshon. Rocheleh spent a good part of her first evening home talking quietly with Devorah, and afterward Devorah told me, "Our daughter is grown," and there were tears in her eyes.

Later that night, I was sitting at my desk with the drawing pad open, and Devorah was in her bed, reading, when someone tapped on our door. It was my mother. She was in her housedress; a kerchief covered her head. The Rebbe's office had just called, she said. My father was returning the following day from Israel.

The next afternoon, a hot windy dust-blown day, Baruch Levinson brought him in from the airport, and I stood in the doorway of the house with Devorah and Rocheleh and watched my mother and Avrumel hurry along the cement walk to the car, this one new and gleaming. My parents exchanged greetings but did not embrace, and Avrumel sprang forward and was suddenly in my father's arms, hugging and kissing him, and my father held him and, singing a Ladover melody, did a little dance with him right there on the sidewalk in front of the house and in the presence of neighbors who had come out to greet him. I glanced at Devorah, and she caught my eyes and looked at me a moment, troubled, and looked away. Baruch Levinson brought my father's bags into the house, said to me cheerfully, "Have a nice day," got into the car, and drove off.

We ate supper quickly and my father went to his office and returned after Devorah and I had gone to bed. I did not hear him come in. The next day he left for his office directly from the synagogue. I took the subway to the warehouse in lower Manhattan where Douglas Schaeffer had stored my uncle's art collection.

In a large, clean, brightly lit, temperature-controlled room, I stood looking at the canvases and drawings and prints arranged for me against white walls by white-garbed workers. The books he had collected were there, too, as were the magazines, scholarly monographs, articles, and notices of my openings through the years. There was my first carborundum print, the one I had worked on with Jacob Kahn in Paris nearly twenty years before and of which the bon à tirer was now in the collection of the widow of Lucien Lacamp, who had written to Douglas Schaeffer, informing him she intended to hold on to it and telling him how astonished and full of thanks she was for the kindness of Asher Lev. All I could think of when Douglas told me about the letter the previous morning was Lucien climbing the stairs to my apartment with the artist's proofs of my first carborundum print and Lucien helping me carry Rocheleh through the rainstorm to the hospital and Lucien blown to pieces by the bomb in the restaurant on the Rue des Rosiers.

I stood there in front of Uncle Yitzchok's art collection and was lost in the wonder of it, its loveliness pressing against my eyes and filling me with joy so I suddenly wanted to do a dance about the room, its radiance touching my eyes and mind and coursing down to my hands so I felt I needed to do something with my fingers, and I opened my drawing pad and turned to a fresh page and stood there, sketching forms and noting color patterns, and turned to another page and then another. Then I was lost inside the exquisite otherness of it, journeying like a smooth-moving runner, feeling the twists and turns of its forms and the warmth and coolness of its colors. I copied the structures of the Cézanne and the Matisse and the Renoir and the Bonnard, stood and copied, working my way swiftly through the best pieces of the collection; and finally a workman came in to tell me they needed to put the pieces back, they would be closing in an hour. I stared at him, dazed, not remembering for a long moment where I was. Afterward I left the warehouse and stood a long time in the sunlight and heat, nearly overcome by the abrupt transition from the cool silent loveliness in the storage facilities to the gasoline-smelling din of the street. I took a subway home.

During supper that night, my father asked if we would like to spend the Labor Day weekend in the cottage in the Berkshires; he needed to see the Rebbe, Grandmother needed a vacation, and Asher looked like a few days in the mountains wouldn't hurt him. Early Thursday morning Baruch Levinson showed up with an expensive-looking station wagon and loaded us inside. Rocheleh and Avrumel sat in the jump seat in the back, with the luggage, and sang Ladover camp songs about the power of Torah, the victory of the armies of God, the coming redemption of the Jewish people and the world, and the wisdom and saintliness of the Rebbe. My father talked about his work in Israel and his certainty that the religious party supported by the Rebbe would be a major force in the formation of the new coalition government after the November elections. I asked him whom he thought the Ladover Hasidim would vote for in the American elections, and he said the Rebbe would advise his people to vote for George Bush for President. That meant more than ninety percent of voting Ladover would cast their ballots for George Bush. "We are for family values. We are very happy with the policies of President Reagan." Devorah said she did not like Dukakis; in France he would be regarded as a weak man, full of self-doubt and uncertain convictions. My mother said all the women she knew were against the Democratic Party's position on abortion and would vote for George Bush. Baruch Levinson, steering us along the crowded highways, said everyone in his yeshiva thought Jesse Jackson was an anti-Semite and all were fearful of his influence if the Democrats won the presidency. "Who will you vote for, Asher?" my mother asked me; she knew I voted by absentee ballot. I said I had not yet made up my mind. Avrumel wanted to know why the Rebbe did not run for the presidency. I said in order to be President of the United States you had to be born in America, and the Rebbe had been born in Russia. Rocheleh said even if the Rebbe could be President he would never give up being the Rebbe of the Ladover Hasidim; it was the most important position in the world: the Rebbe was helping to bring the Messiah. Sometime during the trip my father asked me if I had given any thought to my uncle's art collection now that Cousin Yonkel had abandoned any further attempts to oust me as its trustee. I said I was giving it a lot of thought and had not yet made up my mind what to do with it.

There was heavy traffic all the way up to the Berkshires: a tedium of encumbered driving. We arrived in the late afternoon and unloaded the car. My father went immediately to meet with the Rebbe.

The colony is crowded; it feels as if most of the Ladover of Crown Heights are here for the weekend. The paths teem with dark-garbed men and long-sleeved kerchiefed women and baby carriages. Children scamper about in the woods and splash in the lake. Men and women swim separately on opposite sides of the high wooden wall. Our side of the lake is crowded with rowboats.

Along the distant shore, small, elegant-looking sailboats glide across the water like white-winged birds. The air is warm. Occasional winds blow across the lake from the mountains, carrying the scents of pine trees and water and verdant earth.

On Friday morning I stand in the sunlight on the beach and watch my mother and Devorah in a rowboat, Devorah rowing, and see Rocheleh and Avrumel swimming, and I think of the Spaniard's painting *Night Fishing at Antibes*. The last time I thought of that painting I was on the train in Antibes, weeks ago that had been, the day I drew the girl drawing. Why am I suddenly thinking of the Spaniard? My right hand quivers, and I look at my fingers. I have never understood what moves these fingers. An otherness enters them from some realm of power, some restive willful source that showers mysteries upon us just as it sends fearful, raging thunderstorms, as it did last night. We all stood on the back porch of the cottage and watched the storm in the mountains, lightning spearing down out of tumultuous black clouds, and I heard Avrumel recite the appropriate blessing and I asked him where he had learned it, I could not remember teaching it to him, and he said he had learned it in camp early in the summer from the boy who had fallen on the rock: "Blessed art Thou, O Lord our God, King of the Universe, whose strength and might fill the world."

I watch my father coming up the path to the cottage, returning from his meeting with the Rebbe. He walks briskly. People greet him. He stops to talk with an elderly man and peers into a carriage being pushed by a pregnant young woman. He looks at such moments like an American politician hustling for votes. It is good to see him like that, so human, so ordinary. He goes into the cottage. The sun is hot. Devorah waves at me from the rowboat and I wave back. A young man, bearded and dark-garbed, comes hurrying over to me. The Rebbe would like to see me. Now? Yes. Would I please come? I walk quickly alongside him to the Rebbe's cottage.

The Rebbe sits behind a desk in a small office that is bare of everything save the desk and three chairs. He sits in a soft chair, wearing a dark suit, a tie, and a dark hat. A window air conditioner hums softly. He beckons me toward him and motions me into a chair.

He has asked to see me now, he says, because tomorrow night, after Shabbos, there will be many people who will want to see him. How was I feeling? How were Devorah and the children?

He speaks softly. His eyes are alert. His hands seem curled, weary. Harsh white sunlight shines through the windows of the office, cutting the air into stark zones of shadow and light. He sits in shadows, motionless behind the desk.

"The art collection of your uncle, may he rest in peace. What will you do with it?"

"I don't know, Rebbe."

"Your cousin has strong feelings about the collection. It is difficult to reason with him."

"On certain matters, Cousin Yonkel is an unreasonable man."

"Perhaps it would be best if you sold it."

I do not respond.

"He is a person of deep piety and conviction, your cousin, an uncompromising man. Does one have the right to disregard the wishes and feelings of such a person?"

"I will try to think what to do."

"Your Avrumel came to see me yesterday. He has a good head. Has he a talent for art?"

"Not for making art. But he loves to look at it."

"He has a talent for Torah. That I can see. What will you do, Asher?"

"I am thinking of that, too, Rebbe."

He sighs. "Some troubles do not go away as we grow older. They grow older with us. I give you and your family my blessing, Asher Lev."

I went outside and walked back to the beach and stood there watching Devorah and my mother out in the rowboat, and Rocheleh and Avrumel splashing about on opposite sides of the wooden wall. After a while I went into the cottage and got my drawing pad and sat under the tree at the edge of the beach and made a drawing of Avrumel talking to the Rebbe and another of Avrumel swimming.

The next morning the Rebbe came to the synagogue for the Shabbos service. The synagogue was crowded, and a shiver of astonishment passed through everyone when the Rebbe slowly entered, together with the two tall dark-bearded men. All were tremulous with restrained happiness as he sat down on the chair near the Ark. He left soon after the Silent Devotion of the Musaf Service. Afterward some of the men did a dance on the grass outside.

During the dance, I stood next to my father, and he said he wanted to talk to me. After the Shabbos meal. We would go for a walk somewhere. Just the two of us. Together.

We walk in the woods, in air dense with the rich dark smell of rotting leaves. It is cool and moist in the leafy shade. My father wears a white shirt and dark trousers; a small dark velvet skullcap covers his head of thick white hair. I see his mouth beneath the long white beard, the full lips, the start of the firm jaw. Under our feet the earth is ridged with bulging and spidery roots. Huge fallen trees lie here and there across the ground, hoary giants, home to ants and maggots. We walk slowly beneath the embowering oaks and birches and pines. Birds sing invisibly from the branches; insects sail about in swarms, and we brush them from our eyes and lips. Pencil-thin beams of sunlight pierce the trees: dancing dots of light on the earth at our feet.

My father asks me how I am feeling. He is concerned about me, he says. I have lost weight. I seem listless, distant. He is worried that I might be—he hesitates—depressed.

I tell him I am not depressed; I have a lot on my mind.

"Are you still troubled by the reactions to your Paris exhibition?"

"No. That seems to have faded. A healed wound."

"What, then?"

I am quiet.

"Is there any way I can help you, Asher? It hurts a father to see a son this way. It makes no difference what age the son is; it hurts."

"I don't think you can help me. I'll work it out."

He was silent. We walked on and came to the clearing and stood quietly in the shade along the edge. Butterflies played in the sunlight, gliding low and circling lazily over the grass and the flat shining rock.

"I saw your latest drawings," he said. "Devorah showed them to me before I went back to Israel. There will be an exhibition of these drawings in the fall?"

"Yes."

"I do not understand them. I have always had . . . problems with your work, but at least I think I understood it. These new drawings I do not understand at all. Bits and pieces of things, like puzzles. Do you aim deliberately to be difficult? Is that a sign of being modern?"

"Some art is difficult because life is difficult."

"The Rebbe likes to make things clearer, not more difficult. A leader should clarify, Asher, not deliberately confuse. He should bring light to the world. One of our great mystical books is called *The Book of Brightness.*"

"Difficulty and darkness are not the same. When something has many sides to it, it's not easy to show it simple and clear. The world is sometimes very ambiguous."

"God did not create an ambiguous world, Asher. We only at times experience it as ambiguous."

"What else do we have but our experience of the world?"

"We have our faith. We have our work. Our work is to bring God into this world. Look what has been done to this world and its people in this Godless century. It is a horror. Our task is to redeem this horror. We cannot redeem it by offering people ambiguity."

"I try to redeem it through my art."

"An artist redeems through his art?" He seemed astonished by that idea. "Acts redeem, Asher. Acts."

"Art is also acts."

"Sacred acts, Asher. Acts connected to the Master of the Universe. Sacred acts saved you. If you had not remained an observer of the commandments all these years, it would have made no difference that I was your father: the Ladover would have cast you out long ago."

My heart pounded. I stood next to him along the edge of the clearing, watching the butterflies sail back and forth over the grass. "Do we understand everything about the people we know?" I asked.

"Not everything, no."

"How can we expect to know everything about God?"

He looked at me, his eyes narrowing.

"I call that ambiguity," I said. "Riddles, puzzles, double meanings, lost possibilities, the dark side to the light, the light side to the darkness, different perspectives on the same things. Nothing in this whole world has only one side to it. Everything is like a kaleidoscope. That's what I'm trying to capture in my art. That's what I mean by ambiguity."

"No one can live in a kaleidoscope, Asher. God is not a kaleidoscope. God is not ambiguous. Our faith in Him is not ambiguous. From ambiguity I would not derive the strength to do all the things I must do. Ambiguity is darkness. Certainty is light. Darkness is the world of the Other Side. Tell me something, Asher. Do you think Avrumel will be better off if he learns ambiguity from you or certainty from me?"

I said nothing.

"Will Avrumel redeem the world through art?"

"Avrumel won't be an artist."

"Then let him study Torah."

"Who said he won't study Torah?"

"Let him start in the yeshiva here."

"We have a fine yeshiva in Nice."

"His grandparents don't live in Nice; they live in Brooklyn. The Rebbe once said, 'The Master of the Universe enables us to live to see grandchildren so that we can have the privilege of experiencing the world as it was at the Creation. Each grandchild is a beginning.' Like the young trees here in these woods. How many years do your mother and I have left, Asher? How will it hurt you if you let Avrumel spend the next year with us?"

I look at him closely. I know all the languages of his face, every emotion in it, its angers and laughters and fears. I know all the messages he sends when his eyes cloud over or sparkle, when his nostrils flare, his lips tighten, his jaws clench. There is nothing hidden in him now, not the faintest hint of duplicity. He knows nothing. Or perhaps he knows and doesn't know—simultaneously. If an entire community can know and not know something at one and the same time, certainly so can its individual members. Should

I tell him? I will tell him. Now. Papa, do you know who the next Rebbe will be? You. But only if I give my word to the Rebbe that Avrumel will follow you. The Rebbe wants to create a dynasty. You will not become Rebbe without Avrumel, even though you deserve to be, because when you die and there is no one to replace you—not even a child; children have replaced Rebbes before; charisma is heedless of age—there will be worse confusion and dissension than there might be now if the Rebbe were to die—God forbid!—without making a sign regarding a successor. I will tell my father all that. Now. Yes.

He will look at me as if I have lost my mind, for he regards himself as utterly unworthy of succeeding the Rebbe. He, a Rebbe? Unthinkable! A blasphemy! And how is it that I know of this, I, Asher Lev, who haven't lived among the Ladover for twenty years? Am I suddenly a prophet? He will call me a troublemaker, an irresponsible dreamer, an artist, a defiler of Ladover Hasidus and of the great name of the Rebbe, and he will stalk off in a rage.

I tell him nothing.

"You will do your mother and your father a great kindness, Asher, if you let Avrumel spend the coming year with us."

Does he want Avrumel to remain with them for a year—and will it then be another year, and another?—because of the reason he gives, or because he is somehow aware of the condition attached to the sign the Rebbe wishes to give? Is he aware of both—and unaware? Can the mind ride two such separate tracks simultaneously? Concealed ambivalence. Hidden ambiguity. Are we so flawed that we can never truly know our own most secret motives?

"What about Rocheleh?" I ask.

"Rocheleh is not Avrumel." That is his way of saying: Rocheleh is a girl; we must concern ourselves with the men.

"I don't think Devorah will go back without Avrumel."

He gazes across the clearing and is silent. He is telling me by his silence that this is a boundary he will not cross. A man must resolve such matters himself with his wife; no one may interfere. Finally he says, after a long pause, "Devorah is very happy here. She has found a home and a community here."

"So I've noticed."

We go back through the woods to the cottage. Later that afternoon, I see him sitting under the tree near the beach with Avrumel. I walk by. He is telling Avrumel a story about the Rebbe's grandfather.

On the beach that night, after the children are asleep, Devorah says to me, "You look so troubled, my husband."

My parents are with the Rebbe. There are parties in some of the cottages. We hear laughter and traditional Hasidic music and the music of a Hasidic rock band. The sky is black and studded with stars. I feel the sand of the beach beneath my shoes and think of the summers in Provincetown with Jacob Kahn. How memory accordions time and places disparate moments next to one another like photographic slides on a tray!

"I'm thinking of the coming year, Dev."

She is silent.

"We can't leave until after the holidays. The children have to go to school. We should put them for the time being in the yeshiva."

"I have already done that."

A cool wind brushes across the faintly moonlit surface of the lake and sends wavelets rippling against the rowboats. The lights in the Rebbe's cottage are ablaze: meetings. Day after day, meetings. And one day my father as the Rebbe? Asher Lev, artist, son of Aryeh Lev, the Rebbe of the Ladover Hasidim? It sounds vaguely like a blasphemy. Should I tell it to Devorah? Yes. I will tell it to her. Now. Listen to me, my wife—

No.

She will recoil. Or she will grasp at it too swiftly, see it as the fulfillment of the Divine Plan she believes began with her years in that sealed apartment, and she will give herself to it entirely, mindlessly, dissolving herself in it, consumed by it. No. Let it come to her gradually. The Spaniard is right. That day in the rain, stumbling about Paris, looking. The old Jew on the street showing me where it was. The Spaniard appearing suddenly amid his paintings and sculptures and telling me that some truths are best given in riddles. Sound advice. The advice of an artist's rebbe. A demonic rebbe, as it were, from the Other Side. Let the truth about Avrumel be unriddled very slowly, so it does not strike with the force of lightning but is a gentle illumination, like a picture one learns to read color by color and shape by shape, one color or shape at a time.

The wind rises and ripples the lake. A shooting star streaks across the black sky, blazes, and swiftly vanishes. Devorah and I are alone on the beach. I put my arm around her and hold her to me. She came to me so thin and shy that day Max brought her to my apartment, wide gray resolute eyes with pinpoints of darkness in them, a long thin oval face, pale and determined—to finish her work at the Sorbonne, to make some sense of her lost life, above all to overcome the darkness of those two years of entombment. She was one of those who would never ask to be looked at when someone talked to her; she herself had so much difficulty looking at the world. Yet she wanted to face everything, and sometimes it wore her down and she lay in her bed, trying to fall asleep with the lights on. And she wrote stories. And she was a mother and a wife. And I loved her very much. And we were now going to have a strange and unforeseen life. Another riddle.

Suddenly I feel her sag against me. She has remembered something from the distant past. These moments are palpable, these sudden passages into remote memory; they come as real burdens with tangible weight. "The second summer we were in the apartment," she says softly, "it was so hot we could barely breathe. It was like breathing through hot, wet wool. And I remember we couldn't take baths because there was something wrong with the plumbing. One night that summer the Americans bombed a part of the city, and the next day there were roaches everywhere in the apartment. We couldn't kill them quickly enough; they were all over, on the walls and the floors. And it was so hot. I slept with almost nothing on, and on top of my sheet, and I was terrified I would wake up covered with roaches. Sometimes I thought I could hear them crawling around in my room in the dark, on the floor and walls and all over my bed. The concierge told us the whole neighborhood was full of them. He said they were crazy from the heat and the bombardment."

"What happened?"

"After about a week, the heat went away and the roaches disappeared."

"Poor Dev."

"It was a terrible time. Isn't it strange that I didn't remember it until now?"

"Not so strange."

"Asher, I think I want to go back in now and have a cup of coffee and go to bed. Do you think we can go to bed? I know it's beautiful out here, but I think I really want to go to bed."

We lie in my bed and listen to the night. The walls of the cottage are thin, and I hear Avrumel cry out in his sleep: the nightmares of a child. Is he dreaming of his friend who fell with his face on that rock? Why were they playing baseball on a field with a rock? I hold Devorah and listen to the wind on the lake. She is warm and silken in my arms. From time to time she quivers in her sleep. What is she remembering from that sealed apartment? It is a long time before I am able to sleep.

On Monday afternoon we drove back to the city. The next day Rocheleh and Avrumel returned to the yeshiva.

The neighborhood returned to its presummer life. Signs of the coming holidays began slowly to appear. Clothing stores were crowded. There was a heightening of stress, a quickening of the street rhythms, a scurrying about.

The Rebbe returned from the mountains. He did not appear in the synagogue. But lights burned in his home into the early hours of each morning.

I thought to sell some of the prints in my Uncle Yitzchok's collection and establish a yeshiva scholarship fund in his name. But word came swiftly from Cousin Yonkel through the principal that he would never permit his father's name to be even remotely connected to any funds that originated with the art collection, and if I or the school went ahead with the idea, he would take us to court. Cousin Yonkel, it seemed, was demented when it came to his father's art collection: he saw it as crawling with the demonic minions of the Other Side, as a corruption that could spread and poison the air and endanger the entire community. I called Douglas Schaeffer and told him not to sell the prints.

My mother was back teaching at New York University. Devorah tended to the children and went to women's meetings, where she spoke of her wartime experiences and growing up in a Ladover home in Paris and her childhood memories of the months the Rebbe lived with her family in their Paris apartment. She remembers the Rebbe far more clearly than she remembers her parents and relatives. My mother told me that the women were charmed by Devorah's accent and intrigued by her as the wife of Asher Lev. My father made a brief trip to Israel and said little to me about it when he returned. "Meetings and politicians," he murmured, with an edge of contempt in his voice. "Descent for the sake of ascent. We do it for the sake of heaven."

I roamed the neighborhood, drawing. "It is only by drawing often, drawing everything, drawing incessantly," I read in the collection of letters written by Camille Pissarro to his son Lucien, "that one fine day you discover to your surprise that you have rendered something in its true character.... You must *harness* yourself to drawing." I drew endlessly: the faces along the parkway; the machines scarring the road; the children walking to school; the angles of sun and shade on the houses; a dead cat, crushed by a passing car; the Ladover ambulance at its parking station near the headquarters building; people pouring out of the Kingston Avenue subway station during the rush hour; Rocheleh and Avrumel returning home with their schoolbooks amid a crowd of their friends. I did not show the drawings to anyone.

One afternoon I bought a box of pastels in the neighborhood art supply store and made some drawings of faces I saw somewhere inside myself—whitish faces against black-and-red backgrounds. I put the drawings into my attaché case.

A few days later, I bought a small set of watercolors and paper and some mailing tubes and set up on the terrace a card table I hauled out from a closet in the den. I diluted some cadmium red and, with a number 6 brush, washed the hue across the fingertips of my right hand. The color moved into the skin and mixed with the ingrained grime of years and sank into the tiny trenches, forming spiky rivulets. I looked at my hand. It quivered faintly. Then, leaving most of the white on the paper, I painted an old white-bearded man walking along Brooklyn Parkway with a little boy beside him, passing a bulldozer that was tearing up the street. Then, once again leaving most of the white on the paper, I did a watercolor of Avrumel talking to his Shimshon doll, and another of Devorah talking with my mother. The paintings had a strange quality: they were figurative but there were no figures in them. They looked as if they might suddenly dissolve. I let them dry, then rolled them up, slid them into a mailing tube, put the tube into my big valise, and returned the valise to its closet.

Devorah noticed the watercolor set later that day and said, "Asher, are you working with color?"

"I played with it a little."

"And what came of it?"

"I can't tell yet."

"May I see it?"

"It's not ready to be seen."

"Not even by your wife?"

I shook my head.

She sighed. "You are so difficult sometimes, Asher. Are you sure you cannot work here this coming year?"

"We've been through this already, Dev. I lived part of my life here once. I can't repeat myself."

"Asher, I do not understand you."

I told her of a letter Camille Pissarro once wrote to his son about Monet's dealers, who were insisting he exhibit only one kind of painting, the one that had become very popular with collectors. The collectors only wanted *Sheaves*. Pissarro wrote that he couldn't understand how Monet could subject himself to the demand that he repeat himself. He called it a terrible consequence of success. "It's a kind of death to keep repeating yourself and your life over and over again," I said.

"I do not understand. Are all the people here dead? This entire community? Your parents?"

"I'm talking only about *me*, Dev. It's death for *me*."

She shook her head and was quiet. Sadness darkened her eyes.

As we drew closer to the sacred time of the Jewish New Year and the Day of Atonement, I sensed the neighborhood growing more populous, expanding. Stores crowded all day long; street corners jammed solid with pedestrians waiting for lights to change. Every day there were more congregants in the synagogue for the Morning Service; the *New York Times* sold out earlier each morning from the vendor I passed on my way back from the synagogue. I began to hear a variety of languages on the streets and in the shops: Italian, French, Spanish, Dutch, Israeli Hebrew, British and Australian English. Sidewalk vendors appeared: electronic toys for children; pictures of the Rebbe; adult and children's books in many languages. One of Devorah's books was there, in its English edition: *Rebekah Runs Home*. A little girl returns home one day to the apartment where she lives and finds that her parents are being arrested by two policemen. She is about to cry out to her mother, when her mother sees her and screams at her to get out, this is not a zoo or a circus, go home to your own parents. The little girl realizes in an instant what her mother is saying, and she turns to run away, and as she turns she sees the two policemen looking at her and then at each other. She is out of the door and running to her big cousin's apartment in a building nearby, and she runs and runs and scrambles up the dark staircase and rushes into her cousin's apartment, only to discover that somehow she is back inside her own apartment and her parents are being arrested by the two policemen. The policemen turn to look at the little girl and then the little girl wakes up and discovers it has all been a very bad dream, how lucky she is to have her own family, and how wondrous it is for them all to be safe in their own home.

I remarked to my mother one day about the crowds and the many languages I was hearing on the streets, and she said, "They have come here from all over the world to be with the Rebbe for the holidays."

"Every year so many come?"

"More and more come each year. We have grown, thank God."

"Maybe they expect the Rebbe will give a sign."

"What sign?"

"About who will succeed him."

Her face stiffened. She looked past me. "We do not talk about such things, Asher. The people are here to be with the Rebbe, may he live a long and healthy life."

I came out of the Kingston Avenue subway station late one afternoon after a day in Manhattan galleries—at the Marlborough, startling black paintings of landscapes and cityscapes by Alex Katz; at the Sidney Janis, black and white sculptures by George Segal named *The Street* and *Abraham's Farewell to Ishmael*—and saw the crowds on the street. It took a minute or two for me to realize that something strange was happening. The streets were choked with dark-garbed men milling about, darting, walking agitatedly back and forth. Some waved their arms over their heads; some were talking aloud to the sky; some were biting their clenched fists. The air was turbulent with confusion. I asked an old man what had happened, and he said the Rebbe had been taken very ill. A coldness of utter bereavement washed over me, and I looked blindly about, expecting the heavens suddenly to turn black and torrents of blood to come pouring from the sky. In front of the synagogue the crowd was impenetrable, a solid wall of black-garbed, wide-eyed, frantic men. I headed toward the house, wondering where my father was—at the Rebbe's bedside?—and saw men and women weeping openly on the streets and children looking around wide-eyed and people standing helplessly about. I turned the corner into my parents' street and saw another crowd in front of the Rebbe's home, spilling out across the sidewalk and blocking traffic. I went past my parents' house and my Uncle Yitzchok's house toward the home of the Rebbe, and suddenly the perimeter of the crowd in front of the Rebbe's home began to break into fragments; it seemed to go flying off in all directions. Young men went running through the streets, shouting. One raced past me, and I heard him cry, "Thank God! Thank God!" and another cried, "The Rebbe will recover!" and the news flew through the neighborhood: the Rebbe had fainted during a meeting, but it was not serious, only something having to do with low blood pressure, thank God, thank God!

Avrumel and Rocheleh told us later that when the news came of the Rebbe's sudden illness, all the students in the yeshiva ceased their learning and began to recite Psalms. Devorah was giving a talk to a group of women in a nearby apartment when the phone rang with the news; the women immediately recited a chapter of Psalms and returned to their homes. My mother was teaching and found out about it when she arrived home, after it was over.

My father had been with the Rebbe at the meeting. He helped carry the Rebbe to his bed. He was with the doctor. He brought the doctor's diagnosis to the Ladover elders waiting outside the bedroom. When he came home from his office that night and told us what had taken place, he looked worn, ashen. He could not eat and went to lie down. Later, as Devorah and I were getting ready for bed, we heard him go down the hallway, heard his recognizable slightly limping tread and the front door open and close. He was going back to his office and the Rebbe.

Days later, the Rebbe was well enough to stand on the bimah before the entire congregation on the two days of Rosh Hashanah and each day sound the shofar. A motionless sea of white-garbed men stood silent and tense as the reader called out the notes and the resonating sounds of the ram's horn pierced the air of the synagogue. The long notes, the broken notes, the staccato notes, again and again, coming from the shofar blown every year at this time by the Rebbe. The call to watchfulness, to action, to redemption.

On the second day, the Rebbe faltered at the start of the final long note. He tried repeatedly and could not get the note out. The congregation stirred, tensed, leaned forward as if imparting to the small white-clad figure on the bimah its own collective strength to enable him to continue—and he raised the ram's horn to his lips and blew on it a long, pure, sustained note that went on and on and on until it seemed no human was sounding that ram's horn but some messenger from the Master of the Universe, someone bringing a clear musical note from the heavens, heralding transformations soon to come. And when the note came to an end, all in the congregation whispered, murmured, sighed, stirred. Not a word was spoken. Yet everything was spoken. The Rebbe is well. It will be a good year. Thank God! Thank God!

On the Shabbos between Rosh Hashanah and Yom Kippur, the Rebbe stood at his lectern before the Ark and spoke about the role of the Ladover in America and in the world. America, this great land, is a tragic country today, he said. Its best minds can only watch helplessly the ugliness, the vulgarity, the disintegration all around. Who could ever have believed this would befall America? We waste our resources, human and natural. Families are in disarray. Whole sections of our great cities are in ruins. What has happened to us? The destiny of the Ladover is to collect broken souls, to bind up broken lives, to save Jews and thereby, in doing our share of the work of redemption, help save America and the world.

Asher Lev sits in the synagogue between his father and his son, listening to the words of the Rebbe. How clearly the words come to him from this small, saintly, aged man. For more than two hundred years the world has tried to save itself through secularism, the Rebbe says. And where are we? Two world wars. The Holocaust. The atomic bomb. Blood and devastation. Is it better for man to live with uncertainty? Is the answer of Freud an answer? We should simply learn to accept our position as strange sick creatures? Is the answer of Nietzsche an answer? We should learn to live gladly as guests in a murderous but fascinating world that cares nothing about our presence? That was odd, the Rebbe mentioning Freud and Nietzsche; he quoted only from Rebbes and the Rabbis of the Talmud when he spoke in the synagogue. Perhaps there was someone in the congregation he was addressing directly. Freud and Nietzsche, he went on. The two extremes of secular life. Stoic acceptance and gay defiance in the face of—nothing; in the face of indifference, boiling violence, inexorable chaos; in the face of—the Other Side. Two hundred years of this. Enough. Jews must return to Torah. The world must return to God. There must be a center to human life or, God forbid, there will be no human life left on this planet. A man may not live alone. A man is part of a larger world. Even a great man, a creative man, a man who needs solitude, even such a man is part of a larger world. To live alone, apart from a community of men, is to live in death. I listened and looked at him and realized with cold shock that he was talking to me, directly to me. I wondered how many others realized that. Many, I was certain. I saw myself as part of this community and this country, concerned about both their futures. What was happening to our world was unbearable to me. But I had no illusion that I could ever change anything. I could only do my part by doing my own work and playing out the string of my own aberrant gift. Could one love only if one was present as part of the flesh and sinew of the beloved? Could one not love also as witness and distant participant? "The Jewish world will return to Torah and to its Father in Heaven," the Rebbe said. "And then surely the final redemption will come. May it come speedily and in our day. Amen." And the congregation thundered, "Amen!"

All of Yom Kippur the Rebbe was in the synagogue, and fasting—that entire day. He spoke before the Memorial Service about the souls of those who shaped our lives and who were with us still, every moment of our waking and our sleeping, ancestors, parents, and friends, who walk with us, talk with us, share our sufferings and our joys. And even those among us whose parents might have been cruel to us, God forbid, for reasons we can never understand, even those among us who live in the mystery and the anguish of a broken relationship with a parent—still we owe them our lives, and we must remember them at least for that. I closed my eyes as he spoke and saw Jacob Kahn and Anna Schaeffer, saw them clearly, and saw too, yes, the Spaniard somewhere along the edge of my vision, saw him nod in silent acknowledgment of my gratitude for his mysterious presence in my life—that Spanish renegade Catholic pagan hedonist demonic genius present in the life of a Hasidic man born in Brooklyn to Hasidic parents who were giving all the strength of their lives to Jews and to their sacred community. Another riddle!

After the Closing Service the Rebbe sounded the shofar, a single long clarion blast, and Yom Kippur was over.

The day before, in the early afternoon, I had telephoned Aunt Leah, Cousin Nahum, and Cousin Yonkel and asked them to forgive me for whatever pain I had inflicted on them during the year. Aunt Leah and Cousin Nahum said simply, "I forgive you." Cousin Yonkel said he would forgive me, but only because Jewish law required it, and he hung up. In the synagogue, thin, dry, and quivering with rage, he looked at me out of cold slitted eyes, then turned his back. Cousin Nahum shook his head and shrugged and rolled his eyes to the ceiling.

On the way back from the synagogue after the Yom Kippur Closing Service, Avrumel said to me, "The Rebbe really knows how to blow shofar. Will you teach me to blow shofar, Papa?"

I told him I was not good at it.

"Your grandfather blows shofar very well," my mother said. "He will be happy to teach you."

"Grandfather?" Avrumel said. "Will you?"

"It will be my joy," my father said. He and Avrumel walked on ahead together through the night streets.

On the terrace the next morning, I did a watercolor of the Rebbe sounding the shofar. I did it mostly in white and showed it to everyone during supper that evening.

"I like it better than your drawings," my mother said. "Your drawings I don't understand."

"Why did you make the Rebbe's eyes white?" Avrumel asked. "The Rebbe's eyes aren't white."

"Papa sees them as white," Rocheleh said. "He feels them as white. When will you understand that?"

"What else is white in the picture?" I asked Avrumel.

"The Rebbe's tallis," Rocheleh said.

"Your name is Avrumel?" I asked.

"The Rebbe's beard," Avrumel said. "The siddur in front of the Rebbe. The air all around the Rebbe. The sun coming through the windows."

"And who is in all these?"

He thought for a moment. "The Master of the Universe?"

Devorah and Rocheleh were looking at Avrumel. My parents were looking at me.

"You like the picture?" I said to Avrumel.

"Ah, yes, Papa!"

"It's yours."

"Papa!" He looked radiant.

"For your collection."

He was suddenly in my lap, hugging and kissing me. Then he went out of the kitchen, taking the watercolor with him.

"A nice gift," my father said, smiling.

Later, I looked into Avrumel's room. He sat at his desk, doing homework, his red hair covered by his dark velvet skullcap. The Shimshon doll was on his bed. Someone, probably Devorah, had carefully tacked the drawing to the corkboard over his desk, piercing only the farthest edges of the corners, which would easily be covered later by the frame. I looked at Avrumel and at my watercolor of the Rebbe. He was not aware of me standing in the doorway, watching him.

In our room that night Devorah said to me, "It is a very beautiful watercolor you gave Avrumel."

I stared at the picture of the Rebbe on the wall over the desk and said nothing.

"Are you sure we cannot stay the year, Asher?"

"I want to go home, Dev. This isn't home."

"Your parents, the children."

"I've already got the plane tickets. The Sunday after Simchas Torah."

She nodded sadly. "The children are happy in the yeshiva here."

"They'll be happy in the yeshiva in Nice."

"One year, Asher. Only one year."

"It's not one year, Dev. Ten days became five months. It's not only one year."

Her eyes widened. "Asher . . ."

"We're all going home after Simchas Torah. Two and a half more weeks, and home."

She sighed. "You are a strange and stubborn man sometimes, my husband. I do not like you too much when you become this way. It is as if ice enters your soul."

"I'm afraid of this place, Dev."

"Afraid of your own parents' home?"

"This place will consume me."

"I do not understand—"

"I need it as a place to return to, but not to live in."

"Asher . . ."

"We're going home, Dev."

She sighed and shook her head.

The next day I went over to the art supply store and bought a small case of oil paints, some brushes, a bottle of turpenoid, and a pad of canvas paper. On the terrace, using the card table as an easel of sorts, I began to sketch from memory, with washes of oil diluted in turpenoid, some of the canvases in my Uncle Yitzchok's art collection: the Cézanne, Matisse, Renoir, Bonnard. From time to time I referred to the drawings I had recently made of the canvases during my visit to the warehouse. Then I made an oil sketch of Avrumel. There was no one in the house. It took a while for the paintings to dry. I put them into my valise and did not show them to anyone.

I was putting the card table back when the phone rang. A voice on the other end, deep and authoritative, said, "I would like to speak with Asher Lev."

"This is Asher Lev."

"Sholom aleichem. This is Rav Yaakov Reisner. I am on the Rebbe's staff."

"Aleichem sholom."

"The Rebbe would like you to meet with him."

"When?"

"Tonight. At eleven o'clock."

"All right."

"Please be on time." He hung up.

A few minutes before eleven that night, I came out of my parents' house and walked along the street to the home of the Rebbe. I went past the tall dark-bearded men who stood on the porch. My father took me into the Rebbe's office and stepped out and closed the door.

The Rebbe sat behind the desk, a small figure in a dark suit and a dark hat. He beckoned to me and indicated the chair in front of the desk. I sat down, feeling his eyes upon me.

"You are well?" he asked softly.

"I thank God."

"And your family?"

"Thank God, all are well."

"Your exhibition of new work is opening soon, I am told."

"Only of drawings, yes."

"I wish you much success."

"Thank you."

"You are returning to France?"

"Yes, Rebbe."

"To work?"

"Yes."

"You need not return."

"I feel I must, Rebbe."

"An exile need not last forever, Asher Lev."

"Wherever I live, it is exile. Even here. But I cannot live here."

"Your family will return with you?"

"Yes."

"You are certain?"

"Yes."

"Very well." He sat very still behind the desk. There was a pause. He stirred faintly. "There is never an end to our work. It is not given to us to complete it. Who completes his work? That is the way of the world, Asher. Only the Master of the Universe completed His work. And it is said that even the Master of the Universe needs humankind in order truly to complete the Creation. Without man, what is God? And without God, what is man? Everyone needs the help of someone to complete the work of Creation that is never truly completed. Everyone. An artist, a Rebbe, everyone."

He sat gazing at me from behind the desk. The house was silent. I felt his eyes upon me; they seemed without pupils, burning, white. I closed my eyes a moment and when I opened them he was no longer there, the Spaniard was there in the Rebbe's chair, staring at me out of eyes that smoldered like torches, and then the Rebbe was there and then again the Spaniard, like two transparencies vying for the same space on a white screen. I heard the Rebbe talking to me and closed my eyes and opened them and saw him clearly.

"You will be with us for Simchas Torah?" he asked.

"With God's help, yes."

"And Avrumel?"

"He will be with me, God willing."

"Good," he murmured. "I give you and your family my blessing, Asher Lev."

I walked in the darkness beneath trees that were turning color now, leaves beginning to fall in the autumn air. Someone was walking behind me and when I turned it was only a fluttering shadow in the darkness and I knew it was the Spaniard, but when I turned again it was the shadow of the Rebbe, walking beneath the trees upon fallen leaves.

The Rebbe was in the synagogue for the festival of Succos. More Ladover had flown in after Yom Kippur, and it seemed the walls of the synagogue would burst outward from the crush of people and I heard there were fistfights among some of the men jockeying for space and seats. My father and I had built a succah on the back terrace of my parents' home, and the children and Devorah decorated it with dried fruit and drawings. Avrumel drew a picture of his Shimshon doll dancing with a Torah scroll, and Devorah mounted it with tacks on one of the walls. Rocheleh made half a dozen large white cardboard cutouts of Torah scrolls, which Devorah suspended with strings from the roof of the succah.

We ate in the succah. Guests joined us for some of our dinner meals: a professor of philosophy from Columbia University; a congressman from Washington; a physicist who had worked on the Manhattan Project; an artist from Safed who painted castles, clouds, mystical animals, and Hebrew quotations, and whose work was selling well and on occasion even appeared on postcards and calendars made in Israel; a professor of biology from the Sorbonne; a vice-consul from the foreign ministry of Israel. In the course of a conversation around the table, the Safed artist said he had been to the gallery and had seen the show of my new drawings.

"Absolutely I do not like them. They gave me nightmares. What do you hope to accomplish with such work?"

"I don't hope to accomplish anything. I just do it."

He said he didn't understand what I was talking about. The conversation went on to another subject.

Four days later, on the eve of Simchas Torah, the festival that celebrates the close of the yearly Torah-reading cycle, I went with my father and Avrumel to the synagogue. The crowd in front of the building was so thick it reminded me of the day not so long before when I had emerged from the subway station into a boiling sea of anguished Ladover Hasidim made frantic by the news of the Rebbe's sudden illness. And I remembered, too, the crowd on the parkway nearly half a year earlier for Uncle Yitzchok's funeral. The crowd parted for my father, and I walked behind him, carrying Avrumel.

We entered the synagogue. All the benches and stands had been removed. The floor was bare, save for the bimah and the masses of men milling about. I caught glimpses of Cousin Yonkel and Cousin Nahum. My aunt was no doubt upstairs in the women's section. She had said little to me since my return from France in early July and greeted me with hesitant nods the few times I had met her on the streets of the neighborhood.

The Rebbe entered the synagogue from the door near the Ark, accompanied by the two tall dark-bearded men. A moment later, the Evening Service commenced.

The voices of more than three thousand people rose and fell in rhythmed sound. My mother and Devorah were above us, behind wooden screens, in the women's section. And Rocheleh. I worried it might be too congested and too airless up there for Rocheleh; she had begun wheezing and sweating during the Kol Nidre Service on the night of Yom Kippur—the pupils of her eyes tiny, her nostrils flared when breathing in, her lips pursed when breathing out—and Devorah took her from the women's section and got her a cup of water and walked home with her and helped her through postural drainage and put her to bed. But Rocheleh would not stay away from the Simchas Torah celebration; all her school friends were there; if she felt the onset of an attack, she would go outside immediately. Rocheleh.

Avrumel stood between me and my father, praying from a book he held in his hands and swaying slightly back and forth. He was dressed in a dark suit and wore a white shirt, a dark tie, and a dark cap. He looked like a man in miniature.

It was warm in the synagogue, the air heating from the press of bodies. An undulating mass of dark-garbed, dark-hatted men, praying. The Ark was opened, and two men began to remove the Torah scrolls and hand them to those whose names were called out by one of the elders. The crowd stood still, waiting, a low hum of conversation vibrating the air. Behind me someone was talking about the stock market. Someone else was lamenting the fluctuations of the American dollar in European markets. I thought I heard my name mentioned, but I did not turn around. Avrumel, perched on my shoulder now, watched in fascination. He had been to Simchas Torah celebrations before, in Nice; but the crowd there was small. He was waving a small paper flag garishly decorated with amateurish drawings of Torah scrolls.

"How goes it, Avrumel?" I asked him.

"It goes well, Papa," he said happily from over my head.

The first of the circuits around the bimah began, led by my

father, who had put on a prayer shawl. I heard his strong nasal voice above the murmur of the crowd, chanting the traditional prayer. "O Lord, deliver us! O Lord, let us prosper! O Lord, answer us on the day we call!"

Someone began a Ladover melody. The crowd swelled with song. The men carrying the Torah scrolls danced and sang. I watched my father dancing with the scroll he held in his arms. His eyes were closed; his head, covered by the edge of the shawl, was raised. He danced in rapid movements, and I was astonished at his agility. The dancing went on for a long time, and then the scrolls were transferred to another group of men, and another circuit began, and then another and another. My father stood next to me now, Avrumel on my shoulders, in the front row of the tumultuous crowd around the bimah. At one point the dancers went weaving through the crowd and took the Torah scrolls out to the street and danced there awhile and then returned to the synagogue and gave the scrolls to yet another group of men. All the while, the Rebbe, garbed in a white robe, sat in his tall-backed cushioned chair inside his small enclosure, watching, clapping his hands from time to time, nodding. On either side of him stood one of the tall dark-bearded men. It was hot in the synagogue and I was sweating and singing and then someone was offering me a Torah scroll and Avrumel was lifted off my shoulders by my father and I danced with the scroll. Somewhere close by I saw Cousin Yonkel dancing with a scroll, but he would not look at me. I held the scroll as something precious to me, a living being with whose soul I was forever bound, this Sacred Scroll, this Word, this Fire of God, this Source for my own creation, this velvet-encased Fountain of All Life which I now clasped in a passionate embrace. I danced with the Torah for a long time, following the line of dancers through the steamy air of the synagogue and out into the chill tumultuous street and back into the synagogue and then reluctantly yielding the scroll to a huge dark-bearded man, who hungrily scooped it up and swept away with it in his arms. The singing and dancing grew, swelled, dance after dance; now the children doing a dance of their own, Avrumel among them; now the white-bearded elders dancing, their arms clasping each other's shoulders, my father among them; now all the others dancing, I among them, and standing beside me, clasping my shoulder, was Cousin Nahum, and we danced and he smiled at me and I felt him squeeze my shoulder, but afterward his brother, Cousin Yonkel, came over, and they walked away together.

The crowd milled about in a momentary pause. Then a silence fell upon the synagogue. I turned to where all were looking and saw that the Rebbe had left the enclosure. He wore a tallis over his white robe and a white skullcap, and he carried a miniature Torah scroll encased in white velvet. A large area was being cleared on the floor by a phalanx of dark-bearded men. Inside that area, a wide uneven circle, the Rebbe began a slow dance. He moved with infinite care, his head entirely concealed by the tallis, his feet making tiny steps back and forth and sideways: an uncanny mystical dance with the Torah and the Master of the Universe, while all watched in enraptured silence. Then he raised an arm, and the synagogue exploded into a Ladover chant, and feet stamped, and the Rebbe's arm moved back and forth slowly over his head, the wrist arching, circling, the other arm holding firmly the small Torah. How could so old and frail a man dance like that? The floor vibrated to the thunderous stamping; the huge chandelier swayed. The Rebbe lowered his arm and there was immediate silence, and he danced very slowly across the floor in the silence and came to where my father stood, next to me, and reached out for him, and my father joined him, and they danced together gently, as if in slow motion, the Rebbe's left arm now holding the Torah, his right arm upon my father's shoulder. The crowd clapped its hands and beat the floor with its feet. I saw bearded faces nodding and eyes staring and mouths open, as if in some kind of anticipation, and then the Rebbe seemed to be leading my father toward the edge of the circle, toward where I stood, with Avrumel on my shoulders, and there they remained, slowly dancing in front of me and Avrumel, and I felt eyes upon me, the clapping and the stamping now deafening—and then the Rebbe raised his head very slightly and I could see his eyes in the shadows of the tallis, and I stood there looking at his eyes, deep burning white eyes in the white shadows of the tallis, and I saw my father looking at me and then at the Rebbe, and I felt all the eyes in the crowd looking at me and all the eyes of all the generations of Ladover looking at me and the voice of the mythic ancestor I had not heard in years suddenly loud in my ears, uttering sounds that were not words, and I reached up and lifted Avrumel over my head and handed him to my father—and I felt the noise in the synagogue abruptly cease, waves of silence begin from those near me and spread beyond to the walls and the ceiling as my father and the Rebbe moved away from me in a slow dance, Avrumel in my father's arms, clinging to my father with one arm and waving his paper flag with the other, the three of them dancing away from me and suddenly the noise returning to the synagogue in a deafening surge of sound and I thought the floor would crack and the walls give way—and I stood there listening to the sounds of an infinite hope and watching my Avrumel in the arms of my father, the two of them dancing with the Rebbe and the small white-garbed scroll of the Torah. I do not know how long that dance continued, because I backed slowly away from it and through the crowd and out of the synagogue and felt suddenly the cold night air icy on the tears on my face and a hand reached out from the crowd on the street and grasped mine and it was Jacob Kahn and we walked away from the crowd and beneath the trees of the torn-up parkway, and that is all I remember about that night, that is all I remember.

Afterward no one remarked on it. What was it, after all? Simply a dance. My father and the Rebbe doing a dance with the Torah. Every year for years now, my father and the Rebbe danced together with the Torah. What was so unusual about it that people should openly talk of it? The Rebbe was well, thank God, as was my father. And Avrumel? Well—it was a dance, that's all. The three of them had danced a Simchas Torah dance with the Torah. What was Simchas Torah for, after all? That was what you did on Simchas Torah. You danced. Together.

I heard the phone ring and, a moment later, Avrumel's voice saying, "Papa, it is for you."

I went to the phone.

"Asher Lev?" The voice sounded indistinct, hollow.

"Yes. This is Asher Lev."

"The artist?"

"Who is this? I can hardly hear you."

"A friend."

My heart leaped. "Max? This is an awful connection. Where are you calling from?"

"My name is not Max. I am not one of your goyishe friends. I have advice for you, Asher Lev. Go home."

My heart froze.

"You have worn out your welcome here. Listen to my advice. Go back to your contaminated Saint-Paul."

"Go to hell."

"It is you who will go to hell, Asher Lev."

"Why don't you tell me your name?"

"This is the Angel of Death. I know who my customers are. You are going to hell. Do you hear me?" Anger was displacing caution. The voice was edging toward clarity. "Get yourself out of here before there is trouble."

"To threaten a life is to commit a transgression."

"Look who is talking about transgression! Your art is the greatest transgression of all! It desecrates the name of God! Leave us! Your presence contaminates us all!"

The line went dead.

I hung up the phone and stared at my trembling hands.

Avrumel came out of his room. "Who was it, Papa?"

"A wrong number."

Late that night, with Devorah asleep and the lights on, I made a drawing of the Angel of Death. I drew him with slitted black eyes and a long sunken face and a thin raging ugly mouth. I signed and dated it and put it into a manila envelope. The next afternoon, Friday, I walked over to the post office on Empire Boulevard and mailed the envelope to my Cousin Yonkel.

It is a disturbed Shabbos. Devorah and I talk together a long time in our room. I feel myself moving back and forth between resignation and rage. I can barely contain the anger. What kind of God creates such situations? He gives me a gift and a son, and forces me to choose between them. If I speak these words, my voice will be loud. They will all hear me, my parents, the children. Devorah will be aghast. I would be hurting her, when it is Someone Else I really wish to hurt. I sit at the desk and she sits on her bed, and we talk quietly and make plans. Again and again she asks why I cannot work here. Again and again I tell her. Then we explain it to the children: I will be away for two months, then return for Chanukah; then about three months, and back for Passover; then four months, and the summer. We would see about the summer. We would plan things from now on step by step. My parents listen in silence.

On Sunday they all accompany me to the airport—in a new and spacious van driven by Baruch Levinson. In the terminal, Avrumel tells me he really does not want to stay here after all; he has talked it over again with Shimshon, and they want to come back with me to Saint-Paul. I tell him I will be back for Chanukah. Only two months. Rocheleh says two months is a long time and she will miss me, but she understands why I have to go back. "Papa has to work by himself," she explains to Avrumel. "It is what Papa does." My parents are silent. Devorah's eyes are moist. "Travel in good health and return in good health," she says to me. We do not embrace. We have said our goodbyes earlier, in our room in my parents' home.

I walk alone in the crowd toward the security area and I turn and there they are, in the distance, looking at me. They wave and I wave back. My father holds Avrumel in his arms. Avrumel waves Shimshon at me and I wave back again and walk through the security zone and on toward the gate to the Airbus.

I call Max before I unpack. Then I call John. I go out to the terrace, feeling gritty and light-headed with lack of sleep. The morning is cool. There is a stark air of unreality to this Mediterranean world, its trees and gardens and sparkling sea, its green valleys and hills and mountainous outcroppings. Self-exiled to this Garden of Eden! I see Jameel working among the fruit trees. There are birds in the branches.

Max and John come over to the house, and we sit on the terrace.

They listen intently. I say nothing about my father and his future as the Rebbe of the Ladover Hasidim, nor about Avrumel as his heir. I simply ask them: How do you say no to aging grandparents who feel a need to have their grandchildren close to them for a year? Max is suspicious. John looks sullen. Do they hear in my voice the rage I am trying to conceal?

"You are sure those people have not—how do you say it?—washed your brain?" Max asks.

"Hate to say it, Lev," John tells me. "Best part of your family stayed in Brooklyn."

The truth will come to them slowly as the months go by. Pieces will fall into place. Like a riddle.

They take me to the café in Saint-Paul for breakfast. We continue talking. There are few tourists.

In the house alone, later, I unpack. The new Shimshon doll, which I brought back with me in my valise, I now put on Avrumel's bed. The house is very quiet. I lie down on my bed and fall asleep and wake hours later bathed in sweat. I shower and make myself a cup of coffee and walk dazed in the warm noon air to my studio.

The scents and smells that lie thick in the air of the studio wake me fully. How I love these smells! I open the blinds and let in the sunlight. The huge empty umber-washed canvas gazes at me. I stand in the studio, looking at the canvas. After a while I take it down off the wall and roll it up and put it away. Then I tack onto the wall a huge length of white canvas. It glows in the sunlight that filters through the glass brick roof of the studio.

Douglas Schaeffer sends me the reviews of my show of new drawings, which is still running in New York. The critics write about "odd new forms," "cluttered passages," "horizons beyond the recognizable," "multi-dimensionality," and "subtle simultaneity." One critic calls the work "bewildering, enigmatic, strangely moving." Another calls it "a mélange of movements toward new horizons that unfortunately unravels before it gets far."

The drawings that remain unpurchased after the show closes are acquired by Douglas for his personal collection and for the gallery.

Two of the drawings I retain for my own collection; a third I remind Douglas to send to Paris, to the widow of Lucien Lacamp.

One afternoon I sit on the terrace, looking through the catalogue of the New York show, and am able to glimpse for the first time the matrix underlying this new work of my hands. There are possibilities in this flood of forms. How strange to have worked for so long and not to have seen them before now; how strange to be seeing them only dimly even now. A turn here, a rearrangement there. A subtle use of multiple station points; a fusing of section views with perspective views. Yes. Something moves in the shadows beyond the terrace, and I raise my eyes and see the Spaniard. He stands looking at me, his face calm, his head slowly nodding. "Begin from nothing," he says. The fires of hearths and forges burn in his eyes.

Douglas calls me. What should we do with my late uncle's art collection? he asks. I tell him to let it sit in storage. I will pay for the insurance and storage fees. For how long? he asks. For a long time, I tell him. Maybe fifteen, twenty years. "My son will know what to do with it," I tell him.

It is early November. Max is in Paris. The print he made during the summer, using the carborundum process I taught him, has sold out, and he is now making another, using the same process. Afterward he will go to Canada and Japan. The China trip is off for the present.

John roams about his property or sits on his terrace, writing. On occasion he comes over to the house and we talk. There is almost always the smell of alcohol on his breath. Sometimes I help him walk back home.

I eat breakfast in the café in Saint-Paul and often skip lunch. Claudine prepares supper. I spend the days in my studio, and Shabbos in Nice with a journalist for the *Nice Matin* and his family. He is a Ladover and a specialist in jazz. The weather is cold. It is surprising how cold it can get here. The mistral is often bitter, and sometimes I hear shutters banging as it blows. There is mist and the start of the winter rains. The tourists are gone.

Devorah and Rocheleh and Avrumel. I see them everywhere, especially Avrumel. Beings of imagined presence. I have a recurrent vision: Avrumel sitting in the green armchair in my studio, hugging Shimshon and watching me paint.

Avrumel is watching me paint Avrumel as he will one day be. He will be grown and wear a dark suit, a white shirt, a dark tie, and a dark hat. His beard will be red. He will sit in a room gazing at the paintings in my Uncle Yitzchok's collection. I paint each of those paintings as they were once painted by the painters themselves: Cézanne, Renoir, Matisse, Bonnard, Soutine, Chagall, and the others. Avrumel will know what to do with those paintings. A Rebbe must know many things. Why not also how to value art? I will teach him.

I walk to the grave of Jacob Kahn. Standing on the knoll in a chill north wind, I recite chapters from the Book of Psalms. Tanya is not well. She sleeps a great deal. It is difficult for her to talk.

My father stops off at Nice in mid-November on his way back from Israel. He is exultant over the results of the elections in both Israel and the United States. He is deeply but indirectly involved in negotiations to form the new coalition government in Israel. Devorah and the children are well. He spends the night and flies back to the United States on the Airbus. He sleeps in Avrumel's bed.

Devorah writes me regularly. The Rebbe is not well. God give him strength, God give us all strength. My parents are fine. Rocheleh's medication was recently changed by the doctor; she is a young woman now. Devorah has agreed to write a series of articles on famous Jewish women for the Ladover weekly newspaper. She has also begun a book for religious Jewish children on how to live with asthma and other lung illnesses. It will include, she tells me, a special message from the Rebbe.

Weeks of longing and solitude: twin muses of creation. How the work now flows, whitish forms against backgrounds of eerily tinted blacks and reds: strange images in sealed rooms. My brushes push and pull densely textured oils across the surface of the vast canvas. I use palette knives. I use my fingers. Sweeping motions and the sense of being taken over by the Other as the hand does its work—moves and circles and thrusts and lays on paint and gouges for texturing and then no memory at all but the smells of the paints and the sweat on my face and chest and in my armpits, drenching sweat, and the need to urinate but no time for it and the hand going on, possessed entirely now by the Other. Did the Rebbe know that I wanted, needed, to be alone now; that I would choose not only for the needs of the Ladover but also for needs of my own? Did he count on that, on the helpless self-centeredness of the artist's soul, as he danced with my father and the Torah scroll in front of me and Avrumel that day? Another riddle.

Devorah writes me. Avrumel has lately taken to ignoring Shim-shon and insists on walking to school by himself.

A Note on the Type

This book was set in a film version of Granjon, a type named in compliment to Robert Granjon, but neither a copy of a classic face nor an entirely original creation. George W. Jones based his designs for this type on that used by Claude Garamond (1510–61) in his beautiful French books, and Granjon more closely resembles Garamond's own type than does any of the various modern types that bear his name.

Robert Granjon began his career as typecutter in 1523. The boldest and most original designer of his time, he was one of the first to practice the trade of typefounder apart from that of printer. Between 1557 and 1562 Granjon printed about twenty books in types designed by himself, following, after the fashion, the cursive handwriting of the time. These types, usually known as *caractères de civilité,* he himself called *lettres françaises,* as especially appropriate to his own country.

Composed by American–Stratford Graphic Services,
Brattleboro, Vermont

Printed and bound by Fairfield Graphics,
Fairfield, Pennsylvania

Typography and binding design by
Dorothy Schmiderer Baker